HEART IN DIXIE

A NOVEL

NICHOLAS BOULER

Author's Note

This is a work of historical fiction and is, to the author's ability, true to its time. Among other things, this means that the story contains demeaning and offensive language about Americans of African descent. **This includes use of the epithet "n*****."** I hate that word. I felt I had to use it, however, in order to be historically accurate. More important, however, is that I felt that readers too young to have lived this story should understand that, in those days, many people could use that word with no thought of how, literally, hateful it is.

To repeat, this is a work of fiction. It is clearly inspired by actual events during the Civil Rights era, particularly the career of George C. Wallace. But this book won't teach you anything specific about him; the book is not "about" Wallace. *Heart in Dixie* is about a current of political thought that has always been part of America and, as this is written, has helped to elect our current president. But it is also a love letter about this special place where we were "southern-born and southern-bred."

No specific reference to any person living or dead is intended or should be inferred. Every conversation, newspaper "article" and transcript is a work of imagination, unless attributed. Nothing in this book has ever appeared in the *Atlanta Constitution*.

For Jean

and

Alissa, Clara and Dorie

My four "stout pillars that hold up all"

Prelude

They do not know they are Southerners; that's how young these boys are. If born in an earlier time, the age to catch tadpoles.

They take their surroundings for granted, as the young are privileged to do, and don't find it odd that a State Patrol car regularly parks outside the yellow brick house up the way. They can't imagine that the old man who never comes out of that house was once famous; the street they live on is named for him.

Like all little boys they long for excitement. So they can barely control themselves this morning when suddenly sirens wail and two police cars and an ambulance screech to a stop in front of that yellow brick house, all lights flashing, one hundred times better than an older brother's video game. The boys sprint across the neighbors' yards, right through the flowerbeds, to arrive at the house just as the ambulance attendants roll a metal bed to the porch steps and then carry it inside. A policeman sees them and shoos them away and they walk back home, dawdling, sorry to leave the action, but glad for a pretty exciting morning on boring old Davis Street.

Part One

They Do Things Differently There

This Was An Important Man

Rebecca Tanner was having a good day. Earlier in the week she had gotten a lead on a secret meeting between two small-town council members and a local developer, a meeting state law said should be announced and open to the public.

"Good potential, if you prove it," her editor had said. "Could be the section front." That was all the encouragement Rebecca had needed. The story made the front page of today's Metro section, not a small achievement for a junior reporter at a paper as big as the *Atlanta Constitution*. So she was feeling pretty good about things when Jeff, that editor, came over and tossed a printed e-mail onto her desk.

"One of the stringers sent this in," he said, as she quickly read the first two lines.

SEGREGATIONIST GOVERNOR HOSPITALIZED
DAVIS'S CONDITION SAID CRITICAL

Rebecca looked at Jeff, then read the message again, rubbing her bottom lip with a forefinger.

"Ex-governor of Escambia? Is that the Davis we're talking about?"

Jeff breathed an exaggerated sigh. "Your encyclopedic knowledge is a constant comfort to me. This was an important man. He moved America to the right; hell, he may still be moving it. You have to guess which state?"

"Don't be a jerk," she grumbled. Jeff was always kidding her about being one of his youngest reporters, as though he had to explain who was president before Clinton, in case she might think it was Lincoln. But her only problem with this part of history was that she was a midwestern girl from Indianapolis and she was only twenty-four, so a lot of the civil rights leaders and history were not familiar to her. After all, it was 1999; a new century was about to start. Civil rights was a pretty old story.

Rebecca looked thoughtful. "This guy lived at the time of Martin Luther King, and he's still alive?"

"Not for much longer, I suspect. But lots of his supporters probably still are. And we need their stories. This was a segregationist governor who ran for the president of the United States. He won 10 percent of all the primary votes cast. He won Michigan, for god's sake. We need to understand how that happened. That's why I have to get you over there. I think Delta has a…," Jeff stopped, looked, then leaned closer to her. "What's wrong?"

Rebecca hadn't realized it would be so obvious she didn't want this assignment. She had just been wondering if she could do this with phone interviews. That would be a big enough interruption from the local politics she loved to cover. But Jeff was talking about making her actually go to Escambia.

"I'm not sure I'm right for this one, Jeff. I'm from Indiana, remember? You Atlanta people know all this civil rights stuff, but it's like the Civil War. It's a local thing, you know? I mean, I've never even been to the Cyclorama," she said, referring to a painting-in-the-round at a local park depicting Sherman's fiery march through Atlanta.

Jeff shook his head. "Give me a break. Nobody from the South lives in Atlanta if they can help it. Even after eight months, you know that. Anyway, how could you ever take Groves's job one day if you don't know the civil rights stories?"

Rebecca caught her breath. Gary Groves was the *Constitution*'s Washington correspondent, and acknowledged to be one of the best in the country. Rebecca dreamed of someday getting that job; to hear Jeff mention even the possibility was a thrill.

"You've done good work on these local stories since you've been here. This one will give you a chance to stretch." Jeff said. "There are lots of things about those years we still don't know: what was the civil rights movement like on the other side? There were lots of segregationist governors, so what made T. J. Davis so appealing? Who supported him? What legacy did he leave?" He stopped and looked at her for a moment. "You up for that?"

Suddenly Rebecca's concerns about being away from the office had melted. She could feel the grin spreading across her face.

"I won't let you down, Jeff"

He gave an amused snort. "I hope not, I'd hate to have to run your ass off and get somebody else. Now go home and pack."

Rebecca made several calls, arranged for one of the secretaries to cover her phone for a few days and was getting ready to leave when Jeff came back by.

"I almost forgot," he said, holding out a book to her. Rebecca read the title: *Long March for Freedom: The Battle for Civil Rights in Dixie.* It was not a book she recalled from her Indiana childhood. "I had this in my office," Jeff said. "Think of it as one of those 'for morons' books. It'll help you navigate the alien terrain."

Forty-five minutes later Rebecca was putting clothes into a carry-on when it suddenly occurred to her she wasn't entirely sure where Escambia was. She found an atlas in the bookcase.

There. A long narrow state, one of the four tall rectangles of the Deep South, marching west from the Atlantic: Georgia, Alabama, Escambia, Mississippi. Capital city: Montville. Population: 2.8 million. Oh great, she thought, the whole state has fewer people than Metro Atlanta. There are probably half that many cars up on blocks. She noticed the light blinking on the phone message machine, and pushed the button.

"Hey, it's me," a recorded voice said. "Looks like a late one. You go ahead and eat; I'll heat something when I get there. Love you."

Imagine that, she thought, Paul having to work late. That only happens about twenty times a month. Still, he was sweet to call. She clicked the TV remote, just to have voices in the apartment. With *Hollywood Today* in the background she scanned the atlas article on Escambia.

The first white settlers moved into what was then called Western Georgia in the late 1700's...Geologically, flat coastal plain runs northward from a narrow coastline along the Gulf of Mexico, changing in the midsection of the state to the rolling hills of the Appalachian Piedmont which become more pronounced along the northeastern border with Tennessee... For most of the twentieth century major industrial development centered on steel smelting at Carnegie, the largest city in the state...Insurance, banking and other service industries have dominated the economy in recent years. Agriculture, however, continues to play a major role in the central and southern regions. Major crops are corn, soybeans, and cotton... International trade flows through the port city of Bienville...State government operates from the capital city of Montville in the center of the state.

The television show began a segment about a new movie "star", not yet 20. Who needed that? Rebecca pressed the remote to find CNN and went back to packing. The book Jeff had given her on the history of the civil rights movement went on top of her carry-on, along with the obit file she had remembered to pick up on her way out of the office. When she first joined the *Constitution*, after having worked on a weekly and a small daily in Indiana, it had been a surprise to learn that most big papers kept pre-written obituaries of public figures on file so that important dates and details would not have to be researched from scratch when a death occurred. If T. J. Davis did die, updating the obituary would be her job.

After packing she went to the tiny kitchen to pour a small glass of wine from a bottle of Paul's that cost more than a week of her lunches. Paul felt life was too short for cheap wine. He wouldn't have approved of a mid-day glass, either, but Rebecca needed strength for the call she had to make. She dialed the number and waited for three rings.

"Hello?"

Rebecca sagged a little at the sound of the voice she had known longer than any other.

"How are you, Mom?"

"Your dad and I just got back from a nice walk. How are you, Honey?

"I'm fine. I got another section front today. So things are good."

"Send us a copy. Dad loves to see them. And how's Paul? I'm sure he's working hard."

"Yes, Mom, he's putting in a lot of..."

"Hours. I'm sure. At his office."

She pronounced it AW-fice. Mom was not much for subtlety.

"Mom, Paul has to work very hard to ever make partner."

"I thought he was going to be your partner. When is that going to happen?"

Rebecca sighed. No time to go through that again, and no point.

"Look, I called to tell you I've got to be away for an out-of-town assignment." She began to explain about T. J. Davis, the civil rights era governor of Escambia, and was surprised when her mother interrupted.

"Wasn't he the racist down there? Put Dr. King in jail over voting or restaurants, something like that? You're going there?"

"I don't really know the details, Mom." Rebecca aimed the remote like a weapon, fanning channels like Paul does, stopping at a music video. "That's why I have to go."

"I don't know if you should." Now there's a shocker, Rebecca thought, Mom has an opinion on this, too.

"It's my job, Mom. We don't vote on it." The song was not one she knew — nice beat, though. She'd watch for the end credits, she might want the CD.

"Are you still there?" The Voice, annoyed. Oops.

"Sorry, Mom. I was just making a note."

"How long will you have to be there?"

"Maybe three weeks, I don't know."

There was a long silence.

"Mom?"

"You be careful," she said, slowly, as though weighing every word. "That place you're going to, it's not like Indianapolis. Before you were born, they had lynchings there, and bombings. They let police dogs loose on children."

Rebecca was startled. Where was this vehemence coming from? Her mother was the least political person she knew. But all she said was,

"That was a long time ago, Mom."

"I know, Honey. And I don't want to be unfair to those people, really. But you be careful."

Rebecca considered herself neutral on the South, though she did think of it with a capital letter. But here was her mother, making it sound like part of the Third World. And then, as she had been doing all of Rebecca's life, her mother read her mind.

"It may be different now, I don't know," Mom said. "But in the Sixties, Escambia wasn't really a part of America. It was another country."

Margaret's Puzzle

I n his garden, Gordon Halt felt he understood what the world was all about. He recognized this feeling was illusory, but that did not make it any less pleasant. In a southern garden there was order and beauty and even history and culture. The black people talked about soul food that nurtures one's being as well as one's body, and Gordon thought of the garden as food for his soul. Especially this garden, the product of his own hands, made from plants he'd known all his life.

Years ago, when he and Margaret had moved to this two story brick house, the subdivisions had not yet reached this far out and he had been able to afford these three acres to have room for the plants he loved: the honeysuckle that grew on a short section of fence put in for just that purpose; the dogwoods that spread in the rippling shade cast by over-arching oaks and soaring, rail-straight pines. Almost thirty years ago Gordon had brought small magnolias from the family home place and planted them to mark the side property line. Now they formed a forty-foot wall of green, with polished leaves big as napkins and plate-sized blossoms of snowy white. In the spring clouds of their fragrance could transport Gordon back to his childhood or make Yankee visitors swoon.

It seemed to Gordon that he would know this place even if he were brought here in a croaker sack, blindfolded. Friends tried to tell him that everyone feels that way about home. Let a Scotsman tell you about the highlands or a Russian about the steppes, they would seem just as certain that no other place was like this place. But walking in this garden that seemed almost holy to him Gordon thought, for the thousandth time, that only in the South were men so firmly tied to place and to the past and to all those who had loved this land long before he was born.

Standing beside a spreading Pink Perfection, he reached up to pull a large bud from one limb. Gordon used a fingernail to pry apart the hundreds of tiny future camellia petals, tightly folded into this elegant spiral with a precision he could hardly imagine. He had done this dozens of times but his wonder at the design had never lessened. Everywhere he looked, it seemed to him that nature embraced complexity, preferred intricacy. It made him wonder if the engineers, rather than ministers and rabbis, are truly God's representatives on earth.

He heard his name called from inside the house. "Gordon, Hon, have you forgotten you were on an errand?" Any time he was out of her sight for twenty minutes Margaret seemed to think he had developed Alzheimer's in the interval. God love her, she didn't mean to aggravate him so.

"I'm on my way," he called toward the kitchen window. "I was just checking on the garden for a minute. Didn't realize there was any hurry." Not that he could hurry, the way his joints were acting up. When he was young, old folks had called it sciatica. His HMO doctor (Gordon called him the "homo doctor," but he didn't laugh) called it rheumatoid arthritis. But Gordon wondered if that kid really knew anything. He had wingtips older than that doctor.

He crossed the yard to the utility room that formed one wall of the carport. He slowly bent to pick up a charged battery, then carried it back to the house and hooked it up to Margaret's wheelchair.

"Thank you, Hon," she said from her place at the table. Before her, the newspaper was open to the puzzle page. Margaret was a gifted solver of word games, especially of the letter-substitution cryptic puzzles. He leaned over her shoulder to see her working on a short one.

Gsv kzhg rh mvevi wevi. Rg'h mlg vevm kzhg
— Uzfopmvi

"It's a quote, you see. Two sentences. The dash means that word is the author's name." She had explained it to him a hundred times over the years, yet each time she nearly giggled with enthusiasm, certain that today, at last, he would become as excited as she.

That had not happened yet. He leaned over to kiss the top of her head. "I'll be on the patio if you need me," he said.

Walking through the den he picked up his book and went out the double doors to the patio where he settled into the wooden chair Edward had bought for him a few years ago. He had thought it silly at the time; it claimed to be an "Adirondack" chair but Gordon was almost certain no one in the family had been within 200 miles of the Adirondacks. And what was sillier, the chair came in the mail - well, one of those trucks, but it amounted to the same thing. Gordon felt that if you needed something for the house you go to Rich's, as his mother used to do.

He settled in with a contented sigh and soon he was deeply into *The Mayor of Casterbridge.* Since his retirement Gordon had taken on the project of reading the GREAT BOOKS, a designation he thought of without irony in capital letters. It did not seem remarkable to him that there should be a list of such books, agreed upon by educated people, anymore than that there should be "great" (as opposed to inferior or mediocre) food, baseball teams, or music. He was aware of the criticism that these lists are elitist, made up of works by dead white European males. But since Gordon was already in three of those categories and was none-too-far removed from admission to the fourth he had decided that he, if anyone, should support these classics.

Besides that, this book's plot - a man under the influence of drink sells his wife and child to a gypsy - seemed thoroughly modern in its weirdness. Any large city now produces a story just as strange every month. But the novel did what the newspaper never could — followed the characters to show the consequences. This was the appeal of literature to Gordon, the idea that some order and sense could be made from the randomness of daily life, and he could be lost in these pages for hours at a time.

But not today, apparently.

The sound of a ringing phone broke through his concentration. He heard Margaret's chair come to the door. She glared at him and extended the cordless phone. The next thing he heard was a voice that was once as familiar to him as his own.

"He collapsed, Gordon." Barbara Davis sniffled into the phone, her shallow gasps making it hard to hear the words, or to understand how bad it was.

"Where did they take him?" Gordon asked. Her response would answer the biggest question.

"GreatHealth," she said. A hospital, then. So he was still alive.

"What do I need to do?"

"Can you come, Gordon? Tell Margaret it would only be for a little while. Can you, Gordon?"

Gordon said he would. Margaret would not be happy, though it had been so long since there had been anything between him and Barbara it seemed more like a rumor he had heard than like anything he had lived through. Women, apparently, saw these things differently. He and Barbara had been to dinner occasionally and kissed rather enthusiastically a few times. That much had gotten back to Margaret and he could never convince her there had been no more to it. Truth, it turns out, is not always a defense.

"Why is she bothering you with this?" Margaret asked after he clicked off. "You could have a heart attack yourself."

"You know she doesn't have that many people to call. Besides it's not for her; it's for him. I owe him some attention."

Before the accident, she would have stomped out of the room. Now she only turned the chair away from him, letting the whine of the electric motor serve as his rebuke.

Gordon was perturbed now. His reading time was shot and his wife of a lifetime was peeved with him over something that never really happened 25 years ago. He could have laughed at the absurdity of it.

As a young man he had imagined that if one could live past seventy he would be able to look back on his life as a finished work, almost the way he might look at a performance, and perhaps learn something. But having reached that point, he found no coherent view, as though the lighting on the stage was so poor that critical details were missing, or the cast suddenly recited the lines from Act III before finishing Act I. Memories came and went, maddeningly without warning. A random phone call ruined a peaceful morning with unsought recollection.

Gordon had first met T. J. Davis at a football game. Gordon didn't so much recall that scene now, he seemed to move into it, or be dragged; that's what memory was like, a film clip showing over and over in a theater you can be yanked into, instantly. In his mind he saw the yellow and orange leaves of oak, hickory and persimmon, skitter across the University quadrangle. Suddenly he was on his feet, without pain, kicking those leaves out of his way as he made long strides to the stadium. Life, not just the weather, was perfect. He was twenty years old.

Vanderbilt was the opponent for that day's game, so there was little anxiety about the outcome. Even before the State U's glory days of the 1960's, Vanderbilt was about as likely to beat a Crimson team at home as Jesus was to come back to conduct the band at half time. Thus the crowd could fully concentrate on a key purpose of the event — socializing. A football game was not quite as good for this as a funeral, since the people you wanted to see were much more scattered out. But many of them were better dressed.

Climbing the stadium steps with his date, a pretty tri-Delt whose daddy owned the bank in Poe, Gordon had to stop several times to wave to friends and acquaintances. The girl grinned at him.

"I'll bet you wanted these seats up so high so you could impress me with all the people you know," she said.

"You caught me," he said, squeezing her hand because it seemed like what a gentleman would do. He couldn't help, though, being disappointed that she would think he needed to impress her.

"Gordon! Hey, up here!" A tall man in an expensive plaid jacket was waving his arms to get Gordon's attention. Rob Burris was a senior class SGA rep Gordon had interviewed for a student newspaper piece about dormitory issues. Burris, a bit of a blow-hard, fancied himself a mover and shaker. Gordon liked him well enough, though, and Burris's love of seeing his name in print was a useful weakness.

"Want you to meet our next sophomore senator," Burris said as he clumsily maneuvered a stocky boy with tousled black hair into Gordon's face. The stranger's jaw was shadowed by stubble and his posture betrayed a country boy uncomfortable in the suit Mama had bought for him to take to college. But at least he knew to dress for the game. He probably preferred overalls, but the Crimson men would no more wear denim to a game than they'd wear earrings.

"I'm Thomas Jefferson Davis, call me T.J.," the stranger said in a growlly drawl. "Robbie tells me you write for the paper."

Gordon knew Burris hated being called Robbie, so he couldn't figure why Burris was still smiling.

"That's right. When there's something to write about."

The boy made a face that Gordon considered an attempt to grin. Like the suit he wore, the expression was unaccustomed and calculated, ending up as a smirk.

"Well, it's nice to meet you." Davis turned the grin on Burris as though to share some imaginary spotlight with him. "Robbie is gonna let me be on the ticket for that sophomore SGA slot." He turned back to Gordon. "Oh, and this is my assistant, Billy Trask."

He motioned to what Gordon could only think of as a slab of humanity. The only men in the entire stadium bigger than this Billy Trask were wearing uniforms on the field. The "assistant" seemed to tower over his friend (boss? Gordon wondered) and everyone else around. He was watching the field, though, and let a grunt and a wave suffice to acknowledge the introduction.

Gordon smiled. "We don't see many sophomores with assistants."

Davis smiled back, but his eyebrows contracted, canceling any mirth. He knew he was being teased, and didn't like it, but let it pass.

"You don't see many sophomores like me, period. We're gonna have a lot of information to let the voters know about. This is an important campaign."

"I'm afraid that may be quite a surprise to the students," Gordon said. The tri-Delt giggled and squeezed his arm. "But it's good to have enthusiastic candidates."

"Oh, I'm plumb loaded with enthusiasm. And I got lots of ideas. I'd like to talk with you about them."

"This may not be the best time." Gordon looked at the thousands of fans who were now standing for the kickoff, beginning the long "Gooooooo" that would change to a thunderous "Crimson" when the kicker's foot touched the ball. He yelled over the din.

"Tell Rob to call me. We'll set something up."

As the young Gordon turned to walk up the concrete steps of the stadium the roar of the crowd faded, suddenly, and much more than it should have after the kickoff. The light pressure of the girl's hand on his arm became insistent, rude, almost shoving him, and her voice was now ridiculously low.

"Gordon, I thought you were going to the hospital."

Gordon looked up into his wife's face, shamed at being caught daydreaming. The quintessential old fart. He could see in her eyes the continuing quest for signs of senility, but she had the grace not to interrogate him.

"Edward called to say the *Constitution* is sending someone to do a story on Governor Davis," she said. "They figure this is his last trip to the hospital and they want to be ready. He was sure they'll want to talk to you, so he wanted to give you some notice."

"Sure. That's fine." Gordon said.

Margaret gave him a slight smile.

"Edward said he didn't mind if you talked to the competition," she said in a stagey whisper, "but save the best stuff for the family sheet."

They both laughed, sharing the family resistance to being of any help to the competing paper in the much larger city.

"Maybe I shouldn't talk to their guy at all," Gordon said.

"That's what I told Edward, but he said that wouldn't be right. He said you're a part of the history of the Davis administration, a bona fide source."

Gordon groaned inwardly. A part of history. How Father would have loved the thought of that.

Margaret reached out to hand him the newspaper she had been working on in the kitchen. "Seems like this is an appropriate message for today," she said. At first he didn't understand what she meant, but then he read her neat handwriting under the puzzle she had been working on.

Gsv kzhg rh mvevi levi. Rg'h mlg vevm kzhg

The past is never over. It's not even past

Uzfopmvi

Faulkner

They Want to Move the Flag

W hen the seat belt sign blinked off, Rebecca finally released the death grip she had on the armrests. She was not the world's best flyer. She took several deep breaths, then reached under the seat ahead of her to wrestle out the bag containing her heavy "laptop" computer, as they called it. Carrying this through airports, she had wondered if pregnancy would be like this. She kept hearing that new light models were being developed all the time but by the time one of those made it to her end of the food chain they would have fixed that "Y2K" problem she kept reading about but didn't understand.

She pulled out the file containing the standby obit for T. J. Davis. If he did die she would be responsible to fill in the blank spots and supplement the story with details of his last years.

(HOLD for use) *<<OBIT>>*

DAVIS, Thomas Jefferson (b.1924 d. ——)

The combative former governor and segregationist firebrand Thomas Jefferson Davis, who waged the most successful third-party campaign for president in United States history, died today at the age of

——

Davis had been hospitalized at _____(hospital) in _____(city) since _____. He had been suffering from _____ for the last _____ and was known to be in declining health. Hospital officials said _____. _____, his _____ were with him at the time of his death.

18

"Davis became the central oppositionist figure of the civil rights era, with his frequent statement that 'Segregation is God's Way.' It is no exaggeration to say that Davis was every bit as central to white reactionary forces as Martin Luther King was to the black Americans seeking reform," according to R. Barnes Woodston, a historian at Emory University and author of a best-selling history of the civil rights movement, *Long March for Freedom.* *"And remember, King was never a candidate for President of the United States."*

Rebecca noted the reference to the Woodston book, the one Jeff had given her for background.

Davis's political career began as an elected judge in his home county in southern Escambia. He attended the famous 1948 Democratic Convention in Philadelphia which nominated Harry S. Truman for his own term as president and Davis stayed behind with his mentor, then-governor and populist John "the Giant" Partain when many southern delegates followed Strom Thurmond in a walk-out over segregation of the military. Thurmond founded the Dixiecrat movement that controlled Southern politics over the following years, throwing both Partain and Davis out of office.

While he began as a moderate, or even liberal, on race issues, Davis learned the lessons of the Dixiecrat movement and in 1958 he defeated Partain for the Democratic nomination to win his first term as governor, in a campaign almost entirely based on opposition to school desegregation. In that campaign the Ku Klux Klan, then a major force in Escambia politics, supported Davis.

Davis won the governor's office three more times, serving longer than any other governor in modern times and dominating his state as few governors of any state have ever done. His influence spread much farther, however, as he expanded his opposition to civil rights to include a protest against big government "pushing around the little man." He was able to channel frustration over school busing into a national political campaign that made him a serious contender for the Democratic nomination for President in the 1968 campaign. His appeal became even stronger four years later when he mounted the most successful third-party campaign for President in U.S. history,

winning several primaries outright before suddenly ending his cam-
paign without explanation. Years later historians learned Davis
attended a secret meeting with then-president Richard Nixon only
days before his withdrawal from the race.

Now, with his death _____*** years after the end of his last*
term as Governor it may be said that the tumultuous civil rights era
has finally ended. (**ed. note: he left office in 1974)

Rebecca made notes in a new steno pad about the obit's references
to "Giant" Partain, the Davis presidential campaigns (which she had
never heard of), and the meeting with President Nixon, then returned
the folder to her case and removed the Woodson book Jeff had given
her. She quickly saw that this copy was Jeff's own, filled with penciled
underlining and marginal notes. The index revealed more than 100
references to T. J. Davis or the state of Escambia. She listed the page
number references in her pad and got to work. By the time the plane
landed she had filled a dozen pages with notes and interview questions.
She made a point of having her questions cover the subjects Jeff had
made written notes about in the book.

* * *

The luggage carousel came to noisy life as an electronic display lit
up with her flight number and the word "Atlanta" while a rotating
beacon sent flares across the ceiling. Rebecca almost laughed at the
pointlessness of this activity. Montville might be the capital, but its
airport had only two small carousels, side by side, so the elaborate lights
and alarms that would be essential in Atlanta or Chicago seemed bogus
here.

Driving into town, a matter of only five miles, she passed acres of
Holstein-dotted pasture that reminded her of home. Closer in, though,
rows of shabby wooden houses, staggering on concrete blocks and
weathered to gray under patches of peeling paint, were another matter.
These dilapidated shacks where ragged black children played in patches
of dirt did not remind her of anything except pictures she has seen of
third world countries.

Even downtown, only two or three of the newest office buildings strained past twenty floors. The street made a long curve to the right and suddenly opened to a large grassy square, beyond which a broad boulevard ran up a prominent hill. At the top, the state capitol presided over the downtown area, its white marble shimmering in the spring sunlight. Impressed in spite of herself, Rebecca decided to park the car and look around.

The stately dome and columned entrance high atop a marble staircase recalled the capitol in Washington, but the smaller scale seemed so much more approachable, a place where ordinary people really might aspire to govern themselves. Or, she suddenly thought, a place where a small-town ego could imagine taking control.

How often, she wondered, would this Governor Davis, this man she had to write about, have stood in this spot and had this same view. What would he have been thinking?

As Rebecca started back to her car she saw a group of men at the side of the roadway. Some waved placards energetically to attract passing cars. "Our flag, Our heritage" she read on one, and then "One Dixie, under God" on another. She approached a solidly built man in a short-sleeved plaid shirt and denim jeans. He was older than she would have guessed from a distance; gray liberally sprinkled his wavy dark hair and his hands and face were weathered. As she approached he turned to pick up something from a folding table set up on the sidewalk.

"I'm from out of town," she said. "What's up with the signs?"

"They want to move the Confederate flag off the capitol, and we don't want 'em to." He spoke slowly, almost shy, which surprised her in someone of his size.

"Like in South Carolina?" she said. She had seen stories come over the wire about the protests by the NAACP that had recently begun in that state and recalled that these were the only two states that still flew the Confederate flag from government buildings.

His mouth twitched at the corner. "Yea, pretty much. We don't have a thing in the world against the black people voting and whatnot, but they ain't satisfied with that. They want to wipe out ever' trace of the South."

As he spoke, he passed a handbill to Rebecca. She noticed a jagged scar on the back of his hand, which was reddened and calloused; his muscles did not come from the gym. She glanced at the flyer quickly, just enough to see "Heritage — Not Hate" printed in large letters across the top of the page and a circular logo of some kind at the bottom. The man absently rubbed the scar with two fingers.

"Who is 'they'?" she asked. "The civil rights groups?"

He shook his head, as though embarrassed to point out her lack of sophistication. "If that's what you want to call 'em. They're more like civil hate groups, you ask me."

"Just so I'm clear, though, these groups are asking to take the flag off government buildings, right? Not all buildings or museums or whatever?"

"Oh, sure, that's what they say now — 'just get it off the Capital.' But you know how that goes." He twisted his lip at the deviousness of his opponents. "If they get our flag off the capital, next thing they will get it wiped out ever'where." He turned again to the table, picking up a stack of papers. "Want to sign a petition and help us out?"

Rebecca smiled as she held up a hand. "I'll think about it. Like I said, I'm from out of town." The lack of logic in that statement did not appear to faze him.

"You have a good one," he called to her as she walked away.

Back at the car, she looked up to see the flagpole on the very top of the dome. From the pole streamed three banners: Old Glory, as her dad would refer to it; one she had never seen before, which must be the flag of Escambia; and one other, of blue bars filled with white stars diagonally crossing against a red field. Before she moved to Atlanta Rebecca would have sworn this last flag existed only in books. After she came to Georgia she had seen it in five inch tall versions bunched on a rack at off-price gas stations, but here it was waving from the dome of a state capitol as though the last 150 years had never happened.

I'm Not From Here

T he redbrick home of the *Montville Courier* took up a large city block. An imposing entrance framed in marble reminded Rebecca of every newspaper building she'd ever seen in old movies. From the side of the building she could hear the roar of forklift trunks trundling in and out of trailers parked at the loading dock. She walked to the corner to watch for a few minutes as pallet after pallet of folded papers was loaded. Talk about low-tech, she thought. Why had she fallen for this part of the business? Print! Paper and ink trying to compete with CNN! Were they all crazy or what?

Fifteen minutes later she was in Edward Halt's office. "Start with this guy," Jeff had told her. "His family has been in the newspaper business since before Escambia was a state. There's nothing that goes on that the Halt's are not involved in. His grandfather, Gordon Halt, was a key staff member for Governor Davis. His great-grandfather won the Pulitzer Prize. If you get in with them you can find the stories that didn't get in the paper."

Edward was in his forties, with that reddish brown hair they call auburn, and green eyes that seemed to be smiling before he spoke. He was dressed in a tweed sport coat and a bow tie, giving her the impression that he might have just returned from a prep school reunion. His speech was relaxed and soft in a way she had come to associate with older southern men.

"So my buddy Jeff wants a story on Governor Davis?"

She smiled to herself, wondering how he would spell the word he had just pronounced as Guhv'nuh.

"We have the obit from the public figures file," Rebecca said, "but it hasn't been updated for some time."

Edward nodded. "I pulled ours out to have a look at it this morning. Of course we updated within the last six months just because of who he is."

Rebecca was a little surprised. At the *Constitution* only Jimmy Carter and a few dozen others warranted that kind of attention, and she said as much.

Edward gave her a small smile and moved his tiny glasses farther down his nose. She had made a mistake somehow and this was his gentle correction.

"If you're surprised, you shouldn't be," he said. "Even after all this time Davis is much more important to our state than Carter is to yours, I suppose because we have less to be proud of. Many Escambians still think of him the way Americans years ago thought of FDR." He paused and for a moment Rebecca was afraid Edward thought he had to tell her who FDR was, but then he went on.

"And sometimes the same people revere both men. Many of our citizens have never recognized anyone who came after him as a legitimate leader." He had been watching her face while he talked. Now he looked down and snapped the cap on a fountain pen. "We may not be happy about that, but we try to be fair in assessing why that might be."

Rebecca saw a chance to redeem herself. "That is what I want to write about. Why was he such a huge force? What part of the South was he appealing to?" She tried to sound committed in the hope of overcoming any doubts he had about her preparation.

He whistled. Not long or loud, just as if to mean 'good luck, you'll need it.' But all he said was, "How much do you know about the Davis years?"

"Not a lot. I'm not..."

"From the South? I know," he said, smiling. "Jeff told me when he called that you would need some, let's see, he called it 'orientation.' You're too young to know the history directly, but that's no sin."

"I'm trying to learn," Rebecca said, leaning over to take a book from her bag. "Jeff gave me this for background."

She handed the Woodston book to Edward, but saw instantly this was, damn it, another mistake. He made a small grimace, almost as though the book had an unpleasant odor.

"Not the one I might have recommended," Edward said mildly.

"It's written by an Emory professor." Why was she defending this book she had barely begun reading?

"Quite," Edward said, handing the book back. "The idea that Emory is a Southern school is a widely-held misperception. Of course, much of the material about Governor Davis is accurate, but I frankly thought the tone was more, well, negative than someone who understands the South could justify. I hope this is not your model for the story you plan."

"And I hope you don't think I've decided what to write before I start a story." Rebecca tried to keep her voice level.

"I'm sorry," Edward said. "I didn't mean to offend you. I only meant books like this refuse to grant that anything has changed here. We are not the same place we were in the Sixties."

Rebecca told him she'd keep that in mind, but she made a mental note of his defensiveness. She expected to see this in many of the people she talked to.

"Jeff told me no one could do the story of Thomas Jefferson Davis without talking to Gordon Halt," she said to change the subject. "Do you think your grandfather would be willing to see me?"

"I've already mentioned that to him," Edward said.

"I don't want to waste his time with questions that are common knowledge. How about the *Courier*'s morgue?"

Edward laughed. "The Governor was in office for four terms. You can't make much progress on the clips, there are too many, but there probably are some summaries. And you can meet Miss Amy, a Southern lady of the old school. That alone will justify your trip."

Was any grown woman really called Miss Amy, Rebecca wondered, when someone from the Midwest wasn't around?

More Like a War

Miss Amy turned out to be the librarian of the *Courier*, the custodian of the "clips" which were, simply, stories from the paper which had, for generations, been cut from the printed pages and placed in folders according to subject. The process had changed, of course, once newspaper stories began to be written on screens rather than paper, but computerization had only been around for about 20 years. The *Courier*, as Miss Amy had been anxious to inform Rebecca at the earliest opportunity, was founded in 1828, making this small daily older than *The New York Times*, which dated from 1851. After that revelation, Miss Amy was positively giddy in revealing that *The New York Times* was brought to greatness by a Southern family. Mr. Ochs had learned the business as publisher of the *Chattanooga Times* in Tennessee. By far the largest part of the history of the *Courier* was not on computer, but in the clip files, referred to as the "morgue."

Miss Amy ("nearly everybody but my husband calls me that, so you do too," she had insisted) was not a small woman. As tall as Rebecca at five seven, she was broad and solid as she strode between row after row of cabinets in the morgue, a group of cramped and garishly lit rooms deep in the interior of the building. Her size made Miss Amy's voice, a high, soft drawl, a surprise.

"Gracious, we do have a lot of material on the governor. It seems to me like we have had several pieces over the years giving a recap of his career. Those would give you the most information the quickest." She put her right hand to her chin in a gesture that could be titled "contemplation," then selected a drawer to open.

"This looks right," she said withdrawing several files and spreading them on a nearby counter. She looked through the clipped stories, in deep thought, seeming to talk to herself.

"Donnie Mason wrote this one. He was a nice young man, from one of the Ivy League schools. He went to the St. Petersburg paper after his wife left him. That was a sad thing."

Rebecca was thinking this was going to be a long process if Miss Amy was going to recite the professional and personal history of every byline she saw.

The older woman turned and handed the folder to Rebecca.

"This has a few updated stories that will give you a start. I'll keep looking while you read these."

The story by the abandoned Mr. Mason was written near the end of the Governor Davis's first term and, as Miss Amy had promised, was a perspective piece.

Thomas Jefferson Davis had seemingly come out of nowhere to defeat John "the Giant" Partain in the 1958 race for governor of the great State of Escambia. Partain, who was called Giant because of his six foot five inch height, had been a populist of the Huey Long variety. He was for spending money on education and good roads so farmers could get their crops to market. He was suspicious of the power company and the banks and especially the Escambia Land Bureau, a group that claimed to be a farm lobby but, according to the Giant, was only truly interested in keeping taxes low on the huge acreages held by mostly out-of-state mineral and paper companies. The Giant claimed he lost office because these groups, fearful they would be required to pay a fair share of state taxes, had bankrolled Davis as a way to regain control of the state house of representatives.

Davis's supporters naturally told a different story. They pointed out that Davis, as a state legislator had been a supporter, practically a protégé, of the Giant. It was only when the Giant's antics became an embarrassment to the state that Davis decided to run.

The story Rebecca read had been written in November 1961. She smiled at the delicate language the writer used to describe the Giant's "antics." Among other transgressions, the then-governor had been accused of "sharing" a hotel room with "a woman not his wife." The language seemed almost a parody in its gentility. But she could imagine her mother reading this story, finding a restraint in the choice of words that would not be unwelcome even now. Rebecca recalled that a few years back she had read, in *Newsweek* of all places, a graphic description of how gay men might spread the AIDS virus. It was hard to imagine news writing had changed so much.

There were other "antics" related in the story, but the one that apparently sealed Davis's eventual win was a televised debate — Rebecca was surprised such a thing was possible so long ago. It seemed that the Giant had been so intoxicated on camera that he had not remembered the names of his own children.

In the final weeks of the campaign the Giant claimed the debate had been fixed and repeated his warning that the office of governor was being bought by the big-money forces. But it was useless.

T.J. Davis was swept into the office he would not leave for two decades.

That night Rebecca had dinner in a chain restaurant before returning to her room at the chain motel. She wrestled her computer onto the table and connected the modem wire after unplugging the room phone. When the electronic growling ended, indicating a connection had been made, she checked her email and left messages for Jeff and Paul.

Lying in bed, she scanned the Woodson book, thinking history would make her sleepy if all else failed. But every page seemed to contain some graphic account of a beating, a shooting or a bombing. The civil rights movement, to judge by this book, had been more like a war against habits of life that seemed almost unimaginable now. The so-called Freedom Riders, for example, were simply people riding on Greyhound buses through a series of southern towns. The only aspects of the trip that were protests in any way were that passengers sat where they wished and, when in local stations, they refused to use separate waiting rooms, restrooms and entrances for blacks and whites. Yet that was enough to cause violent reaction by townspeople, nowhere more so than here in Escambia.

Just before she closed the book for the night, she flipped back to the introduction, intending to learn more about the author, but finding another penciled note from Jeff, this one in the form of a big star in the margin beside a line of text that had been heavily underlined:

The past is a terrible place to live, but some people can make a home nowhere else.

She Knew the "Big Picture"

G ordon Halt lived in Glendale, a fashionable older section of Montville. Driving to his house, Rebecca had the impression of going into parkland. The lots were not huge, one or two acres, but were heavily wooded with old trees. There were none of the spindly pear trees seen by the hundreds in new developments, planted in a fruitless effort to make tract houses look permanent.

Mr. Halt proved to be a stately man, slow moving not just because of age but also a certain natural formality. His face was smooth, lighted by cheery green eyes under graying brows, and his white hair was carefully combed. His manner was so animated and friendly she would have taken him for a younger man than she knew he must be, but when they shook hands she felt the slackness of age, as though the bones withdrew slightly from the skin.

"I have enjoyed meeting Edward," Rebecca said. "I can see the resemblance."

The old man smiled slightly. "That's more of a compliment than you know. When I see Edward, his father seems to smile back at me."

Miss Amy had told Rebecca that Mr. Halt's only son, John --Edward's Father--had died several years before in the same car crash that crippled Mrs. Halt.

"It must make you happy to have Edward at the paper."

"The newspaper has always been central to the family. Even though we don't own it anymore, having Edward continue the tradition gives me great pleasure."

He led the way from the entrance foyer through a formal dining room where Rebecca counted eight chairs around the long table and at least four more against the walls. An original landscape painting on one wall faced a huge multi-paned window giving a view onto a lovely garden. They then came into a paneled den with a large desk, a sofa covered in stripes of green and tan, and two armchairs. Two walls were covered with framed awards and photographs; the other featured floor-to-ceiling bookshelves. As in the dining room, a large window looked onto the garden. Gordon Halt settled into one of the armchairs and motioned for Rebecca to take the other.

Rebecca retrieved a notebook and recorder from her bag but felt in no hurry to begin the interview. Miss Amy must be having an effect on her; she didn't want to appear abrupt. "Does it always smell this good in here, Mr. Halt?" The most wonderful scent filled the cozy room -- yeasty, cinnamon and somehow warm, like Christmas cookies.

"Call me Gordon, please. Mr. Halt was my father." He grinned, and then tilted his face up to take a noisy sniff.

"You caught Margaret in her baking mode. She can't get anywhere near a peach without making a cobbler. You'll have to help us test it in a bit."

After getting Mr. Halt's permission to turn on her recorder, Rebecca explained that she knew the "big picture" about T. J. Davis's importance in the state. Now she wanted to talk to people like him who had been on the scene when all this history was happening. She asked him if he had felt strange, going from an editor to a campaign staffer.

"You were already a notable figure in state government yourself, since the *Courier* was the paper of the state capital."

Gordon nodded, as he would do after almost every question.

"I suppose that's right," he said. "I had been Capitol Editor for some years and I had a bit of influence. I thought the move to the governor's staff would give me more."

"That would raise eyebrows in some journalism schools."

"I don't see why." Gordon tugged slightly at his collar. "There have been plenty of news people who have become speech writers and press secretaries."

"But surely not at your level. It was your own paper. You weren't afraid of hurting the *Courier's* reputation for impartiality?"

"No. The *Courier* had someone to make sure that was never in question. If anything, I wanted to protect the administration from the paper, not the other way around."

"You're referring to your father, I take it? He must have been disappointed that you would work for an administration he did not support."

Gordon stirred in his chair, lifting himself up on the arms seeming to look for a comfortable position. He looked at Rebecca, his eyes narrowing slightly.

"I don't think your readers are likely to be interested in that kind of question."

"But Mr. Halt," —she noticed he didn't correct her this time— "you are a big part of Governor Davis's place in Escambia history."

This flattery clearly had no effect on the old man. "But my relationship with my father is certainly not." He smiled as he said it, as though he were still being modest. But beneath his gentle manner, Rebecca recognized that he was addressing her as Jeff would, as her editor. He expected his word to settle the matter. As though his body reflected her thought, he relaxed back into the chair before he spoke again.

Gordon said he had not always been a supporter of T. J. Davis. The governor had been in office several years before Gordon did any work for him. But Gordon told her he had been impressed with Davis "since the first time I ever spoke to him" at a college football game. That first meeting had apparently assumed the power of myth in Gordon's memory, judging by the loving detail in which he recounted it.

Like nearly all men of their age, Gordon and Davis had their college years interrupted by World War II. Both men left the University to serve, though they had no contact during their absence. On returning to Escambia, Gordon finished a degree in journalism and joined the family newspaper. T. J. Davis transferred to the law school — Rebecca was surprised to learn that at that time it was not necessary to have a degree before entering — and became active in campus politics, the usual first step for future state leaders. After graduation, the future governor returned to his hometown and Gordon again lost sight of him for several years, until Davis came to Montville as the youngest member of the legislature.

"How did that happen?"

Gordon smiled at her.

"The usual way. He worked very hard and he got a lucky break. The incumbent died. In some ways that was the story of his entire career. He loved campaigning, loved shaking hands and remembering family connections. And many times something happened to create an opportunity where there had not been one before. Such as the debate in which Giant Partain defeated himself.

"Even the school desegregation issue could be called a case of Davis luck. We look back at the famous 'boycott' of black students from the University as something of an embarrassment, but at the time it galvanized the voters and gave the governor a power and authority much greater than he would otherwise have had. So, hard work and lucky breaks at the right time were the keys. But that's true for every famous man, I suspect."

Rebecca wondered about calling the deaths of two men "lucky breaks" but, of course, Mr. Halt was right. It was only realistic, not morbid, to recognize that death, like alcoholism or a sexual affair, is a fact of political life that often changes elections and careers.

Gordon staunchly defended the Davis against the charge of racism. "It was very much overblown. I don't think Governor Davis had a hateful bone in his body. He did make use of rhetoric; I admit that. And, this being the South, the rhetoric tended toward the excessive. We are emotional people and we speak with passion when calm would be more becoming. But recognizing that, and the historical period that produced him, I think Governor Davis deserves much credit for restraint during his years in office. In retirement, he frequently repudiated the excesses of those years."

Rebecca made notes of this speech without comment. She wouldn't have expected Mr. Halt to say that Davis was to blame for the buses being burned and the Freedom Riders being beaten in downtown

Montville and she didn't want to begin challenging him in this first interview. She would have a chance to ask others how T. J. Davis's apologies for those times had been received.

Mrs. Halt (Rebecca smiled to think she would undoubtedly say, "Call me Margaret, Hon.") came to the door, announcing that the cobbler had cooled enough to serve. Rebecca thought how strange it was that there were no footsteps to announce her, just the low hum of the wheelchair, and she felt for a moment her usual awkwardness around disabled people. But Mrs. Halt was as cheerful as Rebecca could imagine anyone being, and the feeling faded.

As they followed Margaret to the sunny kitchen, Gordon whispered to Rebecca, "You might make a fuss over the cobbler. She got the recipe from her Momma." Then he gave her a wink that Rebecca thought was as flirtatious as it was conspiratorial.

She did not need any encouragement to "fuss over" the cobbler. It sat proudly on the kitchen table, the light from the bay window glittering on the glazed and sugar-sprinkled crust that swelled over the sides of the tin pan.

"A friend brings the peaches from Chilton County over in central Alabama," Gordon said. "People call Georgia the peach state, but I don't know that they have any better than these, especially when Margaret gets a hold of them."

Mrs. Halt smiled as she reached over to pat her husband's hand. "Don't embarrass me in front of company." She picked up her fork again and said to Rebecca, "Besides, I could make a much better crust when I was younger. These hands can't roll out the dough as well."

Rebecca truthfully said she could hardly imagine a crust being better, then turned the conversation back to work.

"The books and news stories talk about how incredibly popular Governor Davis was, but I haven't seen anything that explained why."

Gordon smiled at her with a certain warmth, as though he were an old uncle. "I tend to forget how concerned young people are with 'why.' I guess we never really know. My own thought was that he understood the need plain people had to be taken seriously. He said it's okay to be country and to talk slow and to resent being pushed around by the government. People responded to that."

Rebecca considered that recent presidents had included Jimmy Carter and Bill Clinton before asking, "Did Southerners have a problem being taken seriously?"

"Oh, I think so." He sipped his coffee. "I know you'll say the Southern Senators have always been among the most powerful. Look at Jesse Helms and Strom Thurmond, to this day, and Newt Gingrich and Trent Lott. But I don't think there is any serious question that in the South we were second class citizens."

"Didn't the South bring some of that on itself?" Rebecca thought the events of the civil rights movement must have produced a lot of negative feelings about the South. Her own mother was an example.

"By the war, you mean? I suppose that argument can be made."

"War?" She felt as though she had wandered into a completely different conversation.

He grinned mischievously, "I was speaking of the War Between the States. Perhaps you've heard of it?"

Actually, Rebecca had barely heard of it. The war took up only two days on the history curriculum in an Indiana middle school. And anyway, that was not what she had meant.

"That's a little far out there for me, Mr. Halt. I was talking about the violent resistance to civil rights. Wasn't that a factor in how Southerners were thought of?"

Gordon was quiet for a long time. Rebecca thought that for the first time she had said something he didn't have a ready answer for.

"That is an excellent comment, but it points out the difficulty in our generations being so far apart — I don't mean in years only, but in emotional attachment to events. For someone your age, the civil rights years are the distant past and the war is as ancient as the Roman Empire. For me, the civil rights years are recent, a part of my own history, while the particular attitude toward the South that I am talking about is much older. That attitude, the second-class status of Southerners, was established during Reconstruction and had not begun to be weakened until T. J. Davis came into office."

He sipped his coffee and dabbed his lips with a cloth napkin before continuing. "You won't understand, but the War Between the States seemed recent to Southerners my age. When we were children it was constantly referred to. I grew up in Salem, on the Tecumseh River that forms the border with Mississippi, and my family knew two or three ladies who were widows of much older husbands who had fought in the war.

"We were the defeated ones, after all. As a young man I occasionally traveled to New York or Chicago on business for the paper. On those trips it was very clear I was considered an odd creature, hardly to be expected to keep up with complicated business discussions. If I was treated that way as a fairly prominent member of an important family, you can imagine how the working men and women of the South were treated."

"You do mean the white working men and women?"

Gordon's eyes narrowed.

Rebecca continued. "I mean, the black working men and women were accustomed to that treatment, right?"

He looked at her guardedly, as though they had not been introduced. "We are all glad those days are over," he said.

"I understand," Rebecca pressed, "but, at the time, racism was a large part of Governor Davis's appeal. Isn't that true?"

"I've already said that he wasn't a racist."

"But he used racism, didn't he?"

Gordon's face tightened as though an unpleasant taste was on his lips.

"You think that's the only story there is in the South, racism? It was a complicated time. I'm sure if he were not lying unconscious in that hospital, Governor Davis would say that he followed the people in that regard, more than he led them. But it's a complex story. And it was half a century ago. It's hard to judge a man fairly looking back."

"You don't think he should be judged for what he did, the role he played?"

"I didn't say that. I said it's hard to be fair in doing the judging."

Rebecca wasn't convinced, but she wasn't here for a debate. She tried another tack.

"I read that in all his campaigns, Governor Davis was never seriously challenged except by a..." she looked at her notes, "a Michael

DeWitt, the lieutenant governor?" Rebecca could see she had surprised the old man again.

"You have done some research, haven't you?" he said.

He stared into her eyes for a long moment, but then his alert expression changed, his face falling as though he had heard disappointing news, or remembered some, and she knew they were finished for the day.

Like, with Two Syllables

Rebecca's notebook, which had been empty when she arrived in Escambia, was now crammed with notes, most of them describing a world as exotic as Haiti or Kazakhstan. She had learned that, during the civil rights years, nearly one-third of the citizens of Georgia, Alabama, Escambia and Mississippi — the "deep" in Deep South — had been African-Americans. She could appreciate this now, living in Atlanta, but when growing up in Indianapolis black people had been as rare as, well, grits.

She had also learned, having never really understood it before, that the old Supreme Count case, *Brown v. Board of Education*, had mattered because there were places that had completely separate school systems for black children. Separate buildings, separate staffs, everything. The state of Florida even made its free textbook system entirely separate. The result was that if a schoolbook was intended for a black school it was separated from "white" books from the very first moment it entered the state. That book was transported in trucks carrying only "black" books and stored in warehouses used only for "black" books, as though a book might spread contagion.

She also found that some things were different than she expected. The Brown decision, which held that "separate but equal" schools were inherently unequal and therefore illegal, was one. She had long known the title of the case but now she learned that particular famous Board of Education was located in Topeka, Kansas. She had thought the case involved only southern states.

* * *

"Do you like Atlanta?" Miss Amy pronounced the verb "lye-ke," with two syllables. She had brought two cups of coffee to Rebecca's table and now shared a break with her.

"It's so big," — bee-ug — the older woman said without waiting for an answer. "Why now a days it seems as big as New York (nu-yaw-uk) doesn't it?"

"It is a major city," Rebecca agreed. There was a brief silence, something rare when Miss Amy was around, before she spoke again.

"But you're not from Atlanta, are you?"

Rebecca laughed. She had never thought to question a person she had barely met about such a thing. Things were definitely different here.

"You caught me," she said.

"It's no crime," Miss Amy laughed, "but we can usually tell. Now let's see, I'd say you're from the Midwest, maybe Ohio or Missouri?"

"Indiana. Pretty close."

"I think it's fun that we still sound different. Don't you think it makes people more interesting to have some differences?"

Rebecca agreed that it did, not saying that some differences might not be a good thing. She was thinking of the attacks on the Freedom Riders she had read about last night, but then realized how unfair that was. Those beatings had happened 35 years ago, before she was born.

"I got to spend three months up in Pennsylvania, years ago." Miss Amy was also thinking about the past. "I worked in a company's records department up there, sort of an internship.

Rebecca looked longingly toward the files she needed to read, her coffee almost finished, but Miss Amy missed the hint, continuing.

"And it was the strangest thing, people would come in this big room, people I knew, at least on sight, they would come in and get a file they needed, or pull a report down and read it. Then, when they were finished they would leave, walking right by me just pretty as you please."

Rebecca was puzzled. She had heard Southerners were story-tellers, but this "story" didn't seem to have much of a point. Miss Amy apparently read that thought on her face and giggled like a young girl.

"Oh, see, you're just like them. You don't see what was strange. They didn't speak when they came in. They would walk right past you, do their business and then leave without a word."

"Oh," Rebecca said, apparently without sufficient conviction.

"See?" Miss Amy was so into her story she hopped a little in her chair. "That's the way they looked when I asked about it. One of them said, 'Amy, I've already said good morning to you when we first came in.' Miss Amy's face registered amazement as she added, "Like that was all the helloing you'd do all day!"

"Well, Miss Amy," Rebecca said, "you can feel free to say hi to me as many times a day as you want to."

The older woman gave a big grin. "I promise not to overdo it." She picked up the empty coffee cups and walked back to her desk. Rebecca turned back to the clip files, traveling back to the 1960's.

Rebecca entered another name into her pad and, later, remembered to take it with her when she accepted Miss Amy's invitation to lunch.

People Do Like to Talk

R ebecca dug her fork into the steaming pile of wilted leaves on her plate. "I have friends in Atlanta who eat these."

"Now, Hon," Miss Amy said, "you sound like an anthropologist. This is not strange food; this is real food. Collards are my own choice for the classic southern green. Though some people would give that title to turnip greens."

Rebecca chewed the soft mass of collards, while thinking that turnips were a root vegetable, weren't they? Are there green turnips? She was also thinking this was substantial food, to be worked through like a piece of steak. The dense, smoky flavor reminded her of spinach but turned up and with a mineral edge; spinach on steroids.

Miss Amy had gently suggested that a non-native could not really explain the South without a first hand experience of the local cuisine. No place better served that purpose, in her opinion, than this large dining room in what appeared to be a private house. "Tucker's," Miss Amy had called it. Formerly a boarding house, the widow had planned to close the place after Mr. Tucker passed, but the luncheon spreads were legendary and customer pleas were so piteous that Mrs. Tucker was prevailed upon to continue opening her dining room for lunch (only) as a public service.

"She feels it's her contribution to the cultural life of our city," Miss Amy confided in a low voice.

Rebecca stifled a smile. When she talked to Paul last night he had kidded her about being in the "boonies." "What's the difference between Escambia and yogurt?" he had asked. "Yogurt has a live culture." Rebecca decided Miss Amy might not find that amusing. Instead she asked, "Is it my imagination or do you know everybody in town?

"Oh I don't think so. But a Southern lady does feel a certain duty to be well informed about her community. And, like yourself, I am at least a tiny bit in the newspaper business."

She tittered. It was a word Rebecca's mother sometimes used and it sprang to mind for the tiny half laugh Miss Amy made.

Rebecca suddenly put down her fork and retrieved her notebook. "I've got this list you might help me with," she said. "The clips have all these names - it's like I need a program."

Rebecca placed the list beside her plate and, as they ate, Miss Amy explained who the players were.

Gordon Halt had been the last chairman of the family corporation when the paper was sold to the giant Newmann chain in the late Sixties. And, as Rebecca also knew, he worked for Governor Davis for a number of years. She asked Miss Amy if people at the paper thought that was improper.

"It wasn't at the same time," Miss Amy said. "He would never do that. He left the paper during those years."

Rebecca asked about Michael DeWitt. Miss Amy recalled him well. "His people were from up in Carnegie, in the steel business somehow. His daddy was rich as Croesus. Fine man. Michael had been a rival of Governor Davis for years."

Rebecca recalled that DeWitt had died long ago, in a car accident. "There was a lot of talk about that at the time because it was right before the election," Miss Amy said. "People do like to talk."

That left Fred Middlebrooks who, Miss Amy pointed out was the Reverend Fred Middlebrooks. He had been the most important civil rights leader in Escambia, Miss Amy said. And yes, he was still alive. In fact, she thought he was still teaching an occasional course at the University.

Miss Amy looked thoughtful as she dabbed her mouth with her napkin.

"Now that I think about it, the last time I saw Reverend Fred he was sitting right over there." She motioned to a small table under one of the large windows that faced the street.

"He likes the collards?" Rebecca asked with a grin.

Miss Amy tilted her head toward Rebecca, keen to detect any hint of sarcasm.

"Everyone likes the collards, Hon. But the Reverend, I've heard, especially likes that table. They say that was where he sat the very first time he ever came in this room." Miss Amy lowered her voice, as though spreading an unsavory rumor. "It was white only then, you know."

"Hmmm," Rebecca said. "I wonder what that felt like?"

The older woman looked at her for a moment before speaking.

"He got himself arrested, so I'm sure he remembers. You should go and ask him."

The Special Collection

T he University of Escambia was not famous for very many things. On the phone the other night, Paul had been a little cruel about the institution's academic reputation. (What do you get if you drive slowly past the UE campus? A degree!)

"Hell of a football team, though," Rebecca had noted, defending this place from her reporter's sense of fairness. Even in far off Indiana, as a child she had heard her uncles discuss the prowess of legendary coach 'Bear' Butler.

The University gained notoriety in the civil rights era when Governor Davis refused to peacefully integrate it and turned a confrontation with federal authorities into the fountainhead of a political dynasty. The governor's repeated pledge to "chain the schoolhouse gate" against black students had been a source of political symbolism and power for him long after black students had been admitted despite his show of resistance.

At exit 106, Rebecca steered the rental car down the ramp to a stop. Signs on the highway led her to the campus. Her rental car passed dignified old brick buildings and blank modern ones that seemed to debate architecture across tree-lined streets. She found a parking space a few blocks from the central quadrangle and walked toward the bell tower. Miss Amy had said this was the heart of the campus and the best place to get oriented. The tower (her map referred to the structure as "The Chimes") was built of colonial red brick, with a wooden cornice near the top and a cupola trimmed in white. Rebecca smiled to herself thinking that the locals probably would not refer to this style as "Federal," but the stately column would be completely at home in Williamsburg.

She unfolded the email response she had received from Professor Middlebrooks. He would not be able to meet with her until next week, but suggested that the university library would be of value.

"Our Butler library will never be confused with the one at Coumbia, of course." In his message, the professor pointed out that the state had a college or junior college in almost every town that had three traffic lights, and with so many institutions to fund the legislature did not have the money to make any one of them of national quality.

"But for what you need, which is the story of T. J. Davis and Escambia, there is no better place," he had written. "The Library has every resource imaginable about the history, ecology, geology, and every other "ory" or "ology" you can think of about Escambia."

Rebecca easily found the imposing structure, climbed the stone steps to the elaborate entrance and walked past the card catalogs, rows of wooden chests, filled with small drawers fronted by brass pulls. She wondered if anyone ever used a card catalog now as she stepped into the ancient elevator. The door was a folding metal gate, giving her the impression of being in a large birdcage, which, noisy and slow, carried her to the reference department on the third floor.

"Talk to Mrs. Fieldstone," the Professor had said. "She'll be glad to help you."

The stern matron standing near the marble counter looked as though she'd be far from doing any such thing. With her scowl, severe dress and rapid movements, Rebecca thought Mrs. Fieldstone looked like a prison matron in an old black-and-white movie, a woman who might be happier guarding inmates than books. She stepped forward abruptly, as though to forestall any show of initiative by an outsider.

"What *materials* would you be wanting to see this morning?" Rebecca had hoped Professor Middlebrooks might have talked to this woman to make an introduction, but if that call had occurred Mrs. Fieldstone was not responding warmly to it. Rebecca explained her assignment and her need for information from the collections to present a rounded picture of the Davis years.

"A rounded picture, indeed," Mrs. Fieldstone sniffed. She turned with a gesture, an order really, that Rebecca should follow and walked to a stairwell, then up one floor and down a long corridor to where a double door was set into an alcove. The words "Special Collections" were painted in gold on mottled glass door panels.

Once inside, Rebecca saw that she had entered an entire department, comprising at least three large rooms she could see opening off the central hall where she stood. Dark wooden bookshelves climbed every available wall while a group of ornate desks for staff members took up the center space.

She followed the librarian into one of the smaller rooms where metal shelving was filled with tan storage boxes. Each box bore a neon yellow label with the name of a publication, a number and the time period. Box number 5456 was marked "Crimson - Spring Semester - 1942, Box 1 of 3."

"There are work tables against each wall," Mrs. Fieldstone said. "Please take only one box at a time to look through. When you finish with one, place it on the reshelve table at the end of aisle 18. Do you understand?"

Rebecca nodded.

"Do not reshelve the boxes yourself."

"I understand," Rebecca said, in case nodding was not enough.

Mrs. Fieldstone seemed about to say something, but turned and pointed to one of the smaller rooms.

"In the room on the left are published volumes related to the civil rights era generally and Escambia history. The room on the right may be of more interest..." the librarian turned back to look at her, "for your purposes."

It suddenly occurred to Rebecca that this was the first time since she'd been in Escambia that anyone had been actively rude to her. As she thought about why that might be, Rebecca was inadvertently staring at the librarian.

"Well?" the older woman asked.

"Have I offended you in some way?"

If Rebecca had thought such directness would throw Mrs. Fieldstone, she was mistaken.

"You have not, Miss, but I must confess I do not care for your business."

"Newspapers?"

"Dirt." She spat the word out. "That's what you're looking for. Dirt to embarrass the governor and embarrass the state. Just like all those times before."

Rebecca felt the need to defend herself. "I'm just trying to do a balanced story. That's what…"

The older woman cut her off, speaking with emotion,

"By talking to Fred Middlebrooks? You think he's going to give your story balance?

Rebecca thought again about how emotional this material was, even though to someone Rebecca's age it seemed too ancient to matter. This was exactly why she had told Jeff she didn't want to do history in the first place.

"Look," she said, "I haven't even met the professor until yet. You don't know me but I'm a good reporter. I even work for a Southern paper. I've got no reason to tilt this story one way or the other."

The librarian bit her lower lip but did not say anything. After a long moment Mrs. Fieldstone turned on her heel and continued where she had left off.

"The room to your right is where the University maintains its copy of all theses and dissertations done by graduate students, at least all the ones that relate to Escambia history. I know that Mr. DeWitt and Governor Davis have been the subjects of a number of those. Indexes are here in the central hall."

Rebecca went to the indexes eagerly, finding many references to Davis, DeWitt, and fewer to Halt and Middlebrooks. There were references to three different dissertations on the 1958 election for governor in which Davis had defeated Giant Partain. She also found a one-line description of a manuscript for an unpublished book, Pressing Business — A Newspaper Publisher in the Civil Rights Era South, which appeared to be a history of the Halt family newspaper, and a list of reference numbers for numerous boxes of miscellaneous materials for unfunded research. The entry indicated these miscellaneous materials were not cataloged.

Rebecca was pleased. She had spent much of her college years doing research of one kind or another and most days had not been nearly this productive. Of course that depended partly on the subject. She had often spent a week researching some topic and been lucky to find a helpful paragraph.

With popular subjects like civil rights, the problem was the oppo-site — too much material, not too little — and therefore the difficulty was in finding some fact, some connection, some meaning that had not already been analyzed and dissected a hundred times.

Which raised another problem — one she had thought about a lot but had not admitted, certainly not to Jeff. When she worked on political stories at the paper, they were small-scale pieces with just a few sources, and those not difficult to locate. Since she was doing the digging, she could be an authority. She hoped that voters found her stories interesting and helpful, but she was honest enough to admit there wasn't much at stake for readers to get excited about.

As Mrs. Fieldstone had already demonstrated, however, this story was different. How could she pretend to be an authority? Many of the people who lived this story were still alive. And another thing. This was not obscure history. This wasn't like a change of rules that usually made little or no difference in the daily lives of average readers. This story involved the world being turned upside down in a generation at the very most fundamental levels. It was a story that made heroes of the people on the professor's side and something close to demons of those who had opposed civil rights. It was a story about opening sores that, decades later, were still sensitive to the slightest touch. What hope did she have that some writing of hers would do more good than harm?

She finished making notes on the last of the dissertations, replaced the file in the box and, with several grunts, managed to move the heavy box to the reshelve table. The sun slanted low through the window as she stretched her back and shoulders. She had filled many pages of a legal pad with notes and mulled the possibility of quitting a little early, then changed her mind. She was near the end of the list she'd made that morning of possible sources and all she had to look forward to was the long ride back to Montville and a fast-food dinner. She looked for the next item.

"Section LL, drawer 3."

She followed the trail of drawer labels around to Section LL in a dark corner of the room. Drawer 3 was not labeled but 2, above it, was. The drawer was heavy to open but inside she found only 14 thin files most of which were entirely off subject and took up only a few inches of the drawer. The moveable divider had been slid forward to hold those up and behind the divider Rebecca found three large manila envelopes, lying flat and nearly out of sight.

The crumpled brown envelopes were bulky and surprisingly heavy. She wrestled one out and read on one side the hand-written words "Oral History Project — Davis Administration." Rebecca checked her list of the items from the indexes, but saw no reference to "oral history." She reported this to Mrs. Fieldstone.

"So," the older woman said acidly, "you found a treasure." She told Rebecca what the younger woman already knew. Most research libraries have large amounts of material they don't know about. "It's obvious, really. People have papers and things they know should be saved and they give them to us because saving things is our job. Often the items come from old offices or warehouses and are thrown into boxes more or less at random. Then we have budget cuts and downsizing and as a result we often don't have staff to go through all the boxes and tell us what we have. But we can at least keep them safe until a need for the material arises."

As they talked Rebecca removed five large plastic reels from the envelope. The reels were smaller than motion picture reels she had seen and were nearly full of narrow brown tape.

"This looks like the tape on cassettes," Rebecca said.

"Recording tape is exactly what it is. Before your time, as most things are, this would have been played on a large machine we called a "reel-to-reel" player. You see, this reel is full and the machine wound the tape onto an empty reel as it played."

"Can we find a machine to play these?"

The librarian rubbed her throat absentmindedly before answering. "I don't know if that's a good idea. As I said, we have no idea what's on the tape."

"Right." Rebecca nodded, her eyebrows raised. "That's actually why I thought playing it might be a good idea."

"I need to check with my supervisor to see..."

Now it was Rebecca who moved to protect her territory.

"This is a public research institution and this material is part of an open collection. Professor Middlebrooks invited me to use the library. Be sure to tell your supervisor that."

Miss Fieldstone scowled and walked away to use a phone out of Rebecca's hearing. A half hour passed after which Rebecca was allowed to sign out the tapes, but only to take them to the multi-media lab in the basement, where a reel-to-reel recorder had been located. A shaggy haired communications major with an ear stud set up the large boxy device.

"Be glad you didn't need an eight-track. Unh-unh... We <u>don't</u> have one of those."

When he was ready, Rebecca handed him the only reel that was labeled, with a small white rectangle bearing the typed name "Billy Trask."

"I don't guess you know who that would be?" Rebecca asked.

"No way," he replied. "Judging by the age of that label he could have signed the Declaration of Independence. You ready?" When Rebecca nodded, he pushed the "Play" button.

"Mother" Sounds Way too Formal

TRANSCRIPT
Interview: Billy Trask
Position: Chief of Staff   Date: [unknown]

Gordon is a' OK fella, but, really, I never understood why the governor wanted him around. I know he had his reasons, and the governor's a sight smarter than me, that's for sure. But I just thought Gordon was so much different than the rest of us.

Hell, when I first met him he didn't even drink. I always think that's a bad sign, but maybe I was around too many Baptists growing up. And he was such a hoity toity. You know his family owned damn near the whole county, which is funny 'cause his daddy was the newspaper guy who was about half communist to begin with.

And that name of his. He didn't even have a nickname like the rest of us, unless you count Mash Miller always calling him Dick-head. He wouldn't even let you call him Gordy, like a regular guy. Didn't say why he didn't like it, but he'd be quick to tell you he didn't. "Please call me Gordon," he'd say. Like it was a title or something. Hell, what kind of name is that, anyway? It always sounded about half queer to me. 'Specially with that flower he always had in his coat collar. And a tie everyday.

But none of that made no nevermind. The governor wanted his advice and opinions and the governor always made damn sure he got what he wanted.

And Gordon was a good enough guy. I got to where I was right friendly with him. And I did get him to where he could knock back a slug of Jim Beam right out of the bottle which, if you'd a seen him when I met him, you'd know was a whole lot of progress.

He was a right interestin' fella to me. Gordon was crazy for the politics stuff, just like the governor was. I never understood that myself. I mean, I loved the governor like he was my big brother, better if you get down to it, but the politics was just a big ole pain in the ass. But not for Gordon. Gordon liked being a big deal. Or thinking he was a big deal, which ain't really the same thing, if you take my meaning.

He didn't have a practical side to him. I figured the politics was something you did so you had a friend in the capital and could make a little money hauling gravel or selling coal or printing legal documents. You know, public service. But not Gordon. That kind a thing wouldn't have been enough money to get his attention. He wanted to do good. What a dick-head.

I got up with the governor mainly 'cause his Daddy and my Daddy had growed up together. It was always kinda assumed that he was going to be a big deal, and I was going to be help for him. It was that way at the University. He'd run for class president or some damn thing and I'd be there to help. I don't think the University had a dogcatcher or I guess by God he woulda run for that. But whatever it was, I'd always be right there with him. Running the mimeograph machine (I guess you probably don't have no idea a'tall what that was), cranking till I thought my arm'ud fall off. And then, of course, that was only the beginning, 'cause a handbill is plumb useless 'til it gets passed out, so I guess you know whose job that was, too.

Then after the University I was working at home, doing some welding and sellin' cars and odds and ends and the governor was running for district judge. It was a little old job, not much more than justice of the peace, but he was running like it was Supreme Court justice, and he needed some help.

You had to get a man's permission to park a flatbed in the parking lot of his store, and you had to find somebody's flatbed to use. Hell, you had to round up some kind of an audience. But I had lived there all my life, so I was good at it. And then, you know, I was with him all the time and listening to him talk about being proud of what we were and somehow, even though I heard the speeches over and over, I got to believing in him.

The campaigning was a lot different then. The towns were so small, it don't seem possible. People didn't really trust politicians any more'n they do now, but back then they was willing to listen to 'em. For a while, at least. It was like entertainment. If a circus hadda come through town, they would a gone out and seen that, too. Or a tent preacher. The politicians was kinda like that. There wadn't no TV.

(Unintelligible)

Pardon me?

(Unintelligible)

What was that word? Oh, I said "wadn't". What does it mean? Well now... let me think. It means "was not." It's a whatchacallit, a contraption. Ha! Wadn't. I never even thought about it.

See now, it's funny you asked about that. I'm sure you're thinking that's just typical old ignorant Southern talkin'. Naw, now don't deny it. I know you're too polite to say so, but that's what you're thinking. Which is a shame on account of ignorance has got nothing on God's green Earth to do with it. See, to us, using the slang and stuff is a way to make you more comfortable. To us, when people go out of their way to use the fancy grammar and the big words, why that's just another way of saying "look how smart I am." It's just rude, if you think about it.

'Course a big part is just habit. We all talk how we learned to talk when we was young uns. I had a reporter in here one time, interviewing me you know, and he asked me about mama. Not my mama, of course. He wouldn't a known her, he just asked me about the _word_. I don't know how it come up, one or two things had reminded me of mama, so that's what I said. And he asked me if that was something I said so I would sound southern.

Well, hell, I looked at him like he'd asked if my mama worked in a whorehouse. "Son," I said, "I don't have to worry about sounding Southern; I _am_ Southern." Then I asked him, "Where you from?" and he said "Virginia" and I began to see the problem. You'd be surprised how many people think Virginia is part of the South. So I said, "Is that where your people are from?" And he said, "My father's family was from Connecticut." Ha! That right there made the problem a whole lot clearer. So I said, "Whose family was that?"

And he said, "My father's"

"Hum. And what do you call your father's wife?"

He gave me this funny look. He was thinking so hard I was afraid his eyebrows might fall off. "My mother?" he says.

"Right!" I said, and slapped him on the knee. "See, that's your problem," I said. "Down here, we think 'Mother' sounds way too formal. That sounds like what the rich folks kids learned to say while they was off at boardin' school. That's just the problem, actually. It sounds distant, like the person is just an acquaintance. So we say mama."

That's part of being Southern, you see? We recognize that talking means a lot more than just the words you use. The sound of the words, how you say 'em, whether it's high or low, loud or soft, the meaning is all of that. That's why it's so easy to insult us. We don't just hear what you said; we hear everything you meant.

{end of transcript}

Rebecca worked the Xerox machine, almost giddy. She made copies of this transcript and several others for Mr. Halt and Professor Middlebrooks, with handwritten notes asking for comment, and called Mr. Halt to say she'd be sending it. But she didn't send any of them to Jeff; she wanted to surprise her editor with how resourceful she'd been after she had a story to put around this research.

Strangers in Their Own Country

T he class was in progress when Rebecca took a rear seat in the high-ceilinged lecture room. A tall, strongly built man stood throttling a frail lectern. Unruly gray hair grew thickly around his bald pate, and gray eyelashes were prominent on his dark face. He seemed too energetic to be Professor Middlebrooks, a man who could not be younger than seventy-five. His voice reverberated in the modest sized hall with the depth and resonance she associated with a speech. Or a sermon.

"You will be voting on these questions all your life. You need to understand how these issues affect your fellow citizens," the professor was saying. "If a politician asks you to vote for a new tax, you should know sales taxes are very hard on the poor, much more so than on well-to-do people. That's what we mean when we call these regressive taxes."

A young man about ten rows from the front raised his hand. Rebecca noticed the student's hair was cut short and immaculately combed, in sharp contrast to his teacher's.

"If the tax is a penny on the dollar and I, like, spend a dollar, I pay the penny. If some poor person spends a dollar they pay the penny too, you know? So what's the big deal?"

"Look again." The professor turned to the calculations that were already on the blackboard. "The working poor must spend a much higher percentage of their income at the grocery store that prosperous people do. In other words, this "equal" tax is much more difficult for the poor person to pay. And the richer people are, the less they feel the effect of the tax."

The well-dressed student was not impressed. "If I make that much money, I should, like, be able to keep it, you know? I mean, I thought that's what a free economy was all about. If poor people don't have enough money shouldn't they, like, get better jobs?"

The professor jammed the eraser onto the tray on the board, but with too much force. The eraser bounced out onto the floor as he spoke.

"Is that what's involved? That the poor don't work hard enough? Do you really believe that opportunity is equally available in this economy? The different burden of taxes is just the tip of an iceberg of inequity. Add in tax benefits: 401K's, capital gains, stock options, things that working class people never even guess at, and the favoritism toward the rich is even more pronounced."

His voice cracked slightly and rose in volume. For the first time he seemed like an old man. "And it works on the other end as well. Public money is spent for infrastructure improvements to benefit those who are already well off. Why is it there are airports in this country that look like the Taj Mahal, but almost no public transit systems that are not near bankruptcy? Why do we ask poor people to pay sales tax to build "public" football stadia with skyboxes that are given away to the team owners to sell for millions of dollars in private profits? Then the owners charge prices so high that working people can't afford to get in these palaces they are paying for."

"The answer is that working class is never included in the system at all. At least they are not included in the benefits. When the system overheats, the working people are certainly expected to pay for it. Ask your parents about the savings-and-loan scandal of the 70's. The bankers said governmental controls were unfair and hurt the economy. But these same bankers wanted the government to continue to guarantee the accounts, so investors would feel comfortable. When the savings and loan system collapsed after controls were removed, it cost working people $500 billion."

Some of the students looked wary, on-guard against this strange attack on cherished beliefs. But most were simply blank, as though their advisors had stupidly signed them up for a lecture given in a language they did not speak.

The professor dusted the chalk from his hands for longer than seemed necessary, his shoulders beginning to slump. When he spoke his voice was low.

"Your papers are due on Thursday. And remember, I don't want to see long quotations." The rumble of papers being gathered and books packed covered his words. "Give me some analysis. Show me how you interpret the material."

His tone was flat. Rebecca imagined a tape playing behind the lectern; he only mouthing the words. The students weren't listening anyway, and she wondered which of those conditions had come first, the one causing the other.

Students were up all around her, moving toward the exit. She pushed through them toward the front of the class, but the professor was gone. One or two of the students were near the lectern and also seemed surprised an old man could escape so quickly.

He could not, however, negotiate the stairs very quickly and it was there Rebecca caught up with him.

"Professor Middlebrooks?" Without thinking, she had reached out to touch his shoulder — and felt him recoil from the contact. When he turned she could see in his tightened brows and down-turned mouth a physical aversion to being approached by what he thought was a student.

"I'm Rebecca Tanner."

"Oh…of course. I had forgotten which day you were coming."

Rebecca could not get over his apparent relief that she was not one of his students.

His office was on the fourth floor. He heated water in a small electric pot for tea. Cups and saucers came from a small cabinet under the window.

"I read that our former governor had gone into the hospital." He rubbed his elbow with some concentration. "All us old ones'll be going before long. Though I doubt the Atlanta paper will be coming over here to do a story when it's my time." He gave a snort at the fickleness of the media and brought Rebecca a cup of tea.

When he had carefully lowered himself into a leather armchair, he he said, "Of course no one ever voted for me as president."

"I'm sure the subject of T. J. Davis inspires strong feelings in you, Professor."

"Not really, not anymore. It's just that Davis's story is not the one I would tell. But then I'm not doing the tellin'. And he is a story of some kind. If there had never been a Governor Davis, I suppose there would never have been a President Carter, or Bill Clinton. Think about that - as we sit here in 1999, we have a President from Arkansas, a Speaker of the House from Georgia and the Senate Minority leader from Mississippi. Losing the war was the smartest thing the South ever did."

He made a dry chuckle and shook his head.

"I'm being ironic I'm afraid. In truth, the tragedy of the South stems from the fact that losing the Civil War made southerners strangers in their own country, the only Americans ever to live in an occupied territory. Most of the violence of the civil rights era could have been avoided if southerners had not had an inferiority complex. Do you know the historian, C. Vann Woodward? He wrote a book called "The Burden of Southern History" and made that point. History is a burden down here. If not for that fear of being second-class, the people would not have picked a demagogue like Davis in a million years."

He stopped to sip his tea, giving Rebecca a chance to catch up with her note taking. She had several questions she wanted to ask, but the Reverend had not provided an opening so far.

"One problem feeds on the other," he continued. "The feeling of inferiority makes people fight back, so to speak, by rejecting anything offered by the 'superior' group, whether politics, culture, whatever. People like Davis gave voice to that rejection and enlarged it. So, for example, if education is something that is valued in the North, we will automatically ridicule it here. The only real problem with my students is that most of these kids have no idea why they're at a university. They don't place a high value on education. This is just where you go after high school. And, yes, I do blame Davis for that.

"He used this phony pride issue — 'Stand up for Escambia,' 'Be Proud of Escambia' — as a way to gain political power because he benefited from everything staying the same. He never cared what damage that attitude had caused to the state. So we get kids who think that any change is an attack on their worth or their "heritage." In theory, that sounds like it might be good, but in practice what it means is these kids think they are fine the way they are. They shouldn't have to learn anything new or deal with anything that challenges their most simplistic beliefs."

He stopped to sip his tea and, Rebecca suspected, take a breath. She had been stealing looks around his office while he talked. The walls were covered with pictures and certificates. She could not see details, but she recognized many of the photos as reprints of newspaper pictures. One in particular, even from this distance, looked familiar. It was a shot of a low-slung building with a flat roof extending out well past the building walls on both sides.

"That picture is in the book!" she exclaimed, causing the Professor to jerk slightly. She was remembering the glossy version in the book Jeff had given her to read for civil rights background. In the Woodson book's clear print, atop the roof, a greyhound and three letters B-U-S. "That's where the Freedom Rider beating happened."

He looked at her as though she had materialized like a genie out of a bottle.

"No one your age ever recognizes that picture. That's where one of the beatings happened, yes. That's the old bus station, which is still standing downtown in Montville."

"It doesn't look historic, does it?" she said.

"The civil rights movement was a poor man's revolution. Our goals were so very modest; as a result our monuments are bus stations and Woolworth's lunch counters. So, no, it doesn't look like much."

Rebecca had read that two buses came from Birmingham on that morning in May 1965. For much of the way they had been followed by carloads of white men, heckling them and occasionally firing gunshots. A few miles from town one of the buses had been run off the road, down an embankment. The other had gone back for the riders, who had to cram into it. Suddenly it occurred to her why the professor had this picture.

"You were on the bus that day?" she asked.

"I looked back, as our bus pulled away, to see the other bus was now surrounded by this crowd of shouting white men, shooting the windows out. They attacked the vehicle as though they could stop the whole movement by killing that one bus.

"The white men were no longer paying any attention to our bus, so I asked our driver to stop about 100 yard away to see what would happen. Soon, clouds of black smoke poured from the shattered windows. They had set the thing afire, as though they wanted to make it seem like a huge Klan cross." He cleared his throat and ran a hand over his forehead. "I don't know what it is they like so much about burning things."

A People United in Heart

J ust at the part in Hardy's novel where Henchard, the anti-hero, is about to win his campaign for Mayor while hoping his sordid past would not catch up with him, the doorbell rang. Gordon muttered under his breath.

"I'll get it," he yelled.

When he got there a large cardboard envelope had been left on the porch. Stooping with some pain to retrieve it, he saw the name of the Atlanta reporter.

He returned to the den, reluctantly putting his novel aside to deal with real life. He wondered which would turn out to be more reliable. Inside the envelope he found a note from Rebecca reminding him she had referred to this transcript in her telephone call yesterday. Her note was clipped to several typed pages.

TRANSCRIPT:
Interview: Billy Trask
Position: Chief of Staff   *Date: [Unknown]*

I 'spect I've known T. J. longer than anybody. Other than his Daddy, of course. I been with him since grade school and most of that time has involved politics. That's the god's truth. That man has been running for something long as I've knowed him. He had an uncle who was a county commissioner and somehow being around his uncle made T. J. want the political life.

He had a good start on it 'cause between his uncle and his Daddy they knew everybody down there. T. J.'s Daddy was a preacher back then, you see, and had baptized, married, or buried somebody in just about every family in a hundred miles. So T. J. came by it naturally. And he was friendly; one of those people what never met a stranger. He was president of the senior class, lead man in the class play, all that stuff. He was never in the running for valedictoran [sic] of course, but that was probably intentional. He was plenty smart, but he knew the voters don't want to have smartness thrown up in their faces all the time. That was part of how people-smart he was.

The politics got serious early. He was still in high school, must a been about 15 was all, when he got me to helping him with this idea to write a letter to every single member of the Escambia state legislature. He wanted to be appointed as a page for the summer. What a job that was. I copied letters for him, by hand I'm talking about, and addressed them envelopes 'til I thought my arm'd fall slap off. And don't you know I pitched in my little bit of allowance to help buy the stamps.

Well, you can bet T. J. got the job. Them House members hadn't never seen nothing like this kid. T. J.'s Daddy went up to visit him once during that summer and took me along as a reward for what I'd done to help. T. J. took me around and introduced me to legislators, grown men, as though he was one of 'em. It was amazing. Late one afternoon all the visitors had gone and we had the whatchacallit, the big lobby thing, pretty much to ourselves. I remember it now, that big circle hall with the dome curving over it and the light coming in the high windows straight across to the opposite wall, the sun was so low. There's a little brass something in the center of the floor and suddenly T. J. walks over to it with these long steps and plants himself right on that plaque, and stands up real straight, like a statue. Then he pulls a piece of paper out of his black suit coat pocket and starts making a speech. Can you beat that? Just a high school kid.

I teased him about it, but inside I was really impressed.

"Great place to practice," I told him. He looked at me in this weird way and said something like, this is more than practice. It was his destiny is what he meant. 'I'm gonna be governor of this state,' he says. I gotta tell you, I believed him — partly because the whole thing was almost religious like. And partly because T.J., I'll say this for him, he ain't never been bad to bullshit a whole lot. Time I known him, if he said he was gonna do a thing he pretty much done it.

So, looking at it that way, I got pretty excited myself back then, 'cause even if I was just a boy I could picture it that being the best friend of a governor might be a pretty good deal for me. And don't you know it has been. (laughter)

I always thought everything started right there, in that rotunda under that dome. Writing letters was one thing, but hearing T. J. actually say he'd be governor, that was like I was hearing some kind of a sign about my own self. Like I was Paul on the road to Demopolis [sic] in the Bible. Suddenly it wasn't all just about him. I was a part of it. It was my future, too. I put my hand on his shoulder and asked him if I could have that paper he had been reading from. He asked me why and I told him I thought this was a day I might want to remember. He looked at me real close for a few seconds, like he hadn't really seen me before, then give just a little bit of a smile and nodded his head.

"Yeah," *he said,* "you just might want to do that."

(Do you still have that paper?)

"You bet I do. Really ought to give it to the lib'ry (sic) but I ain't *wanted to part with it. It's over there in that box. I could read it for ya."*

(Yes. That would be great.)

[Sounds of moving in room, drawers opening and closing.]

"O.K. Here goes." *(throat clearing):*

'It is joyous, in the midst of perilous times to look around upon a people united in heart, where one purpose of high resolve ani... animates and acta...act-u-ates the whole - where the sacrifices to be made are not weighted in the balance against honor, and right, and liberty, and equality. Obstacles may retard — they cannot long prevent - the progress of a movement sanctified by its justice, and sustained by a virtuous people.'

[Sounds of paper rustling]

"Good, ain't it?"

[End Transcript]

Think Cain and Abel

R ebecca sipped from a china teacup while the Professor finished
reading the Billy Trask transcript.

"Most interesting," he said, placing the transcript pages neatly
onto his desk. "You say there is a lot of this?"

She grinned like she'd found free money. "Hours of tapes. It's
fantastic. But there's no explanation of why the tapes were made or
even who made them. We had to do an Internet search to figure out
that Billy Trask was associated with T. J. Davis."

The professor leaned over his desk. "To say he was 'associated' is
putting it rather mildly," he told her. "Trask was the Governor's closest
aide and the one who was with him for the longest time." The
Professor described him as "a goon, as much as anything," but assured
Rebecca he was, indeed, at the center of power in the Davis administration.

And Gordon? The Professor said the tape provided a pretty accurate thumbnail portrait of a man who was famous for his formality.
Rebecca recalls she had that impression in her interview.

"I wouldn't call his style formal myself," the professor said. "I'd
call it stiff. But that was minor compared to the other things about
him."

"Did you know him well?"

He smiled and waved his hand toward the photo-tiled wall. "I'm
sure I've got a picture with Gordon here somewhere. I knew him, but
never understood what he was up to. A lot of people were shocked
when he cozied up to Davis. Not because of the newspaper connection
itself — a lot of editors were racists themselves and others did not want
to lose the advertising that would flee if a paper was too critical of T. J.
But the *Courier* was different — always had been.

"In the old days, before the movement really started, nearly every state had one paper and one editor who was known for being at least somewhat progressive on the race issue. Ralph McGill, who, as you should know, was at the *Atlanta Constitution* and Hodding Carter at the*Independent* in Greenville, Mississippi, are just two examples.

"Gordon's father had been that man for Escambia. He was a statesman; a true newspaperman who felt that honest reporting should make a difference. He lost readers and advertisers sometimes, but they always came back in the end and, like several of the others, he won the Pulitzer Prize.

"For black people in those days, the *Courier* was about the only bright spot where white people were concerned, and there was an assumption that Gordon had been trained by his daddy to carry on the tradition. So for Gordon, of all people, to work for Davis was a shock of some significance.

"What was worse was that by helping T. J. Davis, Gordon was making an active decision *not* to help someone who could have been the governor the state needed. Because, you see, there were alternatives. North Carolina had Terry Sandford during this time, Florida had Reuben Askew, Tennessee had Lamar Alexander...you get my point. We had a lieutenant governor who could have changed the history of Escambia..."

Rebecca read from her notes, "Michael DeWitt?"

"Right...yes." He gave her a look that said interruptions were not welcome, but then continued. "DeWitt, in the early races, could well have won if he had gotten support from men like Gordon Halt. But when someone as influential as Gordon didn't support DeWitt early, it set everything back, especially since everyone knew Davis and DeWitt had known each other for years. Still, DeWitt stayed active in state affairs and was a viable candidate in that last election — and then the accident happened. Just before the election, when our hopes for him were at their highest. Most of us black voters in Escambia decided God must have something against us."

"So, were Michael DeWitt and Governor Davis rivals during all their careers?" Rebecca asked.

"Longer. They were students here at the same time, and the rivalry, as you call it, was evident from the first. But rivalry is not nearly strong enough. Don't think Coke and Pepsi; think Cain and Abel."

"But aren't you being a little unfair to Gordon Halt? Governor Davis swamped his competition, surely Mr. Halt's being on the other side couldn't have changed that?"

The Professor stared at her, scrunching his eyebrows to a solid line of bushy white.

"Since he never tried, we don't know, do we? Anyway, the point is not whether he could have changed anything, is it? The point is whether he was on the right side. Isn't that the only question any of us can answer about right and wrong — were we on the right side?"

Silence stretched out as Professor looked out at the trees in the quadrangle.

* * *

After the computer stopped that grinding, whirring noise that told her the modem had connected, Rebecca read her daily email from Jeff. How, she wondered, should she respond to his simple question, "how was it going?" It was going fantastically, she supposed. Of course it was. Who could have guessed she'd find this treasure trove of tapes? How lucky could a reporter be?

But somehow she didn't feel jubilant. Taking a sip of white wine from the plastic motel "glass," she could not help feeling that she was a trespasser in this territory - the past. And like any trespasser, capable of doing great harm. The first tape had been an unflattering portrait of Gordon Halt, by a person who never expected to have his remarks surface forty years after he spoke them. Could she write a story about that tape without being a form of thief? If nothing else she would be a thief of someone else's peace and privacy. But Jeff had sent her here to write stories and, so far, this was the story she had.

She took out the Woodston book and read for most of an hour but her concentration was poor. Finally, she remembered to plug the phone back into the wall. It began to ring immediately. She picked it up, expecting to hear Jeff's voice and was surprised by a deep drawl.

"Miz Tannuh, this is Fred Middlebrooks from the University? I hope I didn't wake you. It occurred to me that since you are writing about Governor Davis and Escambia you might like to join me on a little field trip?"

"Thanks for thinking of me, but my time is pretty limited. This place where you're going, is it far from here?"

"That's what makes the trip worthwhile for your story," the professor said. "It's about 50 years away."

Rebecca laughed and shook her head. What reporter could refuse an offer like that?

Gordon Had Been Present at the Beginning

G ordon threw the transcript pages onto the kitchen table, causing Margaret to look up from her puzzle.

"What's wrong?" she asked, mildly startled.

"It's just this girl reporter. She's only been here a few days and she finds *this*," he said, pointing. "These tapes are in our backyard but the story will be in the g.d. *Constitution*." Gordon considered the adjective part of the proper designation for the paper in Atlanta.

Margaret grinned, the reading glasses making her green eyes huge. "Is this just friendly competition or are we being just a tiny bit obsessive?"

Gordon shook his head. "Say what you will, but your grandson is the editor of the *Courier* and this won't look good. That girl said there are a dozen of these tapes. God only knows what's in them if somebody was smart enough to keep buying Billy drinks."

"Boys will be boys." Margaret bent back to her paper and penciled in a few letters before speaking again. "All this was an awfully long time ago, Dear. It may not be such a big scoop for Edward to lose, after so long. Remember, not everyone was there, like you and Billy. The history may not seem so important to the average reader."

Gordon stared at the top of his wife's head, wondering how she intended him to take her remark. God knows, he loved her and would be lost without her. But God also knew she could say things that just drove him crazy. Was he supposed to feel better that his own paper had not done a very good job in finding a story, or was he to feel worse because the work of his life was now part of ancient history? Good old Margaret.

"I'm sure you're right, Sweetheart," was all he trusted himself to say. She was right, of course. He should really feel both better *and* worse. Wasn't that pretty much how life was most of the time? When you think of it, the glass is *both* half empty and half full. Your own outlook, perhaps even your mental health, depends on how you choose to regard what you see and experience, but your decision doesn't change anything in the real world. Only time reveals what were the right or wrong decisions. And, as Margaret has so helpfully pointed out, by the time enough years have gone by to reveal the "truth" no one much gives a damn what happened anyway. We live with the results of all those things done in the past but we don't have the patience or resources to understand and learn from them.

Gordon scratched his ear absently and looked back at the table where he had placed the envelope and the note from the reporter. Re-reading her note he saw something he had overlooked before:

"One of the people I'm interviewing told me the rivalry between Governor Davis and Michael DeWitt was intense. When we speak again, could you provide me with your perspective on that issue?"

One of the **negroes** you're interviewing said that, Gordon thought. Who else would still be trying to embarrass the Governor about the Michael DeWitt episode? Now that *was* ancient history. He hadn't given a thought to Michael in years and didn't want to now.

Gordon had been present at the beginning of the rivalry between Davis and DeWitt. How strange; he could close his eyes and make himself see the crowd of students still gathered, the speeches still unspoken, still to come in this memory that may, by now, exist nowhere else.

This was the last political rally before the 1941 Student Government Association elections. In his campaign literature Davis described a South with much to teach the rest of the nation about essential values and ethics. The great challenge, he said, was to resist the temptation to modernize excessively in an effort to become "more Yankee than the Yankees." This might mean rejecting certain kinds of economic development if control did not come with it. He felt too many southern leaders were willing to let northern firms "re-institute the sharecropper" by giving the South the dirty and difficult plant work while keeping for the Yankees the management jobs and power that drove the plants.

In spite of himself, Gordon was impressed. But he could see what Davis apparently could not, that this program of his bordered on a real philosophy and was just too grand for college kids.

And besides, Davis was facing Michael DeWitt. Golden-haired, tall and slender, Freshman Favorite, DeWitt was the scion of a North Escambia steel family. He was nearly a half-foot taller than his opponent and for a time during the middle of the campaign he arranged to be photographed beside Davis at every opportunity. It was said of DeWitt that he never met a stranger and would rather make a speech than get laid, though he had ample opportunity to do both.

Aside from his physical attributes, DeWitt had the considerable advantage of the major Greek backing. No small thing. Davis was fraternity too--Robert Burris had secured a bid for him--but there was no steel mill ownership in the Davis line and with no "legacy" help, that was the only bid he got. (Michael had been the third generation of his family to attend EU, while many members of the Davis family couldn't reliably spell "college," let alone get into one.) Like neighborhoods and churches, fraternities are divided by class, and Davis's was unmistakably lower.

But if he ever recognized he didn't have a chance, T. J. Davis never let it show. He talked about an SGA that would recognize the "specialness" of the South in preparation for a time of turmoil. He eloquently argued for a cohesive student body, saying "we are all Escambians, and will be after we leave this place. That's what matters, the things that will remain." This infuriated the Greeks, including many of his own supporters, when it was interpreted as an approach to the vast majority of independent students.

In his memory, the lights in the auditorium lowered, the drone of nearly 500 students fell to a buzz, and Gordon turned to a clean page in his notebook.

"I have been talking this last month about what the Student Government Association ought to be all about," Davis began, "and I feel like a lot of you have been listening. First is, the SGA ought to be run serious. It ought to be careful with its money because that's our money it's spendin'. We need to know that student money is going for student purposes. I'm gonna make sure that happens.

"Second thing though, is that SGA ought to have a role in helping the students understand the responsibility we are all gonna have for the state we love when we get out of this here University. We'll have to decide what we want Escambia to be, and then we'll be responsible to do it. Do we want Escambia to just be another state as much like every other part of the country as we can make it? Do we want to think like every other part of the country and sound like 'em?

"Now my opponent, who I think a lot of, is a fella with a great speaking voice. I think anybody would say that about Mike. He sounds like he could be on the radio. But, he don't sound like us much. He's got what they call a polished voice and he knows all the big words but he don't have a lick of an accent that I can tell. And I'm wondering, is he listening to them fellas on the radio so he can learn to talk like that? Is he afraid of sounding like he's from Escambia?

"I think maybe those are things we should be thinking about. We've got a history and heritage here in Escambia most places can't come close to. We need to hang on to it and build on that, not throw it out so that we can become more like everybody else, just to attract these northern businesses?"

Davis waited for applause. As the audience saw him waiting, they politely provided some. But Gordon had thought at the time that most of the listeners were probably like him, so stunned to hear a candidate in one of these silly races actually say something that they were unprepared to react.

Davis could not completely conceal his disappointment that an expected tumult had not come. His tone changed suddenly.

"People have said we're the underdog in this thing, and that may be. But worse than losing would be to win without any principles, to not care about any issue except whether you win. That is something T. J. Davis will never do. So I ask you for your vote and I look forward to serving you in the SGA."

He stopped and looked at the crowd, waiting but not yet finished. "And for a lot of years to come."

He gathered up his notes while the applause started. It did not involve the entire crowd, but it was enthusiastic, at least until it was interrupted.

When applause and whoops broke out in the rear of the hall, Gordon turned to see DeWitt striding down an aisle holding high over his head an Escambia state flag so large it draped to his shoulders.

At the base of the stage he handed the flag to a fraternity brother who carried it behind him as DeWitt mounted the steps and took over the lectern.

"Go, Crimson!" he shouted.

"Go, Crimson, go!" the crowd shouted back. He held both arms over his head as the cheers continued. Suddenly he seemed to notice for the first time that the microphone was pointed downward to a place well below his chin. "I'm going to have to change this from where my little buddy had it." He laughed and grabbed the mike, twisting it up toward his face.

A group of his supporters laughed in the front, then the laughter spread generally and Gordon thought whatever points Davis might have made had just been erased from the memory of most listeners.

DeWitt raised a hand to quiet them. "You know that flag stunt had a point. I think Mr. T. J. Davis is confused about a lot of things. We're not voters yet, and he's not running for Governor, though I'm sure that's just a matter of time." More laughter.

"But love for Escambia is something I do agree with him about. And I could tell by the reaction when I brought that great flag in, you all love it just as much as I do." Cheers broke out from most parts of the hall. "Sounds like Mr. Davis may be confused about that, too. What do you think?"

Shouts of "yeah" and "damn straight" came from scattered spots around the auditorium.

"I'm glad he thinks I have a nice voice." He stopped and searched the front rows, as though looking for Davis, then stopped and waved a hand. "Thank you for that little buddy." A few snickers in the front quickly spread to scattered laughter. DeWitt looked up to the crowd again. "Is that a bad thing? You want your SGA to be quality representatives. Because make no mistake, people will judge the University, will judge *you* based on the people who represent you in the SGA."

"This election is not about other states. Where did that come from? Do you know?

Again, scattered parts of the crowd seemed anxious to participate, sending up shouts of "NO!" and "Hell, NO!"

"I don't know either. Maybe Mr. Davis is confused about that, too. When you go to vote on Thursday, think about the real issues. Think about having an SGA that presents the best possible picture of *you*, the students, to everyone who deals with the university. I think I can do that. I can stand tall to represent *you* about real issues on this campus, not made-up, half-baked ideas about some far off influences. You need to think about whether the other candidate can represent you as well."

The shouts started again and Gordon began to feel DeWitt might be going overboard with the fraternity brothers he had planted in the audience to build response. Now they answered the implied question, shouting "No, No" and "We want Mike! We want Mike!" This kept up for several minutes, involving about half the audience. On stage, DeWitt picked up his notes and walked off stage, waving and smiling. The cheering continued for a considerable time after he was gone.

After the program ended, Gordon headed to Fraternity Row to gather the obligatory quotes from the candidates for his story.

DeWitt had a quote prepared, no doubt typed by one of the sorority girls who hung around his group. He talked about what a privilege it was to be a candidate and repeated some themes of his speech.

Gordon had more trouble finding Davis. A brother at the frat house suggested he try O'Malley's, a working class bar far off campus. Davis and several cohorts were around a table in the corner. Gordon approached, but was not noticed behind the bulk of Billy, Davis's gargantuan "assistant."

"They didn't really listen to you, T.J." Billy was saying between bites of a suitably large hamburger. "They gonna have to hear the message a few times before it registers."

"That's right," a kid with a rash on one cheek spoke up, but Davis was not mollified.

"They let him make fun of me," he mumbled. "They liked his good looks and him carrying that flag so much that they didn't notice when he had nothing to say." Davis chewed his bottom lip while his face reddened. "And goddamn," he slammed his fist on the table, "the bastard called me his little buddy and they laughed."

In the silence that followed, Gordon spoke. "Can I quote you on that?"

Davis had looked up, unpleasantly surprised, to see someone scribbling in a notebook. He forced his face to relax into a weak smile as he recognized Gordon. "Why hell no," he said, calm now. "Don't write that. It makes me sound like a crybaby." He took a swallow of coffee, and then peered over his cup. "Besides, you were spying. You play fair don't you, Gordon?"

Gordon looked at the candidate for a moment considering how easy it was for Davis to surprise him — by the issues of his campaign and by invoking an old fashioned virtue. *Lucky for you I do*, Gordon thought as he scratched out the words he had written.

"I need a quote," he had said to the candidate.

"Well, put this. 'I don't care if I win — I care about saying what needs to be said.'"

Gordon wrote, and then closed his notebook.

"Can I buy you a beer?" Davis called.

Gordon held up his pad.

"I'm a reporter on duty and you're a candidate. But some other time."

Gordon was walking toward the door when he heard the voice again.

"Gordon…"

He had turned to look at Davis, surrounded by his supporters. Davis held up his cup of coffee in salute. "There *will be* … another time." Cheers and laughter rang around the table.

Back in his den, a lifetime away from that night, Gordon smiled at the memory. How typical of the governor to try to come up with some theatrical exit line. He was famous for the half sentence with the dramatic pause. And there seemed to always be appreciative audiences for even the most cornball gestures.

Gordon stretched and rubbed his shoulder, stiff from sitting in one position, then saw the transcript still lying on the table. Something about what he had read earlier now nagged at him. He picked up the pages and found the "speech" Davis, as a boy, had given in the Capitol all those years ago. Reading it again, Gordon laughed out loud. How could he have missed it before? Billy had been a little more impressed than he should have been. Of course it was good. All the reviews had said so back in February 1861, when Jefferson Davis had spoken those words in his inaugural address as President of the Confederate States of America.

It's Mostly Politicians

"Do we have to take all these little two lanes? We'll never get there, wherever there is." Rebecca was sitting in the front seat of Professor Fred's car, an enormous and ancient Buick

"This is the only way to see the county," he said, and I don't like interstates, even if there was one."

Rebecca looked ahead to see another tight curve approaching. "I love the interstates. They let you save some of your life to actually spend at your destination."

Professor Middlebrooks harrumphed. "Young people are unbearable," he drawled. "Besides, there are no interstates to the past."

They rode in silence for a while. The music from the radio gradually dissolved into static. When she pressed the scan button Rebecca heard three successive evangelists, each in the middle of sermons that seemed weirdly vehement for a weekday morning. She turned the radio off, wishing she'd brought her Walkman cassette player. Outside, dense pine forests flanked the car, unchanged for the last ten miles. She wondered if they had entered a national park. Professor Fred corrected her.

"It's all private. Most of it belongs to the big national paper companies. They own thousands of acres in the state. That's part of the reason these counties seem empty. Out-of-state landowners contribute to the political pressure groups to keep taxes low. With such low taxes there can be no local services. With no local services new business doesn't come in, which is the way the landowners want it. New businesses would require new infrastructure that would require taxes. And new businesses would raise wages, which the landowners also don't want. T. J. Davis didn't invent the system, but he never tried to change it, when he was the only governor who could have." Rebecca had to keep herself from smiling at the professor's love of speech-making.

"That's why I called this a trip to the past," he continued. "Life in these counties hasn't changed in sixty years. You're going to see how things were when Davis was in office, conditions he didn't even try to improve. He wasted his huge political following. He didn't rock the boat."

He turned into a gravel parking lot in front of a single-story building of mustard-colored brick. A hand-made sign was propped in a window: "We Care Community Services Center."

Inside, Professor Fred said a few words to the receptionist, who left the room. Soon an attractive, matronly black woman entered, obviously delighted to see the professor.

"Freddy Lee!" she said, enfolding him in a two-armed hug that looked potentially dangerous to someone of the professor's size and age, but he returned the embrace with enthusiasm, then turned and introduced Rebecca to Ida Mae Brown.

"She's one of the originals," he said. "You don't know the history of Escambia if you don't know Ida Mae."

In the next two hours Rebecca learned that the We Care Center performed three functions in its plain brick building. The noise she heard came from the Head Start classes. This was a federally funded program that taught pre-school children basic skills to prepare for first grade. When the children left at noon, some of the classrooms were used for adult education and counseling. These classes included reading since, Rebecca learned, thirty percent of adults in the county could not dependably read one of Rebecca's stories in the newspaper. The percentage was much higher for the black adults who made up most of the Center's clientele.

The third major function of the Center was to provide health care, especially for expectant mothers. This service was done in a spare room that had been sparsely furnished with worn but functional medical equipment. A nurse practitioner opened the clinic three mornings a week.

Ida Mae Brown led them to a far end of the corridor where another handmade sign was attached to one of the doors: "Clinic is OPEN."

Near that door, their backs against the wall, six pregnant girls sat in cheap metal chairs to wait for their appointments. Rebecca noticed that two of them were white, the only whites she had so far seen in the building. None looked old enough to be out of high school.

"This county has an infant mortality rate higher than the Dominican Republic," Ida told them. "Lots of reasons," she said ahead of Rebecca's question. "These are very young girls, you can see, so that is part of the problem. They're poor or they wouldn't be here. There's not an obstetrician in the entire county so prenatal care is unheard of except for the people with cars and time to drive for hours." She stopped in the hall and turned to face Rebecca. "But it's mostly politicians."

Rebecca almost smiled. The older woman made it sound as though she thought the politicians were impregnating these girls. Rebecca wondered if there were any issues in life that didn't come down to politics for Ida Mae Brown. She thought of asking, but there was not much chance to get a word in. Ida Mae could match the professor as a talker.

"The right-wingers who control the legislature don't want these girls to have birth control," she continued. "They think abortions are sinful, but they won't vote a nickel in taxes to provide medical services or decent nutrition that keep more of these children alive."

As they walked back to Ida Mae's office the Head Start classes emptied noisily into the hall. Ida pointed to where a little boy in a worn orange sweater walked beside a gray-haired man with mahogany skin and the still-stout build of a former athlete. The boy holding his hand barely came to his waist and could keep up only because the man took pains to walk slowly. They talked and laughed like old friends and Rebecca thought they would make a terrific poster for Grandparent's Day.

Ida Mae greeted the old man enthusiastically.

"Mr. Turner, how you doin' today?" Ida Mae put a hand on the man's forearm as she spoke.

"I'm passable well, Ms. Brown. I hope you are too."

"Did Jamal tell you he's becoming quite a reader?" She caressed the boy's head as she spoke. The old man laughed.

"He was just telling me about that. Pole, tell Ms. Brown what I told you."

Jamal scuffed a toe against the floor and looked up shyly. "He told me to keep my mind on doing my job."

"That's right," his grandfather said. "And what's your job?"

Jamal stood straighter, as though reciting in Sunday school. "Learn everything that teacher knows!"

"That's my Pole alright," the grandfather said. "You done good. I'm gonna have to find a nickel for you." He took the boy's hand and they walked out to the parking lot.

"What was that name he was calling the boy?" Rebecca asked after they had gone.

"Oh, he was saying 'pole. Short for tadpole. Mr. Turner has called Jamal that from birth because he was so small. He was very premature. His mother still has some pretty big problems. She was Mr. Turner's last child, a late one, and always pretty wild. She had trouble with school and dropped out, so pretty soon she had problems with drugs. She lost control of her own life and hasn't been able to do anything for the boy's. Thank God for Mr. Turner or Jamal would be just a wild animal.

Rebecca thought of her own mother who had always been present for her like an angel or, just as often, a warden. But there was never an issue of Mom putting anything else ahead of her. Then she thought of those girls down the hall, soon to be mothers themselves.

"So, not everything is political?" she asked.

Ida Mae Brown looked at her quizzically.

"I mean," Rebecca went on, "some people make bad choices and ruin their own lives. Not everything that happens to people is political."

The older woman's face hardened into what Rebecca imagined was her standard mask for debate. "I find that successful people want to believe that they created their own good fortune. And it is true that a few people, percentage-wise, do rise above impoverished backgrounds. But the system should not be stacked against average people just because they're black. Average white people can still get decent medical care and education. That's all we're talking about. Make the playing field level and then we'll agree with you that the ones that fail deserve to."

Walking back to Ida Mae's office Fred came alongside.

"So, you're soaking up the true Escambia experience?" he asked.

Rebecca thought it an odd question. "Is that what I'm seeing, the true experience?"

"It is for half a million of Escambia's people. I hope all this makes it into your story."

Rebecca only nodded. She was a little disappointed at his lack of subtlety.

Probably Just a Mistake

The morning traffic was heavy and Gordon could not get around a trailer in front of him. He finally reached the exit to Great Health Medical Center. A CNN remote broadcast trailer and two small vans from the local network affiliates were set up near the main entrance. In the old days — how he hated that expression, but could not stop thinking it — Gordon would have gone to great lengths to find a way to enter the building without being caught by a camera or microphone, but these trim and coiffed reporters had not been born when he left public life. Being old made some things simpler.

The group of demonstrators had grown since yesterday, as word spread. There were about twenty today, all men, mostly in jeans and polo or open-neck print shirts and work shoes or sneakers. A cute blonde reporter was holding a microphone up to an older man who outweighed her by two hundred pounds. Gordon recognized Doug even at this distance. A few signs, hand-lettered on poster board, leaned against a folding table. "God Bless Governor Davis." "Honor our Heritage," were typical messages. A small banner across the edge of the table read "Sons of the Confederate South."

"Gordon!" a voice called. He turned to see the interview had ended and the big man was striding toward him. "I've been meaning to call you," he said.

"Hello, Sonny. Your dad here?"

"Yeah, he's in with Barbara." Sonny looked up as though he might point out Governor Davis's room amid the hundreds of windows. "I wanted to talk with you about doing somethin' for a memorial for the Governor. You know, make some speeches for the fundraising, that sort of thing."

"I don't know why not," Gordon said, "as long as it's here in town. I don't travel well anymore."

"No sir, that won't be any problem." He extended a hand the size of a phone book, "We'll be calling on you."

Inside, Gordon went to the information desk to see if the Governor had been moved overnight. He noticed a fancy, color brochure describing how the new corporate hospital structure would revolutionize health care. His son had been born in the appropriately named Providence Hospital that was run by a group of nuns (*Is there a word for that?* he wondered. *A herd of nuns? A bevy?*) and was proud to be non-profit. The other large hospital in town, more prosaically named Montville Infirmary, also had been non-profit, and Gordon supposed he had thought all hospitals would be. He did not remember the care in those institutions being inferior. And why would it be? Those hospitals must have had more money to provide care since that profit has to come from somewhere.

When he got to the right floor the colored nurse offered to help him, probably thinking at his age Gordon would not be able to find a room by its number. A rumpled security guard seated by the door recognized Gordon and nodded. Several magazines lay on the floor beside his metal chair. The nurse wished Gordon a nice day, a smile of unwarranted cheerfulness revealing gleaming teeth. Gordon thanked her and entered the dimly lit room.

To the left a privacy curtain blocked his view of all but the foot of the metal bed. Beyond the bed, hazy light filtered through the closed window blinds. There was a low rumble behind everything as though blood was pumping through the building's veins. The profusion of flowers and plants, along with the low light, gave the odd impression the Governor was being treated in a green house. To the right of the window Barbara rose from a small chair and came to Gordon.

He gave her a hug. Dropping his hand he knocked four get-well cards off a small table covered with them.

"Don't bother," she said as he bent to pick them up.

From the foot of the bed, Gordon could see the Governor's face, withered with age and illness.

"You think he looks bad," Barbara said. It was not a question.

Gordon did not answer. Back when he was starting in the newspa-per business he would occasionally write crime stories that featured what the cops called a deathbed confession. But in those days he thought of the term as just a cliché. Now it looked pretty obvious this ugly metal contraption with its motors and cables and stark white sheets would be the deathbed of Thomas Jefferson Davis.

The Governor's ragged breathing seemed like distant thunder. Why is this decay always such a surprise? Gordon wondered. Is it because we spend all our time pushing the thought of it away, to make daily life bearable? Making the most common thing, death, the most mysterious and forbidden must have the effect of making it inexplicably shocking when the fact can no longer be avoided. This was the most powerful man in the state for two decades. Now he was as frail as the autumn leaf a strong wind blows down the block.

Gordon suddenly remembered that he had once talked with the Governor about this very thing. Not surprising when they had talked about so much.

"Gordon, did you ever see anybody die?"

"My wife's grandfather died in that old cane rocker of his on that wide front porch at the white house. He was giving Edward a pony ride on his knee, like you do. Bouncing him up and down. That was his favorite thing to do. I guess Edward was six or eight years old and just a ball of fire but he would sit there quiet as you please as long as the old man would bounce him. So when we heard him yell to us, we knew something was wrong.

"I think Pawpaw must have just passed right there and stopped pushing that rocker. When the motion stopped, Edward tried to wake him and when he never answered, Edward called out for us. That's how we knew."

The governor nodded. "I like that story," Davis had said. "Mine died in his own bed, right there at home. He asked for all of the grandsons to be sent in and he had a private word with us, then asked us to bring the rest of the family back together. Then when we were gathered round he said, "I guess that's all of it."

Standing here looking at this frail man who used to be so big in his life, Gordon was frustrated that he could not remember the occasion that had impelled them to speak of death. He knew they had been drinking, so it was late in the last term, but he could not remember why.

"You know, don't you," T. J. had said, "that we will be the last ones who have any idea about death being something natural. The younger ones think these hospitals is how it's supposed to be. Damn shame. They are nothing but factories for dying."

Gordon sighed, remembering those words as he scanned the cold bare room. God, how the Governor would hate this, he thought. He loved crowds and noise. He was never comfortable in small groups.

He turned back to Barbara.

She was still a good-looking woman. Of course she was nearly 20 years younger than he, which didn't hurt. That age difference had always been a problem for the Governor; people thought she was an opportunist. But unless she was a great actress, she must be very much in love with her husband; her distress, Gordon thought, would be hard to fake.

"He always thought an awful lot of you." She dabbed her nose with a tissue. "He always said you were the brains of the outfit."

Gordon thought this was not quite the compliment Barbara intended, considering the competition. Speaking of...

"I saw Sonny down stairs. Is Billy here?" he asked.

"He was here just a bit ago. He's making arrangements and calling people. He's been very good."

Gordon did some thinking as they walked into the corridor, but did not speak.

"Speak of the devil," Barbara said.

Glancing up the long hall, Gordon saw the familiar hulking figure 30 yards away. Even at this distance, Billy Trask was an imposing figure. White haired, over seventy, he still had the build and bulk that practically screamed "muscle," in the crime movie, not bodybuilding, sense of that word. Billy was almost as physically intimidating as the first time Gordon had met him at that football game when their lives were just beginning. Gordon had no doubt Billy was still filling that role of "assistant," unwilling to admit he was powerless against this threat to his beloved boss.

"Gordon," the big man bellowed. "Where you been, boy? I ain't seen you in a coon's age."

Billy grabbed him in a bear-hug, forcing Gordon's nose into the big man's shoulder, a torrent of emotion making Billy forget that Gordon abhorred physical displays. It had always amazed Gordon that a man so physical should be completely unable to mask his feelings but, whether murderous rage or childlike mirth, it was always right there on Billy's face. His red eyes threatened to tear as he spoke.

"It don't look good for him, Gordon."

"No, Billy, but he's had a great life. He's a legend."

"How we gonna do without him."

"We'll get by, Billy."

The big man looked at Gordon, the effort of thought knitting his brow. "I never have before."

Gordon had never felt close to Billy. Their backgrounds were too different, and their roles in the campaign had not required that they work together. But he was suddenly struck by something close to tenderness for this man unkind people had frequently referred to as the Governor's "goon." At some level he had been the Governor's friend in a sincere way.

This caused another fragment of memory to float into consciousness. They had been discussing something, who knew what, and Gordon had addressed the Governor as he always did when Davis stopped suddenly and stared at Gordon for a long time.

"You still callin' me Governor." Davis had said, shaking his head.

"Still."

"Why don't you call me T. J., like everybody else?"

"We've had this discussion, Governor."

"We did? What did we say?"

"I said, your friends call you T. J. And people who want to suck up to you. We're not friends and I don't have to suck up."

Davis had laughed out loud.

"You know Gordon," he had said, wiping his eyes, "you are one ungrateful son of a bitch."

Gordon kissed Barbara's cheek and promised to come back soon. He reached up to tap Billy's shoulder and motioned for him to stay in the hall when Barbara went back into the room. When the door closed behind her, Gordon told Billy about the call he'd received from the Atlanta reporter.

"She said there are dozens of tape recordings you provided for an oral history of the Davis years. Do you know what she's talking about?"

Billy was silent for a moment, and then shook his head.

"Nope. Nothin' I can think of."

"It would have been years ago," Gordon prodded.

Billy grimaced. "Everything was." He reached to place a huge paw on Gordon's shoulder. "It's probably just a mistake."

Out of the mouths of boneheads, Gordon thought. If anything could be certain about the existence of these tapes he'd bet it was that they would turn out to be a mistake of gigantic dimensions. Unfortunately, if he also had to bet whose mistake it would turn out to be, between this aged behemoth, racing toward senility, and a young, aggressive reporter from a major daily newspaper, he knew where he'd put his money. But he just shook his head as the elevator arrived.

The elevator doors parted to reveal a space as large as a cave. He was alone in the car and was suddenly overtaken by a memory he never entirely escaped. He had been in this oversized elevator before, years ago, and knew it was the only one that could travel to the basement.

As many crime movies as Gordon had seen in his long life, it still came as a surprise that the police actually do have to ask people to come down and identify bodies. What a cheesy theatrical gesture, yet how terrible, how cruel and invasive. Cruel because you think, *if they need identification, then maybe it's not him. Maybe it's, please God make it, someone else.* And that is more cruelty, you wishing a terrible thing on someone else. But you have to face that truth about yourself that you've never suspected. Rather than have your son be dead you would gladly not only wish that someone else's son would die but, good God, *you would kill that stranger's innocent son with your own bare hands* if that would undo what you fear is now done.

That night fifteen years ago, when the police had called him to perform that duty in the basement of this very hospital, was not only the most awful memory of Gordon's life, it repeated for at least a few minutes every day. Straining for a silver lining, all he could come up with was the fact that Margaret's broken body had kept her in that room on the sixth floor, heavily medicated and so not required to stand by the metal table while the attendant pulled back the sheet covering their son's face and...

"Sir? Excuse me, Sir." The young negro man in green scrubs was pushing a cart full of soiled white linen into the elevator, which had not moved. Gordon had not pushed any of the buttons.

"Ground Floor OK?" the young man asked, his face full of pity, as he reached to the panel and pushed '1.'

If You Were Writing About Belfast

R ebecca passed her first night in Greenville at the Wagon Wheel, a "Traveller's Inn" according to the neon sign that hissed and blinked and appeared to be even older than the Professor's car. Taking two rooms in the concrete block motel, they nearly doubled the normal occupancy rate. The occasional logging truck roared by on the potholed county road, but otherwise the night was tranquil.

Rebecca called her mother to report in. Rebecca told her yes, she was still in the Deep South and no, she had not seen a single person wearing a white sheet.

"At least the phones work."

"Mom," Rebecca scolded, "if I said something like that about Ethiopia or Cambodia you'd be disappointed in me."

"O.K., O.K., you're right. I'm sorry. The whole place can't be Tobacco Road, can it?"

Rebecca didn't know what tobacco had to do with anything and was too tired to ask. It did sound like Mom was apologizing, so she didn't push her luck.

Next morning she was back on the "tour." Rebecca might resent the way the professor's tour of Greenville was so obviously scripted — *see there's no public transportation; see how primitive the medical care is; see how this group is isolated to prevent "infecting" other areas* — but she had to give him points for showmanship.

Their group was walking down the halls of the public high school and Rebecca had already taken in the vinyl tiles peeling up from the floor and the walls streaked under the leaking ceiling when something light brushed her head. She let out a startled squeal, fanning her hair violently, thinking in these surroundings a bug or rodent must have jumped on her. Ida Mae bent to retrieve something white and flat as an index card from the floor.

"It's just a piece of the ceiling. It's an old building." Her eyes were as sad as though she were personally responsible.

Rebecca turned to Professor Fred. "O.K., I give up. If you want to convince me the schools are neglected, I'm a believer. You don't have to throw things at me."

"I wish we could time that to happen when the representative visits. That may be what it takes, for the building to just fall in on him. For some reason just seeing all this doesn't seem to make much of an impression." The sweep of his hand had taken in the dented and rusted lockers, the classroom doors with cracked windows, and the broken chairs stacked at one end of the hall. "The school's neglected, sure," he said, "but that's only part of the story. I want you to understand *why* it is."

Rebecca almost winced. He was doing it again, going into full professor mode, as though other humans existed only to be grateful recipients of his knowledge. She wondered what effect that attitude had on other people. Were they as resistant as she was to being "educated?"

For now she held her tongue, following him on a tour of classrooms where two or three kids shared one book and broken windows were patched with masking tape. In one, they listened as a teacher read aloud the questions to a history test because the school did not have money to fix a broken copy machine. Rebecca kept an eye out for creatures that might scurry across the floor and realized she had missed the last question being read. The students, it suddenly dawned on her, must face that problem every day.

The next stop on the tour was the private high school, what Ida Mae referred to as the "white school." This surprised Rebecca. "I thought your whole point was that the schools are segregated," she said to Professor Fred. "Can you go there?"

"I'm perfectly welcome to visit. The tax laws require that they claim to be open. They may have one or two black students; I'm not sure."

It was certainly different. The halls were not just clean, but bright. The building was quiet, the students orderly as they moved from class to class. And they were white. Rebecca's first impression, which she did not share with Fred, was that this was like the school she had attended in Indiana. A pleasant, well-kept facility where you could take for granted that the ceiling would stay in place and you could have your own copy of a history test. She was honest enough to admit that she felt more comfortable here than in the public school. She did not want to think too much about why that might be, and was glad to be distracted from this line of thought by Professor Fred's lecture.

"What's happened in the rural areas is that whites have abandoned the public schools and built these academies. So there are two systems side by side, a private one 90% white and a public one 85% black. The real point is that the whites are the taxpayers because they have virtually all the jobs that are above minimum wage and they own virtually all the property. The South has traditionally had very low property tax because of that ownership, together with the out of state companies. Once whites abandoned the schools, mostly due to integration, there was a halt to any increase in support for public education and, therefore, no money to keep the schools up. The result is what you saw this morning. No taxes, no services; no progress. Southern history in one sentence."

Professor Middlebrooks pursed his lips and wrinkled his brows, as though maybe he was listening to himself and thinking he might be pushing too hard — or maybe not, for he kept going.

"What made this even worse was that T. J. Davis created a community college system forty years ago, to pay back some political debts, and that system drained what little money would have gone into public high schools. What few resources the state was willing to provide had to be divided between duplicate facilities. Take teachers. If a good one goes to the community college, doesn't that mean there is one less good one for a high school? At the same time, the high schools had become so poor that the graduates were not qualified to benefit from a community college even if it was worth a damn."

He finally stopped, giving Rebecca a chance to ask a question.

"You blame this on ex-Governor Davis?"

"I blame it on a vision that says no taxes is good and holding black people back is good. And, yes, that is a vision the people got from T. J. Davis."

"But he's been out of office more than a generation," she observed. "Can you really blame everything on him?"

"He cast a very long shadow," the professor said. "We still haven't moved out of it."

Rebecca made notes on her pad, still thinking about what he'd said yesterday about the ideas he hoped would get into her story.

"I know this is important to you," she said, "but I can't do this story with you as my only source. You said the private school principal won't talk to me, but somebody from that side is going to have to."

"Sure, sure," he said. "I've got some ideas about that." He seemed distracted for a moment, rubbing his right earlobe as though he had never noticed it before. Then he pointed a finger at her. "I knew there was something else. We were talking about Gordon Halt before. Remind me to ask Ida Mae about that when we go back to the Center."

Over the next few hours, phone calls were placed and Rebecca overheard complicated negotiations that reminded her the professor had been a working politician who must have dealt with press issues hundreds of times. Finally he came back to where Rebecca stood talking Tom.

"O. K., here it is. One of the mothers will meet with you. She can be identified as a parent active in the PTO, but no name and no verbatim quotes. Paraphrase is O.K."

"You can meet at the café tomorrow," Professor Fred said. "Call her Sue, that's how you'll know her."

* * *

When she called to report in last night, Jeff had teased her, saying that he was going to call her series "Diners of the New South." Easy for him to make fun. But in towns the size of Greenville there was no place to meet except the diners, so at two o'clock Rebecca was at Ray's Waffle Hut with her steno notebook open on the wood-grain Formica table. A clunky ceramic mug of steaming coffee sat to one side as she made notes in the loopy handwriting Jeff also kidded her about.

Jeff also congratulated her. The first story in her series was in today's *Constitution*. He had placed it prominently on the "Regional" section front and a small promo for the series was on page 1. Jeff was pleased with what she had done so far, but Rebecca knew she could do better. The first story had only re-hashed the history she had pieced together from other people's work with the help of Miss Amy. ("Do they really call her that?" Jeff had asked.)

He had been excited about her trip to Greenville ("That's good initiative, Becko") and her discussions with Professor Fred. Jeff wanted to get both sides. He was less concerned than Rebecca herself about the possibility that the Greenville trip was just a road show to give her a pre-packaged view of black life in Escambia.

"Don't worry about that," Jeff had said. "Of course it's a biased view. The blacks feel they have been damaged by this history you're writing about. You can't expect them to provide a balanced picture, anymore than you could expect the Klan to. Providing balance is *your* job."

She placed her pen on the nearly filled pad and picked up the mug of coffee. That was when she saw the slender woman who had come up to the booth.

"You must be the reporter," she said quietly. "I'm Susan Tate."

Rebecca stood with a smile and the two shook hands. Rebecca ordered coffee for her guest and they sat on opposite sides of the table. Susan asked if she was enjoying her visit to Greenville, but did not seem overly interested in the answer. She showed no signs of nervousness, which was unusual for new sources, and began the interview herself.

"They said you wanted to talk about the Academy?"

Rebecca nodded.

"Why my child goes there?"

"Yes."

Susan looked down at her coffee. "You don't have children."

Rebecca hated it when they tried to draw the reporter into the story. "No, I.."

The woman looked up suddenly. "It wasn't a question. If you had children, it would never occur to you that there was a choice. You've seen both schools?" Rebecca nodded and the woman continued.

"Let's just say the visible differences are the least important. I wouldn't mind my kids going to a run-down school if it was safe, there was good teaching, and if learning was a priority. But none of that is true at the public school."

"And you think that's because it's mostly black."

Susan's eyes narrowed and Rebecca realized she had hit a nerve.

"They said you're not from the South."

"Does that matter?"

Sue rested her face in her cupped hand. "If we were sitting in Belfast having coffee and you asked why my children went to a Catholic school, do you think it would help if you knew the history of the Battle of Orange? It matters because if you're from a place then lots of things don't have to be explained." She turned toward the window, a slight grimace tightening her mouth. "The problems of the public school do begin with it being mostly black, but not in simple ways. The public school has more drug use, more girls getting pregnant, boys going to prison and almost nobody going to college. The middle class parents are not going to stand for that."

"But don't those problems partly happen because children like yours have been taken out of the school?"

"Maybe, but look at me." Sue lifted her collar with the fingers of her right hand; the edge was frayed. "We're not middle class. Besides, I think there's more than that going on. Something essential has dropped out of the black community. But maybe I'm wrong, so let's say you're right and the problem is that the high achieving kids leave the public school, what difference does it make? If the middle class parents pull out and I want my kid to be middle class someday, don't I have to follow them? Do I have a right to sacrifice my child's education to make a point, even if I wanted to?"

Rebecca leaned closer to the other woman. "But that's my question. Why does it have to be a sacrifice if parents like you come back to the system and make the public school work?"

Sue shook her head. "The problem is too big. The schools in this part of the state have never had much money to begin with. This is not a prosperous community and we don't have the taxes some of the bigger cities do. Most of the property is owned by people who don't live here, so there's no support for higher taxes for the schools and people who can afford to get their kids out, do. And once the public school became 50% black, that was it. Even if you wanted to fight it, your kids are only going to be there for four years. While you're fighting, their one chance at ninth grade goes by, then tenth, then eleventh and you're still fighting and they're graduating with a crappy education and you haven't changed a thing. Did you ever see anything in government change in four years?"

Susan took a sip from her coffee, dabbed her mouth and folded the paper napkin neatly before looking up. "So I deal with the system I've been given. I wear this ratty blouse and I drive an eleven-year-old car with bald tires so I can pay private school tuition. I don't like it; my own nephews went to the public school because my older sister and her husband couldn't afford to do for them what we do for ours. So my nephews got the "education" the blacks get 'cause the system works that way. It's not a question of do I like it, or is it fair or anything else. It's only a question of recognizing how things work and doing whatever you have to so your child is not a victim."

What Is Awful About Hope

B ack at the We Care Center Rebecca remembered.
"Professor, you asked me to remind you of something about
Gordon Halt?"

"Yes. Right." The old man turned to Ida Mae. "Didn't you tell me
one of your teachers has some connection to the Halt family? Rebecca
is interested in Gordon Halt's work for the Davis administration."

Ida Mae looked puzzled for just a moment. "Which one of them
was that? Carnetta, maybe? I'll get her."

Carnetta was dark and slender with short black hair and a buoyant
energy that Rebecca thought must be useful in the classroom. The only
problem Rebecca could see was that the teacher was so young. How
could she be of help on this story, which was turning out to be
anthropology as much as anything?

"Carnetta," Ida Mae began, "this lady is a reporter and she is
interested in the Halt family. Didn't I hear somewhere that your family
had some connection?"

The young teacher's eyes widened. "That old man's still alive?"

Rebecca leaned forward in her chair. Edward was not old, of
course, but Gordon Halt certainly fit the description. Did Carnetta
know Gordon Halt?

"I never laid eyes on him, and I don't know a first name, but I
know there was a Mr. Halt whose family my great grandmother worked
for — and I do know he was a newspaperman."

Rebecca felt that familiar tingle she got when discovering a lead,
but she was almost afraid to ask the next question: "I don't suppose
your great-grandmother is still alive?"

Carnetta laughed. "The Lord's not ready for her yet. That's
what she always tells us. She's still right up there in Montville."

Rebecca made a note to look up the patron saint of reporters, to give thanks and light a candle.

"And she knew Gordon Halt?"

"I don't know any of the names. All I know is she says she worked for the Halt family a hundred years."

Rebecca traded phone numbers with Carnetta before she went back to work. Fred turned to Rebecca. She was too excited to want to listen, but had to be polite.

"Before we get out of here I want Ida Mae to tell you about the old days. She knows as much about the Davis years as anybody."

"Now don't you make me sound old," she said, slapping his arm lightly. "I climbed from the crib to pass out handbills."

The professor laughed. "Now tell Rebecca, the first campaign you ever worked on was…"

She shook her head, smiling. "Michael DeWitt for Governor. I'm not too likely to forget that. I've still got a box of buttons in the house someplace." Ida Mae laughed and slapped her hands together. "I see now, you want her to hear my speech about how different things would have been if Michael DeWitt had won? Lord knows you've had to listen to it enough, haven't you Freddy?"

The old woman leaned toward Rebecca. "It's the God's truth, though. I still think we had a chance to have Mike DeWitt win and I still think he would have changed things. You don't get progress without leadership and all the leadership the state got from T. J. Davis was the wrong kind - not much different than having the Klan run things directly.

"But Mike died, of course, so we never got to find out if things could have been different. Lots of us still haven't gotten over that completely, that's what's awful about hope. When you have hope like that and then something rips out that hope before it can blossom, that's the hardest thing there is. If he had just lived through the election and gotten beaten, it would have been so much easier to live with than never knowing."

She turned to the professor. "Did you tell her about that time they bombed your house?" Ida Mae laughed at Rebecca's expression. "You didn't know that, I see. Yes, our Freddy was a soldier in this war. The

Klan threw a bomb that blew the front porch clean off his house. A group of us heard about it and went over that night to see if we could help and after the firemen and police left we were sitting in the living room when there was a knock on the door. I was closest so I went to open it, and there stood the lieutenant governor, Michael DeWitt, bigger than life.

"He came in and sat for awhile, just to be there and to let us know how ashamed he was that people the same color as him could have done something so cowardly. Not that there was much he could do about it. He'd have been impeached if the white folks found out he had come, but I think every black family in the state knew it in a few days."

"That was the first election after the Civil Rights Act passed, so most of our time was spent on voter registration. You should have seen it. The biggest problem was persuading people who had been beaten for even trying to register that this time could be different. It took a lot of persuading and it would have gone much slower, but so many of the colored folks knew that Mr. DeWitt was a good man. If it hadn't been for him there wouldn't have been any good reason to worry too much about voting. With him in the running, though, it seemed like change was possible.

"So, yes m'am," Ida Mae Brown said and nodded her head vigorously "I sure do remember that campaign."

Someone Should Do A Book About Him

I t was still daylight when Rebecca made it back to Montville, though after 8:30. She'd left the professor and picked up her car at the University, then driven back. A long day.

Dinner came in a bag from a drive-through window. She called her Mom from her motel room to report that she had returned safely and yes, they continued to have electric lights and running water in the South. She then took a long shower and propped up in bed, leaning a three-ring binder open against her knees. It appeared to be a scrapbook — almost the kind of thing you would expect a young girl to keep on a teen idol.

During the drive back she had made the mistake of observing off hand that it was surprising so many people mentioned Michael DeWitt to her, teasing the professor that he must have prompted people to mention a man who seemed to be one of his favorite subjects.

"Truthfully," she had asked, "isn't he pretty much forgotten?"

The professor had given her a funny half grin and turned to the box of papers on the seat beside him. He had pulled out this binder and said, "Maybe that's something we should change."

Inside it there were newspaper clippings, faded to a dark tan, covering speeches DeWitt had made, conferences he had gone to, bills he introduced when he was lieutenant governor. Rebecca kidded the professor that this was almost like a stalker's journal. He had laughed and said it wasn't quite like that, though he had at times been almost obsessed with DeWitt. He said he had always intended to write a book someday.

There were photographs of political meetings along with old campaign brochures, now crinkly as October leaves. At several places there would be five or ten pages of typing, with titles like "A New Kind of Politician" or "A Progressive Voice for Escambia" that could, themselves, have been campaign literature since they were obviously written by a devoted follower.

Rebecca read names she had never heard of, names of campaign managers, press agents, and supporters. All were possible sources, if any of them were still alive.

Other sheets contained typing Rebecca recognized as interview notes, none of them less that ten years old.

October 23 Brewster, Escambia

Mae Allen Jones

"My mother was present when Mr. DeWitt visited a family whose Father had been lynched. He was right there in their little house, with the preacher and Mr. DeWitt led a prayer and stayed to eat some chicken pie with them. He didn't have to do that."

[When would that of been?]

"Lordy, a long time ago. Would a been in the 1950's, I believe."

[What did white people think?]

"Wadn't no white people knew about that, I don't expect. Wouldn't a done him too much good for white people to know it." [she laughs]

Burton James, a friend Carnegie, Escambia Dec. 4

"It's hard to say what you remember most about a man who meant so much to you, and hard to decide how much you want to say to some stranger. Does the family know you're planning to do this book of yours?

"He seemed more alive than most people. He had so much spirit. Of course, he could let it get out of hand. I remember he just about got thrown out of school over a teacher he thought was a bad man. And, of course, I remember his driving. You know he was crazy about cars. Always wanted something newer and always wanted to go faster! I remember in college he spent months saving up the down payment for a Triumph sports car and then, before he'd owned it six weeks, took a turn too fast and broke an arm and three or four ribs.

"He was the saddest feller I ever saw while that car was getting fixed. But when he healed up and could drive again it was like he hadn't learned a thing. And that wasn't just when he was young. We were going all over the place in that last campaign and he scared me to death every time I rode with him. He never changed. [voice breaks] I guess that's obvious, considering."

Darryl K. Parkman Political Advisor. Atlanta, GA
March 28
"I've always thought someone should do a book about him. Even considered it myself...People remember DeWitt as a hero, because he was more liberal — he would never have said that; he would have said more 'reasonable' — than Davis, but hell, a lot of people were. Hermann Goering may have been more liberal than T. J. Davis.

"Michael DeWitt was a leader. People got excited about him because he really did have principles. He could let those principles be a weapon, though, against whoever didn't measure up. His approach was almost military, with himself as the general. He wanted commitment, he wanted people to be PRECISELY on time, and he wanted obedience. If he persuaded you, that was fine, but he wanted obedience whether you were persuaded or not. He told me when I argued with him one time, 'Tommy, the world is full of people who disagree with me. Some of 'em are running for office — go work for them.' I loved him, but I have to say the separation in his character between righteous and self-righteous could be as thin as the crack in a china teacup.

"Michael didn't even disagree with Davis all that much on the details — I guess a lot of people don't want to hear that, but it's true. The major differences were about style as much as anything. The Boss didn't like Davis's reactionary style and the pompousness of Davis's phony populism. Michael wouldn't have liked a real populist all that well either, but a phony populist like Davis drove him crazy.

"And Davis surrounded himself with these "buddies" of his who moved in on state businesses, just thugs really. DeWitt hated that and always said that what he'd do first if he was elected was to clean out that nest of vipers that hung around T. J. I remember that Billy Trask was one of the main ones. Pretended to be this simple country boy, like everything was too complicated for him. Right. He missed his calling by not having a chance to join the Mafia.

"The only one of the Davis people Mike DeWitt had any respect for was that Gordon Halt. A lot of progressive people hated Gordon because he should have been on our side. Michael didn't though. He said we should understand that Gordon had a vision he wanted to protect, and he somehow thought Davis could help him do that. Michael always thought Gordon would see the light and come over to our side eventually. But we never got the chance to see if that would have happened."

Rebecca turned another page, her eyelids heavy. The very next item was the lengthy clipping from the *Courier* reporting DeWitt's death in the car crash and saying it made Davis's election a certainty.

Behind the *Courier* clipping was another, this one on thinner newsprint that had not aged well. The typeface was so crude it might have been from an old Underwood and the columns were ragged so that many lines ended with hyphens. A handwritten note on the page read *Escambia Bugle* with a date in 1970.

This story was much longer on the page owing to the size of the type. Rebecca thought her old high school paper had looked like *The New York Times* compared to this rough format, but the writing itself was not bad. Compared to the *Courier* version this one was more conversational and more emotional. Statements like, "A powerful force for meaningful change has been taken away from Escambia politics" and "A man of elemental decency and Christian temperament, DeWitt had no like in state politics," filled the page. It sounded more like a eulogy than a news story, but Rebecca was not completely surprised since this was likely a black newspaper and her trip to Greenville had taught her how DeWitt was revered in that community.

There was also a poetic touch that the white paper had not had. The writer quoted a local minister who said there had been a story that two members of another congregation, elderly sisters described as "white ladies," had heard three blasts from a car horn the night of the car crash that killed DeWitt. Apparently the sisters' house was quite close to the crash site. There was much speculation as to what significance might be given the horn blasts. The sisters had wondered if they might have been a call for help, but police officers who investigated did not encourage that idea since death appeared to have been instantaneous. The minister telling the story was quoted as saying, "It seems fitting to believe the blasts of that horn were the call to his final reward of a good and faithful servant of the Master."

Rebecca was suddenly seized by a deep yawn. Thinking what a long day she had put in, she looked again at the date of the accident. This man had been dead for thirty-three years. The story, if there was one, would keep while she got some sleep.

She closed the notebook and turned to put it on the night table, spilling some loose papers as she did so. To hell with it, she thought, she'd get them tomorrow, and leaned over to switch off the light. But as she leaned she found herself facing a laughing man in a white shirt and loosened tie, a beer bottle raised high, as though in greeting or salute to her.

If she had not just finished reading the account of his death, she might have just turned off the light. Instead, she bent to pick up the photograph and studied it under the lamp. Michael DeWitt, born before her own Father, dead before her birth, was pictured here at about the age she was now. Happy and confident, totally ignorant of the future she knew awaited him. Looking into those long-dead eyes, Rebecca felt like a trespasser, or a peeping Tom, and then she had a thought of the strangeness of written history. All these names, all these reputations, at the mercy of later writers who try to imagine how it felt to live so long ago, with ideas and under conditions that can now only be guessed at. How could she hope to get it right?

Looking at the face in the picture, she imagined Michael DeWitt was wishing her luck. She would need it.

Being Old Really Must Be A Bitch

R ebecca spent the next morning connected by modem to her office to type up her notes. After lunch she drove past the small guardhouse — like an extraordinarily pretentious phone booth — at the entrance to Glendale. Rebecca thought "subdivision" was an awfully plain word to describe this group of half-million dollar houses. Gordon Halt had said that when he built his house this area was mostly forest, but it had since become the most exclusive residential area in Montville. She slowed the car to let the young security guard see how harmless she looked, giving him a smile and a little wave.

Mrs. Halt had prepared peach scones, placing them on a tray with coffee and juice in the den. Rebecca could not remember getting this kind of treatment from a source before.

"I was interested in the transcript you sent me," Gordon said, touching his mouth with a cotton napkin. "Billy is quite a talker."

"Is he telling the truth? Was he that close to Davis?"

Gordon looked thoughtful. "He was the closest person to Davis for the longest time. That's certainly true. Still, I suppose his capacity for, or interest in, telling the truth is not greater than other people's. Probably less that most."

Rebecca raised an eyebrow. "Not exactly a ringing endorsement."

"I would just say you should verify whatever Billy says on those tapes. That's all."

Rebecca paused to take a bite of scone, getting a bit of sweet peach that took her mind off the interview.

"These are unbelievable," she said.

"She does a good job for an old lady," Gordon said with a smile, "but the peach thing is wearing me out. We had pork loin the other night with some kind of peach something and the season is only half over. By August she'll be making peach teriyaki."

Rebecca laughed, then sipped from her coffee cup.

"I haven't been back by the hospital. How is the governor?"

Gordon shrugged. "The same."

She leaned over to open her bag where it sat on the floor, pulling out yet another notebook and flipping it open.

"I'm curious about Michael DeWitt."

"Why, for heaven's sake?"

"He's part of Governor Davis's story, isn't he?"

"Some people used to think so," Gordon said. "Maybe some of the people you're talking to still do."

"Well, they were bitter rivals, weren't they?"

"Competitors, certainly. Especially early on. I remember when it started. They were opponents in a student government election at UE."

Rebecca watched him touch a long, crooked finger to his temple. The hand shook slightly, a faint tremor she had not noticed before. She shuddered inside, afraid he would say "it's all still right in here," or some equally awful cliché. Being old really must be a bitch.

"It was our sophomore year and there was a campaign rally," he said, beginning a long and not entirely coherent story about Davis being short and having to adjust the microphone, and feeling he had been made fun of. Rebecca thought she'd need more coffee if this were to run on much longer. But Gordon seemed to be summing up.

"So they were certainly competitors. But bitter rivals? I wouldn't say so. I don't think two people can be bitter rivals if one of them is never competitive. And no matter what your new friends are telling you, Michael DeWitt was never serious competition for Governor Davis."

Rebecca looked at her notes.

"But you just said DeWitt won the student government election?"

"Only because he wasn't there long enough for students to really know him. And I know what you're going to say next — he held statewide office before Davis did. But that's because Giant Partain appointed him to fill an unexpired term as lieutenant governor and he got reelected as an incumbent. Those were flukes. He was always too liberal to be governor here. When the people found out what he was really like, he wouldn't have beaten Davis at a DeWitt family reunion."

Rebecca bent forward to be sure she had started the tape recorder. Despite the vehemence of his words, Rebecca thought Gordon seemed calm about DeWitt, not quite bored because that would have been rude, but certainly not agitated. She had thought he might be, just because the professor seemed so certain that DeWitt was a titanic force in Escambia history. Maybe there was nothing to this DeWitt thing after all.

"And his politics was just part of it," Gordon continued. He was a wild man, a loose cannon. You never knew what he'd come up with next, just to keep the pot boiling. He had no regard for history or tradition or any of those things that give life an anchor. He wanted things to be the way he thought they should be, regardless of other people's opinions."

Rebecca thought her puzzlement must have shown on her face because Gordon continued.

"Mike DeWitt and I attended the same high-school, the private school here in Montville. He was boarding because his family was in the steel business in Carnegie, about three hours to the north. Anyway, we had this old coot of a science teacher named Walton that everybody called Nine-Ball because he didn't have a hair on his head. Nine-Ball was mean as a snake and graded unfairly, but basically he was just old and cranky.

"Every year Nine-Ball would perform what he called an experiment to prove there was no such thing as rape. I know, I know," Gordon said in response to a look from Rebecca, "not very politically correct, but this was a long time ago. It was stupid, but harmless. At least to everyone but Michael DeWitt.

Gordon shook his head, then sipped from his coffee cup.

"Michael wrote letters to the student paper, to the principal, even to the school board making this terrible allegations about cruelty and so forth and insisting the teacher be fired. And he wouldn't give it up when his missives were ignored. He would interrupt that teacher's classes and put Vaseline on his car windshield.

I suppose such things are common now but in my day any kind of disrespect to a teacher was unthinkable. If it had not been a private school to which his family was so closely linked, Michael would have been expelled. As it was, he was suspended for a month and had to do his work from home. But Michael didn't care. He thought he could do anything he wanted."

Rebecca rubbed her cheek for a moment, then said, "But he was right, wasn't he? I mean that teacher sounds pretty awful."

Gordon shifted in his seat.

"Even if he was, is that enough to justify what he did? Can you excuse bad conduct just by saying you're right?" He snorted at the idea. "Anyway, it shows why he could never have been governor. Not of *this* state. Michael DeWitt had no respect for authority."

Later, walking out to her car, Rebecca commented on a spray of small yellow blooms on a trellis. Gordon laughed.

"I'm glad you noticed that particular flower. I had guests here from Massachusetts a few years ago and they thought I was kidding them about that plant. I actually won a bet when they looked it up and found out that yes, by god, it is *Confederate* Jasmine."

Rebecca smiled, less at the story than at his pleasure in telling it. Where did that come from, she wondered, that happiness at being from one particular place?

They Get Along Pretty Well

Rebecca ate at a cafeteria after leaving Gordon's house. Margaret, his wife, had invited her to stay for dinner (*or supper?*) but she had declined. Everyone she met invited her for a meal, which was nice, but she was beginning to think this story was going in a direction she might not be able to predict. Some distance would be a good thing.

She bought a bottle of white wine to take back to the room. She had filled the sink with ice from the machine down the hall, thinking about the two versions of Michael Dewitt she had gotten from Gordon Halt and Professor Fred, before she noticed her message light was blinking.

The motel operator told her the call was from Carnetta and gave her a long distance number. Rebecca had not expected to hear from the young Greenville teacher so soon, but some sources really got into the idea of helping with a story.

A child answered the call on the second ring.

"Hello?" the small voice said.

"Hi. May I speak to Carnetta?"

"Hello?" the child repeated helpfully.

This continued for several repetitions until an adult took the phone and eventually Carnetta was located.

"I'm going to be in Escambia day after tomorrow if you'd like to go with me to visit Grandma," Carnetta said. "I'm going to take the baby over to stay with her, so you'll see three generations."

"How old is your baby?" Rebecca asked.

"Not mine, my cousin's. That's a long story. Anyway, see you Thursday."

Rebecca's next call was to the hospital where a business-like voice assured her there had been no change in the Governor's condition. He had not regained consciousness.

Rebecca hooked up the modem wire and logged on to the *Constitution*'s mainframe. She read her email and sent a status report to Jeff. She also sent the piece she had done based on her visit to Greenville, "a place where time stands still." She grimaced at the cliché but hoped the copy desk would polish the wording. She needed some rest if that was the best she could do. Besides, no sooner had she typed the words than she had second thoughts.

Despite the poverty and unfairness she had seen in Greenville, any fair observer coming here for the first time would notice that, from a distance at least, white and black people seemed to get along pretty well. She couldn't stop thinking about one fact, simple but overwhelmingly important — there *were* black people here, lots of them. Anyone from the Midwest would notice that first. At the University, in the newspaper office, at the shopping mall or in restaurants, the public was mixed.

She had to get that across in the stories. As different as this place was, something about it was working, not perfectly, but to some degree.

The story Gordon Halt had told about Michael DeWitt came back to her. Thinking about it, she realized Gordon's reaction to the story had fascinated her as much as the story itself. *Is it enough to be right?* Gordon had asked. *Does that justify any kind of action, however extreme?*

Rebecca sighed, thinking that in her life she had never had to ask that question. Her generation had not had the battles over civil rights and military service these old guys had dealt with. A new century was about to begin which could surely bring unexpected challenges, but things had been pretty smooth for her generation, at least in big ways. There was a small war over Iraq's invasion of Kuwait, but it was nothing like what her dad had told her of Vietnam. The American soldiers were all volunteers.

She had dealt with some pretty serious issues, but those were personal. She had not been called upon to be part of a group and she had not missed that. But if she had to respond to Gordon Halt's question she thought she would say *yes, being right on a moral issue probably does justify some pretty extreme conduct.* Hadn't her dad raised her that way? Do the right thing and have the courage to live with the consequences?

She suddenly realized she was staring at the screen without typing anything. She hated to think what Jeff would say if he could read her thoughts. *Too much thinking, not enough facts. Let the story tell itself.*

She logged off, unhooked the phone cord and put it back in her case. By then the wine was chilled. She poured it into the flimsy plastic cup provided in the room, thinking *how depressing is this?* Sitting on the bed, she plumped the two pillows together against the headboard and leaned back. Because nothing else was on, she watched a reality show which required contestants to perform weird or disgusting acts. It was strange, but after about ten minutes of watching, the program itself seemed like a weird and disgusting act - much more depressing than wine in a plastic cup - so she changed channels until she found a Braves game. Good ol' TBS. She was almost certain her dad would be watching at home and the thought made her calm, though normally she found baseball boring. She watched until the wine made her sleepy, then turned everything off and snuggled under the sheet.

* * *

Carnetta had not been sure how to get to the motel so Rebecca had arranged to meet her downtown, leaving her car in the *Courier* parking lot. With the temperature at 93 and the humidity higher, the air was like a curtain you had to move aside as you walked. In the distance Rebecca could see dark clouds piling for the daily thunderstorm that would rain down for only five minutes, just long enough to convert the sweltering streets into a sauna.

Now, though, as they drove, the sun blazed down on the small frame houses that lined the broken asphalt streets. The neighborhood was both better and worse than she expected. The houses were plain but, unlike those she had seen in Greenville and in other parts of the city, these were not shotgun houses of warped and unpainted lumber. These were small, mostly neat, brick or siding residences that, in other cities, young lawyers or bankers would move into, spruce up and make trendy. The difference here was that no sprucing up had occurred for a very long time. While some of the houses were well maintained, most had shutters with missing slats or roofs made gap-toothed by missing shingles.

Every few yards along the potholed street, curbs were littered with beer bottles and broken glass. And the noise was oppressive. Rebecca didn't think they were near the airport, but a roar seemed to be almost constant.

"It's the one with the green roof in the next block," Carnetta said, pointing. She had told Rebecca there would be no white people in this neighborhood, a remark that reminded her what the professor had told her in Greenville. "Residential patterns are the most persistent vestige of the old forced racial separation. Schools are integrated by legal compulsion, businesses by economic necessity and law, churches by principle, but neighborhoods can only be integrated by individual choice." The physical conditions of the houses she saw around her reminded Rebecca of the decrepit public school building in Greenville. And like that school, she suspected, if white people *could* leave this neighborhood, they did. The question, of course, was whether the black people would do the same, if they could. But that was for some other reporter to worry about; she had all she could handle in the story she'd been assigned.

"Watch out for the glass," Carnetta said, as Rebecca steered the car to the curb.

Opening her door, the roar she'd heard earlier became deafening. Rebecca felt like an idiot for not realizing what it was. Just a hundred yards behind the house, rising like an apparition in a Spielberg movie, was an enormous section of Interstate 20, swooping in a wide curve, supported sixty feet in the air by massive concrete columns. Rebecca's first thought was *why would anybody build a house here?* but then she realized that, of course, the houses had been here first. These people didn't have the political power to keep the Interstate from tearing up their neighborhood.

Carnetta was looking at her as though she could read her mind. "The lucky ones had their houses bought for right-of-way and could move. Granny's house was too far away to be taken, but the noise makes the place impossible to sell. And, of course, there's no exit from the Interstate, so the lot isn't valuable as commercial property either.

You Can Sure Tell She's White Folks

C arnetta's Granny Weeda turned out to be a stooped elderly woman, bent like a wind-blown tree, her thin arms like branches protruding from the short sleeves of her cotton print dress. Her hair was stark white and pulled back in kinked waves to a loose bun on her head. Her movements were slow and made Rebecca think that moving at all might be too great a challenge for her after all these years, but her eyes were not just bright but hard, as though daring you to assume that the mind inside was as weakened as the muscles you could see.

* * *

Weeda watched the baby crawl across the floor toward her Aunt Carnetta and the white girl, and thought how strange it was to live so long. *I was already an old woman when Carnetta was born. What an angel that one was, and here she is now, still coming to see me once a week and looking out for this new one almost like it was her own.* Weeda frowned to think about the baby's mother, Carnetta's older cousin. *How could them two be so different and they both my own blood? Carnetta always wantin' to do something for other people and Rosetta wantin' everything done for her. Did the Lord ever make a more selfish girl than Rosetta? All she could do was complain about how hard life is and then use that as an excuse for being no-account.*

Weeda had never had patience for whining and it made her sad that whining was such a part of Rosetta's character. She couldn't see that her situation was no worse than most people faced. When <u>hadn't</u> things been hard? When <u>had</u> there been any money? She knew what Rosetta was feeling, better than her granddaughter did herself. She knew what it was like to want to just lay your head on the table and quit.

But women with children to raise didn't do that. That's what Weeda couldn't forgive and Rosetta couldn't accept. When the children come the mother has to think about them, not herself, and do what's got to be done. Weeda had never quit, all those years she had worked for the Halt family. She did good work every day, even if she did put her head on the table every now and then. She did good work even for that white lady who never appreciated her.

That's what the white girl wanted to hear about.

"Old Mr. Halt was always good and fair to me," Weeda said, "as much as he could be, things being what they were. He probably wasn't quite as good a man as he thought he was, but he was as good as white people got. That wife of his, now, she was another story all together." *She was way too good for a town like Montville and she woulda been real quick to tell you so,* Weeda thought. *'Plantation royalty is what Mrs. Halt wanted to be, so what a shame there wasn't plantations no more. Just towns that was run like there still was."*

"I guess you mostly interested in Master Gordon?"

Rebecca nodded, a puzzled look on her face.

"Funny I still think of him that way, 'cause that's how his Mama wanted him called, like he was a little prince, I guess. I reckon he's got to be 70 or more his own self by now, ain't he?"

Later, Weeda felt as though she had been talking for hours, but she knew it couldn't have been that long. At least not long enough for this little girl reporter to be tired; she had more questions than a three year old. Weeda had told her about the old white house in Salem, where the Halt family had lived when she first started working for them. She wasn't nothing but a girl herself then, maybe 15 but coulda been younger, helping in the kitchen and looking after the baby, that was Master Gordon, what had just been born.

Weeda shifted in the uncomfortable chair to avoid the edge where a spring was beginning to poke through. She looked up to see that the white girl was still here, talking to Carnetta. But was that right? It seemed like too long. Weeda hated it when she couldn't keep time straight, but that seemed to happen more and more now. Carnetta said the white girl was from Atlanta, but she didn't sound like anybody who'd learned to talk in Georgia. Weeda motioned to her granddaughter to come over.

"Y'all help me get the baby fed and bathed and then you need to get on home before it gets too dark."

The white girl heard and piped up. "We don't have to hurry. We can help get her to sleep."

You can sure tell she's white folks, Weeda thought. *One thing never changes about 'em, you cain't tell 'em nothing. She's gonna stand here in my own house and tell me how 'everything is going to be just fine' and 'don't worry about anything' when, God bless her, she don't know nothing. She don't know about the squealing tires in the street, the guns fired from cars, the beer bottles crashing on the sidewalks or into the side of the house. She didn't know about the miserable, mad boys, full of whiskey or drugs, shouting cuss words at the top of their lungs or the women in other houses or on the streets, crying from pain or fear or just crazy. The white girl is thinking of how things are at <u>her</u> home, in <u>her</u> neighborhood. She don't know nothing about this place. She can't even imagine it.*

Weeda raised herself from the rickety chair, wincing with pain and effort and took lurching steps with the walker to cross the room and stand beside the two girls.

"Listen to me now. Y'all think old people don't know nothing, but you listen. You all help me get this baby fed and then you g<u>o</u>, you hear?" She felt exhausted from the effort of trying to make them understand, but she could see a light dawning in the white girl's face: this was serious business.

"This is not a good place to be after dark. Y'all don't want to be outside. You listen to Grandma"

* * *

Rebecca could hear what she had not noticed before. While she had been tending the baby the interstate noise had subsided slightly and been replaced by something much different. Now she heard dull but heavy thumps, actual vibrations, of the hugely amplified bass line of music playing in slow-rolling cars as they cruised the pot-holed streets. Rude shouts punctuated the pounding, seemingly from one car to another. She heard a muffled crash, as though a light bulb had fallen off a shelf somewhere nearby, and the quavering wail of a would-be singer, seemingly high on something already, though the sun had barely set. In the far distance she heard a pop that she hoped was a car's backfire. She looked at Weeda

"Put that baby in the bed, back this way," the old woman said, leading them into a room next to the tiny bath. "I shoulda gotten y'all out of here long time ago."

Rebecca placed the child in a flimsy baby bed. She noticed that screws on the upright corner pieces needed tightening, and made a mental note to offer to come back and do that. The rails seemed too far apart, as well. She knew there were rules about that, to keep a baby's head from getting caught between, but the rules would have applied to beds much newer than this one — and would have been meant for babies with fewer problems than this one.

"Just push that up against the wall, please, so I got room to walk." Rebecca did as she was asked, lining one end of the bed up with the window frame in that wall. Then she gathered her notebook and she and Carnetta walked the few steps to the front door. Carnetta reached up to turn on the porch light.

"No!" Weeda shouted. Rebecca nearly jumped out of her skin. "You don't want to draw no attention to yourself. Be ready to go when you open the door and get in the car quick as you can." She leaned over to give Carnetta a kiss, saying, "Thank you, baby. I'll see you in a day or two"

Outside, the noises were more sinister. Unmuffled cars rumbled down the block. The drunken singer was still at it, wailing from a porch half way up the block. Rap from car amplifiers thudded against Rebecca's chest, felt as much as heard.

Carnetta closed the steel security door behind them. Rebecca noticed burglar bars she had not seen before, saw them on virtually every house and wondered what happened to the people inside if there was a fire and the door could not be used. Walking to the car, Rebecca felt herself slumping to become smaller, less visible.

Another car slowly passed the house and moved beyond them as Rebecca reached the curb. Fumbling with her key, she saw a flash of red, then white lights came on to her left. The car that had passed was now backing up. Shouts came from the car, and a young man's head poked from the side window. Rebecca motioned for Carnetta to stay on this side of the car.

Yellow light from the few streetlights that were working drifted through the trees overhanging the street. Rebecca had the feeling of being closed in, as though on a lighted stage, controlled by someone else, where anything could happen.

"Yo, where that little whitey come from?" The shout came from the car which was now almost beside Rebecca's. She fumbled with the key, finally getting it to turn. The dome light seemed as bright as a rising sun. Rebecca clambered in, then heard a voice behind her.

"Y'all get away from here. Ain't nobody talking to you." Carnetta was staring down the men in the car. The back door opened and one of them started out.

"Don't be that way, mama. Come here and let me talk to you."

Carnetta shouted, "Get away from here before I call the cops." Rebecca gunned her engine and Carnetta jumped in the passenger seat. There was a loud thump as a thrown beer bottle hit the back of their car.

Rebecca sped to the corner and was about to turn when Canetta shouted for her to stop. She had been watching behind.

"They're not following us. I want to see what they do." Rebecca turned off the lights but left the car running. Carnetta rolled down her window and they could hear the boys, now all standing in the street, shouting at each other. As they watched, one of the boys went to the door of Weeda's house. He yelled and banged on the security door, then grabbed the handle as though he would shake it from its frame. The porch light did not come on. Carnetta picked up Rebecca's car phone and called the police.

The Occasional Hysteric Female

G ordon found it interesting to be interviewed, and also appalling. He wondered if his reporters in the old days had been like this one — so self-righteous, so sure she knew the answer before she asked the question. At least he hoped his reporters had not been so emotional. The young woman from the Atlanta paper was red-faced and, a rookie mistake, talking much more than she was listening. He would have to be patient with her.

"I had to drive by a private guard to get here," she was saying. "Did you know that?"

Gordon assumed it was a rhetorical question, unless she thought his age prevented him from noticing the circumstances of his own daily life. He gave a small shrug.

"It seems so strange after all I've seen in the last few days."

Gordon had no idea <u>what</u> she had seen, but he supposed she would not leave him in the dark. He didn't want to be smug. She was young, after all. But she would really have to learn not to get emotionally invested in her stories.

"You seem distracted," he said.

She rubbed her forehead with her fingertips. "I shouldn't let it show," she said, "but we sit here in this lovely home talking about the charm of the South and the Davis heritage and the tie to Reagan and now Bush as though that is something to be proud of. But we don't talk about the fact that most black people in Escambia live in some version of a ghetto, without medical care, schools or police protection."

Gordon straightened his collar, a gesture he had often found useful, like clearing the throat. Years of dealing with the occasional hysteric female employee had taught him that it was important not to respond too quickly to these emotional flashes. Better to take a little time, answer anger with reason.

"I'm sorry you're distraught, young woman, but I think you're being unfair. What you describe is not a southern problem. I can't really believe things are so much different in Indiana, or New York, or anywhere else. I'm not sure what you expected. Do you think a maid should be able to live where I live? I doubt that happens even in communist countries."

The girl bit her lip, but he could not tell if she knew she was out of line or she resented the rebuke. Whichever it was, when she spoke it was with more control.

"I'm not saying poor people are treated differently. Maybe that's what I should be saying, but I'm talking about race. I'm talking about black people getting different treatment *because* they're black. Isn't that the real legacy of Governor Davis?"

They heard at the same time the low hum of Margaret's chair. Gordon turned to see her at the door. She asked if anyone would like coffee. They both refused, with matching, equally fake, smiles. When she left, Gordon turned back to Rebecca.

"It sounds as though you've already decided."

Gordon watched the girl's face soften, as though it only now occurred to her that she was losing her required objectivity. She looked down at the notebook in her lap, then back up at him.

"I don't think so. I have seen some things that disturb me and I've been given one explanation. Now I'm asking you if there is another one."

Gordon shook his head and felt his mouth tighten involuntarily. An explanation? Of course there was. Just as there was an explanation for the violence in Northern Ireland. But could this, this <u>child</u> understand an explanation based on an intimate appreciation of a century of history? He doubted today's schools had prepared her for any such thing.

"There is so much you cannot understand that..."

"That's a cop-out. Make me understand."

She put her notebook on the lamp table and bent over to retrieve the recorder from her bag. She placed it on the coffee table between them as Gordon said, "It's a long story."

Rebecca looked at him with that thin, fake, smile.

"I've got lots of time," she said, and pushed the "Record" button.

Part Two

Get Your ♥ in DIXIE ... Or Get Your 🐴
OUT!
—*Civil Rights Era bumper sticker*

I Never Denied We Were Different

A sense of personal history and tradition requires two things: blood and geography. Don't all people want to know 'who am I?' and 'where did I come from?' Gordon Halt had always been able to answer those questions because his family had been in this place since before Escambia was a state, when the land belonged to a dozen native tribes the white men lazily called Creeks, in a land the white man's map marked as "Western Georgia," stretching all the way from Savannah.

"The first of my family to come here was Travail Chancey, the founder of Mother's family in Escambia," Gordon said. "He came from North Carolina in 1820 with a wagonload of possessions that he had transferred onto a barge at Memphis. The river was the only reliable way to move heavy loads. Travail was bringing a printing press, his most prized possession, which was the heaviest item ever brought here up to that time. The state of Escambia didn't exist yet and Salem was just a clearing in the woods then, an unlikely place for a tradesman but since agriculture appealed to him neither by talent nor inclination Travail decided to try the one trade he knew.

"His father had been a printer in North Carolina, but by 1818 Wilmington was an old, established town where numerous printers divided up a volume of business that would have made only one rich. Travail's Father encouraged him to think of moving to the territories, where opportunity awaited the man brave enough to seize it. His father helped him to repair a broken down press, bought from a bankrupt firm, and wished him Godspeed.

"Travail set up his press in the front room of a small cabin and in a few years was producing handbills for the merchandise store and programs (at half price) for the three small local congregations, two of them Baptist groups who disagreed on the precise meaning of our Father's words. His frequent rounds to the stores and churches to gather the information for the advertising and bulletins made Travail well known in the village and inspired him to begin the Butler County *Herald*, a single-page broadside that was the first newspaper of any kind in the central part of the territory. This was a modest affair indeed, but it was a newspaper and more importantly it was first."

Gordon chuckled quietly. "It's better to be lucky than smart, they say. Anyway, when Salem became the territorial capital, quite a lot of printing was needed and Travail's fortune was made.

"It was not until after the war, in 1874 I think, that Travail's grandson, my maternal great grandfather, built the large white house on the bank of the river. The house was a present for his wife on the occasion of the birth of his first son, Mother's Father. Mother always said the Chancey family considered that house to be her grandfather's pledge that the family would stay in this place and prosper. They were determined not to become casualties of the war."

Gordon took a drink from his glass of water, and cleared his throat. Margaret always teased him about his stories being endless, not meaning that there were a lot of them. But what could he do, with his background and Uncle Buck as a role model, but tell stories?

He saw the slight smile on the reporter's face and imagined how he must be boring her. "I'm sure this is more than you wanted to know."

She reddened slightly. "Oh no, I'm interested. It's just that the concerns about a war that was so long ago seem strange to me."

"Of course," Gordon says, nodding, "I can't explain it myself, but you asked why we are as we are. I will tell you Mother took the idea of family survival so seriously she went to some trouble to be sure I was born in that white house."

If he closed his eyes Gordon could still see his Uncle Buck, his face tanned and arms muscled from days of hunting and fishing, his dark curly hair covered by a feed-store cap. When he was small, Gordon had thought Uncle Buck was the most fun of anyone on Earth and he could see that the older man enjoyed his company as well. His eyes danced every time he told Gordon the story.

I remember that day you were born, your Daddy took you from your crib to go meet Papa, like it was a formal introduction. 'It's a boy, just like I promised,' your Daddy said, like you were a new prince. At this point, no matter how many times he told the story, Uncle Buck would laugh out loud and say, *Which I guess you pretty much turned out to be,* and tousle Gordon's hair.

Your grandfather was old by then but his face lighted up when he saw you. He rocked you in that high back chair he had with the cane seat and back, and I can remember that the whump, whump sound as the runners clumped over the porch floor slats made a lullaby for you. When you started crying your Daddy handed you to one of the colored girls, and then us men toasted your mama with glasses of bourbon splashed with a little spring water.

Thinking of Margaret's teasing, Gordon decides not to share that story. It's not even his own memory, of course, just what he was told. Over and over.

"When I was little we seemed to spend half our weekends at that house. It was a wonderful place to be a boy." He had a vision of the woods that grew thickly between the house and the river, where he had spent long summer weeks with his buddies, Pokey Norris and Booger Bradley. Tree branches metamorphosed into Winchester Rifles and the three boys, on behalf of white men everywhere, once again cleared the Creek from these woods forever.

"I remember one summer when Father had made a rule against playing on the river bank because the spring rains had been so heavy. This prohibition presented the attraction of any parental injunction, which is to find a way to disobey it while technically being in compliance." Gordon laughed. "I had watched a Saturday matinee of a Tarzan movie when the loin-clothed hero used a long and suspiciously well-placed vine to propel himself across a raging river. That very afternoon my buddies and I actually located a vine-equipped tree so tall, with vines so long, that a healthy swing would carry you out over the very center of the river without you setting even a toe where it was forbidden to be.

"Unfortunately after many swings the vine broke and I fell into the muddy bank. I still remember that long, soggy walk home. My mud-filled shoes squeaked with every step, I smelled of river dank and every minute brought me closer to Father's rage. But when I got to the house, my luck changed; no one was there except Weeda. Father and the uncles had gone hunting and Mother was playing bridge at the parsonage. Not that Weeda was sweetness and light, you understand."

"Wait a second." Rebecca looked up from her pad. "Weeda?"

Gordon was startled by the question. One thing that made the girl a good reporter was that she didn't normally interrupt.

"You're talking about the Weeda I visited, who was a maid for your family?" she asked. Gordon nodded. "My God," she said, "I knew she had worked for you for years, but you're saying this happened when you were a *boy?*"

Gordon nodded. "And dinosaurs roamed the earth. I've always heard negroes don't age like we do, so you might not think it, but she's 10 or 15 years older than I. I think she was basically born in my great grandfather's house…"

"The white house?"

"Not *in* it, precisely, but her family would have had a cabin on the homeplace. There must have been 200 acres, and she was around until my own son went off to college. I suppose that doesn't happen much anymore, but it wasn't so unusual back then. People from outside are always surprised at how closely we all lived back then."

Rebecca smiled and shook her head, making Gordon stop. "What?" he asked.

"You said 'people from outside'. You mean outside the South? You can see that sounds odd."

"You're the one that started this, young lady. I never denied we were different. I thought that difference was what you wanted to talk about. Anyway, Weeda probably fixed the first peanut butter and jelly sandwich I ever had, and I'm pretty sure she fixed the first one my boy ate.

"She was tough as nails on me." Gordon continued. "But she would cover for me, too, sometimes. We were pretty close there for a while, all things considered. Anyway, when I walked in with all that mud on me, she was fit to be tied."

What on earth have you done to yourself?" he could almost hear Weeda asking. *Ain't I heard your Daddy tell you a thousand times not to go near that river this summer?*

He remembered explaining that he was playing <u>above</u> the river, not in it, and that he was an innocent victim of the fates. Weeda found this argument less than compelling. *You put yourself in the way of fate, Master Gordon.*

"She clucked and fussed over me even though she was mad about it, drawing a bath and laying out clean clothes. A year earlier she would have bathed me, but I had put a stop to that when I turned six. When she finished there was no trace of my adventure.

"What about the other black people," Rebecca asked, "and black children? Were you close with them?"

"That would depend on if you were city people or country people. During the week, in Montville, we were city and so the only negroes I saw were Weeda and the yardman. Later Weeda had a couple of kids who would be around sometime. But on the weekends we went to Salem, to great-granddaddy's big white house and we were like country people. That meant I would see the negro men who slaughtered hogs and hoed cotton and the women they were married to and their kids and we'd play and whatnot like kids do."

"And that was OK with everybody?" she asked.

Gordon was sitting with his right leg crossed and noticed his shoelace had come untied. He fiddled with the loose lace, thinking of times Mother had expressed concern about his playing with "picaninnies." This was another memory he wouldn't share.

"That was just fine," he said. "In the country."

She made a little "hum" and nodded, then wrote something in her notebook. Gordon had a vision of the young Margaret Mead gathering information about impossibly strange tribes in the Pacific. He hated this analyzing, and was wondering how to politely end this session when she spoke again.

"That makes me think of something I've been curious about. What is the first thing you remember that made you know the South was different?"

He snorted. "The North is different. The South is normal."

She smiled, as though letting him know she did not expect to win that debate. "OK, OK, but when did you first think of yourself as a Southerner?"

Gordon was an introspective man by nature and he had seldom been asked a personal question that he had not, at some time in the past, asked himself but he was taken aback at this one. It had never occurred to him that there might have been a time when he "became" Southern, yet clearly such a thing happens to everyone here.

He was quiet for a long time, but then he felt something float to the surface of that murky lake of memory like a dislodged piece of driftwood. Mentally picking up that fragment and turning it over, holding it to the light, he could see that, yes, this was the one, the true answer to her astounding question.

"I must have been six or seven, just a little younger than when I fell into the riverbank. Grandfather had a neighbor in Salem, a widow lady named Miss Nancy Willoughby, and the kids would go over to her house and have cookies and lemonade some afternoons and, as the price of admission so to speak, we would listen to Miss Nancy tell us about the Siege of Vicksburg. We liked cookies and stories so we were happy to sit and listen while Miss Nancy recalled the horrors the Yankees had inflicted on that beautiful Mississippi city.

"Vicksburg sat proudly on the highest bluff on the southern half of the Mississippi River. God himself might have designed it as the site for a river fortress. The Yankees had identified control of the river as a central part of their strategy for the war early on, and they devoted some 150,000 troops to taking the city, but the Confederate resistance was fearsome and the continuing battles wore down to a draw. Then the Yankees, under the personal command of U. S. Grant, developed a new plan.

"The significance of the battle was that it was a siege in the true sense. Like the Greeks at Troy, the Yankees blocked the city on all sides, intending to break the spirit of civilians through starvation and terror. Unlike the Greeks, the Yankees had artillery, guns and cannon of all sizes, so that terror could be generated very easily in a population with no means to flee. Even the burning of Atlanta was not so great an atrocity against civilians.

"Some accounts say that during the height of the siege, from May to July of 1863, as many as 50,000 shells hit the city each day. Most of these were not simply cannon balls but were exploding shells, aerial bombs. They rained in all day and at night, the burning fuses of hundreds of shells at once streaked the sky like a meteor shower. The firing from across the river was continuous and civilized life as it had been known came to a halt.

"Miss Nancy was seven years old. Her father, normally a cotton merchant on the bustling dock, was away with the 2nd Battalion, Mississippi Infantry. Her mother, Amanda Stewart Gregory, tried to keep a home intact for Nancy, her grandmother Rachel, and Rachel's sister Mabel. Their days were spent scrounging for whatever food was available and cooking for the troops defending the city. When the shelling began, their comfortable home became too dangerous to stay in and they joined thousands of other women and children in caves in the cliffs that had been set up for use as shelters. Each night they tried to rest amid the cries of the young children and the thunderous explosions above ground. Each day they came out to find new buildings collapsed and new fires to be extinguished.

"Miss Nancy told us her only joy during those months was her little dog, Tot. He was a terrier her father had given her for a birthday present and they were never separated until the shelling started. Pets were not allowed in the caves at night, so every morning when the women and children came out, Tot would be there waiting for her. Then one morning he wasn't."

Gordon smiled to himself, thinking how the small detail always made the story. Who knew how many people had starved to death in Vicksburg? Yet when Miss Nancy told the story the saddest part was always little Tot.

"She told us it was years later before her father admitted that Tot had probably been taken away to be eaten. There were no domestic animals left in Vicksburg. There are even stories that butcher shops would hang rats in the window, dressed and ready to cook, just as the chickens had always hung there, because that was the only meat there was. The Confederate soldiers were fed "soup" made from ground chick peas and hulls and any leftovers that had ever been part of a plant, but instead of nourishing them it often caused intestinal problems as bad as dysentery.

"'That's what the Yankees did to us,' Miss Nancy would say as we sat on her porch. 'They made us eat rats, and even our beloved pets. They starved us, but they never out fought us. And we survived, so you children could remember. And remember you must. The South will always survive.'"

"Vicksburg did fall; without food or supplies it had to. The surrender came on July 4, 1863. So, will you be surprised to hear that Miss Nancy's favorite day to tell that story was July 4th? It was actually a tradition in many Southern families to use the day to commemorate that battle and the cost to civilians, almost as a day of mourning. Independence Day as you think of it was not celebrated in Vicksburg for 125 years."

Gordon leaned over to pick up his coffee cup and take a sip. Then he took a deep breath and composed himself; he was surprised and a little embarrassed at how much the story could still affect him.

"That's a very long answer to your question," he said, "but when I first heard Miss Nancy tell that story, I knew I was Southern."

The girl nodded but said nothing, making notes on her pad. Gordon could hear the faint hum of the recorder. He thought about how one memory brings another and recalled a childhood nightmare involving evil men who threatened to kill his dog, Buddy. He decided not to mention it to the reporter, but in his childhood nightmares the bad men always wore blue coats.

The President Was Not Even on the Ballot

A fter spending the morning with Gordon Halt, Rebecca felt she had re-entered the twentieth century when she got back to the *Courier* office and could connect her computer modem to the net. She scanned the *Constitution*'s web page, looked at the editorials, then downloaded her email.

> *From: janders@atlcnst.com*
> *To: rtanner@atlconst.com*
>
> *Re: T. J. Davis Assignment*
>
> *I've attached more of the transcripts. Good Stuff. I wish we had room to run it all. Pick the best; definitely great background.*
>
> *I was doing one of these backgrounders once and my editor clipped a quote for me that I've always remembered. Under the circumstances, you might find it interesting.*
>
> *"The past is a foreign country; they do things differently there." L. P. Hartley*
>
> *Keep doing good work.*
>
> *Jeff.*

Six blue icons marched across the bottom of Jeff's email, each one containing the transcription of one of the tapes from the University library. She sent these to the printer, to have some reading for tonight, then packed her computer bag.

She stopped at a drugstore on her way back to the motel and bought a real wineglass. As soon as she came through the door she saw the message light blinking. She called the desk and was told a Mr.

Gordon Halt had called to invite her on a drive to the town of Salem. She quickly called him back to confirm the trip.

Rebecca poured wine into her brand new glass. Time for more reading.

TRANSCRIPT

Interview: Billy Trask

Position: Chief of Staff   Date: (unknown)

After we got out of college, T.J. and I went on back home to Clayman County, looking for something to do. There was a year of fooling around, with T. J. going to every kind of meeting and church social there was until one of the local judges ran for the legislature and there had to be a special election for his seat. T. J. won that first race for judge right handy, and for a while it was like he had everything he wanted. He told me it was like his life was finally beginning, that nothing up to then had meant anything.

Turned out what he meant by that was the election itself. The actual work was something else. Oh, there was parts of the job he liked, like bringing in the juries when a case needed one, 'cause then there was a chance he might meet someone he didn't already know. When that happened, he'd add the person's name and something about 'em to one of them scraps of paper he kept stuffed in his pockets all the time. He always thought it was a good day if he met just one new person.

I don't reckon it much matters, but I think folks felt like he was a pretty good judge, tried to do right and all that, but the truth was he just wasn't all that interested. Now if he had a case involved an insurance company or something like that he would brighten up some 'cause he'd have a chance to show he was on the side of the little man (there wadn't no banks or insurance companies in Clayman County). But most of the cases was one little man suing another one, since there was just about nothing down there but little men, and T. J. just hated those cases. 'Cause, see, he was the judge and the judge has got to decide the case and that means somebody's got to lose. And that somebody was a voter. That put T.J. into agony and he would delay things as long as he could in the hopes the case would settle. And sure enough, most of 'em did.

But after a couple a years the gloom (sic) was off the rose, as they say, and T.J. was looking around for something different to do. Then State Representative Cadwaller helped us out. The legislature was just ending its session up in Montville; this woulda been in the Spring of 1946. Old man Cadwaller had gotten real fond of one of his secretaries during the term and celebrated the coming vacation by going off with her to a lakeside cottage at Caldwell Gardens, a location whose proprietor could be counted on for discretion.

The story never completely got out, but the version I heard was that the secretary was helping the representative research various sexual activities that had Latin names and were illegal in Escambia. These activities proved to be too taxing and by the time the local sheriff responded personally to a call from the Garden's proprietor, Clayman County was without representation in the state legislature. I heard the family decided to have a closed coffin at the funeral because, after working for six hours, the undertaker couldn't get the smile off the dead man's face.

There ain't never been anybody in Escambia who could get votes the way T. J. did. He loved the campaigning so much and worked at it so hard that he couldn't understand why anybody wouldn't vote for him, even the niggers. He could win 80% of the vote and still feel like a failure for not getting that last 20%. Lord knows it wasn't for lack of trying. He campaigned all the time. If we was out on some dirt road and drove by a little country church where they was having a funeral, he made us stop the cars and go slip into the back rows. Then we'd go out to the graveside and T. J. would shake every hand and tell the new widow that even back in town we had all heard what a fine man her late husband was. He was a wonder.

So in 1946 we went to Montville, to be in the legislature. Two years later we were at the Democratic National Convention. We was in tall cotton there for a little while. Whew, it sure didn't last long, though. T. J. and I argued for years about that convention. That was the only bad political decision I ever saw him make."

I Have To Judge Men By What They Do

H er wine glass was empty. Rebecca put the transcript on the bedside table and poured another glass, thinking about what she'd just read. She knew the Democratic Convention of 1948 was held in Philadelphia and, according to the Woodson book Jeff had given her, was the beginning of a major shift involving the South. As always, the issue was race. Harry Truman was president and head of the party. In the final days of World War II he had signed an executive order desegregating the U.S. Army. Black and white soldiers would now serve in the same companies, more or less side by side. The practice of separate companies (basically a separate army) for black soldiers, which had begun during the Civil War, was abolished.

Professor Fred had told her that it didn't take white Southerners long to realize that if equality took hold in the army there would be big problems when the soldiers came home. A popular song of the war, referring to the way travel broadened one's perspective, had asked "How you gonna keep 'em down on the farm, after they've seen Paree?" Southern politicians asked themselves how you were going to keep negroes in separate waiting rooms after they had lived and worked together with whites in the military.

But according to the Woodson book Truman had a lot more he wanted to accomplish. The party platform adopted in Philadelphia contained an entire civil rights plank of four major parts. Truman wanted to make the desegregation of the military permanent, abolish the poll tax, pass a federal law against lynching, and create a Federal Employment Practices Committee. This group would monitor jobs paid for by federal funds, to prevent racial discrimination.

The mere discussion of these plans caused a literal revolution on the floor of the 1948 convention and provided the first state-wide exposure for T. J. Davis. Southern delegates were determined to stop Truman's proposals on race by denying Truman the Democratic nomination for re-election. When it became clear they lacked the votes to force him off the ticket, a militant group led by the charismatic young governor of South Carolina, J. Strom Thurman, agreed to march from the convention, taking the South with them. Once again Rebecca marveled that events that seemed so remote to her had such lasting effects. Here in 1999, Strom Thurman was not only still alive, he was one of the most powerful members of the U.S. Senate.

The dissidents became known as Dixiecrats, and for days they pressured all southern delegates to join the walkout. Every delegate from Mississippi did, along with half the delegates from Escambia. The pressure placed on T. J. Davis by the Dixiecrats was the subject of speculation for decades after.

"Because, when the day came, T. J. stayed with the loyal Democrats. Can you imagine that?" Professor Fred had asked Rebecca, shaking his head as though he could hardly imagine it himself. "The man who would become the national symbol of resistance to civil rights was a supporter of Harry Truman."

Rebecca understood the significance from her own reading. Six years after the convention, Davis would be a rabid segregationist.

"Why do you think he stayed?"

Professor Fred had given a tiny shrug of his shoulders. "I think it was hard for him to imagine not being a Democrat. His people had been Yellow Dogs since the war. You know what that was? A Yellow Dog Democrat was a Southerner who would vote for a yellow dog before he'd vote for a Republican. You see, Lincoln was a Republican and the black office holders during Reconstruction were all Republicans. Young people tend to forget that, since nowadays it's always the Democratic Party that gets the black vote. But the Republican Party was brand new in the years before the Civil War; Abraham Lincoln was the first Republican nominee for president.

"Southerner's were always reliably Democratic, at least until Lyndon Johnson's presidency. That was the Civil Rights era and the Democrats were the party of civil rights. So the South began to be uncomfortable in the Democratic Party. Then Ronald Reagan came along basically saying the country had done all it needed to about civil rights and it was okay to pull back from social programs. That's when the South turned Republican.

"But we are talking about 1948 and back then what T. J. Davis wanted was to win elections. In 1948 he couldn't imagine winning without being a Democrat, so he stayed at the convention."

Rebecca had reminded him that some historians thought that he stayed because he wasn't really a racist at heart, that he only did what was required to get elected.

The snort Professor Fred had given at that was so out of character Rebecca had been startled. "I am a black man," the professor had said. "I don't understand the talk about what's in white people's hearts. Maybe God can evaluate that, but I have to judge men by what they do. Look what happened after 1948. If T.J. Davis wasn't a racist, judging by what he did and what he supported, then there never was one. The word has no meaning if it doesn't apply to him."

Rebecca carried her wine glass the few steps back to the small chair and resumed reading the transcript.

We had a good time in Philadelphia and the Giant, old Governor Partain, was real proud of us but there was hell to pay when we got back. The Dixiecrats was the most exciting thing to come along in a great while. And wouldn't you know, Strom Thurmond decided to hold his separate Dixiecrat convention right here in Escambia. It turns out a bigger percentage of the Escambia delegation walked out than any other state except Mississippi, even bigger than in Strom's own South Carolina, so putting the convention here was the reward. And don't you know it was just like pouring gasoline on a dog bite for T. J.? Everybody at home was wondering what got into him, why he wasn't with the new party. Why, the Dixiecrat movement was so strong it took over the state party and in 1948 Harry Truman, the President himself, was not even on the ballot in Escambia.

That wouldn't a mattered to me. I wadn't going to vote for that nigger lover no matter what, but the terrible thing was that 1950 was an election year for T.J., to keep his statehouse seat. I don't guess I need to say that wasn't about to happen. He went back home and campaigned as good as he ever did, but he was pissin' up a rope. Nobody wanted to talk about anything but the Dixiecrats. Him not being one made him just like Harry T as far as anybody at home could tell. He got whupped good. He and the Giant both got throwed out like they was yard dogs.

"But you know what? He didn't let it faze him. He just got right back to work at home, mending fences and reminding folks what a good fella he was. And in 1954 he signs up to run for governor, pretty as you please. He's toned down some of the progressive stuff you understand, but he's still mostly talking 'bout good roads and schools and makin' the taxes fair. He's trying to keep the race stuff kinda low key, which I didn't understand but I figure, hell, he's the boss.

"But whatever he's saying, I'm thinking I got to do my part so I talked to some of the folks I know and I arranged an endorsement for him by the Klan. State-wide, I mean, not just one or two counties. It was a big deal, I'm telling you, but he turned it down. Even knowin' how much it hurt me with those people, he turned the damn endorsement down. That got off with me bad, I'll tell you. Closest I ever came to packing my kit and going to work for someone else. I told him to leave the convention in '48 and I told him to take this endorsement and he turns me down both times. I was pretty pissed, I ain't gonna lie about it.

"It all worked out though. I told the Klan boys to get in with John Paddington. He wadn't half the man T.J. was, but right at that minute he was a hell of a lot smarter. The Klan endorsed him and he kicked T.J.'s ass in the election. So I made my point, I guess.

"One thing about T.J., you didn't have to hit him in the face with a wet mop to get his attention. He learned pretty quick and you can bet that when the time rolled around for the 1958 election, he had decided that if the voters of Escambia wanted a candidate to talk about race then, by God, he wouldn't talk about nothin' else. He got all us boys over to his house right before the Dobson rally that year to tell us that he would be running again and that this campaign was gonna be a whole different animal. 'Boys,' he told us, 'they out-niggered me last time but I'll be goddamned if they ever out-nigger me again.'"

On the History Route

M ontville had barely disappeared behind the low hills of central Escambia when Gordon became bored with the sameness of the drive. He knew Edward considered him an old fogey, a Luddite opposed to anything new, but he would reluctantly admit some modern things, like the Interstate system, were probably good ideas at some level. Driving must be much safer on them — no two-way traffic, no surprise hairpin turns but, indeed, no surprises of any kind.

Still, it disappointed him that he could never convince Edward that with all this "improvement" much — indeed it seemed a whole world — had been lost. The very concept that travel itself was an experience, distinct from whatever happened, or didn't, at one's destination, had disappeared completely. Now the goal was to anesthetize the kids with CD players and those little hand-held games to achieve the equivalent of suspended animation during interstate driving.

Gordon thought of the innumerable drives his family had made between Salem, where Grandfather lived, and the capital at Montville. The idea that the cars weren't air-conditioned in 1932 was, to Edward, a sign of intentional cruelty, but Gordon would point out that no one missed what they had never had. Every twenty or so miles in those days the road wound through a small town, presenting inviting opportunities to examine fresh produce or get an RC Cola from a painted metal chest in which icy water was circulated around bottles lined up in metal channels. Gordon thought he was so clever when, at age five, he could guide the bottle through the channels to the gate where, if a nickel had been deposited, the bottle could be lifted out to the clank of the gate mechanism opening and then shutting back. Few accomplishments since had given him more satisfaction. He noticed an approaching exit ramp and turned down it.

"I thought we stayed on this another 40 miles."

Gordon turned to Rebecca and shrugged. "This trip is all about history, isn't it? We're going to use the history route."

He had intended irony, but it occurred to Gordon in that moment that Route 40 indeed was his history. The road connecting Salem, his birthplace, with Montville where he had come of age and made his career was an artery carrying his history as much as those in his body carried his blood. He steered the car onto Route 40 and felt his mood improve.

"When I was a boy," Gordon began, "we took trips to visit cousins all over the South on little roads like this, and it used to amaze me that an uneducated clerk in one of the little country stores could nail your accent within 30 miles. As soon as you asked for a pack of gum, you had tagged yourself as surely as if a postmark had been stamped on your forehead while you slept."

You folks ain't from around here, the clerk would say, not being nosy, but merely interested in new sources of information. Everyone would talk with you, about the weather or how low the river was. Not like now, he thought, where there might be a word or two but no more than that. The conversations were scrupulously fair; for every bit of information you might share, there would be a scrap coming back to you so that soon you'd hear about the crops, and weather and roads here (wherever here was). You had the feeling you had actually been somewhere and learned a little something and you gradually understood that this feeling was what "travel," meant.

The girl beside him gave a long sigh. "It does amaze me that the government has spent a gazillion dollars on the Interstate and we're not using it. This is going to take forever."

Gordon smiled. He could imagine Edward saying the same thing. "Don't you mean, 'are we there yet'?"

"Hey! I'm not *that* young," she said good-naturedly, and they both laughed. Several miles passed in quiet, then she said,

"Tell me more about the politics. I talked to Fred Middlebrooks, you know, at the University. He said the Dixiecrat movement in 1948 was the beginning of the really ugly white resistance to civil rights. Is that right?"

Gordon felt his face tighten. He growled at her.

"Why don't you ask me about slave ships and the invention of the cotton gin, if you're trying to make me angry? 'Ugly white resistance'? There were lots of people who thought that the government's highhandedness about the race issue was the wrong way to go about it. There was room for disagreement without it being resistance."

"I'm sorry," she said. "That was not a good way to put it."

Gordon took a deep breath, then relaxed his grip on the steering wheel. "No, it wasn't."

"But things did change after that," she continued. "The transcripts I found say that T. J. Davis turned to racist politics as a political strategy after 1948. You had not supported him earlier, and your father never did. I'd like to understand how that happened."

Gordon thought again how unlikely it was that someone so young could ever understand. "I was at the 1948 convention and..." He stopped because the girl had made an audible gasp. Gordon thought she would not look more surprised if he had said he'd been in the Ford Theatre audience the night Lincoln was shot.

"Anyway," he said, shaking his head, "Davis stayed at the convention even though a lot of us thought Truman had gone much too far. When I went to work for Governor Davis eight years later, Michael DeWitt called me and asked if the 1948 convention was the reason I did it. And I think it was part of the reason. I believed that Davis was like me in that he wanted what was best for the South."

Lush green fields and stands of pine and oak sped by the car in crystalline sunlight.

"Maybe we were wrong about what that was. I don't know."

Gordon bit his lower lip. Beside him, Rebecca made notes in a steno pad. He sighed. He must be getting used to this. The note-taking seemed to bother him less than it had the first few times. Maybe it helped to be outside of his house. He had been dreading these questions about the past, but now it occurred to him that talking could be something he needed to do.

He had intended this route to be comforting, but the view of a land that had changed so much was hardly that. Time and again the car passed a decrepit house, falling down in the dusty sunshine, the last trace of a family that had once planted, tilled, and harvested this land but was now — how could this be? — gone, as thoroughly as the Creek Federation or last summer's cotton.

This absence, testified to by the houses flaking their shingles like dandruff and sagging further each year into their foundations, would have disturbed Gordon less, he suddenly realized, had the fields likewise been left to ruin and neglect. But everywhere he looked acre after acre showed crops nearing harvest, as though spirits rose from the black earth at night to care for the plants without human intervention.

All, he suddenly realized, was separation. The growing of the crops was now separated from the ownership of the land, the ownership separated from individual human families, the sale of the crop separated from the hands that produced it. What had been a complex web of blood, labor, pride and tradition now was broken into discrete pieces, none of which cared whether its efforts benefited any particular crop or region, let alone any particular community. Community — the word itself, in this capitalized sense — would seem embarrassingly sentimental to the corporate forces that now controlled farming.

Mile after mile the scenario repeated itself. In over an hour he had passed thousands of acres but fewer than a dozen people actually working in the fields. When he passed a huge field in which a mammoth combine was being run by a single operator, Gordon wondered — is this a farmer now? Did this solitary figure live in Salem, in one of the brick apartment buildings, or in "manufactured housing," tethered to the ground on a rocky spot not good for anything else?

Can you really be a farmer if even your home has no real roots in the earth? Gordon wondered.

The first traffic light they'd seen in nearly an hour glowed red at a modest intersection. Downtown Salem. Gordon pointed ahead, telling Rebecca that if they went about a mile they would cross the T. J. Davis Bridge. "This one is the west bridge, which crosses the Red Warrior River into Mississippi. There are two others named for him in the state. Once you cross the bridge, Oxford, Mississippi would then be about a one and one-half hour drive to the northwest. Oxford would be a good field trip for you; that's where Faulkner lived."

Gordon turned left, driving slowly through the dying business district. He leaned forward for a better view from the car and pointed to a deserted storefront. "That was Mr. Watson's Variety Store. Do you know what a five-and-ten was?"

She nodded. "My dad told me. It was a store that sold small things, buttons and stuff, right?"

Gordon wanted to give her a gold star. "That's right. I stole something there once, as a boy. It was a little jar of candied beads, for cake decoration. The boys I played with came up with this silly dare that was supposed to prove toughness or manhood or some other trait eight-year olds would have no idea about." He could still remember the sleepless night he had and the arguments when he wouldn't turn over the candy to be eaten by his friends. "A few days later when I went to put the bottle back I was so nervous I knocked a dozen off the shelf. I told Mr. Watson I tripped on a shoelace."

"Doesn't sound like much of a crime," Rebecca said.

"I suppose not, but I still get a pang about it."

"But you undid it, didn't you? If you had confessed, you would have been forgiven, so you should forget it."

"I don't think that's all there is to it, but never mind." Gordon was sorry he had brought it up. On some subjects there really is a gulf between generations that cannot be bridged. How can repentance ever make up for violation of a principle that was supposed to be fundamental? If the violation can be easily forgiven, the principle couldn't have been deeply felt in the first place.

Mr. Watson's window that had been decorated with great care for every season of every year was now as blank and indifferent as the screen of a broken television. But in his memory Gordon can still see the piles of red, yellow and brown construction-paper leaves, the burnt-orange footballs, and the jerseys of crimson and white Mr. Watson would put up in the window each September to remind passing shoppers to buy those back-to-school pencils, notebooks, binders and lunch boxes at Watson's Variety. The children in Salem first learned to recognize the changing seasons by watching this space. The Easter bunnies on fields of shredded plastic grass were a promise of spring weeks before robins appeared. The only white Christmas Salem children dreamt of was the one that appeared right in this window each December.

"You'd be surprised how much trouble went into decorating these stores for holidays." Gordon said absently. "It was a real town, crowded with shoppers." The girl beside him nodded her head, but looked bored.

Mr. Watson's displays were always the most elaborate in town, but by no means the only ones. The empty store Gordon's car was passing now had once been Blaylock's Jewelry which had festive windows to coincide with the wedding and Yule seasons. Fairbank's Fashions for Men, which had been on the next corner for forty years would feature themed displays for Father's Day and Back-to-School. Even Markum's Drugs, which lasted until the big chains came to town, would have glamorous arrangements of perfumes and colognes in jewel-like bottles, resting on black velvet and lit dramatically from above.

The traffic light up ahead turned red, bringing Gordon back from his memories to a reality of empty buildings or cut-rate businesses attracted by the low rents of a failing commercial center. The broad window that had once been Fairbank's pride was now an expanse of plain glass through which he saw a large room with cast-off clothes and household items rudely piled on cheap folding tables set end-to-end. At the front of the store a bored, middle-aged woman sat at a cash register. Without leaving his car, Gordon knew her story, knew she was making minimum wage and would make no more even if she made this junk look desirable. Unlike Mr. Watson, Mrs. Blaylock or Mr. Markum so long ago, she would never have her name on the door.

After having a hamburger for lunch, Gordon and Rebecca got back in the car and started driving south. Within two miles of downtown Gordon steered the car into a large shopping center anchored by an enormous Wal-Mart store. He grimaced at the bluish concrete building, easily the biggest structure in the county.

"What a monstrosity," he said, thinking the store was a window-less monolith far less attractive than a well-designed prison would be, as heavy on the spirit as on the pavement. The parking lot was as large as a small farm, and more than half full.

"My God," he said. "If all these cars were downtown they would fill nearly every parking space."

Rebecca shook her head. He expected her view would be entirely different. "People wouldn't be here if this arrangement wasn't better for them, would they?" she asked. "Prices are lower, it's more convenient, something."

Gordon bit his lip. Pointless to talk to young people, he knew that. He didn't know why he kept trying.

"I know the prices are lower and people need that. But isn't it clear that the community can't support both places, this shopping center and the downtown? Did anyone understand that when this monstrosity was built? Did we intend to put Mr. Watson and the men's store out of business just so we could buy mops and shampoo for a dollar less?"

Rebecca didn't say anything, and Gordon realized there was little she could say, after all. She was too young to have created this system; she just lived in it. Gordon grimaced as it occurred to him that he might have to say exactly the same thing in his own defense. *Gordon didn't create that world, you know. He just lived in it.*

He turned the car around in the lot to get back on the main road.

"Enough macroeconomics," he said. "Let's get back to history."

They drove in silence for six miles then turned onto County Road 38. This two-lane turned into a gravel road that bisected a cultivated field before dwindling into a mere trail through a grove of pecan and oak. Three hundred yards up that trail a clearing opened, and there it was.

You're a Smart Boy, Ain't You?

T he old house was a decayed relic from another century. Gordon could imagine this rotting hulk through Rebecca's eyes, without the softening gauze of memory, as a pathetic apparition that might have existed in this decrepit state for generations. The left rear corner was partially collapsed, the roof broken, leaving the back bedroom exposed to rain and stars. The old wood, unpainted for years, had weathered to a dank mossy brown. The front walls still stood and from this distance the porch looked surprisingly complete, but it was clear that the time was not far off when the last corner post, overtaken by rot and forgetfulness, would surrender its burden. It occurred to Gordon that memory alone was holding the place up — his own thoughts of the time he had spent here as a very young boy — and that when he was gone and no one would think of this structure at all, that would be the day the black soil claimed it at last.

"We called this the Old Homeplace when I was a little boy. My great-great-grandfather built it about 1800 and I think my great-grandfather was born here. These were on my mother's side. She was a Thomas and her great-grandfather started the family in the newspaper business."

Gordon walked carefully over the uneven ground.
"When he was ready to marry, my grandfather built the white house about three hundred yards in that direction," he said, pointing to a stand of rhododendron at one edge of the clearing, "but this one was still used a lot when I was little."

Reaching the porch, Gordon gingerly touched, then grabbed, one of the porch posts. He shook it with some force, gratified when it held firm. The porch deck was made of narrow tongue-and-groove running out from the wall of the house, now buck-toothed where slats had rotted away over the years. Gordon looked up to survey the ceiling and, seeming satisfied, turned to sit on the porch edge, his feet scraping the ground.

He saw alarm in Rebecca's face.

"Is that a good idea to sit there?" she asked. "This place looks like if you sneeze, it'll crumble."

"Your concern is appreciated; fortunately, I don't have allergies," he said. "I guess this old place is in about as good shape as I am." It occurred to him that since neither he nor the house had that much longer anyway, going together might be highly poetic, but he did not share the thought. Young people don't know what to do with death and he didn't want to sound morbid.

"The first time I sat here when I was little my legs would swing free, nowhere near the ground. I was the youngest of the cousins by several years, so I would look off across the road, wishing I was with them playing in the woods. I had to stay here with Aunt Florrie and Weeda, who would be," he turned to point toward the wall, "in rocking chairs just there, each with a big ceramic bowl full of peas to be hulled or corn to be shucked."

He looked at Rebecca with a smile. "If we are very quiet I can hear them behind us right now. *Whump, whump, whump,* the rockers going back and forth on the porch deck. The cousins used to sleep in this house even after the family moved to the big white house. It seemed like camping out.

"My father was always busy with the paper, so usually Mother brought me on the weekend visits, which were frequent. She was very close to her family and this was where they had been for generations.

"Mother's younger brother, Uncle Buck, was just supposed to look after me, but he became almost a second Father. He taught me to hunt and to clean what I killed and not kill anything I wasn't going to eat. He taught me to tell when the scuppernongs were ready to pick and how to avoid poison ivy and sumac. He also taught me some things my parents would rather I hadn't learned. Useful things, though, for the most part."

Gordon looked up at Rebecca. "I don't suppose you've ever cleaned a squirrel?" The young reporter laughed out loud, a response Gordon found entirely satisfactory.

"I'll take that to be a 'no.' It's an interesting process where the head is removed, then slits are cut into the fur. Next, working from the slits, the fur is peeled away from the flesh below, as one peels a banana. When the peeling is done all the way down to the rear feet, those are severed and the fur is discarded in one piece."

Gordon noted with satisfaction the look on Rebecca's face, indicating she might have heard more about the process than she really wanted to know.

"Your face reminds me of Mother's," Gordon said with a laugh. Mother's disgust at the process was even greater than Rebecca's seemed to be, as Gordon well remembered. But suddenly he could remember Mother making that face when she called squirrels 'nigger food.' He had not thought of that in years. And he recalled that Uncle Buck had been offended at this characterization, saying plenty of people were glad to eat squirrel if it was the only meat they could put on the table. It was, in any event, a matter of honor to Uncle Buck that every boy should know how to make a meal from the woods because you never knew what the future held.

"They aren't bad." Gordon said, looking at Rebecca as he shifted his weight on the warped boards. "With biscuits and gravy, you'd be surprised. There's a lot of waste though. Something like crawfish, if you've ever eaten them." Rebecca did not ask for more details. She was, as always, writing on her steno pad.

"This doesn't really have anything to do with the Davis years," he said.

"That's okay." She folded a page back over the cover. "I'm interested in what it was like back then. This place and those times produced Davis. That interests me." She tapped her teeth with her pencil. "Tell me more about things your uncle taught you."

Gordon rubbed his chin, thinking what a huge influence Uncle Buck had been in his youth. "There was so much, its hard to…" Then it was suddenly there in his mind, the right story.

One November morning in his childhood broke unusually cold in Salem. Gordon awoke in the old house and watched his cousins get dressed to go hunting. Clouds formed when they breathed. Gordon jumped out of bed, eager to go with them, but Uncle Buck came in.

"Nope," he had said, "too cold for you, little fella. You stay with me this morning."

When the cousins had been gone for hours, the sun well up and burning off the early haze, he and Uncle Buck had walked to Mr. Dixon's store, Gordon reaching up to hold his huge hand and running to stay with his long strides. On the way, Uncle Buck had taken a detour off the road.

"I want to show you some magic."

"I like magic," Gordon had said.

They tramped through tall wild grasses for what seemed like miles, measured in an eight-year-old's steps, until his uncle stopped him. "Here," he said.

The grass stalks blocked Gordon's view in every direction. "Where?" he said, "Where's the magic?"

"See if you can find it. You're a smart boy, ain't you?"

"I *am* a smart boy," he said.

"Well then, be smart. Use your ears to find the magic."

Gordon looked around and began to listen really hard. He heard a car rumble by on the road they had just left. He heard voices in the distance. Then he realized he was hearing something else.

"Water!" Gordon said suddenly.

"Good boy," said Uncle Buck. "Find the water."

Gordon cupped his hands behind his ears, then turned his head from side to side until he could tell the faint splashing was right in front of him. He walked forward, one step then another, pushing the grass stalks out of the way. Soon, he stepped into a clearing where the ground had sunk to form a small pool.

From one end of the pool a metal pipe rose about three feet, then elbowed ninety degrees and ran parallel to the ground for another foot or so. Water poured out in a steady stream with a gurgle and a splash.

"Ain't that something?" Uncle Buck said. "No pump, no electricity, no valve, no handle. Just water. One minute it's in the ground and the next it's right here where we can put a bucket under that pipe and get all we need."

"Like magic!" Gordon said.

"I told you. And you know, it has run just like that since your granddaddy was born. Nobody knows when it started or if it's ever gonna stop." Uncle Buck laughed a booming laugh. "Close your mouth boy, before a bug flies in there."

Seventy plus years later, sitting on this porch while the young reporter stood near by, Gordon laughed out loud again, just as he had that morning as the cold water splashed over his outreached hands.

He looked up at Rebecca. "I guess 'artesian' was the first big word I ever learned."

So, It Wasn't Just Rednecks?

G ordon remembered that Uncle Buck had taken him across the
street to the old country store. He had poured a cup from the
coffee pot sitting on a pot-bellied wood stove that roared in one corner
and then joined the circle seated round it. It made Gordon proud that
all the other men knew his uncle and, even though several were much
older, they all seemed to listen to him. Mr. Dixon, the store's owner,
brought Gordon a biscuit stuffed with ham and the boy gobbled it
while listening with half an ear to the conversation around him.
Suddenly he jerked around, having heard something he felt he wasn't
supposed to. The men were laughing until they saw him looking. Then
for a time they got quieter.

Gordon hadn't thought of that day for decades, but now details
came back to him. There had been something not quite right about
that day. Something had been said, it must have been what the men
were laughing about when he turned around.

He shook his head, thinking for the hundredth time how difficult
it was to be old. He shifted his weight on the old porch. "There was
something that was said that caused a problem," he said to Rebecca. I
remember asking my father about it. That was a mistake. Father
was furious and for a time Uncle Buck was not welcome in our house."

"Something your Uncle said?" Rebecca suggested.

"Oh," he said, twisting his lip up, "I'm sure it was just a family
thing. There was some tension there, I do remember that at least."

"Hmm" The young reporter made another note in her pad, as she
curled in her lower lip. Gordon had seen the expression many times on
reporters who thought important information was being concealed. He
couldn't do anything about what she thought. Besides, he almost

preferred to have her imagine he was hiding something than admit that he really didn't remember.

He rose from the porch with some difficulty and motioned for Rebecca to follow him back to the car. He found a trail wide enough to drive down to the river so he could show her where he had swung on vines as a boy. He was surprised how scraggly and thin these "woods" seemed. As a boy he had thought them as dense as a rainforest. Returning to the main road he pointed out the house where Miss Nancy Willoughby had lived. He saw Rebecca struggle to place the name.

"She's the lady who told us children about the siege at Vicksburg," he said.

Rebecca nodded. "I didn't ask before, but where is Vicksburg?"

Gordon laughed. "Sorry. We old folks always assume everyone in the world knows the story. Vicksburg is in Mississippi, on the most prominent southern bluff overlooking the river. From that bluff the Confederate Army could control the river south of Memphis to New Orleans. That's why the North thought the siege was justified."

The sun was low in the sky when they started back to Escambia. Cool shadows leaned across the narrow road while coral-ridged clouds seemed to float in a sea of deepening blue. Gordon had read somewhere that this is called photographer's light. He was about to point out that, by pouring through her notebooks, she was missing this beautiful light when Rebecca spoke.

"As a boy, did you call black people niggers?" She said it without emphasis, as she might ask if he liked Chinese food.

"What a question." He knew that sounded like he was buying time and he supposed he was. "Why would you ask that?"

She looked at him blankly; he felt she was consciously trying to keep any emotion from her face.

"In one of the old news clips I read where one politician called another a 'nigger lover,' and it made me curious."

Gordon's chin suddenly itched and he moved his right hand off the wheel to rub it.

"I don't know. I'm sure I've said it at times, long years ago. It was what negroes were called, to some extent. You knew people who said it so you said it as well."

"So," she said, as though the answer really didn't matter, "it wasn't just rednecks?"

Gordon turned to look at her but her face was toward her notebook. "No... I suppose not."

He saw pages of typing in her lap, in addition to her pad. She asked if she could read something to him.

"This is another one of the Billy Trask transcripts," she said. "He's talking about growing up in Escambia and how simple Christmas was," she explained. Then she began to read:

> *All our toys, what little we had, was made for us, which young 'uns today don't understand, 'cause they think homemade things is just pretty much pitiful, but looking back on it I think toys was better then. I mean, that little spool tractor I got for Christmas when I was eight was a whole lot of fun to play with and if the rubber band broke, or the matchstick winder, why you just got another band or a stick and hooked it up and you was all set playing again.*

> *Nowadays everthing for Christmas has to be store-bought and the kids have to wait until they watch the TV commercials in September to know what they want. It's like they're robots or something. Then they don't understand why they're so disappointed Christmas morning when the toy don't do all the fancy stuff it did on TV. And god knows if it breaks or the battery gives out the damn toy is just a worthless piece of junk.*

> *It was lots better back when we was kids. We'd get a ball or a spool tractor and the girls'd get a doll Mama made 'em from some cloth and buttons. There wadn't no disappointment 'cause we knew we was real lucky if we got anything at all. My daddy would cut the bottom out of a big cardboard box to make a flat piece with a border about an inch high, then fill that with oranges, satsumas, apples, pecans and nigger-toes and it would seem like one of them forms (sic) of plenty. It was lots better than now.*

When she stopped reading and looked up Gordon thought she had the most puzzled expression he had ever seen.

"Nigger *toes?*" she asked in disbelief.

"Oh Lord." Gordon laughed ruefully, knowing his reaction would be misunderstood. "You won't believe this, but I never thought of the word that way, as two words."

"Well, duh," she said, if Gordon heard her correctly. Gordon wasn't sure what that sound was intended to convey, but he went on.

"They were nuts, to eat, but they were different from pecans and peanuts and walnuts. We had those all the time but these nuts were exotic. I guess that's why they were only available at Christmas. These nuts weren't round like a pecan or walnut and their color was a dark grey, like slate. They were long and slender and had three sides. You had to use a nutcracker because the shell was very hard and inside the meat was large and smooth and …"

"That *word* is what you called them?"

He nodded.

"As *children* you were taught that word?"

He shrugged, and concentrated on his driving. The trees on each side of the road hurried past the car as though they were late for a meeting. After a few minutes, Rebecca had another question.

"Just out of curiosity, what kind of nut is this really?"

Gordon could feel the right corner of his mouth turn up as it did when he felt awkward. He really needed to change the subject. She didn't give him a chance.

"You don't know, do you? That's unbelievable."

"I don't eat nuts that often," he said, sounding lame even to himself.

She shook her head, shuffling her papers more violently than Gordon thought necessary.

Like a Time Warp

I t was past nine before Gordon arrived home after dropping Rebecca off at the motel. Margaret called out to him and said Sonny wanted him to call, to talk about the monument he wanted built for Governor Davis.

Gordon decided he could wait to call Billy's son back. He put the message on his desk and went to the kitchen to heat some milk. After taking the mug from the microwave he poured in a little bourbon and walked to the den where Margaret was watching an old movie on TV. She turned the volume down as he came in.

"How was your trip?"

"Interesting. For both of us. I have the feeling this reporter thinks she's been kidnapped by aliens."

Margaret laughed and Gordon felt better. Maybe it was the bourbon.

"Honey," he asked, "what's the real name for a niggertoe?"

She caught her breath like a schoolgirl embarrassed by a dirty joke, covering her mouth with her hand.

"You *didn't* talk about that, surely?"

"The reporter brought it up," Gordon said. "I haven't even thought of that word in forty years. It was like a time warp in a science fiction story. But I couldn't remember what the real name of that nut is, so she thinks I'm a Klansman, or worse."

"Oh dear."

Gordon waited for wifely reassurance that, of course, *no one* would think a man like Gordon was a Klansman or worse, but Margaret seemed to have been drawn back into her movie and didn't say anything else. Gordon sipped his milk while, on the screen, Spencer Tracey talked to Kathryn Hepburn about office automation. Why was he wasting his time worrying about today? He didn't care what that child from the Atlanta paper thought and why should he? She could not possibly know what things were like back then. He had not mistreated anybody and he was damned if he was going to let some kid make him feel as though he had something to feel guilty for. He put the trip to Salem out of his mind and watched the movie with his wife, the past retreating pleasantly away from him.

But hours later, tossing in his bed he had a dream.

Weeda was there in the dream, as she had always been there when he was growing up, and Gordon was in grade school. The details were fuzzy, but the family was living in the white house and he was angry because Weeda wouldn't let him do something. He couldn't remember what it was; only that Weeda had been completely unreasonable. Whatever he had wanted to do, he had been sure, was not objectionable by any fair-minded person. The child Gordon had decided he simply could not deal with her anymore.

When Mother came in he had told her Weeda had to go.

"She's just a bossy ol' nigger woman and I think you should fire her," Gordon, as a boy, had said.

Mother mussed his hair affectionately. "Don't let your father hear you. You know you're not supposed to use that word." In his dream, Gordon realized that he had known without asking which word she meant.

"Uncle Buck uses it," he had said, knowing she would not criticize anything her baby brother did.

"He doesn't use it about colored people like Weeda," Mother said soothingly. "Niggers are shiftless and lazy and no account. They steal and cheat to get things they haven't earned. Niggers don't know their place. Weeda's not like that. She works hard to take care of her family and ours. She doesn't give anyone a minute's trouble. I don't want you acting ugly to her."

In the dream Mother straightened his collar and smoothed his hair back into place with a warm palm. Then she turned him around by the shoulders.

"You scoot to the kitchen and tell Weeda you're sorry." She slapped him playfully on the bottom to speed him off. "God knows what I'd get if I had to replace her."

In his dream the young Gordon walked toward the kitchen that loomed far away down a hall that seemed to stretch a mile, as though he looked through the wrong end of a telescope. He walks and walks but he doesn't seem to get closer. He walks faster but even that doesn't seem to help; he has to go faster and faster and then faster yet. He feels anxious and then panicky, suddenly realizing he needs to use the bathroom but there's no time, he has to get to that kitchen so that...

Suddenly Gordon was awake in his own bed in the house he shares with Margaret and he realized it was only a dream. It didn't mean anything, he thought, but he recognized something true in it, and it made his heart pound in his chest. He lay awake for long minutes, then realized something new had floated into his memory. All those years have faded or compressed, he couldn't say which, but something had happened, some key had been turned, and he now knew something he didn't know this afternoon, something he hadn't known for more than sixty years.

He knows the story Uncle Buck told in Mr. Dixon's store.

Uncle Buck's Story

R ecalling the story now, the scene itself became more real in his mind than any dream, more real than the sheet under his back. That piece of biscuit with warm, salty ham from so long ago was in his chubby, little boy's hand once more, the sweet yeasty smell was in his brain, and he heard again that voice he knew so well and loved so much.

"I heard an interesting story this week," Uncle Buck had said, still said in Gordon's memory. "Seems like Henry Stanks and Buster Grimsley was out fishing on Hunter's Branch, just in from the river. They'd been out there a good while and hadn't done worth a damn, so they went to pull up the anchor chain and try somewheres else. Well, it was snagged on something and they had to pull like all hell, but it started coming on up and Buster said, 'Well, we won't go home empty handed,' and they laughed about that.

"When it got up close to the surface they could look down and see something glinting all silver like and then they got a hook on it but when they pulled to turn it over this arm swung up out of the water, like this thing was reaching out for Buster." Uncle Buck's voice rose and he leaned forward and reached his arm out for effect. "Buster screamed and let go of the pole and damn near fell out of the boat. They wadn't too far from the bank so they paddled over and pulled this thing they had up on the land and that was when they saw it was a body. Turned out to be a twenty-year-old colored guy, all wrapped up in chain around his neck and waist. Couple a hours later Sheriff Cole came on out there, and the fellas came back and brought some more fellas with 'em, interested to see how the Sheriff was going to handle such a case. The Sheriff took a long look at the body and finally turned to his deputy, shaking his head. 'Ain't that just like a nigger to steal more chain than he can swim with?'"

Laughter had boomed from the group of men, and now echoed in Gordon's head, resonant and deep, good natured and warm with fellowship.

Father had been so angry.

Gordon took several deep breaths and willed his heart to slow. There was a familiar painful pressure in his groin and after a few minutes he turned out of bed to shuffle slowly to the bathroom.

Seeing Mrs. Roosevelt

G ordon put his breakfast dishes in the sink, poured another cup of coffee, kissed Margaret on the top of her head and walked to the den to read.

He had been making good progress through *The Mayor of Casterbridge*, but had trouble getting back into the story. He read for a few minutes, sipping his coffee from time to time, but the pages turned slowly. His mind wandered from the story on the page to the one in his head, the one the reporter had pushed him into, the story of his life.

He rubbed his eyes. The dream had interrupted his sleep, which wasn't that unusual, but this time he had thought about the dream long after it ended. His subconscious must be working overtime. He wondered if remembering the artesian well story and the embarrassment of having the reporter ask about those damn nuts at Christmas had triggered the dream. It annoyed him to think that he might be susceptible to such simplistic and involuntary workings of the mind.

He supposed the reporter would be quick to say he had a guilty conscience, that he was a closet racist and that was why he had supported Davis all those years ago. He wasn't going to waste his time dignifying such an idea with a denial, but it was complicated. He was shocked by the story about chains - that was probably why he had forgotten it so completely. But Uncle Buck was almost as important to him as Father. He couldn't think of him except with love. Besides, Father's ideas had made a strong impression on him where negroes were concerned, starting with a trip they made together over to Alabama when Gordon was just a teenager.

They had stayed at the Bankhead Hotel, the nicest in downtown Birmingham and for breakfast Father ordered stacks of pancakes.

Gordon could still recall the heavy silver forks and spoons, and the small ceramic pitcher, warm to the touch, of maple syrup.

"Go easy on that syrup, son," Father had said, with a big grin. "Yankees like it, so it might not be good for you."

Gordon laughed at the little joke, thoroughly enjoying himself. He could not imagine what could have caused Father to bring him along on this trip but whatever it was Gordon was all for it. He loved his father, really, especially when he was like this, happy and smiling much more than was usual.

"This is a great day for the South," his father said. "It's lucky that you're almost a man, and can appreciate what you will see this day."

Gordon had seldom seen his father so enthused, except on family holidays. Was that what this was, he wondered, some holiday Gordon had never heard of? Father sipped from his coffee cup, patted his mouth with an enormous cotton napkin and, as though reading his son's mind, spoke.

"Let's buy a diary for you, Son, and make today the first entry. Yes!" Father slapped the table lightly with his palm. "October 18, 1938, we'll write, at Birmingham, Alabama. E. Gordon Halt attends the first convention of the Southern Conference on Human Welfare. Then you'd never forget what happens today."

Here in his own house sixty-some years later, Gordon smiled to think how pleased Father would be, after all the disappointments, if he could look down and see that Gordon never did forget.

Even now Gordon could almost taste the huge forkfuls of pancake and feel the weight of the carafe of hot cocoa as he filled his cup for the third time; all the while Father talking away, as excited as a child on Christmas morning.

"Right now," he said, "just think of it. Eleanor Roosevelt is in this same city with us, perhaps in this very hotel, having breakfast just as we are. By God, it's a great day!"

Father sighed deeply and took a huge swig from his coffee cup. His pile of pancakes was nearly untouched.

"Eat up, son. We must go and be part of history."

Gordon sank the fork into the dwindling pile on his plate. He actually thought Weeda's pancakes might be a little better, but the surroundings and Father's excitement more than made up for that.

After breakfast they had walked up 20th Street toward the Municipal Auditorium.

"I want you to remember everything about this day," Father said. "Someday you'll tell your grandchildren you were here."

He had not been a child that day, as Father had observed, but Gordon wondered if he could possibly be remembering all this at firsthand? Every family has certain stories that are especially meaning-ful, and for that reason are told often. This one had been repeated so often by Father that Gordon could no longer be sure which part of his memory was "genuine" and which part had been implanted in his brain by multiple repetitions. Still, it seemed to him that he could remember the rush of air from the huge outer doors of the auditorium when Father pulled them open. And his memory of faces, didn't those have to be his original memory in order to be so vivid? But the words, they must be a different matter. For Gordon could recall whole discussions in the voices of the participants. Surely some of that must be later embellishment, even if unintended.

How else could Gordon remember that they were barely inside the large lobby when Father tapped his shoulder and said with a wink, "That fellow is in the business," motioning surreptitiously toward a spindly man in a creased suit? This gentleman puffed deeply from a cigarette, then flicked the butt toward a distant ash can, leaving a smoky arc in the still air. Gordon and his father watched the man walk a dozen steps before he drew up short to avoid plowing into a group of much larger men, knotted in conversation.

"It's a great day for Alabama, by God, it is," said one of those men. "Yes, it is, Hugo," one of the other men in the group said, slapping the first man on the shoulder, "and you've done more than most to make it happen."

The first man gave a big smile. At the same time Gordon saw the spindly man outside the group pull a steno pad from his coat pocket and flip back the cover. The man who had spoken first saw that motion at the same time, and spoke again.

"My friends I'm afraid the arrival of the press will force us to cut short our discourse."

He motioned with a huge flannelled arm for the others to proceed into the arena. Then he turned back to the reporter.

"Always a pleasure, John."

"The honor is ours, Mr. Justice Black. This is quite a gathering you've got here."

The big man beamed.

"I should say so. Some of the most distinguished men in all the South."

"And some of the blackest," the reporter answered.

The Justice's eyebrows narrowed.

"As it should be," he said.

"Really?"

"Now John, I hope you don't feel some obligation to be as prejudiced as your readers?"

"Not at all, Mr. Justice. But I feel a very strong obligation to know a story when I fall into it. This is the largest mixed-race meeting I've ever heard of in the State of Alabama. A sitting Supreme Court justice and the wife of the President are in attendance. Give me a break, Judge. In these parts, that's a pretty damn big story."

The justice rubbed the side of his nose so hard he might have removed a freckle.

"I'm sorry to hear you put the issue in those terms, John. The real story is our reason for being here — political equity. Where we all sit is trivial beside that."

"Not to my readers, your Honor."

"John, please. Write the real story. Write about the message, not the seating arrangements."

As those two men began to walk away, others came over to greet Gordon's Father. Young as he was, Gordon had frequently seen this happen, Father treated as almost a celebrity, and making his usual joke. "I'm Edwin Halt and I'm in the history business."

This day, the people who greeted his father were different than Gordon was used to. Gordon remembered how he tried not to stare, having been taught it was rude. But it was hard not to. If he had been older and known more, he would have stared because so many of the men who crowded the hall were famous. He had heard his father mention the name Hugo Black many times. But he had not recognized that the heavyset man with the unruly black hair and bushy eyebrows talking to the reporter was Justice Black, appointed by FDR to the U. S. Supreme Court only six months before. Even at the age of sixteen one person Gordon did recognize was the most famous woman in America, whose homely face reminded him of Aunt Gerty, on his mother's side. Gordon had never seen Father as emotional as when he shook the hand of the president's wife.

Still, it was not the fame of the visitors that made Gordon have to watch his manners. The reason he had to strain to keep from staring was something any Southern child would have noticed. Many of the people who crowded around to say hello to his father were negroes and — this was the strange thing — negro people dressed up for church, in suits and ties and shined shoes and crisp, clean shirts. Gordon listened as these people talked to his father just like people on Commerce Avenue would have talked to him when he visited the Escambia capital. Naturally Gordon would tend to stare at something so different from anything he had seen before.

He had not realized colored people *had* dress-up clothes. It had never occurred to him before and he wondered why. He decided that he had never seen colored people doing things they could do while dressed up. The colored people he knew were like Weeda and cleaned houses and cooked, or like L. G. and mowed yards and carried trash. None of these negro men he saw in the auditorium looked like they had ever carried any trash.

The other thing he had noticed that day, that any Southern child would have, was the way they sounded. Gordon realized that all these well-dressed people sounded more or less the same. He had closed his eyes and listened and realized he could not tell whether the person speaking was colored or white. He could never remember that happening before. You didn't have to look at Weeda or L. G. to tell they were negroes, not if you could hear them. It had seemed to Gordon that day as if that was how it should be, that since the negroes looked so different they *should* sound different. Hadn't God made them? And didn't He decide what they sounded like?

And these people were all together. Gordon couldn't remember seeing that before. Now that he thought of it, every group he had ever seen was all white. He might see Weeda or L. G. with his parents, or some other white person, but he never had seen groups of white people and negro people all together, walking around in a mixed up crowd, and all dressed up to boot.

After a while everyone had gone into the main hall and speeches had begun. Gordon found this considerably less exciting than the hubbub in the lobby and he had gotten semi-comfortable leaning against the back of his metal chair, his eyelids drooping, when suddenly the sound of whistles being furiously blown came from the rear. Father jumped up so fast Gordon was jolted awake.

"Damn them!" Father said. "What are they doing?"

Gordon stood in his chair to be able to see over the crowd, to find a dozen or more police officers scattered across the back wall and blocking the entrances. In the center of the line, several officers blew the police whistles that were threatening to deafen everyone in the huge room. Near those officers was a white man in a white shirt, without a tie, wearing glasses and a hat. That man motioned to the officers around him and the noise stopped. He then turned back to the people in the hall and shouted.

"Who's in charge of this gathering?"

One of the negro men had already come down from the stage and was walking toward the man in the hat, but the white man held up a hand to stop him from coming closer.

"Hold it right there, Rufus."

The man stopped in the aisle. The white man in the hat looked around the room and then yelled again.

"Y'all better get a white man up here for me to talk to, before I get madder than I already am."

The man Father had said was Justice Black came down the aisle to the him. Gordon had thought it was funny that Mr. Black was white, but this didn't seem like a good time to mention it to

Father, who was walking up the aisle to get closer to where the two men were talking.

"…important people here, who've never been in Alabama. We ought to avoid making a bad impression, Commissioner," Mr. Black was saying.

"Judge, the folks in Jefferson County don't elect me to make impressions. They elect me to enforce the law. And the law is that coloreds and whites don't sit together. Hell, you practiced law here, you know that as well as I do."

"Look, Bull, no one is gonna know where the negroes sat, if we don't make a big deal of it."

"I'm gonna know. And if I know, I gotta do something about it. Now I'm telling you to separate the seating or the meeting is over."

"These people are citizens of the United States, Commissioner. All of them. I don't want some of them treated differently in this meeting."

"Well, Judge, I reckon you shoulda had your meeting in Philadelphia or someplace where that constitutional crap woulda bought you somethin'. You ain't at the Supreme Court now and this ain't Washington. This is my city and what I say is what we're gonna do. My police officers here are getting mighty itchy to arrest somebody, and if you keep ignoring me that's what I'm going to let them do. Now get the seating separated or this meeting is over. You hear?"

Mr. Black's face was red and Gordon thought his chest was shaking, but he didn't say anything else. A group of the police officers began to set up a rope line on plastic cones set up in the middle of the aisle, dividing the room lengthwise. There was some talking from the stage, and then a tremendous hubbub as the white people all moved to one side of the rope and the colored people moved to the other. Just as things had quieted and it seemed the program would go on, Gordon heard a new murmur over his shoulder. Eleanor Roosevelt had asked a negro man to help her move one of the metal chairs. She walked to the middle of the aisle and moved the rope off of one cone, letting it fall to the floor. She then placed the chair squarely over the rope, stood before the chair for a moment and then lowered herself onto it as though onto a throne.

The hall that had been thrumming with noise a moment before was now as quiet as a library. A young officer at the back of the hall started toward the First Lady, causing several of the men in the crowd to leave their seats, as though to defend her, but before the officer had gone more than a few steps the man in the hat reached out to take his arm. With just a head nod he sent the young officer back to his place.

The speeches started again, but it seemed to Gordon that the audience was not paying attention as much as before. Gordon didn't feel sleepy at all anymore.

At the end of the day, Gordon had no trouble keeping up with his father's slow steps as they walked back to the hotel. "This will make us look like rubes to the rest of the country," Father said. "Mrs. Roosevelt was here and we wind up looking like hicks."

What Every Sensible Person Knows

F ather had said almost nothing on the drive home to Montville. The next morning he sat at the breakfast table reading a newspaper from Philadelphia. In his distant memory, Gordon was picking at his oatmeal when he heard a grunting noise. When Gordon looked up Father was shaking his head, looking disgustedly toward Mother. Then he read from the paper.

"The burly police commissioner of Birmingham broke up the meeting to enforce a city ordinance that members of the two races must be seated separately."

"I don't see why you're so upset, dear," Mother said.

"Because the man has no subtlety. There are ways to do things that don't make Southerners look barbaric."

"I'm not so sure it does makes us look bad. I think all the colored people are used to sitting in their places and we are all used to sitting in ours." Mother turned to Weeda, who was about to remove the bowl of oatmeal Gordon had hardly touched. "Do you think the colored people mind having their own places to sit, Weeda?"

"I'm sure the *negro* people don't want to make a fuss over it," Father interrupted.

"No sir, Mr. Halt," Weeda quickly agreed.

Father went on, "but I don't think that's the whole issue...Weeda, would you excuse us, please? You can finish clearing these later."

When Weeda had gone, Father said, "I wish you wouldn't do things like that."

"I wanted her opinion," Mother said, folding her napkin and laying it beside her plate. Gordon fussed with his fork.

"You wanted to embarrass her," Father said. "Do you think she is free to tell you what she really believes about these matters? I think it's unkind."

Gordon could almost feel Mother tense. "I see," she said, "I'm a terrible person for saying what every sensible person knows, but there's nothing wrong with you dragging our son off to some race-mixing meeting, is that it? Gordon shouldn't be exposed to things like that."

"That's absurd and you know it. He needs to know that negroes are people the same as we are."

"The same as we are? Now who's being absurd?"

Father crushed the napkin he had been holding, then threw it onto the table. "Gordon," he said, "you may be excused."

As he climbed the stairs to his room, Gordon could hear the argument continue - though his father would have called it a discussion. Gordon noticed that his parents "discussions" generally required that everyone else be excused from the room.

He couldn't remember this happening when he was younger, and that made him sad. He was a teenager and so was at war with one or both parents about a hundred things, but he loved them and depended on their happiness. He couldn't understand why Father would intentionally do things to make Mother unhappy, especially unnecessary things like the meeting with the colored people. If Mother was distressed about that, then many other people they knew would be as well. Why would Father want to be a part of causing so much unhappiness? The family had done pretty well with things as they were, hadn't they?

* * *

Margaret's tapping on the door frame brought Gordon back to his den in 1999. "Lunch is ready."

He nodded, closing the book he had hardly looked at.

"You seemed a hundred miles away," she said with a smile.

"Hmm," he nodded, "or years."

He put the novel on the table by his chair, then slowly pushed himself upright and followed Margaret to the kitchen. Not that he had much appetite. Gordon felt sourness in his throat and a jumpy rhythm in his chest. Rebecca was due to visit again in a few hours, no doubt still appalled by the Christmas story from their drive yesterday. He was angry at himself since there was no reason for him to be defensive and he thought of calling her and canceling the interview. But that would make him look defensive if anything would, wouldn't it?

Simple Hypocrisy

S he was right on time. Gordon heard the doorbell ring just as the antique clock in the den struck two.

"That was quite a trip yesterday," she said when she had settled into her usual chair. "Thank you for sharing all that with me."

Gordon was almost surprised at her pleasant tone, but then realized he had no reason to be. She had almost always been pleasant and professional, except that one time when she fought being upset about where Weeda had to live.

"We were talking yesterday about the 1948 convention," she said. "I'm trying to piece together the main events of that time and I'm thinking the *Brown* decision would be next. Could we talk about that, and how it affected Escambia and Governor Davis?"

Gordon nodded, rubbing the arm of the chair with his hand. "I think that's right. I've often said that if the average American knows the name of any Supreme Court case at all he will know either *Rowe vs. Wade*, the abortion case, or *Brown vs. The Board of Education*, the one on school desegregation. But did you know that school board was in Topeka, Kansas?"

Gordon looked for her reaction and was disappointed that it consisted of only "hmmm." Surely, he thought, she could see his point. The South took the brunt of the civil rights campaign largely because of simple hypocrisy. The rest of the nation wanted to make the South look different, but things were not that good for negroes anywhere in America in 1954.

"I was at work the morning the decision came down. I came back to the *Courier* after graduation from the University. My father had been delighted to have me "in the business" where he thought I belonged and to tell the truth I was poorly equipped to go anywhere else. But I was not especially comfortable there. I suppose most young men go through that stage where one is waiting for one's "real" life to begin.

"I was re-writing a minor story that morning to the accompaniment of the irregular clack of the Associated Press teletype. The paper also subscribed to UPI and IPA, but those two machines were silent for a time. The AP machine finished its story and there was several minutes of "normal" newsroom buzz, seasoned with the perpetual ringing of the brass bells inside the heavy black telephones on each desk." He smiled and looked at her. "I'll bet you've never heard an honest-to-god brass bell ring inside a real telephone. It was a wonderful sound."

Gordon could still remember how the UPI and AP machines had burst into clamorous activity that morning, the individual letter blocks on slender steel levers slamming into the paper more than four times per second. In just moments the IPA machine joined in, and he could remember that each machine seemed to scream for attention, "read me! read me!"

A sports reporter whose desk was backed up to Gordon's looked up. "Somebody musta died," he said.

Tom Blake, the managing editor, had come out of his corner office and torn off the strands of paper that by now hung to the floor, the clacking machines adding more each minute. He chewed on an unlit pipe as he read, then yelled to his secretary "I'm going up to the Boss's office," meaning Gordon's father, the publisher. Tom had passed Gordon's desk to reach the stairs.

"The Court has ruled in the *Brown* case," Tom said.

"Who is Brown?" the sports reporter asked.

Within a few minutes everyone in the building had known that the Court had decided separate educational facilities for the races were inherently unequal. Gordon had read the news stories, with quotes from the decision itself, and found himself disagreeing with almost every word. Later, he had visited his father's office.

"Have you seen the wire stories?" Father had asked.

"I'm sorry to say I have," Gordon had said.

His father looked at him a long time.

"We have an important role to play in this, Gordon. The press can set a tone for reasonable implementation and acceptance of this very difficult ruling."

"Acceptance? Is that what you think the answer is?

"No. I don't think it's an answer," his father said, "because I don't think there is a question on the table. A Supreme Court ruling is the law of the United States. There is no question whether the law will be obeyed. Not if we're a civil society, rather than just a tribe."

Gordon had looked at his father's face, which he could easily imagine to be his own in thirty years, and thought how strange it was that such similar faces could cover such great differences of thought, value and aspiration.

"You're glad of this, aren't you?"

"I think it's the right decision," Father had said, "but no, I'm not glad of it. I'm not glad that we have permitted the treatment of the negro to deteriorate to the point that this decision was necessary."

"This will tear the South apart."

"It will change the South, that is certain," Father replied. He had spoken quietly, as though reason and calm had a place in this dispute. "It doesn't have to be destructive if we provide leadership."

"You're the one who taught me to love the South. How can you be so calm about it?"

"I didn't teach you to love everything about it. That was your mother's doing. I've always felt the situation of the negroes had to improve."

"That's unfair, and you know it." Gordon had crossed his arms over his chest, to give himself strength. "I don't like the way negroes are treated either. Their schools *are* inferior, I know that. But the Court could have ordered that "separate but equal" be enforced. They did not have to destroy a system that is probably best for both races." He had to take a deep breath before he could go on. "You and Eleanor Roosevelt want to improve things for the negro. And that's fine, so do I. But what if you can't have both things? Eleanor would give up the distinctiveness of the South for some slim hope of helping the negro. Would you do that?"

A profound silence had followed that question while Father con-sidered what Gordon had said, really considered it as though it had been spoken by another adult, and in that silence Gordon felt a shift in the earth's crust or perhaps the alignment of the planets. He had entered a new phase, or a new place. Not manhood itself, his time in the war had already provided that change, but perhaps an end of "sonhood," of being in the shadow of his paternity — the first steps on a path clearly separate from his father's.

At last Father answered. "I pray it doesn't have to come to that choice."

Gordon shook his head. "I don't see how it can be resolved any other way. And when that question has to be answered I'm afraid we'll be on different sides."

Gordon left the office late that night, so long ago, knowing his life had changed forever.

Now, he suddenly realized that he was staring out of the den window at the crepe myrtles wilting in the hot afternoon. He wondered how long he had been daydreaming, but he saw Rebecca was waiting patiently, her eyes tactfully diverted to her pad.

"I remember," Gordon said, "walking across Fourth Avenue to the company parking lot that night. I had a 1949 Ford, the first car I'd ever owned — I still think it's the best car they ever made. Before I drove away, I looked up at the corner office on the fourth floor, where the light still burned, and I knew, as well as I know my own shoe size, that Father had stayed late to work on an editorial for the Sunday edition. I could almost see him, choosing his words even more carefully than usual, scratching out the not-quite-right ones to be replaced by the that's-more-like-it ones, all to urge calm and restraint."

Rebecca nodded her head. "Is that one of the editorials that was mentioned in the Pulitzer Prize award?"

"It was the first of them," Gordon said, pulling on the lobe of his right ear. "Unfortunately, it was soon answered by a group whose faith in the printed word was significantly less than that of our family. I was called at home one Sunday night by the weekend editor.

"'You better get down here, Gordon. We got a little present from the Klan.'

"By the time I drove into the parking lot two police cruisers were there. The bright lights of the cruisers were overwhelmed by a burning cross, more than 20 feet high and 8 feet across, all of it covered in flames.

I asked one of the officers, "How the hell could they have put that up?"

"'There's a little plot of dirt they dug into between the sidewalk and the curb; not that hard, I reckon,' the officer told me, not seeming very interested in what he thought was more a prank than a crime.

"'This is aimed at my father,' I told him.

"The officer nodded. 'I figured it was a message for somebody.'

"I told him I wanted the police to give my father protection.

He said I'd have to talk to the mayor or the chief, that he was just a beat cop. He started to walk off, but then stopped and walked a few steps back toward me.

"'Wouldn't it be easier if he just wrote about something else?'"

"DIRTY TRICKS," KLAN, RACISM BOOST DAVIS IN EARLY CAMPAIGN

By Rebecca Tanner

MONTVILLE, ES

This is the second story in the Constitution's series on the career and political legacy of Thomas Jefferson Davis, the four-time Governor of Escambia and the most successful third-party presidential candidate in modern American history. Davis's opposition to civil rights struck a chord of anti-Washington feeling in voters that continues to figure in national elections. As this story goes to press, the former governor lies gravely ill in a hospital here.

Davis began his career in the 1940's as a populist under the guidance of legendary Governor John "The Giant" Partain. The two parted ways after the "Dixiecrat" conservatives took over most Democratic party organizations in southern states and became bitter rivals when each sought to return to state office in 1958. This story provides a behind-the-scenes look at that campaign, which began Davis's reign as Governor — and established him as the unquestioned leader of white opposition to the civil rights movement in the South.

"Looking back from this distance, the election of 1958 reminds me of a Greek drama," said Rev. Fred Middlebrooks, a leader in Escambia's civil rights movement throughout the 1950's and '60's. "When T. J. Davis completed the political burial of Giant Partain, he was a modern day Oedipus, killing his father to fulfill his fate. Certainly the Giant would not have felt more betrayed if Davis had been his own son— they were that close at one time."

According to historical accounts, Governor Partain had been flattered and pleased when Davis, then a young state representative, remained at the Democratic Convention after the Dixiecrat walkout in 1948. As a young legislator, Davis had been an effective supporter of the Giant's progressive agenda. But both men had been turned out in the Dixiecrat backlash and neither had expected the public's memory would last so long. T. J. Davis actually lost his first gubernatorial election. In 1954 he had run on a Progressive program of building farm-to-market roads, expanding educational opportunities for the working class and attracting jobs that paid better than mill piece-work and share cropping.

"Considering his later positions," Middlebrooks said. "it surprises people that Davis actually refused the endorsement of the Ku Klux Klan in the '54 election. The candidate who got that endorsement beat Davis in a runoff. Davis did not like losing—I don't suppose any of us does—but he reacted to it differently than most people expected. No one knew that was going to happen, though, until the famous Dobson speech."

Dobson, Escambia, is today a sleepy town of 8,000 that anchors the southeast corner of the state. The interstate system bypassed the town and as a result it has grown smaller over the years but in 1958 the city had almost 30,000 inhabitants. In those days Dobson hosted a huge political rally at the beginning of every election season and it was often said that no candidate had truly started his campaign until he spoke in Dobson. Both Davis and Giant Partain sought the Democratic nomination and both spoke at the Dobson rally. Historians mark T. J. Davis's Dobson speech as a clean break from his moderate, progressive past and his first explicit embrace of racism and the Klan. The question that has hung over his reputation ever since is, was he a racist by belief or did he adopt the prevailing views purely to win elections?

"That's what his friends say, that he 'changed' for political reasons," Middlebrooks said, "but I think that in 1958 he finally decided to just show himself for what he always was. Up until that time he played at being a populist because he wanted to ride Governor Partain's coattails. After the Giant faded and couldn't be of help to him anymore, I think Davis just decided he could take the mask off."

There are other theories. In a 1958 newspaper interview, shortly after his defeat, Giant Partain stated that the change in Davis's position was not motivated by any conviction, but by a simple willingness to do or say anything to get elected. "Davis has become anybody's dog that'll hunt him," the ex-Governor said in a well-known quote.

Previously unknown historical material sheds new light on this decisive point in Governor Davis's career. In researching this series of reports, the *Atlanta Constitution* has discovered a large number of audio tapes in the archives of the University of Escambia that have been forgotten for more than thirty years. These tapes were made after T. J. Davis had left office for the last time, probably in the late 1970's, perhaps as part of an intended oral history pr*oject*. Because many of the tapes record interviews with Billy Thrash, Governor Davis's life-long friend and most trusted political aide, they provide intimate details about the inner workings of Davis's campaigns and administrations that have never before been made public.

As a result of this discovery, the *Constitution* has learned the story of T. J. Davis's political "conversion" in the words of an actual participant in those events. That story is one of bigotry and political trickery that is unpleasant to read. **Parents are cautioned** that most of this material is not appropriate for younger readers. Indeed, some of it will be offensive even to adults but the importance of the story requires that the record be complete. Because of the controversial nature of the material, excerpts from the recorded tapes will appear in italics. These are the words of Billy Trask and this is the story of the famous Dobson speech:

The tension was so thick you'd a needed a scythe to cut it. We hadn't been on the same program with the Giant since the campaign started. His people thought of T.J. as a traitor and all, and were really pretty ugly about it. The Giant himself just glared at us every chance he got, red-faced as always, half lit but also like he was about to bust. I noticed his doctor was with him. That made me think his own people thought he might explode.

The way this program was put on, the little local races were done first - they figgered if the governor candidates spoke first, folks might not stay to hear the dog catcher speeches - and a skinny fella with this real intense look came to the microphone. His name was Jack Meeks and he was running for some little nothin' job, commissioner I think, and he starts up on how the school desegregation cases is going to destroy our towns. He said the niggers were gonna get all excited about this right they supposedly had, that nobody down here had ever heard of, to go to the same schools as white kids, and when that happened, why, all hell was bound to break loose. It was some speech, and I remember the crowd just went crazy.

On the tapes, Billy Thrash describes the powerful effect hearing this speech had on T. J. Davis, as though it confirmed a change in approach Davis was still undecided on:

This little nobody, Jack Meeks, showed with this speech that the path T. J. was about to start down was the right one; you could see in T. J.'s face he had been changed. Like Paul, in the Bible, struck blind on that road to Demopolis. [sic]

No verified transcript of the Dobson speech has ever been found. Contemporary newspaper accounts of the speech Davis gave that night vary but the following excerpts are in all reported versions:

"The Washington know-it-alls and liberal, so-called intellectuals have got these college degrees with the letters on 'em, Ph.D., STP, PDQ and I don't know what all, but they ain't got walkin' around sense. They wanna come in here, to our home, and stir up resentment and hatred among the nigras that we ain't had before, and I'm telling you I'm not gonna let that happen. These Yankee liberals want to preach communistic amalgamation of the races, knowing full well that is a godless doctrine that flies in the face of the very nature that God created. The differences in the races are the very handiwork of God and it is sacrilege for Washington DC bureaucrats and federal judges to tamper with the system God himself has made.

"We are law-abiding people and the most peaceable in this great nation, but let the intellectuals and the judges hear this. Our fathers before us paid a heavy price for the freedoms that are now being subverted. We are not afraid to pay a heavy price to preserve those freedoms — the freedoms of

race and religion — and our system, created by the holy God, from the attacks of the outsiders who would destroy the life of the South. If that is defiance, then defiant we shall be. Let me lead you in that defiance, to stand tall for Escambia, and the whole of the South."

In addition to what the Trask tapes tell us about T. J. Davis's state of mind on this important day, they also provide first hand information about one of the most famous "dirty tricks" in Southern politics. This 1958 campaign has long been the subject of intense study. The tapes make clear for the first time that Davis's victory was in part the result of an orchestrated plan to destroy "Giant" Partain that began on that long-ago night in Dobson. The following excerpt shows the first subtle step in the plan and confirms the role of the Klan in Davis's first campaign:

"I had a headache by now and so I wandered over to where Dr. Whatley was. The Doc was part of the Giant's inner group. The big man had the blood pressure and all kinds of medical problems and thought having the Doc close by was a good thing. The Doc was like me, waiting for his candidate to be willing to leave, so we shot the breeze a little bit and I asked him if he had any aspirin or anything. He gave me this B.C. powder in a paper, woulda been worth about a nickel, and I gave him $5.00. He looked real surprised, but I had heard some things about him made me think he'd take it and, after jawing for a second that it wasn't necessary, he did. I told him I was always grateful when people did me a favor and I was brought up to show my gratitude, if he knew what I meant. From the quick way he pocketed that bill, I kinda got the feeling he knew.

I walked back over to where I had left T. J. only now I didn't see him but I heard somebody shouting down one of the long hallways that went off the main floor. As I got closer I could tell it was the Giant, giving T. J. holy hell about the speech.

"I taught you stuff, boy. I taught you better than this. You sound like the goddamn Klan." The Giant was yelling mad and almost cryin' at the same time. I could smell the liquor on his breath twenty feet away.

"I sound like the people, Giant," T. J. said. "You can see that, can't you? You heard them. I was saying what they wanted to hear."

"*That ain't your job, to tell them what they want to hear. You're supposed to lead them, goddamn it.*"

There was this silence then, like Giant was thinking over what he'd just said, trying to convince himself. T. J. stepped closer and put his hand on the older man's shoulder, having to reach up to do it. "*I know,*" he said, almost whispering. "*You taught me that and a whole lot more. But I can't lead 'em if I don't get elected. And you know I can't get elected if I'm soft on niggers.*"

Giant shook that big head of his, and I swear I thought that big ole man was gonna start blubbering. But then he got himself together and just said "*not this way*" or something like that.

After the Giant left, I got T. J.'s attention and took him over to meet some fellas I knew from the eastern part of the state. I remember Toby Mullins told T. J., "*I never thought you had the guts to talk about the real issues.*"

"*The schools. Yeah,*" T. J. said. "*That looks like the main thing.*"

"*Nah, hell, not the schools, that's just part of it. The Communists race mixers, that's the real issue. Giant wanted to ignore it. I'm glad you're not going to do that. We can support a man like you.*"

T. J. looked almost puzzled for a moment, as though he was trying to remember where he was. I guess his talk with the Giant had throwed him a little. But he at least recovered his manners enough tell my boys, "*I 'preciate that, I shore do.*" Something like that anyway. Not really enough to make them happy, but I was able to smooth it over later and we got the Klan endorsement we needed.

After the Dobson speech, Davis's crowds grew larger and larger. The participation of Klan supporter groups, especially those of Toby Mullins from East Escambia, made the rallies noisier as well. Newspaper stories from that campaign tell of Confederate flags as big as bed sheets waving at the back of auditoriums. "Stand Tall for Escambia" signs, banners and bumper stickers began to appear all over the state. No one could quite explain why such a plain slogan should become so popular, but by the time of the election many people, when asked by pollsters who they intended to vote for, would answer "I'm gonna stand tall for Escambia."

Even so, ex-Governor Partain continued to run well and the polls showed a close race. But then the first strange event in this very strange campaign occurred.

Where's that Sweet Thing?

Two months after the Dobson conference the police reporter for the local newspaper received an anonymous phone call claiming that Giant Partain was "holed up" with a woman in the middle of the day. In less than twenty minutes, as his story later reported, the reporter was politely tapping on the door to room 428, identifying himself and asking if the candidate was present. He knocked again, and again announced himself. And waited. After twenty minutes had passed and two members of the Carnegie police department and three more reporters arrived at the door, it finally opened, to be filled by the considerable bulk of Governor Giant Partain. Inside the room a shapely redhead stuffed papers into a briefcase. The ex-governor introduced her as Mary Lee Sweeting and described her as a political consultant from Rondo, a very small Escambia community.

The police drove Giant Partain and Mary Lee to the station to be charged. The ex-governor professed ignorance of the local ordinance making it illegal for an unmarried couple to share a hotel room. "Well that's just silly," the Giant told the press. "We just had a meeting. Besides, we're both married." An unfortunate error in the arrest records caused the woman's name to be listed as Mary Lee Sweething. A police spokesman denied the entry was intentional, to embarrass the Giant. "Must of just been a subconscious thing. I mean, she is a fine looking woman. Think if Sophia Loren had a sexier sister. Like that."

The ex-governor protested his innocence for weeks, then paid a small fine. T. J. Davis seemed to take the high road. "I'm sure the Governor has an explanation he will give the people when he's ready. I hope that will be soon."

The Giant waited for the fuss to die down, but when it had not done so after four weeks, he agreed to be interviewed on a state-wide news show. "The good people of Escambia," he said, "know that anyone in this business of politics is gonna make enemies. I've told you all for years about the Big Bulls that run this state, the power company, the Farm Bureau and the timber barons. I've made life tough on the Big Bulls all that time I was governor, fighting for you, and they've always wanted to get me. Jesus found himself attacked by the Pharisees and the might of Rome. It's always been that way."

"Now you folks know me. You know the Giant is just a man. I'm one of you. I got the same weaknesses. I never claimed different. The men that want to bring me down, to make me smaller in your eyes, they have tried every kind of temptation to corrupt me. The Big Bulls offered me power and money. They offered me big cars and fancy clothes. And I said no, every time. But this time they tried something different.

"And I gotta be honest, if you set out to catch the Giant and the bait you use is a pretty red-headed woman, not a girl mind you, but a full-figured honest to God stacked up woman, well if that's your bait, I reckon you gonna catch the Giant pretty near every time."

He asked for forgiveness and a lot of people seemed ready to give it to him. But he never had another rally without seeing a few signs asking, "Where's that Sweet Thing?" And the Davis camp never missed a chance to remind the voters that their man had married the innocent young girl who used to come to the corner drugstore where he worked, when they were both still in high school.

To everyone's surprise, the Giant remained very much in the race after the Mary Lee incident and still had a chance to win. Particularly because something brand new came to Escambia politics that year—a live debate from the studio of WFHJ in Carnegie, broadcast statewide. A good performance, many thought, could have put the Giant back in front of the field. That didn't happen, though. Instead, one of the biggest meltdowns in American political history took place in front of more than 300,000 viewers. Experts on southern politics have argued about what happened that night for the 50 years since. Now, for the first time anywhere, the *Constitution* provides the inside story as told by the key participant, Billy Trask, in a tape recording made more than twenty years ago:

T.J. was amazed that the Giant was still in the race. Like most politicians back then he expected the voters would tear a candidate apart over sex issues. That's why he was so careful with his own little flings. I thought there was other factors in this case. It occurred to me that Mary Lee may have been the wrong choice. She was _so_ damn good looking folks probably thought Giant would'a been queer if he hadn't a wanted to f*** her. It sure didn't hurt him like it was supposed to. My mistake. Live and learn.

The debate was another opportunity to knock the old man out. T. J. felt good about that. The Dobson speech had been working fine all around the state, so he knew what issues to hit. He couldn't use that speech on TV of course, too many people had heard it, but his new talk on the same issues was just as strong. The Giant still wasn't talking about the Brown case, so he couldn't possibly do well in the debate.

But that didn't give T. J. any comfort. "I want to make sure this time, g********. I'm counting on you, Billy." I got the message and went to make a phone call.

The night of the debate the Giant arrived in his usual condition - loud, friendly and moderately drunk. Nobody was particularly surprised. None of us could remember a public appearance when he did not appear to have had a nip or two. Fact is, I doubt he'd a made any kind of sense at all if he was sober.

We were all there early. There was lots of fussing about makeup. That was a whole new idea to these fellas, but the TV people said you had to do it. I remember they had a real hard time with T. J. and only convinced him by telling him Ike himself had to wear makeup to be on TV, or he'd of looked like a ghost on account of the lights being so bright.

After that we still had nearly an hour to go. I was getting a little antsy 'cause a guy I was expecting to see hadn't shown up yet. T. J. studied notes he had made and went over the stuff we had put together about how to stand, talk and look on TV.

On the other side of the studio, the Giant was pacing some, yelling at his staff people while waving his hands around, then running one through his hair. Everything in the world but trying to relax, seemed like. But that was what we was used to with him. Then I saw Dr. Whatley for the first time that night. I began to breathe easier.

The Doc watched Giant for a little while, then went over to the Giant's campaign manager and whispered something in his ear. The two of them then went to the Giant and, one on each side, led him to a side room, the doc carrying that bag of his in his free hand.

Historians consider the debate one of the turning points of Escambia politics. Newspaper reports described the Giant as "knee-walking drunk." His speech was badly slurred. He referred to the memory of FDR as the "great holy hope" of the nation, while tears streamed down his face. Trying to compose himself, he thought to introduce his family but referred to his own wife as "Mary Lee." Since the entire state knew this was the name of the woman he had been caught with at the Tutwiler Hotel, this faux pas did not endear him to the wives in the audience. Attempting to introduce his seven children, he came to the youngest and cutest, a boy of six who looked just like him, and was struck dumb. It was as though the child had been dragged off the street at random, so blank was the Giant's look. But the damage might have been less had he just kept silent. Instead the ex-governor squinted at the obviously uncomfortable little boy and said, "which one are you?"

Even the progressives in the state were put-off by this sleazy perfor-mance. Afterwards his campaign reported that the Giant had been the victim of poor doctoring—that he had reacted badly to an injection given him less than an hour before the debate. At the time this story was written off as a mere excuse, and no excuse could outweigh the impact of those pictures of an addled and drunken man beamed straight to the living room of most Escambia families. This new evidence may cause those events to be re-examined. But nothing can alter the effect of that night. After a truly important career, the Giant left public life as a pathetic buffoon. The era of T. J. Davis had begun, setting priorities, and some would say tactics, that would stigmatize the South through the civil rights years.

You Know the Rules

The phone rang four times before Gordon got to it.

"Have you seen the *Constitution* today? We've gotten a black eye on this one," Edward said.

Gordon would have loved to make his grandson feel better, but in truth it was just as he had feared from the day he first learned Rebecca had found the tapes. No one would understand why the *Courier* had not discovered such historic material in its own backyard.

"We'll have to do something on it," Edward said. "When would you feel like having one of our reporters come over?"

"To talk to me, you mean?" Gordon said in surprise. "I don't know anything about the early days of Davis's career. I wasn't a part of his campaigns at the beginning."

Even over the phone line, Gordon could sense Edward's exaspera-tion.

"I think it's a lot safer for us to interview you than Billy, wouldn't you say?"

Gordon agreed, having little choice, then said goodbye.

Almost immediately the phone rang again. Barbara Davis was alarmed that the story had run while her husband was still in the hospital, unconscious. Gordon explained that the discovery of the tapes would be newsworthy even without the illness, but didn't expect that to make her feel much better. He was glad, at least, that he had answered that call before Margaret could get to the phone.

The phone screamed again as soon as he hung up. Gordon sighed deeply, looking at his unread book on the end table.

He picked up the receiver to hear Billy's deep scratchy voice. It was silly, he thought, to keep thinking of a man nearly eighty by that boy's name, but "William" seemed impossible. Not just too formal; too civilized in general.

"God *damn*, man, what is that girl trying to do to us?"

"Good morning to you, too, Billy," Gordon said. He felt so tired. "You remember I told you at the hospital that she had found these tapes. You seem to have done a lot of talking."

"Like hell I did," the old man sputtered into the phone. "She's faking this. I just know she is. I don't remember no damn tapes."

Gordon sighed, having no desire to be drawn into this particular controversy but seeing no way out.

"I've heard one or two of the tapes, Billy. It certainly sounds like you. I don't think she'd go to the trouble to try to make them up."

A staticy silence lengthened in Gordon's ear.

"Billy? Did she call you for a comment?"

A grunt. "She could have. I don't talk to reporters. Never have. Ever body knows that."

"You know the rules, though," Gordon tried to sound patient. "The reporter finds a story and gives you a chance to explain it and you don't call her back, she goes with what she's got. That's how it works."

"Not this time, goddamnit!" The outburst would have surprised Gordon if he had not known this old man for so long. "You got to make her quit it."

Gordon snorted. As though he could make a young person do anything. "How am I supposed to do that? Besides, how much worse can the tapes get?"

"You sonofabitch. I can't tell if you're trying to be cute or if you really are stupid, Gordon." Deep wheezing sounded in Gordon's ear. The conversation was an effort for Billy, even as angry as he was. "Listen to me," he continued. "Make her stop."

Gordon did not get a chance to protest again. The sharp click of the phone being slammed down cut off the call. He put the phone on the end table where *The Mayor of Casterbridge* lay unfinished. He was much too agitated to read now. He didn't blame the reporter; she was just doing her job. If they had done things differently forty years ago, he thought, there would be no stories for her to find. Just their luck this particular reporter was given this assignment. There were so many lazy ones who would never have found the tapes. Why couldn't the *Constitution* have sent one of those?

Gordon breathed deeply to calm himself. The only good thing about any of this was that the calls had started early enough this morning that he could still spend a little time in the garden while it was cool. He poured another cup of coffee, then went out to sit in the shade.

In her room at the Montville Inn, Rebecca read the *Constitution*'s web page. She never tired of seeing her name in the byline.

She was proud of the story and had gotten an email from Jeff congratulating her on it but, really, she wondered, did anyone care about this old stuff? It was hard enough to get people to read newspapers for current events. She could easily imagine that only a dozen septuagenarians in Escambia—and no one at all in Georgia— would even take the trouble to read the story. Of course one of those Escambians would be Miss Fieldstone, guardian of the University library, she who was so certain Rebecca wanted only to tarnish the reputation of her fair state. Rebecca could imagine that, for sure, she was reading the story, clucking her tongue as she did so. Rebecca could almost hear her — *just as I suspected, only the most unflattering information is worthy to appear in the newspaper. The nerve of the Constitution, to send a Yankee writer to tarnish our Governor's final, noble struggle.*

She lifted her coffee cup to her lips before noticing it was empty. She couldn't work without coffee, so she walked to the lobby for a fresh cup.

Checks and Promises

G ordon looked for patterns in the dappled shade. It would be unbearably hot in the afternoon, but for now he was comfortable, at least physically. He could not hope for mental contentment until all this hubbub about the Davis administration had ended. He found himself thinking of those distant days much more than he wanted to, as though by some compulsion. The *Constitution*'s story took him back to the first Davis inauguration.

The swearing-in had been appropriately serious and the new governor had delivered a well-received speech. But hundreds of contributors, looking forward to a rowdy celebration at the governor's mansion, were shocked when, at 9:30 that night, the new governor took his young wife's hand, waved a farewell over his shoulder, and climbed the fancy staircase to the private living area. There was considerable consternation because most of the important people had not gotten the word that, this year at least, the mansion would not be the site of the party. Billy had made other plans. There was some awkwardness while the word got out, in the now nearly silent mansion, but soon enough the group reconvened at the Federal House, a pretentious motel out on the by-pass.

Billy had arranged for a case each of bourbon, gin, vodka and scotch, to be tended by negro waiters in black tie, and, with the lobbyists from Escambia Power, the Farm Bureau, the Insurance Council and the Lumber Products Association, he staged a party that made many think of the rowdiest days of the late, lamented "Giant" Partain.

Even now, Gordon could remember that Billy was in his element - slapping backs, pouring drinks and extracting checks and promises - and delivering promises himself, not of what he would do but what he could prevail on Governor Davis to do. It had occurred to Gordon at the time that Billy was so clearly at home in this setting that one would have though he himself had been the victor of the recent election. No one present, Gordon thought, missed the message. The governor had gone upstairs early, leaving the party—in every sense—in Billy's hands. More than one of the agents of powerful men present thought there was a sign there, and they had gained their positions by being good at reading signs.

After the inauguration there was a period of quiet. The *Brown* decision had been filed, but not immediately acted on. There was a feeling that the Supreme Court might mean something in Washington or Massachusetts, but that here in Escambia the Court was very far away, in geography and philosophy, from making any impression on "real" people. Gordon recalled those as good days.

At the paper, Father had continued writing his editorials hoping for a "positive" response to the *Brown* decision and, as hopelessly in Gordon's opinion, reform of the state's tax system. As with many states, Escambia's tax system had been a crazy-quilt designed, Father always said, to make absolutely sure that every tax was passed to the lowest-income section of the population as quickly as possible. Thus, the taxes on Escambia Power's revenues were, by act of the legislature, included in its rate base while the largest consumers of electricity were exempted from the tax, making the percentage passed to homeowners that much larger. There were taxes on newspapers, tobacco, alcohol, gasoline, automobiles, clothes, drugs and food but, Gordon had to admit, only the most token taxes on property and virtually none at all on businesses. Father had written that there was enormous opportunity for a governor with Davis's popularity to make this system fair. But the effort would have been difficult and, to say the least, would have required full-time attention. Even before he had joined the administration, it was clear to Gordon that attention was something T. J. Davis simply could not give. He was incapable of extended concentration on any issue that would not immediately generate votes. Tax reform would have gained many, but it would have alienated the money interests who, Gordon knew, could have found an opponent to run against Davis in the time it would take to get a haircut.

A chipmunk skittered across the lawn and dived into a bed of mulch under the Professor Charles S. Sergeant bush. Gordon unfastened another button at the neck of his polo shirt. It was not yet noon but the garden was still and sweat beaded on his brow. Soon he would have to go inside for lunch and perhaps do some reading. But he would have to slow his mind for that to happen, and hold it here and now.

So hot. He thought how Edward had complained as a boy whenever they rode in Gordon's old car. How strange to think that air-conditioning came about in his own lifetime, and late at that. There was no air-conditioning at that first inaugural he was just remembering, or in the house where he and Father argued about that first administration.

Gordon approved of Davis to the extent that his administration stood for pride in the South. Gordon recalled one of his few early editorials had been a column praising the statewide junior college system Davis proposed as a progressive concept. He and Father had even argued about that — "Just a way to create a patronage system," Father had said. "More teachers on the state payroll and all the administrators will be appointed by him." All the while, Father's editorials about a reasoned position on the "race question" continued to be ignored.

Gordon had no particular desire to see the negroes downtrodden, or even denied the vote, but unlike Father, it pained him to see Yankees portray the situation as one in which the only way for colored people to improve was for the South to be ridiculed and diminished. In his memory this had been the case throughout Davis's first four years. Every attack on a negro was not just a criminal act by an ignorant and bigoted minority of white people but, according to the northern press, part of a grand conspiracy to maintain segregation. That some of this ridicule was brought on by the clumsiness of the Davis administration in handling press issues and public relations in general only added to Gordon's pain.

When the lunch counter protests swept the South during the first term, for example, the administration issued statements implying that violent resistance by white customers might be justified. Gordon thought they should have simply defended the enforcement of long-recognized laws.

Events outside of Escambia kept the issue in the national press. From its beginnings with the Montgomery bus boycott of 1955 and the attempt to desegregate Little Rock High School in 1957, the civil rights effort had grown to become a genuine political movement that had started vibrations in southern life that had continued to hum and grow ever stronger. The Davis administration too often seemed tone deaf.

Gordon remembered that his involvement with the Davis campaign for election to a second term in 1962 had started out just this simply. Gordon's only goal had been to influence the Davis message on two points: that neither side, North or South, had perfect knowledge of what was best for the negro people and that the South had a special culture and way of life that deserved to be respected at the same time that its faults were addressed.

So he had decided to visit the Governor. It was a sunny mild day so short sleeves were everywhere on Dexter Avenue, coats having been left in offices.

Governor Davis himself came out to the reception area to bring Gordon back to his office. He stuck out a chunky hand in greeting.

"The Fourth Estate finally visits."

"Thank you for seeing me, Governor," said Gordon.

Davis chuckled. "All those times we talked about politics back at the University, did you ever think this day would really happen? Me and you chatting in the Governor's office."

Gordon smiled, knowing that Davis had never had the least doubt it would happen. They went to the office, which Gordon had expected to find cluttered with letters to be answered and legislative bills and governmental reports to be read. But once inside he saw that the huge desk was all but bare. A picture frame, note pad, a phone. That was it, as though the man who sat there must spend most of his time staring out the floor-to-ceiling windows that rose behind the desk.

"I appreciated the column you wrote about the junior colleges," T.J. said.

"The junior colleges are a good idea."

"Well I hope…"

"Unlike attending the White Citizens Council meetings," Gordon continued as though there had been no interruption.

"The boys are supporters," T. J. began.

"The boys make you look like a Klansman. That won't work outside of Escambia. And you have to understand, this battle *will* be fought outside of Escambia."

T. J. narrowed his eyes. He was not accustomed to being interrupted. "Why do I give a damn what outsiders think?"

"Because you're smarter than you act half the time, or you wouldn't be here. If you let the state look stupid and violent in the national media you are going to lose this fight."

As he spoke, Gordon noticed, framed on the wall, a ragged square of notebook paper covered with a penciled note in crude handwriting.

"What the hell are you talking about?" T. J. asked grumpily. "National media my ass. The evening news is only 15 minutes long and most people don't watch it. Hell, most of my people in Escambia don't have TV to begin with."

"Maybe. But enough of them saw the debate with Giant to make you the governor." He stood up and walked closer to the framed note. It appeared to be patriotic, like a Fourth of July speech a kid had copied. "Robert E. Lee?" Gordon asked, touching the frame.

"What?" Davis had been deep in thought. "No. Jefferson Davis. Part of his inauguration speech I always liked."

"Hmm." Gordon walked back over to where the governor sat. "Look. Most of the people in Escambia don't want the negroes to vote or go to school with their kids - but it won't be up to them. This is going to be a national fight - if you want to have a chance to win it you've got to fight it nationally." Gordon settled into an armchair.

"Colored kids are never going to white schools," T. J. snorted.

"Right. And no Catholic will ever be president. You see how well that worked out."

One thing about T. J., Gordon thought, he would never have made a poker player. When an idea caught his attention, he showed it from a mile away.

Gordon stirred on the garden bench trying to get some circulation into his legs. Sitting too long made them feel like wood, but when his mind wandered he lost track of time. He thought about the girl reporter. She'd probably ask him about his work for the administration. He had not joined the staff. He'd just let her know that he only reviewed speeches and made a few suggestions about which ties to wear and such things.

Not a big deal, he'd tell her, though people back then had noticed that some of Governor Davis's rough edges had been smoothed out. Not a big deal. Except, of course, to Father. She would want to ask him about that.

Gordon remembered how angry his father had been and it made him shudder, still, more than fifty years on. It was absurd. "You're making that racist look presentable," Father had said so long ago, when he'd heard of Gordon's visit to the Capitol. "Is that something you're proud of?"

Gordon had defended himself with the self-righteousness of youth. "Davis loves the South, as I do. I don't feel ashamed of that. We can care about the welfare of the negro without wanting to go to church with them."

He could still remember how Father had sneered. "I don't think I'd mention church when you make your case for that bigot. Do you think God's a racist who's on your side, Son?" Father had rubbed his forehead, then pushed a lock of hair back from his face and laughed bitterly. "Is that it, Son? Do you and Davis think God is *white?*"

Even in the heat of his back yard in summer, the memory sent a chill through Gordon.

We Ain't Interested in Outsiders

P rofessor Middlebrooks stood by his office window, absently stirring the cup of tea held on a saucer in his left hand.

"I know you've read about the attacks on the freedom riders and some of the other civil rights crimes. The young priest shot to death in broad daylight in Selma, Alabama. The white mother from Detroit killed as she drove black students to register to vote. But the truth is those crimes got a lot of attention because the victims were white people who died for the movement. The routine killing of blacks, especially young men, was seldom covered in the media but was a part of our life, growing up."

He seemed to find comfort in the movement of the hickory trees outside his window and did not look at Rebecca as he spoke.

"It was in the nature of those times that the violence was part of the politics. We recognize this is how things work, out in the distant world, and so bombs and mayhem in Ireland or the Middle East have always been accepted as part of the natural order. But we do not think of America this way, at least I guess white people don't. We are supposed to be immune from these contortions, protected by a system of government in which all sides have a fair opportunity to be heard. Certainly Michael DeWitt did not think violence should be part of politics in Escambia. And the story is told that he went to see Governor T. J. Davis to tell him so.

T. J. had been elaborately courteous, opening the door himself, having a negro valet bring in coffee on a silver tray. The two adversaries shared the sofa; T.J. did not want to seem to be hiding behind the great desk.

"You've got to rein the Klan boys in," DeWitt had said when they were seated. "You know that, don't you?"

T.J looked at the floor and shook his head back and forth slowly.

"Michael, I don't know what you mean." Then he looked up and twisted his lips thinly into a "U" shaped grin.

"That's not going to work, Tommy. You may not be telling the Klan to kill these people, but if you say for it to stop, it will stop." DeWitt set his cup on its saucer. "Everyone knows that, you're not fooling anybody."

T. J. had leaned back against the sofa cushion, his eyes closed and his head bobbing slowly while DeWitt talked. He kept it up for several minutes of silence, then spoke without opening his eyes.

"Why do you do that?"

DeWitt looked around the room and saw Gordon Halt sitting quietly in a corner.

"Do what?" Dewitt asked.

"Call me Tommy, like we're still at the University and you're the rich kid who runs everything," T. J. said, his head still bobbing slightly. "You know all that's gone do is piss me off and make me ignore anything you've said." He opened his eyes and suddenly leaned forward. "You know that, but you don't give a damn, do you Michael?"

The legislator walked across the office to the long windows beside the desk.

"This is not personal, Governor. If I offended you I apologize. I came here to try to be of help, to try to help the state. You must see what this violence is doing to us, and to the image of the South."

T. J. had risen from the sofa and walked toward the taller man as he spoke. He resumed his chair behind the desk and turned toward the corner where Gordon sat before answering.

"You hear this? Michael is concerned about the image of Escambia. Ain't that good of him?"

T. J. sneered the last sentence, playing out the delivery for the benefit of his trusted advisor. He got into the part, ignoring DeWitt as completely as if he was only an image painted on the wall.

"You see the mistake Michael is making, don't you Gordon? He's concerned about image when image don't make a good goddamn. Image is how you look to the outsiders. We ain't interested in outsiders, are we?"

He laughed out loud.

"Why don't you take your advice somewhere it's wanted, Michael? The niggers can stop the violence anytime they want to, they just got to behave themselves."

"People are dying, Governor."

T. J. glared at DeWitt, his thick brows knitted together, his upper lip curling slightly.

"Those people, Senator, are doing things to get themselves killed. Hell, its practically suicide. It's not anything that ought to be blamed on me."

DeWitt walked back to where his briefcase rested on the sofa. He picked it up, then rubbed the side of his face with his free hand.

"It's not about blame," he said. "And it's not about you. We can be opposed to civil rights without the killing. That's what it's about. If we are on the side of murderers, what chance do we have?"

T. J. slammed the top of the desk with his thick hand.

"I don't get you, Mike. You just don't learn. You get nowhere with me using that kind of talk." T. J. fumed in his chair for a moment, then turned to lift a file from the small stack at one end of the desk. "Go on, now, I've got work to do."

A spell of coughing interrupted the story. Rebecca waited for Professor Fred to compose himself.

"You're probably thinking I'm making this up," he said finally, "and I'm sure the dialog is not exact, but the meeting was written up in the local black newspaper, probably from an account that someone got from DeWitt." The old man pulled a tea bag from his porcelain cup and strained it over a spoon.

"The thing that is certain," he said, "is that word of the meeting with Davis resounded through the community and was the beginning of Michael DeWitt's transformation into a hero for the black people of Escambia. I think he had always been on our side, as much as a white person in that time could have been and still be in politics, but from that day forward he was more committed to some kind of fair treatment for black people than any other politician."

Letting the Fox Into the Hen House

A fter leaving the Professor, Rebecca bought a hamburger and drink at a fast-food place. She thought about eating in the car but changed her mind and spread out the waxed paper wrapper on the small table and settled into a plastic chair. She decided to make the best use of her time and found Jeff's history book in her bag. After searching the index she found an account of the beginning of Davis's third term. This would put her right at the time the professor had been talking about.

After the voting rights march in Alabama, groups of activists throughout Escambia attempted to emulate the Alabama activists and made efforts to register at several courthouses. These efforts, though noble, had no practical effect and T. J. Davis was re-elected by a record margin.

The beginning of Governor Davis's third term brought no great changes in the pattern of a Davis administration. The Governor's attention continued to be focused on vote getting to the exclusion of any other interest. There was also no great change in the relationship between races. The presidency of Lyndon Johnson saw an unprecedented emphasis on civil rights at the national level and a continuation of virtual revolution against any change at the state levels, particularly in the Deep South.

The most significant event of the first two years was not recognized as such for some time; at first it was almost comical. A seventh grade teacher at the new (and very expensive) middle school in Montville noticed that one wall seemed to get hot whenever it was cold enough to have to use the supplemental heating system. He reported this fact and was informed it was "probably" normal. In a staff meeting another teacher mentioned her windows seemed to be warping and a third said a stain of some kind was growing on one of her walls "like a creepy Steven King kind of thing." There were jokes about the new building being haunted by the people who had lived in the houses that were torn down to make room for it, but no one took the problems very seriously; this was a public building, what could one expect?

That attitude changed when the first teacher came in one Monday morning to find his classroom filled with smoke. Class was suspended for a week while the school was thoroughly inspected. This was, of course, unnerving for the staff and the parents but it was after all a small matter. Much too small to get the attention of the Davis administration, at least for quite some time to come.

Even in quiet times Governor Davis would not have been interested in a local school problem, and 1967 was anything but a quiet time. His stand against the national government on the Escambia University campus had made him a hero to people who felt put upon by an overpowering federal government. Without really meaning to, the Governor had become a national figure. In 1967 he made more than 20 speeches in 15 different states, only five of which were in the Deep South.

It seems obvious now, when the South is solidly Republican, that an extremely conservative Democrat would have been an attractive national candidate. Davis was giving so many speeches and being so well-received that it did not take long for the money men to come calling offering to fund a run for the Democratic nomination for president.

In 1968, Davis entered the Democratic presidential primaries in Iowa, New Hampshire, New York, and South Carolina. He received no less than 5 percent of the vote and actually won in South Carolina. He was not a serious threat to the party's nominee, but he did win the chance to give a major address at the convention. This caused great consternation to the black delegates who argued that recognizing a man like Davis went against the core principles of the Party. The more practical opponents argued that giving a forum to Davis was letting the fox into the hen house. In 30 minutes he would reach millions of people who otherwise would never hear of him, and the party he detested would pay the bill. This particular prediction would come home with special pain four years later.

But four years seemed very far in the future in the time we are speaking of. Looking back it was clear that Davis was at the height of his powers. He could not have known it, and wouldn't have believed it if you told him, but things would never be as good for him as they were in the middle years of the third administration.

The moderates of Escambia and, of course, the black citizens, were concerned that DeWitt had not entered the 1966 gubernatorial race and wondered if he ever would challenge Davis. There might never have been an answer to that question — Michael DeWitt was, after all, a highly respected lieutenant governor of Escambia who seemed to have nothing to gain from challenging the most popular Southern governor in three generations — but, as they must do, events overtook the participants in them.

Two small groups of people intent on their own activities triggered the changes. One group of white men met in secret, at social clubs or even under railroad bridges, plotting dramatic acts of what they considered to be patriotic necessity. The other, a group of senior citizens engaged in that most banal of activities, tourism.

Historians would later remark on the irony that the two events occurred so closely in time. The group of white men set out for the nearby high school at about the same time that the group of tourists from a church home for the elderly climbed into the bus for their ride to New Orleans. The white men left their package at the school at about the same time the tourists ate a box lunch on their bus. When the white men were at home in their beds, the tourists were near to New Orleans. On Saturday, and while the tourists were learning their way around the Vieux Carre, one of the white men drove by the school, disappointed to see it standing. That night, while the tourists listened to the city's own music at Preservation Hall, a group of students slipped into the school for the unannounced rehearsal of a play.

A slow-moving cold front, pushing warm damp air ahead of it, brought soaking rain to the midsection of Escambia.

Later, some said it was a blessing that many of the students had left the rehearsal before the bomb blast ripped the north end from the school auditorium. The site of so many civil rights meetings was laid open to the weather and the abuse of the elements. In the wreckage laid the mangled bodies of five high school students and their drama teacher. Even the steady rain could not prevent the raging fire, fed by the varnished wood floor, the wooden bleachers and a ruptured gas line. The sign that proudly read "Phillips High School" was blown across the empty parking lot a distance of nearly 100 yards.

News of the bombing caused the tourists a somber ride back to Montville that Sunday. Mounds of oppressive gray cloud hung morosely in the air, while the rain never stopped. Hours went by with only whispered conversation, the mood inside the bus as gray as the weather outside and the swish of the heavy tires on the wet roadway becoming a tedious drone. The dreary afternoon faded imperceptibly to darkest night. Many on the bus were asleep by the time the tires hit a rough section of pavement coming down White's Bluff in Choctaw County. Almost home.

Clarence, the driver, must have thought it odd to have the road turn so rough, so suddenly. After all this was not county blacktop; this was a state highway, not even very old. He must have been surprised at how difficult the big vehicle was to control without the benefit of a smooth road. One can only guess at his concern when he lost control of the huge bus and found himself bearing down on the guardrail that had been erected on the road's edge.

What terror he must have felt when the bus, not moving particularly quickly, broke through the guard rail which tore as though it were made of twigs. By the time the rescuers had recovered six dead bodies and twenty-four wounded ones, speculation was already building that poor workmanship in both the roadway and the railing had probably caused the accident. Even Davis's supporters were alarmed when the subsequent investigation revealed that one of Billy's close associates was the responsible contractor for that section of roadway and, for some reason no one could explain, had not been required to bid to get the work.

Whatever his reasons had been before for staying out of a race, DeWitt knew he could stay out no longer. And he didn't just step gingerly into the campaign. He roared into it with all the zeal of a convert. The people of Escambia deserved better than racial violence and corruption. He was going to provide it.

Rebecca made a few notes on her pad, then tossed the remains of her meal in the trash and returned to the University.

We Love a Conspiracy Theory

"**I** know we've talked about this a lot," the old man said as he stirred yet another cup of tea, "but it is difficult to express how completely T. J. Davis controlled the state of Escambia. He had ruined the Giant and he ruined many other lesser figures. Michael Dewitt must have known that to run against Davis would be the end of his political career. The fact that he was willing to do that out of sheer outrage at the death of the young people in that high school says a lot about him.

"DeWitt was no liberal, but he was not willing to classify blacks as subhuman and he was completely unwilling to make the South an outlaw community. He was shocked by the violence that Davis seemed to be tolerating and shocked by the terrible image his beloved South had in the rest of America.

"The interesting thing, surprising really, is that the bombing of Phillips High School actually did make a difference in the campaign. The Halt family paper came out against the governor, which was an embarrassment to Gordon but not a surprise to anyone else. What was a surprise was that some of the larger papers in the state finally criticized the violence for its effect on the state's image. Since the governor personified the state's image, Davis was more nervous about this campaign than he had been since the Dixiecrats were in power.

"And yet even with all that, I don't think the deaths of a few more black people, even high school kids, would have given Davis any serious problem at all if it hadn't been for that bus going through the guard rail. That seems odd, I know, but the allegations of bid rigging in government contracts got the FBI interested and you can imagine that's the last thing Davis needed just as he was becoming a major force in national politics. Corruption could be tied to him directly when the violence could not."

Rebecca wrote fast, jotting notes in her steno pad. She had read a brief mention of the FBI investigation in Jeff's history book. The United States attorney in Montville had been disappointed that the Justice Department allowed Governor Davis to "grandstand" with his speech in the doorway when the University was desegregated, and took out his frustration when the chance for a public corruption investigation came along.

Professor Fred chuckled at the memory. "We had gotten so accustomed to the governor's pomposity, railing against the Washington establishment to build his image, that it was real funny to see the U.S. attorney borrow some of those same tricks. I always figured he was just tired of Davis constantly using the federal government to bait the voters and decided to give a little bit of his own back to the Governor. And of course people are always interested when public money is being wasted.

"The U. S. attorney had the bus crash to work with, and the terrible construction in the high schools and other public buildings. He even made it sound like more than racism was involved in the Phillips High School bombing, as though the bomb was intended to destroy evidence of how poorly one of Billy Trask's buddies had built the building. It was a masterful performance.

"Of course, Davis always made it sound like he should be proud of the investigation. He claimed the FBI was only after him because he was such a successful campaigner he might put their boss, President Nixon, out of work. We always love a conspiracy theory down here and Davis had some pretty good luck with that story."

Rebecca continued to write, then looked up. "But you don't believe that do you?"

Professor Fred looked out the window for a moment before answering.

"If I'm honest, both things could be true; he could've been stealing the state blind on the one hand, and the President could've been afraid of his political power on the other. It doesn't have to be all one thing or all the other." He shrugged. "When you look at what happened, you can believe either version."

He put down his teacup, sat down at his desk and picked up a student essay from a stack on it. "You should ask Gordon Halt about that. He was right in the middle of it."

A Very Old-Fashioned Notion

I n Gordon's den the ticking of the mantle clock was the only sound. The clock was a gift to commemorate the end of his year as president of the Rotary. He was mildly surprised this girl had not asked him about *that*; she's pried into every other part of his life.

He pondered her question about the fourth campaign. The government investigation, Michael's challenge, all part of a life he can barely recall. He almost felt like a fraud pretending to be an authority on those dim, distant times. Of course he remembered that T. J. overreacted emotionally to the challenge from Michael. He was never in any real danger of losing. But that wasn't enough, just to win, it never had been. T. J. wanted every vote; he wanted to be loved. He could never understand why the negroes didn't vote for him; he was trying to preserve their South, too.

The reporter coughed and Gordon looked up. She must have decided he was not going to answer her earlier question, the one he has now forgotten, because after a moment of hesitation she said, "I don't mean to get too personal, but you supported T. J. despite your own background."

He cocked an eyebrow toward her. At long last she was worried about getting too personal?

"My sainted Father, you mean, the beloved Pulitzer winner? We had different views. You may not know, but in my day that was common in families, for fathers and sons to disagree. I think he was appalled that I got into the nitty gritty of politics rather than keeping a gentlemanly distance."

He laughed hollowly at his small joke, thinking how much he loathed this questioning, this raking up of old business long settled, or if not that, at least interred.

"In any event," he said after a moment, "I can assure you the FBI investigation was not something we took lightly.

"T. J. had always been known for his temper, but it was around this time, the race with DeWitt, that his temper became a titanic force, a rage that suggested something Homer might describe."

Gordon had been there when the story broke in the paper. T. J. hated for anything to interrupt the breakfast that the porter always brought him on a tray. So when he saw the page one story about the U. S. attorney's interest in state purchasing practices he called Billy in from his office down the hall, shouting even before the big man entered the room.

"'Goddamnit, I told you to be careful! Doesn't anyone listen to me? I can be destroyed by this kind of crap.'"

"We tried to calm him down, telling him he was the most popular governor in the history of the state, that after his stand against the Feds at the university no one in Escambia cared what the federal government did. He was a hero to the people; nothing would change that."

"Is that how you really felt about him?"

Gordon looked up in annoyance. Every time he began to get his thoughts in some kind of order, this reporter interrupted him with a question. He chewed his bottom lip

"The story disturbed me, I can't deny that. No one wants to be associated with anything illegal. I think the truth is that T. J. didn't know if Billy was stealing or not, and probably didn't care. It was a detail, and details were never his strong point. But I had seen Billy around the people who visited the capitol, and I knew a lot of them were much more anxious to see Billy than the governor. Of course I didn't know what Billy was doing, and I'm sure T. J. never did. I really thought T. J. would issue a statement and the issue would go away. That's what usually happened.

"But then, I knew a lot of things that nobody else but T. J. knew. We had started to get calls from very serious national people, people with influence and money who would not have gotten near T. J. in earlier years. But now he was no fluke, he was about to win his fourth term as governor, which no one had done in this century, and in the last presidential campaign he had won the South Carolina primary, and scored well in others, in a campaign financed with pocket money. He was a genuine contender to become president.

"This amazing possibility was opening up for him just at the time that Billy's foolishness was threatening his reputation. So it was natural he was tense and more likely to blow a fuse than usual. The FBI investigation was a threat to his future; there was no way we would have taken it lightly."

Rebecca put her pencil down and scratched her nose. "You seem to be saying that the candidacy of DeWitt was not a concern at all?"

Gordon smiled slightly, as though she had said something silly but he did not want to embarrass her. "The idea that Michael DeWitt could have beaten T. J. Davis in this state is a joke. I know many negro people think of it as a dream of theirs, but it's just a joke. DeWitt had nothing in common with the people of Escambia and they knew it."

He saw her face wrinkle in thought; she was considering his answer, not just noting it, probably thinking of what her black sources had told her about DeWitt and trying to make the two versions fit.

Gordon watched her bend almost double to rummage through her shoulder bag, resting on the floor. He wondered how many years it had been since he was that limber. She retrieved a paper, straightened and passed it to Gordon.

It was a crumpled piece of notebook paper with writing from an old manual typewriter. Gordon felt a pang at the sight, remembering the feel of metal keys against the tips of the fingers and the magical feeling of seeing words appear on the paper one noisy metal slap at a time. He was wondering if this child had ever even seen a manual when he found himself reading the words on the page.

The only one DeWitt had any respect for was that Gordon Halt. A lot of people hated Gordon, since he should have been on our side. Michael didn't though. He said we should understand that Gordon had a vision he wanted to protect, and he thought Davis could help him do that. Michael always thought Gordon would see the light and come over to our side eventually. But we never got the chance to see if that would have happened.

"Where did this come from?"

She ignored his question.

"Michael DeWitt asked you to join him, didn't he?" she asked.

Gordon looked up at her as though she had shouted a profanity. "Who told you that?"

She smiled, and Gordon felt a bit sick. She was only guessing, wasn't she? Now he had made her feel she had gained a point.

"Nobody told me, Gordon." She couldn't keep from grinning. "Give me some credit; I'm a reporter, after all, remember?"

Gordon smiled thinly, thinking he had to give her more respect. She seemed like a child to him but she was obviously good at this.

"Can we take a break for a minute?" Gordon asked.

He struggled to raise himself from the chair, rising slowly to his feet. When he was steady, he crossed the room to the French doors that looked out over the patio and into his beloved garden. The sight of honeysuckle and jasmine blooming on the section of old split-rail made him resent having to be inside. He was feeling a good deal of resentment, not least at being pushed into the past against his will. He knew this girl (he had to stop thinking of her that way) was only doing her job, but that didn't really help. She was the problem, however good her excuse, with her insistence that he plow these fields of memory.

What should he tell her? She was so smart, that was part of his resentment. She knew that DeWitt had come to see him, she knew that DeWitt had asked him to join the campaign. How much did she know?

It was there again, that familiar feeling that he was adrift in the events of his own life. Every year had seemed so real and so true when he was living it but now, from a perspective so distant it was very little better than hers, he wondered if she somehow knew these events better than he did.

When he turned back toward the room, she had wandered over to the bookshelf as she often did when there was a break in the interview. She peered at the titles on the spines, occasionally removing a volume to read a cover note, perfectly at home.

"My dad is a big reader," she said absently.

Watching her scan the spines, noticing the names of authors, seeking the order that determined which book went where, it was clear to Gordon this young woman must be from a family of readers.

"And yourself?" he asked.

"Oh yeah." She turned to him and smiled with what he imagined was a look of relief, as though she could confess such a thing in his presence without embarrassment; like fellow drunks at an AA meeting. Takes one to know one. She turned back to the shelves, hand up, fingers grazing the spines, literally in touch with the volumes. She would be the type whose favorite afternoon passes in a bookstore, or a library. Just as it occurred to him she was so intent she might have been searching for something specific, a thought that grazed his mind for only a moment, light and quick as her fingers on the books, he saw her stretch to pull a volume from a high shelf.

"He's always loved this one," she said, crossing the small room to hand the thick volume to him.

Gordon felt a twitch near his left eye. "I've always found Dickens very reliable." He didn't add that he had known what the book would be. After all the questions and all the probing of his now-no-longer-reliable memory, it was logical that this would be the book she would find.

"Dad says most fiction tries to escape from life, to serve as a diversion. He says Dickens explores life and asks us to imagine that we did the things his characters do and that we learn the lessons they learn."

"That is, I'm afraid, a very old-fashioned notion." Gordon wondered if this child had any inkling of how offensive her audacity might be considered, but said nothing further.

Rebecca laughed as though Gordon had said something truly delightful. "It's a theory that drives college literature professors crazy. I can tell you that from experience. When dad gave me that one to read," she nodded toward the volume in Gordon's hand, "he said 'the unexamined life is not worth living.' Do you think that's true?"

Gordon took a deep breath, determined to remain courteous in the face of her rudeness. "I don't believe your father is the author of that sentiment, sad to say. As to whether it's true," Gordon shrugged slightly to signal how trivial he found the discussion, "I suspect if most people examined their lives very closely they might well cut them short."

She looked slightly shocked. Good. He continued, "That may, however, be an overreaction on my part just because I don't like being interviewed." He patted the cover of the thick volume, then handed it back to her.

"I think Mr. Copperfield might like to go back home."

She stretched to push the book back onto the shelf, then returned to her chair and placed the steno pad on her lap. She looked up at Gordon, her pencil poised over the page, and said, "I believe you were going to tell me about your meeting with Mr. DeWitt."

Gordon turned back toward the window.

"Was I?" Some of the gardenia blooms were beginning to brown at the edges, mid-summer heat taking its toll.

He remembered being in the aisle with Margaret, the 11:00 service at All Saints having just ended, when he felt a tap on his shoulder. He turned to see Michael DeWitt extending his right arm. Gordon shook hands, muttering the usual pleasantries, which Michael returned, adding "the Peace of Christ", which made Gordon cringe with embarrassment.

Michael had bent close to Gordon's ear and whispered, "Can we talk for a minute?" He motioned toward the front of the sanctuary where the altar was now deserted. There was a small chapel off to one side. There was barely room for the two of them and Gordon realized Michael had picked this place to avoid embarrassing him. Whatever he was going to say, Michael was going to say in private.

"Do you remember the convention in Philadelphia, Gordon? I told you T. J. did not stay at the convention because he was a good Democrat. He stayed because he's a political hack. He does what's good for his reputation at the time, or what he thinks is; whatever the thing is that will win votes for him or keep the votes he already has. Beyond that, T. J. Davis has no ideas or even any human feeling.

"It can't keep going like this, Gordon; this is not what you want for Escambia. I don't blame Davis for all of it, I know he has not killed anybody, but he is to blame for the atmosphere that lets these things happen. God knows he hasn't even tried to control Billy. I don't know that I can make a difference, but I know I have to try. I'm going to announce next week that I'm running against him for the nomination and I'd like to be able to announce that you are my campaign manager."

Standing at his own window, in his own house, Gordon could not now remember exactly how he felt hearing these words. He certainly did not plan to tell Rebecca this part of the story — she seemed to be thinking DeWitt was a hero already and he had no desire to contribute to that — but he supposed he would have to tell her something.

It was so odd to think of that event and try to imagine it fresh, as it occurred, when it had been a fixed part of his ancient history for so long. He certainly did remember, however, his first reaction to Michael's proposal.

"Don't take this too personally, Michael, but why would I support someone who is going to lose?"

It had taken Michael a moment to answer and now Gordon realized that moment had not been for Michael to think of something to say. Michael had known what he was going to say long before asking Gordon for this meeting. No, that pause was for Gordon to have time to listen carefully to Michael's answer.

"Because it's the right thing to do. You want to do the right thing, don't you Gordon?"

This was the part Gordon did decide to tell Rebecca.

"He was always that way, you see, always so sure that he was on the side of right. Little wonder he never had a chance of getting elected."

Rebecca wrote on her pad, then flipped a page over. Gordon thought the noise seemed entirely too loud. The girl looked up at him.

"Obviously, you did not leave the Davis campaign. I wonder, though, was that meeting all DeWitt did to try to persuade you?"

Gordon could almost hear her mind working, churning. How did she know the questions to ask him, the questions he did not want to answer? He had to admit it. She was really very good at her job.

"I suspect you can guess what he did. He talked to my father."

Gordon was astonished to feel the anger building in him over this thing a dead man had done thirty years before. What fools memory makes of us, that we can be punished forever by a past that can't be changed but won't fade. What nerve DeWitt had to go to Father, what gall.

A Fragile and Precious Construction

The last thing Gordon had needed was another confrontation his father over T. J. Davis. It had taken nearly a year to reach some equilibrium in their relationship after Gordon became an advisor to the governor. He and Father had not been close at the best of times, they were much too different, but they had seldom raised their voices at each other over any other subject.

It had started off quietly enough. Gordon had been to the house for Sunday dinner. After the table was cleared, his father invited him to the study, a reliable sign that a confrontation was coming.

"Is there any news about the Phillips High bombing?" His father asked. This seemed a peculiar question since at this time Father was still the publisher of the paper but he knew the governor's office was keeping a close eye on the bombing case, if only because it was mentioned on NBC's *Huntley-Brinkley Report* two or three times a week.

Gordon shook his head. "No one seems to be doing much talking."

Father's eyes narrowed. "I suppose we should be glad the Klan is not bragging about what they've done." He sipped from the cup of coffee he had brought in from the dining room and rubbed the side of his head with two fingers. "There were no Davis bumper stickers on the bodies this time? I suppose you all are happy about that." The skin around Father's eyes tightened as though he expected a response he didn't want. Gordon resented this reference to the killing of three civil rights workers whose bodies had been buried with a bulldozer, into an earthen dam. The victim who was a black man was found with a "Stand Up for Escambia" bumper sticker crammed into his mouth.

What an ugly thing to even refer to. But Gordon didn't really expect Father to fight fair where T. J. Davis was concerned.

Gordon tried to keep his voice level when he answered.

Father looked down and moved a piece of paper from one side of the desktop to another.

"Michael DeWitt came to see me," Father said with excessive casualness. "He plans to run against Davis; did you know that?"

Gordon fiddled with the lace of the shoe on his crossed leg. "He mentioned it, yes."

"How long have you been working for Davis, now?" Father did not look at him as he asked the question, still preoccupied with arranging the papers on his desk. "What is it, six or eight years?"

Gordon could not believe he was going to have to go over this subject again, could not believe that DeWitt would have brought it up at all, could not believe that he would never ever make his father happy. It was harder this time to keep his voice even.

"I've been having so much fun I'm not sure how long it has been." Sarcasm was not really Gordon's strong suit but at least it did make Father look up from his desk. The disorderly papers were ignored now.

"It has been long enough, Gordon. Whatever you thought you might accomplish by being at the side of that person, surely you can see no good is being served by what you're doing. People across the country are shocked by what is happening here and you are helping to make these things happen. I can't tell you how sad it makes me to say such a thing about my own state, but please believe me I only say it from a desire that she will change. T. J. Davis is an evil man, and he does not deserve the support of good people like you."

Gordon's face was burning as though he had been scorched by the sun, or embarrassed by a cruel joke.

"No one is happy about the killings. You know that, and yet you try to use them against us. What you don't say is that things would be even worse if Governor Davis was not providing an outlet for people who disagree with you about the pace of change. I don't claim to be accomplishing miracles. But I am doing some good for my state. I'm not just standing on the sidelines and carping; I'm in the battle every day. What does it matter if Michael DeWitt would turn Escambia into Shangri-la? Everyone knows he can't win. How can I do any good if I'm not in the office, on the front lines?"

Father shook his head, seeming very old. "We say the same things over and over, don't we, Son? And neither of us can convince the other. You talk about how important it is to be in power, at the front lines. But if you can't do what you know is right, what difference does it make where you stand? You have given Davis every chance. You have influence and energy that you could use for the right things; why won't you use it for DeWitt?"

Father was right; they had been over this ground so many times they were both exhausted with it. Father would never understand, or believe, no matter how often Gordon had explained it: Michael DeWitt would never win. Nothing would change, and in some strange way that was a comfort. For if nothing ever changed, then Gordon would not make a mistake if he did not change.

In some way, the essential difference between Gordon and Father was that staying the course was basic to Gordon if not doing so meant the South itself had to change. Gordon knew that Father loved the South as much as he did himself, but what Father could not understand was that, compared to Gordon, he loved it in a different way, less completely, more conditionally. Like Michael DeWitt, Father was willing to say the South had its problems and could be improved by changing. What Gordon knew and what T. J. Davis knew was that the South was of a piece, a fragile and precious construction which, even if some tiny parts of it were wrong and everyone knew it, had to be maintained as a whole because once change was permitted it might not be possible to control. The South was under pressure to change its language, its economy, its social systems, its openness to outsiders, its pace of doing business, its sense of decorum and good manners. But to permit change in any of these could only weaken the other parts, so that in the end the precious and good things about the South (which were the majority) would be buried and adulterated. The region would be only another part of a homogenized America, indistinguishable from any other. All its special character would be crushed under the pressure of modernity and everything Gordon, and those who loved it as he did, cared about would be gone forever.

Gordon's thoughts were interrupted when he felt something touch his arm. This seemed to happen to him more and more, to be in his own thoughts, and then look up and realize he was not alone. This girl from the Atlanta newspaper — God, it seemed she had been in his life for years but he knew that was not right. What had it been? Three days? Three weeks?

It Was a Very Complicated Issue

The girl leaned toward him solicitously.
"Do we need to take another break, Mr. Halt?"

Gordon wiped his eyes with the handkerchief he was surprised to find in his hand. "No, no, I'm fine, let's go on."

Rebecca looked at her notebook, and then asked, "When did your father win the Pulitzer? Tell me about that."

Gordon smiled ruefully. "I know it was a long time ago because we rode a mastodon to the ceremony." The girl smiled politely; she would be surprised to know how long ago it really did seem to Gordon. He told her he had still been in college, of course, but now he thought it might have been earlier, before he went away to the war, but in any event a long time ago.

She asked him if it had been a "big deal," and he agreed that, yes, it certainly had been. The family had gone to New York for the ceremony; Mother could not entirely hide her disappointment that Father was not the sole honoree. They were on the campus of Columbia University before she remembered that Pulitzer prizes are awarded in journalism for a number of different categories. She had been a good sport about it, though, patting Father on the cheek and saying she was the only woman in Escambia whose husband had won a Pulitzer Prize.

"You must have been very proud of him," Rebecca said.

What a tactless question. "Of course. We were a newspaper family, so I had heard of the Pulitzer since I was in the playpen." The truth was it was a very complicated issue. Most people then or now don't know what a Pulitzer is and don't give a damn. The few people in Montville who knew what the prize was were the very ones who were angered by it. But he was damned if he was going to tell this reporter that. She already thought the South was a primitive place, as far as he could tell, and he certainly was not going to tell her that the *Courier* was nearly put out of business by this prize she thought so highly of. Advertisers in Escambia in the 1950s were not impressed. Besides, she already had DeWitt down as a hero; there was no need to add his father to that list.

Gordon had closed his eyes for a moment. Rebecca put here notebook back into her bag. "I think that's a good morning's work," she said.

Gordon invited her to stay for lunch but the girl said she had an appointment, which suited Gordon fine. She asked to come back in the afternoon. He did not object.

* * *

Thinking over the day's session with Gordon as she drove back to her hotel, Rebecca had the thought that there was something in her notes about somebody else's father. She didn't think it had anything to do with Professor Middlebrooks; it would have to be in the transcripts of the Billy Trask tapes.

When her laptop had booted up she opened the transcript files, using a search for the word "Daddy" in each one. It didn't take long to find the one she wanted.

"You know we were saying a little bit ago about how Southerners talk and all. I got a story to prove my point. You got time? When I was about eight or so I got my daddy a Father's Day card. The card said father, which threw me for some reason, like my brain had picked up some kind a warning. But I ignored it, and I got to thinking, well, the holiday is "Father's Day" and all the cards said that, and it seemed like the envelope ought to say the same thing as the card, so on the envelope I wrote "To Father"

Hah! People don't believe this unless they're from down here. He came in the kitchen and saw that card on the table. "To Father." He didn't say nothing but he got this look in his eye and I knew something was not like I thought it was s'posed to be. He turned to look at me while he was picking up the card, with just two fingers at the corner, like it smelled bad. "What the hell is this?" he yells, like I'm in the next county, and then he's grabbing my arm and pulling me close. "Are you trying to get smart with me?" he says. And I'm getting wet-eyed and quivering and I said "no sir" and then he opened the back door amd flicked that card flying into the backyard. "I ain't your goddamn father, I'm your daddy." Hah! Can you beat that? But see, he didn't want me sounding stuck up. That word was so formal, it just didn't hit his ear right. I guess he thought it was like making fun of him, as though I thought I was more high class than I really was."

[Laughter on tape]
"You know, something just occurred to me. I bet you fifty bucks Gordon called his daddy Father. What 'cha bet?"

You'd Make A Terrible Novelist

Margaret had Gordon's favorite lunch ready, chicken salad on wheat toast, and as he ate he talked about the odd feeling this story was giving him.

"This girl," he saw Margaret make a face, "-and I know I shouldn't call her that - this *reporter*, expects me to explain the history of the entire state, when she obviously finds it repugnant."

Margaret put a few apples slices on his plate.

"Her name is Rebecca, dear, you know that. She is only doing what reporters do which is just to make people explain themselves, not the whole world."

Gordon looked at her with narrowed eyes. Did she really think statements like that made him feel any better?

Finishing his glass of milk, he took a cookie from the tray on the table and went to the den to find his book. He was about two-thirds of the way through *The Mayor of Casterbridge* and once again realized how much he preferred the company of characters in books to certain real people (like that reporter), even when the fictional characters were really not very pleasant.

Gordon was deeply into his book when he heard Margaret answer the door. He would have sworn only a few minutes had passed since Rebecca had left the house, yet now here she was back again, like a bad penny. He was amazed that she always seemed so fresh. It seemed to him that they had been working for months, or was it years, of terrible, tedious labor; he felt near exhaustion. Yet here she was, straight backed in her chair and ready to work, he feared, until midnight if need be.

"We were talking about DeWitt entering the race," she said.

"And you already know that he did, and you already know he died before the election." Gordon made a face. "You'd make a terrible novelist. You don't have any surprises to work with." As soon as the words were in the air Gordon realized he had made a mistake; he had left an opening. He knew what she would say before she opened her mouth.

"You've never told this story before, Mr. Halt." She smiled sweetly. "I'm counting on you to provide the surprises. So, tell me what happened."

If asked, Gordon would have admitted that when these interviews began he enjoyed the idea of being a source for this story. He always imagined himself as not just a witness to history but a participant in it. Now, though, he saw a different side to this activity. He was tired in ways he had not been before, ways he had not known he could be, tired in ways that made him frightened that what he was tired of was his own life. His past was a desiccated husk he was being asked to poke and probe like an anthropologist. This examination was an activity he did not enjoy; one that made him wonder why he had ever thought history could be fascinating.

"I assume you want me to remark on my father's decision to endorse Michael DeWitt in the campaign. I also assume, however, that we have discussed the subject of my father often enough over the last few days that you already suspect I have nothing to say on that subject."

"I respect your feelings," Rebecca said with what appeared to be genuine feeling, "but you know I have to ask the question. It must have been embarrassing for you, to say the least."

Gordon sighed and shifted in his chair, his thin arms trembling with the effort. "To say the least," he repeated with a dry chuckle. "Yes, you can have that quote. But also be sure to say that my father's endorsement would not have mattered. The accident didn't change anything. If he had risen from the dead, Michael DeWitt would not have won that election. I know there are many still alive in the state who think otherwise. Well, maybe not many — I have outlived most of the ones who knew what I'm talking about. But I tell you, the people you're listening to are wrong. I was there. I know."

Now the girl looked uncomfortable, fiddling with her pen, pulling her lower lip between her teeth. It was clear she was deciding whether to ask one more question.

"The Governor must have been furious about the endorsement. That was why it was embarrassing, right? You couldn't get the vote of your own father?"

Gordon pushed himself up from his chair as quickly as his worn body could be driven, wishing he had the energy to stomp out of the room.

"That's enough," he said, wheezing. It pleased him to see the look of panic in the eyes of the girl; he was afraid his slow movements would keep her from realizing how angry he was. She started to say something, but he had no interest in hearing it. He held up his hand to hush her. "That's enough."

As he made his way back into the main part of the house, he heard the outside door close behind her.

A Serious National Campaign

A stack of papers crowded the corner of his desk, essays of anxious students, needing grading. Rebecca eyed them guiltily because she was here again taking his time away from his important work. But the professor, as always, seemed eager to talk.

"When Michael DeWitt died in that car wreck, many in the black community thought Governor Davis was responsible. The timing was just too much of a coincidence for us, I guess."

He gave a deep rumbly chuckle, rough and crackly as though things in his chest might be breaking loose. Rebecca wondered if she should be concerned. She had not been around elderly people much at all until this week, so she didn't know what sounds might mean real trouble (though the way things were going she might qualify as a geriatric nurse before this damn series was finally finished). This time all seemed well. Professor Fred hacked loudly two times more, then seemed to return to normal.

Rebecca let out the breath she had been holding. "I remember, professor."

He had turned to stare out at the quadrangle. A row of red maples waved slender limbs like a chorus line in the light breeze.

"But what we thought did not matter and T. J. Davis looked to be on top of the world after that election. He had been elected governor four times; his life-long rival was tragically dead. He not only was essentially the king of Escambia he had become a force in national politics. He was dreaming of Washington, there's no doubt about that." He sipped his tea, then turned back to face Rebecca.

"Of course the problem with being on top of anything is, you only have one direction to go from there." He chuckled at this homespun wisdom and looked again, but without much concern, at the stack of papers on the corner of his desk.

"I have always heard that Davis's phone started ringing off the hook before all the ballots were even counted. He had already been a huge force among those people who thought the central government was too strong, which was mostly the crackers who didn't want anything to change for black people. But for some reason after this election his popularity exploded. They say he was getting calls from all over the country offering money and support for a serious national campaign."

Rebecca made a note of the word - "cracker." She thought of calling Professor Fred on it - he's a black man using "cracker" against others, almost like the "n" word - but she didn't want to interrupt the story.

She enjoyed his memories but Professor Fred had not been inside the campaign, of course. Jeff had told her he was expecting something new in her version of the Davis story and it was becoming clear that the professor had very little to offer. She would have to go back to her most talkative source.

* * *

Transcript:

"...but who ever thought us country boys would have been going to our fourth inaugural ball? I enjoyed all of 'em, but that last one was just unbelievable; like somethin' in a dream. Mainly because it was a bigger crowd of more important people than we had ever been around. Of course, T. J. had given that speech at the national convention two years before, so I reckon I shouldn't a been surprised.

"There was people there from all over the country, there was television from New York and California, and oh my God there was money, money, money. I had hoped for it to be like this, but never really thought it would be. T. J. was different though. I think he had been waiting for this all the time. When I look back on it, it seems to me that he always knew he would have a national role to play. He had just been waiting for the country to find him. And now it had.

"*I will say one thing I didn't like about it. All of a sudden we were running around all over the place, all over the country really. I never did care for that very much. In just the first few months of 1971 we had been to Indiana, to Ohio, even to Pennsylvania and New Hampshire. It was amazing the crowds we got. Thousands of Yankees screaming for T.J. just like they woulda done if they was back in Escambia. I had never been outside of Escambia before and I was about as uncomfortable as a long-tailed cat in a roomful a rocking chairs.*

"*It didn't seem to faze the governor, though. He was pretty much talkin' the same talk as he woulda done right here at home, and he was just about as popular. Pretty soon there was stories about him on the nightly news and articles in Time and Newsweek. It was then we got the call to be on Meet the Nation, the most important news show on television. I believe that was the only time I ever saw Gordon get excited.*

"*We were all in the office when Gordon came in, grinning like the Chester [sic] cat, saying a producer in New York wanted the Governor to appear on the show. Gordon was jumping around so I thought he'd wet his pants, as though going on TV was just like getting into heaven. I was never in favor of it myself; I hadn't lost nothing in the North that I needed to go get, especially not in New York City. I always thought that if New York ain't hell the Good Book could be wrong; there might not be a hell a 'tall.*

"*But T. J., now he was another story. All he ever wanted was a bigger crowd to talk to and Gordon convinced him this was the biggest damn crowd you could get. There was a couple of problems though. The program was on Sunday, for one, and we'd be ridin' from the hotel in a big ole limousine for the other. T. J. didn't much like the idea of people back home wondering why he'd be doing politicking on the Lord's day and he sure didn't want no pictures of him getting out of a limousine bigger than some people's trailers. Gordon convinced him TV was a big enough deal that the home folks would understand that even the Lord would give him a pass to be on Meet the Nation. As far as the limousine went, Gordon said he could keep any pictures out of the local papers and the Yankees would think it made us look important.*

"*Gordon about drove us crazy, making sure we was up and ready to go to the studio that morning. T. J. Davis never slept past 6:00 a day in his life, so all Gordon's worryin' was just so much wasted energy, but that's just how Gordon was. He had to be directin' things all the time and thinking' nobody can get along without him. T. J. seemed uncomfortable while we was in the limo, like maybe one of his old teachers might see him and think he was getting too big for his britches. Me, though, I enjoyed that big old car. We deserved it, was how I looked at it. There was even a little bar in there I would of made use of if it hadn't been a Sunday morning.*

"Poor old Gordon was fussing over T. J. like a mother hen and, wanting to go over questions the reporters might ask. He gave T. J. a memo of some kind with questions he might get on everything from how the banking system works to foreign policy. T. J. looked at it real polite for two or three minutes, but then folded it and tucked it into his inside jacket pocket. 'This is an awful lot of work for nothing, Gordon,' he said. 'You know all they want to talk about is niggers, and I sure don't need to be prepared on that subject.'

"You shoulda seen the sweat break out on Gordon's face."

[Laughter]

"But T. J. was never much of one for preparation. He had a power when he spoke that came to him naturally, from heaven maybe, and I think he felt too much preparing might spoil things. He patted Gordon on the shoulder, telling him to relax. 'I don't need to worry about what questions they're gonna ask, Gordon. I already know the answers I'm gonna give 'em.'

"Gordon looked right miserable, with his advice not being taken and I laughed to myself watching him. He told T. J., just please don't bluster like you do, something like that. It would a made me mad if he had said it to me, but T. J. just laughed. Then Gordon said this wasn't going to be a stump speech like back in Escambia. 'They're going to try to make you look like a fanatic, like somebody who's raving. Don't fall into that trap by becoming bombastic.'

"I remember that word so well cause I'm not sure I ever heard it before. T. J. must a thought the same thing, 'cause he turned to me with this big question on his face and then repeated it, 'Bombastic!' in this booming, exaggerated voice that echoed in the limousine. 'Is that my problem, Billy, am I bombastic?' Then he started laughing, saying it over and over in different ways. 'Bom-BASTIC, BOM-bastic, BOM-bast-IC,' and now getting me laughing too, 'Bom-bas-TOC, Bom-bas-TAR,' and him saying 'like the Klan boys, the bomb-BASTARDS. Hey Gordon, maybe

I can use that in my speech. Vote for me and I'll try not to be such a Bomb-Bastard!' T. J. was laughing until he nearly had tears in his eyes and it was that much more fun for me that Gordon never looked more miserable.

[Laughter on tape]

"They had a room for us to wait in while the show was on. There was a big ole TV in the corner, the biggest one I had seen up to that time, and I remember how funny it seemed that T.J. was there with us one minute, then they came to get him for the show and the next minute there he was on that TV. We watched the governor take the first three or four questions and I looked over at Gordon and he had this big smile of his face. All the tension from this morning had drained right out of him. 'Look at him,' Gordon said. 'He's really doing it.'

"I knew what he meant. Watching T. J. on that black and white screen he was a different fellow. He was quiet and polite and looked for all the world like a college professor explaining things to a class that was maybe not his best students.

[Laughter]

"You could almost see the disappointment on the reporters' faces when this man from redneck country didn't act like a moron. I remember they asked him 'what is the real purpose of what you're doing?' He gave them a little smile, all patient like you would have to be with someone that asks such a damn fool question, and said his purpose was to give the government back to the people. 'This campaign is not about me; this is about all the people like me that the government just doesn't listen to. We don't claim to have a utopia in Escambia, anymore than you all have a utopia here in New York City where a person can't walk in Central Park after dark without getting raped or murdered. Every state has its problems, but those problems are best solved by the people who live there. That's the message my supporters want me to send to Washington. That is my only 'real purpose,' as you put it.'"

It Didn't Turn Out Like We Planned

R ebecca poured a glass of wine and looked over her notes from interviews, the Trask tapes and Jeff's history book. She took a deep breath and started the next section of her reporting.

<Davis Story - Pt.5>
By Rebecca Tanner
MONTVILLE, ES

Even T. J. Davis's fiercest political opponents admitted his appearance on *Meet The Nation* was a huge success. Rather than a racist firebrand, pundits said Davis came across as a calm, reasonably distinguished speaker articulating the need for government to listen to ordinary citizens.

Davis returned to Montville a different man, aides said at the time. Previously satisfied with being Governor as his life's ambition, he now believed he could move to a larger stage. He had always loved campaigning and been bored by the details of actually governing, so it is likely that the eighteen months after *Meet The Nation* were the happiest of his life. These were the months when, in speeches from one end of the country to the other, he found that the disaffected white lower or middle-class voters who were his strength in Escambia were also present in large numbers throughout the nation — including in states that had presidential primaries.

The winter of 1972 was a record cold one for Iowa but the Davis team didn't complain. "The welcome in those school houses and church basements was plenty warm enough. We never knew God had made so many rednecks," an aide was quoted as saying. Mainstream Democrats, troubled by the sudden appearance of Rebel flags on front porches or sprouting as decals on car windshields, moved close to panic when Davis finished a close third in the Iowa caucuses with twice as many votes as even his own supporters had predicted. Coming after his *Meet the Nation* appearance, the showing in Iowa made him a serious contender overnight.

When the Davis campaign garnered twenty percent of the vote in New Hampshire the result was considered an even stronger sign of his appeal. If his message could draw so many votes in a "Yankee" stronghold the Democrats had to take him seriously. In practice, that meant the party panicked.

The Democrats, though not usually known for unity, formed a solid wall to keep Davis out of the New York primary. He put up token resistance in the form of a half-hearted write-in campaign, but was secretly happy to stay out of what he referred to in the press as "the Pinko People's Republic of New York." In truth, the snub gave him a chance to resort to the tactic he had always found most productive: lose but claim you won. This had been his approach after "blocking the gate" to the University. The black students had been admitted anyway, but he could claim the role of defender of state's rights.

Days before the New York primary the campaign ran full-page ads in the Greenville S. C. papers screaming "Davis — the man they don't want you to hear." The ads portrayed him as the man party leaders were "afraid of." He won the primary outright, collecting 26 convention delegates and moving the Democratic Party from panic to outright war.

Davis's response to Democratic party resistance was to create the American Freedom Party. The tapes of extended interviews conducted in the late 1970's with Billy Trask, which have appeared in this *Constitution* series exclusively, give an insider's view of that decision and its unexpected conclusion (the *Constitution* has edited certain obscenities and racially offensive terms, but **parents are cautioned**):

"It was bothering (Davis) a whole lot the way the system was set up. Here he was running against the Washington power structure but having to run in a system they controlled; there was no way that was going to work. I'm surprised how long it took us to realize it. We went through the South

Carolina primary before we got the message real good. We won that one outright, even with the n****** voting against us.

"After that win and the showings we made in Iowa and New Hampshire there was lots of interest from people who wouldn't a touched us with a ten-foot pole before. All of a sudden we had money to travel to hell and back. I remember going to Dayton, Ohio, and thinking these folks live on good flat farmland just like we do. It had the longest, straightest streets I think I ever saw, like you laid it out with a ruler straight out to the horizon. We had three rallies there — one in the park, and two in various meeting halls around the city. After that it was Denver, Phoenix, hell, we even went to California. Weeks at a time we were gone, with T. J. giving speeches and press people following us like we was Waylon Jennings. Except for the war, I reckon it was the longest I was ever away from home. We was on top of the world. I don't know that we ever believed T. J. would actually be president but we woulda had a big hand in deciding who <u>*would*</u> *be. And there's lots of benefits that come from that, I can tell you. But of course, you know, it didn't turn out like we planned.*

"The night I finally got home from that long trip there was a car I didn't recognize on the curb out front and a man with a fancy badge was waiting in my living room. [Laughter]. Yeah, I can laugh about it now, but I'll tell you if you ain't never seen an FBI badge, it'll pucker your *** up real quick."

The FBI agents took Billy Trask to the federal building in Montville that night, to a windowless room with a metal table and four chairs, all painted an odd shade of light green. Trask was prepared to resist questioning. He considered himself a pretty sharp operator and he had watched *Dragnet* for years. He got a surprise though: the Feds weren't interested in asking him questions. They wanted to do all the talking.

They talked about Paul Titus who ran the Titus Coal Company and had made a fortune over the years selling his product to Escambia Power Company. Trask considered Titus a pal and had often had a drink or a meal with him while picking up donation checks for Davis's campaigns over the years. The Feds told Trask the dates when some of those checks had been picked up and how much they'd been for. "We have copies, Billy, if you'd like to see them," they said. Trask decided that wasn't necessary.

They talked about road builders and paving contractors Trask had been friendly with. They even talked about how a good road should be built, what kind of steel and supports go into good handrails and how the state roads Trask's friends had built didn't seem to measure up.

"Just so you know, Billy," they told him. "We've been to see all your old friends. Just so you know." That wasn't what they meant of course; what they meant was they wanted T. J. Davis to know.

About a month later the news stories started, always based on a "source close to the Justice Department," that the FBI had begun a probe into the misuse of public funds in questionable state contracts during the Davis administration. The U.S. Attorney issued a statement saying, "It is our policy neither to confirm nor deny such reports." Everyone who read that sentence thought they knew what it meant.

At first these stories only appeared in Escambia papers and had little impact; a local official who asked not to be identified said at the time, "the folks in Escambia would only have been surprised if a news story suggested politicians *weren't* crooks." The issue could not stay local, however, with T. J. Davis in a different state almost every week campaigning to be president of all the people, not just those accustomed to public corruption. Soon the wire services carried the stories to papers coast-to-coast and questions about payoffs and kickbacks followed Davis at every appearance. The campaign kept Trask out of sight, of course, and Governor Davis used the questions to his advantage, as much as he could. Obviously, he'd tell the crowds, his criticism of the Washington insiders was hitting home. Of course the bureaucrats were trying to shut him up.

But despite the public show of defiance, behind the scenes the stress was taking its toll. Several of Davis's biggest contributors were forced to provide records in response to government subpoenas. The FBI visited Trask's accountant to obtain his tax records for seven years. And a leak from inside the Administration reported that Trask's income had somehow grown to five times what it had been at the end of Davis's first term. Davis kept a public face of unconcern, but in the Capitol building shouting was often heard from the governor's office.

"I told you to be careful...damn it, I told you."

Because Davis had always been indifferent to money, he had badly underestimated the effect it might have on others. And because of his own indifference, the idea that Trask's pursuit of money might be his own undoing was enough to drive him to rage, especially when every week brought some new investigation or subpoena — or worse.

On July 20th, agents of the FBI paid a call to the home of Wallace Brookstone, scion of a prominent Escambia family, the grandson and great-grandson of state senators and himself the elected head of the Public Service Commission. Among its other duties the Commission was supposed to regulate how much Escambia Power paid Titus Coal, so the ratepayers were not abused. When rumors circulated that Mr. Brookstone had been pressured by Trask or Davis to approved high-price coal contracts, he had been politely requested to come downtown to the office of the U. S. attorney and, having failed to do so, was now to be invited somewhat more forcibly.

Two agents stood at the front door but no one came to let them in. As the two discussed what they should do, a third yelled from the end of the house that a car was in the garage. The roll down garage door was locked by a flimsy metal bar that slid into a slot in the rail, no match for the long pry bar that three agents used on the door. Inside the car, the agents found Mr. Brookstone sitting at the wheel, dead for hours, if not days.

As the investigation spread into more and more areas of Escambia government, T. J. Davis tried to deal with the political ramifications by spending ever more time outside the state. His strategy to portray the investigation as a political attack by Washington insiders and intellectuals was successful with his largely working-class supporters. Even though his press conferences in Illinois or Arizona became more and more contentious, the crowds at his rallies continued to grow. Historians looking back at that campaign have said that the center of American politics shifted forever. From then on, Washington was to be viewed with suspicion, and a generation of campaigners (including even those who were themselves U.S. senators) tried to claim the now popular title "outsider," and trumpet a determination to clean up the "mess" in Washington.

This historical shift was still in the future, though, when Davis was hoping to be president in 1972. He was the strongest third party candidate in U.S. history and seemed, despite his difficulties, to be gaining strength every week. But one of the most controversial events in American politics ended his campaign and his dreams of national office.

Transcript: *"I'm not too sure I remember anymore where we was when the invita-tion came. It was some big ole city so I was fairly miserable but they had a fancy auditorium for T. J. to talk in and there must a been 15,000 people there if there was a dozen. Afterwards we was backstage and T. J. was shaking hands and giving the bureaucrats hell, just really enjoying himself when Gordon …uh, you remember Gordon? … [Laughter] came up to him and took him off somewhere. I knew it had to be important 'cause T. J. didn't like to be interrupted when he was campaignin', so I went back to investigate. Soon as I walked in the room where they were, T. J. handed me a business card with a fancy printed gold and blue seal on it, but otherwise just a name. I had to look real close to see that the seal was for the Justice Department.*

"'They want to have a meeting,' Gordon said to me, then turned back to talk to T. J. The Boss's eyes were bright and those bushy eyebrows were bunched close together while he figured this out.

"'What are they offering?' he asked.

"Gordon shrugged. 'Who knows?'

"T. J. paced around the room, his hands jabbed in his pockets deep, like he'd rip the seams out. Then he stopped.

"'Tell him no.'"

"Gordon tilted his head, like he'd a been looking over his glasses if he wore any. 'Are you sure that's what you want to do? Because I think…'

"T. J. waved his big hand, cutting Gordon off like a pushy waiter.

"'No, to a meeting with the attorney general. I've talked to the attorney general enough, after that day at the University.' He gave a little grin, knowing the spot he was putting Gordon in. 'Tell 'em I'm the boss and I want to meet with the boss. I'll meet with the president. Otherwise,

forget it.' Gordon made a face and looked up to heaven as though asking, 'why me Lord?' Then he held up the business card, said 'I'll tell the man' and he was gone.

"Weeks went by. I had meetings with my lawyers and the state lawyers and the FBI and IRS, so you can imagine I didn't have time to think anymore about it until one morning I got a call from T. J. He wanted me to take a trip with him up to Huntsville, Alabama, where they was building rockets for the space program. As was usual, he didn't tell me anything more than he thought I needed to know. He always liked to keep things to himself — I suspect so there was no doubt about who was in charge.

"Gordon was with us, in the front seat by the driver. We set out early and were about three hours out of Montville, which got us up close to the northeast border of the state, when we pulled into a parking space on the Main Street of Whatley, just across from the old railroad station. I hadn't been in Whatley since the last campaign but I recognized Whitey Burgess right off, standing on the curb. Since he knew we would be there at a certain time, he obviously knew more than me about what was going on. Whitey shook hands all-around as T. J. thanked him for his help and apologized for all the secrecy.

"'I don't mean to be so cloak and dagger, Whitey, but I'd appreciate it if you keep this to yourself,' T. J. said.

Whitey grinned, pleased as punch to be asked for a favor. Of course he knew the favor would be remembered when he needed something. T. J. was always very anxious to keep the ledger balanced. 'Don't you worry about me, Governor,' Whitey said, 'I ain't laid eyes on any of you ugly cusses in near a year.'

"Gordon took a set of keys from Whitey and we climbed into his old station wagon, with those oak side panels just a' glowing in the morning sun. I admit I was a little slow on the uptake. Changing cars should have been a big clue. And even when we stopped just inside Huntsville so Gordon could make a call on the pay phone, it still didn't hit me. It was only after we waited at that convenience store for 20 minutes, when the black sedan with four men in dark suits drove up and we pulled in behind their car to continue our drive that I figured it out. I had seen enough

government agents in the last few months to have a good idea that those four fellows were on the same payroll.

[Laughter on tape. Noise of ice and glasses.]

"If you ain't ever seen it, it'll take your breath. Other than the First National Bank building, that airplane was the biggest damn thing I ever seen. They had pulled it way off to one end of the airfield, as far from the terminal as they could get and they had National Guard in jeeps all around it. A couple of the jeeps raced toward us when they saw we had plans to come closer to the plane, but the fellas in the car in front waved to 'em and talked a bit and they let us drive right up to them big stairs that led up to the door. It seemed like a thousand steps to get up there.

"I didn't get to see the president; that was disappointing. T. J. spoke up for me but an aide said only T. J. could go in, so that's how it was. Me and Gordon waited in this sitting room they had with leather chairs and paneling an inch thick that would have put T. J.'s office to shame. I got a drink — they had an attendant there could get you anything you wanted and it seemed like a time to celebrate — and Gordon had one too. He had gotten to where he could knock one back pretty good in the last few years after being a real pain in the ass teetotaler there for the longest. They brought T. J. back to where we were after an hour or so. We went down all those stairs, back to the normal world, and I will admit I walked slow, to make it last as long as possible.

"I gotta tell ya, fellas, I was nearly as excited as the first time I got a (sexual reference deleted). That's the kind of experience it was, knowing T.J. had the clout to get on that plane. That he was the reason the plane was even there. When we got back to the station wagon, we heard those big engines fire up and the plane was rolling before we went through the main gate. I couldn't understand, though, why T. J. didn't seem near as excited as I was. He was talking to Gordon about something, but real quiet like maybe it was where he wanted to go for lunch. In fact, I remember when we got back to the main road I said something to him, like that we really had everybody's attention now, and by chance right at that moment Air Force One screamed off the runway and flew right over our car. And I remember T. J. bent over to look out the window as that plane got smaller and smaller in the sky, with this little half smile on his face, and said,

'Well, Billy, I'll tell you. They're flying and we're driving, so I guess we ain't all that big a deal after all.'

"Of course he knew what had happened in that meeting and I didn't. It would be a while before I found out."

It would be five weeks before Trask and everyone else found out what would happen next. At a press conference outside his office in Montville, T. J. Davis suddenly announced that, having won two primaries and with his polling numbers showing him to be the most popular third-party candidate then or since, he was ending his campaign for President of the United States and throwing his support to the Republican candidate for that office, the incumbent Richard M. Nixon.

"The threat to our democratic institutions is too strong to take any chances in this election. The Democratic Party, which hardly deserves that name, has become so left-leaning and America-hating that I cannot risk the chance that the votes I receive will weaken the showing made by that great American, our president.

"I have much work still to do in my beloved home state and I plan to dedicate myself to that work and to continuing to be a voice for the common man, wherever in this great nation he may reside. Thank you and, to all those common men and women, may God continue to bless you."

Governor Davis refused to take questions from the members of the press that day, so any attempt at explaining this strange turn of events was purely speculation. That speculation boiled over, of course, when three weeks later the Justice Department announced it was closing its investigation into bidding practices in the Escambia state government. No charges were ever brought against Billy Trask.

In retrospect many suspicious people wondered what happened the day Air Force One spent a few hours on that Huntsville, Alabama tarmac. But that meeting didn't become public knowledge until some months later; President Nixon had already begun his second term.

It Was Code, But Not Secret Code

"**I** can almost feel sorry for them," Professor Middlebrooks told Rebecca. "Not quite, you understand, but almost. They were so close, T. J. and Billy, having come so far from being nobodies; they must have thought they were almost there, as though they were stretching out to grab the gold ring that is coming closer to their fingers each time around. And then just like that, as fast as a light bulb goes black, the ring is gone like a mirage which perhaps was all it ever was. All their dreams of being powerful, of being respected, unraveled like a worn hem. T. J. and Billy thought they were going to stop history and get some respect in the bargain — that's really all it was, rednecks wanting to get some respect. You see, that's why I can feel for them — I'm a black man, I know all about the hunger for respect. That's what it is, a hunger. You can't know what I'm talking about if you got into a good school or got a good job without really thinking about it. But I know.

"It had been obvious to me early on that if T. J. had reached out to *us*, to the black people of Escambia, we would have understood him better than anybody. Because we would have known what he was feeling: when he thought the Easterners with their good educations and proper speech were sneering at him, we would have understood; we knew all about being sneered at. And when he looked at college professors and newspapermen making fun of his country accent and he thought, *they're not good enough to criticize me*, we would have known what he meant. We were always abused, and by the least worthwhile white people. But he didn't reach out to us.

"Instead, he catered to the worst elements out of fear that he couldn't attract the best; fearing inferiority, he betrayed the only good instincts he ever had. When he first ran for office he was for good schools and good roads and giving people a chance. He supported government and the things only government can provide. But then he got so crazy for political power, so ready to sell out to any cause that would put him in a spotlight, that he seized on racism and then the code words for racism, so that finally what he said was "get the government out of our lives." And that meant let us deal with of our niggers like we always have. It was code, but not secret code; everybody knew what he meant. But he betrayed the people who loved him most because they did not think through what the code words implied. The fact is that getting government out of our lives is great for the rich folks, but it's a disaster for the poor, and perhaps especially Whites. His popularity made him a traitor to his own best nature. He permitted the Republicans to become the right wing extremists they now all are and encouraged poor whites to abandon the only party that ever helped them, just because it might also help some Blacks. That is the tragedy of T. J. Davis. He could have brought the lower class Blacks and Whites together, and shown them that they should be natural allies; no one else in our time could have done it. But instead he took the easy way, the tempting way of a cheap demagogue, and played right into the hands of our most cynical president."

* * *

Gordon pinched the bridge of his nose and took a deep breath. The glare off the bright paper hurt his eyes as he read these pages but he had wanted to stay outside when the Atlanta reporter came back to see him. Who knew how many days he might have left to enjoy his garden? He looked up at the honeysuckle on the short section of fence, thinking of what he'd just read. She must be nearly finished, he thought, if she's up to the meeting on Air Force One. Thank God. Gordon was so tired of this story.

"Very well, I've read Professor Middlebrooks's statement," he said.

"And?" She was almost childishly eager. "Comments?"

"What kind of comment would you like? What would give your little retrospective a snappy ending?" Gordon could not keep the annoyance out of his voice. "Should I just voice the opposite opinion from the black professor? Is that what your readers expect; point, counterpoint?"

He waited for her to object, to accuse him of being defensive or just crotchety. What he didn't expect was for her to half smile, close her notebook, and walk over to the fence section to lean her face into a mass of honeysuckle and breathe deeply. "It is unbelievable isn't it? That smell and the sunlight through these trees? No wonder you love it."

Give her credit, he thought — if anything could have disarmed him, this approach would have. She turned back to face him. "You are part of the record, Mr. Halt. Anything you want to say is valuable to me."

He handed the typed pages back to her and walked carefully back to the teak bench. He slowly lowered himself onto the seat, and then rubbed the slender wooden armrest with the flat of his hand. "Edward ordered this for me on the computer. He thinks that's a good thing." Gordon shook his head. "You probably do too." He looked at her mock-accusingly.

"Well, yeah," she said, as though there could be no question.

"It's generational, you see, like talking about my political career. You think the modern way is best because it is convenient and gives you many choices, but I know something you don't know. I know there was once another way to do things — that men in small towns sold furniture like this in tiny shops that had the family's name over the door. They raised children and paid taxes and you saw them in church on Sunday and during the week at City Hall and the PTA. Now that independent way of life is gone. But you don't defend the old system because you don't remember it and because no one has tried to point out that, despite it shortcomings, the old system had some real advantages." He rubbed his hands on his thighs, leaning forward slightly. "My career was spent trying to show the South has value and advantages worth saving."

"And you thought supporting Davis would do that?"

Gordon scrunched up his mouth and rubbed his temple. "Davis made people pay attention to the South and because of that I had an obligation to be proud and supportive of him. I felt the same way about

Hugo Black — the great Supreme Court Justice from Alabama who served on the Warren court and was as liberal as any of them. During the civil rights era, extremist groups wanted to impeach Black and asked for my backing. But I spoke against any such idea. A Southerner of national prominence had to be supported."

"But you didn't want black people to vote!" she snapped. Gordon was surprised by the emotion in her voice and she must have surprised herself for she lowered her tone before speaking again.

"I mean, you were on the wrong side of that question, weren't you?"

Gordon reached up to rub the ache behind his eyes. "We weren't opposed to Blacks voting, at least not permanently. We just wanted a reasonable amount of time to make what was a huge transition. But we all knew voting would happen sooner or later."

"And the Klan. They always supported Davis."

Gordon sighed. She would bring that up, of course; they always did.

"We minimized the influence of the Klan. No one gives us credit, of course, but Klan activities would have been much worse in those years if T. J. Davis had not been in office."

She bit her lower lip as she wrote in her notebook, something Gordon had now seen her do a dozen times. He had the odd sensation he had known this young woman for years. He wondered if he should tell her that biting her lip made her look even younger. Probably not. Instead he said:

"I suppose you're glad to be finishing up your story. I'm sure it will be very interesting." There was no harm in being generous; he certainly did not intend to read it.

She stopped writing and looked up at him with the slightest, absent-minded smile. I told my boss at the beginning, history is a lot different than news."

Now Gordon smiled. "My father didn't think so. He believed that old saying that a newspaper is the first draft of history. I think I told you, when strangers asked his line of work he would say, 'I'm in the history business.'" Something shifted slightly in Gordon's memory, an item tilted without actually falling from the shelf, and the item behind was exposed to his recall for the first time in years. It must have shown on his face because the girl said,

"And?"

"I haven't thought of this in ages. When I was still living at home and Father would say that, I would tell people 'I want to be in the history making business.' I must have been insufferable." He smiled at that young man he used to be, but the girl didn't laugh.

"But you were," she said.

"Insufferable?"

Now she did smile. "No, you did make history."

He pushed himself up from the chair with shaking arms. "No," he said. "Not like I intended. The South did change to become as frivolous and shallow as the rest of the country, and as apathetic about its past. I didn't make anything happen. History rolled right over me. That was hard to take, for a long time, but I've gotten used to it."

"My dad says we never really know who we influenced by the way we lived our lives, but we did have an influence that goes on longer than we do."

"I applaud your father's belief in the importance of a human life, and I would not lessen your own assurance in that regard, but I'll remind you that before you started this story you had never heard of Gordon Halt. Few people in this state have, leave aside the country. The things I believed in are gone forever."

Gordon instantly regretted the morbid tone. He could see he had made the reporter uncomfortable. She was still young enough to have some empathy with her subject. She'd grow out of that. Now, though he could see that she was struggling to decide whether to ask one more question. Finally, she did.

"Looking back on it now, did you think you were right to support Davis and segregation? Is there anything you wish you'd done differently?"

Once again Gordon thought he could not take her lightly. She might empathize with her subject like a rookie but she could still get to the heart of the issue. Too bad for her, Gordon thought, that he wasn't so sure he could do that himself.

Part Three

Being Southern is Something Different

Back To Breaking News

The next morning Rebecca checked out of the motel and was at the *Courier* office, saying her goodbye to Miss Amy, when Edward dashed into the room, out of breath. At the same time, Rebecca's pager began to chime. She recognized Jeff's number at the *Constitution* in the display.

"A sniper is holed up in a restaurant in Greenville. A couple of people on the street have been hit already." Jeff's voice was in her ear without introduction. He was in heavy news-gathering mode, somehow implying Rebecca had already fallen behind. "CNN is sending a truck," Jeff said. "Isn't that the town you were in the other day?"

"That's where the daycare center is," she said.

"Yeah. Well, get over there as soon as you can and scope the thing out. You've wanted to get away from history and back to breaking news. See who this nut is and what made him crack. If the story fizzles, you can still get back here tomorrow."

Jeff hung up without ceremony.

"Something's going on in Greenville," she said to Miss Amy.

"Edward told me while you were on the phone. He said CNN already has something about it."

Miss Amy suggested watching the coverage in the newsroom. Several reporters were gathered around the set when they walked in.

"… in just the last few hours. There is speculation in the community that the man in the abandoned restaurant may be Leon Threadman, described as a loner who has lived in Greenville his entire life, but there is no official confirmation on that."

The flat, professional voice came over the jiggling picture of a long, barn-like structure, old and worn, its wood plank side painted long-ago in dark red, now faded and flaking.

"This amateur video is from the scene in Greenville. You can see several vehicles parked askew on the side of the road. There are no details available yet but we are assuming these cars may have been hit by the gunfire that has been coming out of the building periodically. Again, this is amateur video so the quality is not the best. You may be able to see a puff of smoke in just a second...there, from that window on the left...which we assume must be rifle fire.

"We do know several cars were hit in the first volley. This video was taken right after that, so that would be about an hour ago. We are told a man was lying on the ground on the other side of this car, here, and that the police have now gotten to him. At least four people, and perhaps as many as six, have been transported to area hospitals. There is a report that the man on the ground has died, and also that a small child was in the car with him, but there is no confirmation so far. We will have a live report for you just as soon as our people can get in place on the scene."

An hour later, speeding down the two-lane road toward Greenville, Rebecca thought that these falling-in buildings and broken up pavements were beginning to feel familiar to her. She was already forgetting how strange this place had seemed when she first drove into Montville from the airport.

Nearing the small town, she slowed for the school crossings and slow moving logging trucks. Drivers in passing cars gave a little wave, as she had seen them do in Salem when she was with Gordon Halt, and she found herself opening a hand on the steering wheel and extending the fingers straight up to return the greeting. She pulled into a service station to ask directions to the restaurant the CNN broadcast had identified. "You one of them press people or you just nosy?" the red-faced attendant had asked. She assured him she was a professional but he did not seem entirely satisfied. After driving a few more miles she found the streets and lawns were dense with vehicles, like Christmas at the mall, except that many of these were marked with the call letters of networks or local stations. She parked in someone's side yard and walked toward noise and flashing lights. In a few blocks police cars and fire trucks and people in uniform mixed with people carrying cameras and microphones surrounded her in the confused scramble that is any live TV event.

Rebecca flashed her press I.D. as often as possible, but it didn't help; in this crowd, most of the people she showed it to were reporters or camera operators themselves. Finally, a young cop took mercy on her and pointed toward a clump of journalists surrounding a harried-looking officer trying to read from a notebook. It was impossible to hear him over the cacophony of dozens of questions being yelled at once. The officer stopped suddenly and held the notebook high over his head.

"Please let me read the statement, folks," he shouted. "This is what we know about this situation. If this statement doesn't answer your question, then we don't have an answer. You can see this event is still underway. Our investigation is just beginning. This is all we have."

The crowd quieted and he resumed reading.

"At just after 10:00 a.m. today, a black male experiencing car trouble pulled to the side of Powell Road in front of an abandoned restaurant. When he got out of the car, a number of rounds, perhaps as many as thirty, were fired from a semi-automatic weapon. The shooter is believed to still be in the restaurant building. More shots were sprayed at other vehicles on Powell and also into homes across the street. There were a few pedestrians in the area who ran for cover.

"The first victim took several rounds and the car was seriously shot up. A female child was in the back seat of that car and was also wounded. Those two victims were recovered by police and have been transported to the hospital.

"In addition," he continued, "six other individuals in cars that stopped to help were also hit and have been taken to area hospitals. The driver of one of those cars was dead on the scene. We were able to quickly remove the residents of the houses that were fired upon, several of whom were also injured. I believe four of those individuals have also been hospitalized. Finally, flying glass injured one police officer and a reporter for the *Ledger*. I don't believe those injuries are serious."

Rebecca was straining forward to hear when new shouts came from the direction of the restaurant. She looked around to see people pointing toward black smoke just beginning to pour from a boarded-up window. The spaces between the boards caused the thick smoke to flow in wide ribbons, like bands of black crepe unrolling into threatening piles high overhead.

One of the fire trucks began a slow roll toward the smoke. Suddenly gunshots sounded, bringing the fire truck to an abrupt halt. Rebecca could see flashes at one dark window twenty feet or so away from the fire. Soon bright orange flame licked out between the boards of the first window, replacing the smoke. As she watched, the flames appeared in the adjacent window. Oily smoke formed a dense and ominous thunderhead rising hundreds of feet above the restaurant like the special effect representing god or doom in an old movie. It seemed to Rebecca that time had stopped, except for the flame and smoke. Everyone - reporters, cops, and onlookers - seemed hypnotized by the blaze, almost reverential, listening to the roar of hungry flames consuming the building.

Then there was a pop. Quite distinct; Rebecca had no doubt it was another gunshot, but muffled. After a time, she could have been persuaded she had only imagined it, except that people all around her were speculating on its meaning.

The firefighters were the quickest. The hose truck operator yelled at his crew, "I betcha we won't have no trouble now, boys," and climbed behind the wheel. For the second time the truck slowly advanced toward the building, which was now more than half consumed in flame. As the truck approached, the end wall, now pure flame outlining the rows of remaining wall studs, surrendered to the forces of evil and gravity, collapsing inward, the rafters at that end of the building quickly following. The result was a huge splash of spark and smoke, as though the pieces had collapsed into a fiery sea.

After the sparks subsided, the truck moved in, hoses at full flow. This time no shots come from inside. Other trucks join the first one and for an hour the reporters watched the work many of them had dreamed of doing in childhood

The standoff was over. There had been no more gunshots and the fire, though not completely out, was reduced to a smoldering nuisance, like an illicit trash burn. The officer who had read the earlier statement came back, calling out for their attention.

"I have an update, people." The strain of the day was apparent in his voice.

"We have six confirmed dead, all of whom have now been identified. The male and the little girl were James Cooper, 62, and his niece, Rashanna Anders, age 8. In the cars that stopped to help, we have identified Thomas Allen, Roberta Kennedy, and Philip Watson. Finally, Sandra Madison was killed in her home across the road. All of the victims were residents of Greenville. Two other victims are in critical condition at Fairview Hospital. Those identities and conditions will be released by the hospital."

"Did the police start the fire?" Six or eight people were shouting questions, but that was the one Rebecca could hear most clearly.

"We did not."

The floodgates were now open and shouts of "Did you..." "Will the ..." and "Why was ..." erupted all around the officer.

"Hold it, hold it!" He was shouting now. "I can tell you, yes, we think the last shot we heard may have been the shooter taking his own life. That is not uncommon in these situations."

"And not unwelcome?" someone asked up front. The officer grimaced.

Another reporter spoke up. "There was a report the shooter was a local man named Leon Threadman. Can you confirm that?"

"That report did not come from our office. I have nothing on that."

"Was he crazy?" someone shouted from the back of the crowd.

The officer stared out into the crowd for a moment before answering. "We don't use that word for people who are ill. Some kind of mental instability is often a part of cases like this. It's hard to imagine there is any rational reason for it." The officer shook his head, then seemed to remember where he was. "That's just a personal opinion, though. The department has no evidence of that at this time. That's all for now. I'll be at the station downtown in two hours to give you whatever update we have at that time."

Rebecca watched him retreat and then could see the media crowd, as though it were a beast, scan its surroundings for another target to focus its immense attention on. She admitted a prejudice for print, but she thought even Ted Turner could not believe this chaotic, almost violent, process with its pushing and shouting could ever be expected to produce analytic journalism. A terrible event like this, if it could ever be understood at all, certainly could not be understood quickly, without analysis. But this process, which only buried a viewer under a mountain of unconnected bits of rumor, speculation and gossip, was almost a guarantee that comprehension would never be possible. Jeff was right. The reporters were all out gathering all these details, some of which were even true. But where was the story?

The cluster of reporters moved on but she did not go with it. The truth, if there was any, was not here; it was in the story of the tortured or evil soul who had started all this. She stood in the parking lot by herself, thinking, then looked down at her notes. Leon Threadman. He must be a piece of work, if his own neighbors could think he might be the shooter.

She looked up at the smoking remnants of the building, at the confusion and the sound trucks. Is this what you wanted, Leon? For CNN to know your name, if only for a day or two? She flipped the notebook closed. Jeff would say there must be more to it than that.

She started back to where she had left the car. The young cop had told her the press could view the scene close up after it was secured, but that was for television. Seeing the scene was not going to tell her what had been going on in the shooter's mind. That was what Jeff would want to know. The human context made the story and if you could not put the event into a context then it was simply random, like being killed by a tornado or a lightning bolt. Any intern could write those stories.

The human context would require some interviews. The only people she knew in this town were Ida Mae Brown and the group at the We Care Center - if she could only remember how to get there.

We Tolerate A Lot Of Oddness

S he had to stop twice for directions - first at a gas station and then at a convenience store, but soon she was pulling into the parking lot she had visited with Professor Fred and Tom just a few days before. Now, though, the parking lot around the plain brick building was filled and cars overflowed into the street, which seemed odd this late in the afternoon. She drove back out of the lot and found a space at the curb.

Her plan to get a quick interview and move on was shot as soon as she walked into the large front room. The space was packed with people, mostly black women and, as she looked from one face to another, it seemed each was crying or recently had been. The sound of soft sobs came from every part of the room, leaving Rebecca confused and disoriented. Then she overheard part of a nearby conversation and her insides went cold. "…and that sweet little girl wasn't nothing but a baby," the voice said, and Rebecca suddenly understood.

She walked quickly up to a woman she recognized from her previous visit. "The little girl was a student?" she asked. The elderly black woman nodded. Rebecca thought she might have seen the girl when she was here with Professor Fred.

"Greenville is a small town," the woman said. "So we know the folks that die, and if they got killed, we pretty likely know the folks what killed 'em." The woman introduced herself as Sadie Warren. "I seen you here the other day with Pastor Fred." Sadie said she had lived within ten miles of the Center for more than forty years. She was in her sixties but she still worked, "cleaning white folks houses. Least that's what I do for my money work. For my own self I work here at the Center two or three days a week. To be with my babies."

Sadie's voice broke and she dabbed her red eyes with a small wad of crumpled tissue. "Rashanna was one of my babies." She cared for the

249

five-to-nine year olds in the after-school class. "I ain't really their teacher, I'm just a helper you know. I enjoyed my own babies and my grandbabies so much at that age… You feel like you can still protect 'em." She sobbed quietly, her face in her hand.

Rebecca reached for a nearby box of tissues and handed a couple to Sadie. Clouds of crumpled tissue billowed from numerous trash cans. Rebecca almost felt she needed one herself.

"The television mentioned a man who may have done this." Rebecca fumbled with her notebook to find the right page. "Leon Threadman." She looked up at Sadie. "Would anyone here know who that is?" The question seemed bizarre, even to her, but Sadie herself had said what a small town Greenville was.

"We know him. His people have a little store on Mason Street and he'll some time be out there on the corner ranting about one thing and another. He's just a poor ole fellow." Sadie wiped her eyes. "He's not right in the head, but I don't know anybody ever would expect him to do something like this."

Rebecca felt a hand on her shoulder and turned to see Ida Mae Brown, who promptly enclosed her in a hug. Like everyone else, Ida Mae had been crying but seemed composed now.

"I thought you might be here," Ida said. "What a terrible day."

Rebecca asked for some details about the girl, Rashanna Anders. Ida Mae told her she had been coming to the center for three years, since starting kindergarten at age five. She was an energetic, bustling little thing, but had gotten much better in the last year at concentrating when given a "project." And her reading had improved noticeably over the last year. Sadie interrupted Ida to say that she did not do the reading instruction - "I been kinda learnin' my own self." That was handled by one of the younger volunteers, a teacher in the Greenville public schools.

"She was so sweet," Sadie said. "She would just smile so big at you if you paid her any little bit of attention. And if you had to get on to her about something, her little face would just crumple up like a old rag. She wanted to please people."

Rebecca looked back at her notes. "The little girl…Rashanna Anders, was with her uncle…?"

Sadie *hmmphed* and made a sour face. Ida Mae gave Sadie a quick, disapproving look, then motioned for Rebecca to follow her into her office.

When she was seated behind her small desk, Ida Mae said, "Rashanna is like many of our children, she has...had...a difficult home situation. Her mother has had some problems with drugs and like that. Mr. Cooper was the mother's uncle, and he spent as much time with Rashanna as he could, so the she'd have a man in her life."

Rebecca asked about the girl's Father, but Ida Mae looked at her as though that question was not asked in polite society. "I'm a reporter, I have to ask."

"The father's identity is not known to us here," Ida Mae said, stiffly. "We assume he is not part of the girl's life. I think that is why the great uncle has...had...tried to spend so much time with her." Ida Mae rubbed the side of her head. "This is hard for black women to talk about. We have held our society together for generations, and we have pretty tough standards for mothers. It hurts all of us to think there are cases like this. It's rare, I can tell you. I try to think about my own mother, my aunts, using drugs or drinking and letting some baby take care of itself. It's just impossible."

Rebecca nodded, understanding, yet surprised at the depth of emotion Ida Mae displayed. The issue was one a sociologist could explain, perhaps, but the fact was that however bad her mother was, that was not what had gotten little Rashanna killed.

"Sadie said she knew of this Leon Threadman? So you do too, I guess?"

Ida Mae nodded slowly, as though fatigue and grief had slowed her reactions. "His family's lived in town forever. He's been a little off since he was a boy. We always thought he was harmless, but he was definitely sick." She gave Rebecca a small smile, entirely lacking in happiness. "In a small town you tolerate a lot of oddness; it's not scary like it would be in a big city 'cause you know the rest of the family. Guess this time was different though."

Rebecca nodded. She recognized the look Ida Mae wore, the look that said suddenly she couldn't count on anything, her life could be upended at anytime. Newspaper reporters, like cops, see that look frequently.

Rebecca wanted to ask if Ida Mae thought this was racial. Did Leon just not like black people? But some of the victims had been white. And besides, Rebecca felt pretty sure that if Ida Mae could have found a racial angle in this she would not have been slow to point it out. Rebecca decided not to ask.

What she did say was, "I need to talk to Threadman's family. Could you introduce me?"

Ida Mae blinked as though she had just realized that Rebecca was working, not just a sympathetic visitor. The black woman just shook her head.

The Work Of A Lone Gunman

T he police station was only a couple of miles from the We Care Center and Rebecca was there in plenty of time for the next press briefing.

The same officer from the scene came to the front of the large central hall in the blinding glare of the television lights. He was a little heavier than ideal for his five-ten frame but solidly built. He was clean-shaven and the extra weight had not made it to his face; the cheekbones and chin were strongly contoured. He somehow conveyed both that he wished he didn't have this PR duty and that he would do it well.

"As I told you this afternoon, I am Sergeant Murphy of the Greenville Police Department. I would like to begin by relaying the prayers and condolences of our city to all of the families that have been so cruelly stricken by the violence today."

Sergeant Murphy stopped and looked down at the yellow pad in his left hand.

"I have an update from the last statement. The body of a middle-aged white male has been recovered from the scene of the shootings earlier today, and we assume this person must have been the shooter. Preliminary indications are that the body suffered severe burns and at least one gunshot wound. Cause of death will be determined by the medical examiner. I know there was speculation at the scene, but at this time we are not able to confirm whether the gunshot wound was self-inflicted. Also, I do not have anything for you on the identity of the recovered body. Are there questions?"

Immediately questions were shouted from every corner of the crowded room. Rebecca took notes as the sergeant responded.

Someone asked if the shooter was Leon Threadman.

The officer rubbed the back of his neck with one hand. "Let me repeat, I cannot confirm anything about the identity of the assumed shooter. We are waiting on the ME."

A voice near the front asked if the Threadman family was asked to produce medical records. "That is true," the officer answered, "we've asked the family for those medical records, but we've also asked for records of other persons of interest."

"Do the police have any ideas on motive or conspiracy?"

"We have no reason to think this was anything other than the work of a lone gunman."

"Is there any possibility this was a hate crime?" Rebecca looked around quickly to see if she could guess who had asked the question. When she looked back, Sergeant Murphy wore a pained expression.

"We don't have any indication of a motive at all, and certainly not that one." His forehead was deeply furrowed, as though he was weighing his words. "To be fair to our city, I don't think there *is* much hate in Greenville."

"Wasn't Threadman known to be mentally disturbed?" The sergeant's eyes narrowed for a moment before he answered.

"Mr. Threadman has family in our community. I have said we do not know that he is involved in this case. I certainly will not speculate on any unfortunate condition he may or may not have suffered."

Rebecca's reflexes kicked in almost before she realized it. "Have?" she called out. "You said 'he may *have* suffered.' Do you think Leon Threadman is dead?"

Now it was Rebecca's turn to receive the Sergeant's narrowed stare. "I misspoke," he said. "That's all for now."

* * *

She walked back to her car and sat quietly behind the wheel for a few moments, thinking of what she had learned. She was almost ashamed to admit she felt such a sense of relief. Jeff didn't fully realize the pressure he put on all of his reporters to go to the root of every story, and he certainly didn't realize how draining that process could be. Having spent exhausting days chasing the history of the Davis administration she was glad this one would be a quick wrap. Leon

Threadman was a nutcase and, based on Sergeant Murphy's slip of the tongue, had died in the fire, as the police would acknowledge tomorrow. A tragedy for all involved, of course, but not a big story. In fact, it seemed there was a nutcase killing every week somewhere in America. Now that probably is a big story, why do these crimes happen in the United States and not in other countries — but who had the time to figure that out? Rebecca certainly did not plan to volunteer, though she wouldn't be surprised if Jeff's febrile mind suggested it.

No, this event, though terrible, was random, like lightning striking. There is nothing to be learned from poor Leon. She looked at her watch. She could still get to Atlanta and be in her own bed before midnight, finish this thing up by phone tomorrow.

It occurred to her that Professor Fred had been able to arrange her interview with the white woman to talk about the private school. He might know someone who could help her get into the Threadman family.

He answered on the third ring.

"You read my mind," he said. "I was going to call you. There's been a shooting in Greenville, it's in all the news."

She decided not to get annoyed that he might think she didn't pay attention to the news, since that was, like, her career. She just answered, "Actually, that's where I am, in Greenville."

"Ok," he was thinking. "So you know about Leon?"

"Threadman? Yeah." *But I'm supposed to know about him*, she thought. *How exactly do you know about him?* But she didn't think she'd have to ask.

"They told me at the Center that one of their kids was shot."

"I know," he said quietly.

She waited for a moment but when he didn't say anything she went on.

"Some kind of pathetic sick person, apparently."

She waited again. This was not the conversation she had expected to have before leaving Escambia forever; it was turning out to be barely a conversation at all.

"Just a random tragedy," she said to fill the silence. She was about to ask for his help with the family when he finally spoke:

"Did the police tell you there was a note?"

Rebecca squinted, then rubbed the side of her forehead with three fingers. Was he playing some game with her, to keep her from going back to her real life in Atlanta? She had no desire to know about any note - she just wanted to get home - but she knew she had no choice if she wanted to keep working for Jeff.

"What note?"

You Never Know What Connections You'll Find

That phone call went on a good deal longer and was followed by calls to Jeff, at the paper, and to her mom. After checking in at a Greenville motel — Jeff had made the reservation before he ever called that morning — Rebecca had filed her initial story by email, making a reference to a "possible" suicide note and noting that this information was exclusive to the *Journal Constitution*. Jeff approved this wording as being loose enough to run in the paper before law enforcement confirmation could be obtained.

The next day, the Greenville police confirmed that the shooter's body recovered from the badly damaged restaurant had, indeed, proven to be that of Leon Threadman. When the press conference broke up, Rebecca hung around until her colleagues had finished their questions so she could have a word with Sergeant Murphy in private. The officer looked less intimidating close up. His face was sprinkled with light freckles she had not noticed before, but might have expected from the reddish tint to his short brown hair. He didn't seem as old as she had thought, outside the glare of the television lights. He did, however, seem exhausted.

"I haven't heard anybody ask if there was a note?" she said, making it a question like a teenager would. "I just wanted to be sure I wasn't missing anything."

The sergeant looked over his reading glasses. "I don't have anything for you about a note."

He continued to stare at her as she thought that over.

"Does that mean there's not a note?" She tried to sound as though she had not done this job before and needed a nice man's help.

"It means I don't have anything for you. Is there anything else?" He was still staring at her. Apparently he didn't consider helping reporters to be what he was paid for.

Rebecca said "thank you" as sweetly as she could and left.

* * *

So that was how Rebecca came to be standing against the wall at the Threadman home, trying not to be a disruption. Three days had passed since her call to the professor and the press briefings with Sergeant Murphy, since the morning when she had first heard of Leon Threadman, since she had hoped to be back home in Atlanta by nightfall. Since then she had been to Leon's house several times and had come to know members of his family. She had, just this morning, attended his funeral. Now, after the pathetic ceremony, grieving people in the small house surrounded her.

Leon's sister sat with an uncle on a sofa of brown vinyl. A small tear at the edge of a seat cushion revealed cotton batting. A person who had been described to Rebecca as a "neighbor lady" brought coffee in from a tiny kitchen just off this room and placed the tray of mismatched plastic cups on the metal dining table on one side of the room. When the neighbor handed a cup to Leon's sister, she took it with shaking hands, sending a few dark drops to the floor. The neighbor lady bent to wipe it up from the gray linoleum, which reminded Rebecca of the floor of a diner. The sister placed her mug on the ring-stained coffee table in front of the sofa. This rested on a small oval rug of contrasting bands of rust and pale green which was the only floor covering.

Jeff had, of course, been delighted that Rebecca had an "in" into the family, though he was a little fuzzy on how she had managed that. She told him that was why a reporter wants to stay on good terms with sources; you never know what connections you'll find. The professor had spoken to Susan, the private school mom and learned that she had a close friend who, Greenville being a small town, was a best friend of Leon Threadman's sister.

Susan felt Rebecca had been fair with her about the school story, and so she assured her cousin that Rebecca would not sensationalize

Leon's story, that she would make it as balanced as circumstances permitted. In the end, with dozens of reporters crowding the front of the house, Rebecca was the only one who'd been allowed in. Her first visit had been on the day after the shooting; she had not even asked a question that day. The atmosphere of shock and despair would have made an interview pointless; she just stood in the room quietly, letting the sister get used to her. She did, however, finally get to see the note. Covering several sheets of lined notebook paper, hole-punched for a three-ring binder, the writing had the odd spelling and jerky, irregular scrawl of a child's.

* * *

On that first visit to this run-down little house, standing near where she now stood, she had listened to Leon's sister tell Susan about how sick he had recently been, and how agitated by worries that the family could not understand. He had heard voices for years, getting messages from the television or a radio that no one else heard. But lately the messages were aggressive and Leon seethed with anger much of the time, for no reason his sister could understand. Rebecca had hung on every word, but she didn't make notes.

Diana Threadman had watched her brother move farther and farther from reality for the last five years. She took Rebecca through the stages: the first random "oddnesses"— weird leaps of logic, abnormal gestures and a slight ironic smile, as though he was in on some joke he thought you were playing on him, so subtle that only family members recognized anything odd about it, and swings of mood, from bottomless despair to irrational euphoria to sputtering rage, with no apparent outside stimulus, culminating in "conversations" with unseen voices or TV personalities.

"We felt so guilty," the sister said, "that we couldn't make him better."

Afterward, Rebecca had returned to her room at the Greenville Inn and called the office. She emailed in an "aftermath" story, the standard day-after piece about a small town trying to return to normal after a spasm of senseless violence. Did these stories get written anywhere other than America? she wondered. Did Europe or Asia have

"Columbines" or "Wacos" — single words that conjure national nightmares?

Jeff agreed that she should stay in town to cover the funerals. Bulky gray clouds had covered the sky this morning; Leon Threadman would go to his reward in an intermittent light rain. Diana had invited Rebecca to go to the funeral with the family and so, without a camera or notebook, she was the only member of the press in the bland funeral home chapel. A mournful tape of organ music played through small, hissing speakers. Rebecca wondered if these tapes were bought from a catalog, generic funeral music mass marketed for these chapels.

Diana sat with the rest of the family on the front row while Rebecca had a pew to herself a few rows back. The chapel would have held two hundred people, but no more than thirty were present, in groups of two or three. The brown casket sat on its wheeled bier in the center of the alter area, a spray of carnations on top in a field of greenery. A framed picture of Leon in his early 20's and dressed in coat and tie had been placed among the flowers on the casket.

Rebecca had not been to many funerals, but she could tell the young man who walked to the lectern was an employee of the funeral home. He made a hand signal for the taped music to be turned down, and then began reading a form of service. Even given the difficult circumstances of Leon's death, it seemed strange that nothing whatever was said about his life. No family member spoke and the things the young man said were the bland reassurances of a commercial sympathy card, addressed to no one in particular.

It was obvious to Rebecca (though, out of tact, she would not say so when she wrote her story) that the young speaker had never met Leon and knew nothing about him but his last horrible outburst. No school friend, no lover, no mentor spoke for Leon. He was tended by strangers on his way to eternal rest, strangers and his shell-shocked family who perhaps made, after all, only one more set of strangers.

At the graveside, rain drizzled from the green canopy protecting the casket, which rested on canvas straps above the open grave. The young man from the funeral home read the twenty-third psalm. After a prayer, he motioned to an assistant and the casket was gently lowered, slowly disappearing into the ground. Rebecca watched as a pallbearer unpinned his boutonnière and dropped it into the open grave. No one spoke on the short drive back to the house.

He Didn't Never Hate Nobody

R ebecca placed her coffee mug on the dining table, thinking once
again how small these rooms were. A particle board china cabinet,
veneer peeling off one high corner of the side, pressed itself snug
against the wall, barely leaving space for the table. Leon's funeral had
ended one hour before.

"His room is back here," Diana said. It was only three long strides
down the "hall" to the closed door where a length of yellow crime scene
tape lay crumpled on the floor. Diana kicked it out of the way. "Did
you know they really use this?" she asked. "I didn't. I thought it was
just something the police did in movies."

She opened the door and they walked in. "I told the police I
wouldn't touch nothing on the walls, but you can look."

The room was small and overstuffed, with a compact chest, a bed
and an end table. Two metal windows were hung with faded draperies
which Diana now spread open. In the light, Rebecca could see the
small room was furnished for the boy Leon had once been. The single
bed, chest and table were all of oak in a clunky design that suggested a
western bunkhouse. The front of each drawer and the headboard
featured a horse's profile in black metal. A mirror hung over the chest
in a wooden frame with a rope design carved to form a looping lariat at
the top, trailing into a border around the sides.

The other objects in the cluttered room broke the effect of child-
ishness. A large Confederate battle flag served as a bedspread. Two
walls were covered with pictures and clippings thumb-tacked into
groups, a hand-lettered sign above each. So there was an area for
"Confederate Pride," where pictures of soldiers on horseback were
labeled as Robert E. Lee, Stonewall Jackson, and Nathan Bedford
Forrest. Several articles urged that the Confederate flag remain on the

capitol building in Escambia. There were also more modern pictures, black-and-whites from a cheap printer, of various men she did not know and one she did. A balding man held what looked like a short baseball bat in a threatening pose. The name "Lester Maddox" was printed under that one. There were others, usually of white men standing at microphones, but they were unlabeled.

The ones Rebecca recognized were the shots of T. J. Davis. In one he held his fist up to the camera as though about to throw a jab. In others he addressed crowds, either from a formal podium with microphones arrayed before him or, in several cases, speaking to a small group while wearing short sleeves, his tie either loosened or removed. A flag like the one on Leon's bed appeared in each of these pictures, either on the podium or carried by a listener in the informal shots.

This section also featured hand written quotes on 5x7 index cards. Rebecca copied a few of these into her notebook:

"Segregation is God's plan. He separated the races at creation; we merely respect His divine will." — T. J. Davis.

"No colored boy is going to sit beside our sweet little girls at school while I draw breath." - T. J. Davis.

"Our new government is founded upon ... the great truth, that the negro is not equal to the white man; that slavery is his natural and normal condition." Alexander Stephens.

Under a "Black Racists" label a close up picture of a middle-aged black man in coat and tie had been defaced with a large X in what looked like white shoe polish. Where the name was printed below the picture, the last name had been scratched out and written over so that "King" became "Coon." A black-and-white photo with torn edges showed three men on an urban street. One was in a white robe, another held up to the camera a large poster reading "Death to Race Mixers." The "Federal Oppression" section included a clipped article claiming that the 14th Amendment to the U.S. Constitution was, itself, illegal. There was also a picture Rebecca had, by now, seen many times—the famous shot from *Life* showing T. J. Davis in the door of the University of Escambia, denying entry to black students. A nearby rectangle read "Stand Tall for Escambia," a photocopy of a Davis bumper sticker from more than 30 years ago.

Rebecca did not take the time to read everything on the walls. She did make note, however, of a sheet of lined notebook paper, which had been scrawled on in dark marker. "Roll of Honor" had been written in crude block letters and four names entered below that one under the other. The handwriting veered erratically across the page, giving a clear view of the mental distress of the writer. Rebecca copied the names into her notebook: James Earl Ray, Byron De La Beckwith, Roy Bryant, and Bobby Frank Cherry.

Compared to what she saw on the walls, the collection of everyday objects piled on top of the wooden chest seemed weirdly normal. A hairbrush with strands of Leon's hair, nail clippers, letters offering a pre-approved credit card, a coupon for a free drink at McDonalds, deodorant. Above these, a Nazi flag the size of a postcard was taped to the mirror.

Thinking of her own room, Rebecca suddenly wondered, where are his books? She turned to sister. "Did he read?"

"Naw, couldn't hardly. Just short things like *TV Guide*, some sports in the paper." She paused and something she thought of changed her face. She went to the chest, and rummaged in the second drawer.

When she turned back toward Rebecca, she held a stack of loose papers.

"He did have these things." She looked down at them uncertainly, as though these pieces of paper might embarrass the brother she could no longer protect. She placed the stack of paper on the Confederate flag and stepped back from the bed so Rebecca could thumb through the collection. The papers were newsletters and brochures and without looking closely it was apparent they were confederate- or racial-themed.

Diana kneaded her fingers. "We ain't never had no problem with the coloreds. I knew it was his sickness doing it to him. I told him that but he'd fight you if you tried to throw away any of this junk." She blinked hard, making Rebecca think she might cry, but she collected herself after a moment and continued.

"It wadn't really him, you know? Leon was always a sweet man; he didn't never hate nobody."

"I know," Rebecca said, having to say something. She turned back to the bed and picked up some of the papers.

"I notice a lot of these are printed. Did your brother own a computer," she said.

"No, not hardly," Dianna said. "He told me though he learned about 'em at the library and used the ones they have."

"Do you think I could take a few of these?"

Leon's sister looked thoughtful. "There's so many, I reckon it wouldn't hurt nothing. The police have already seen them." She flipped through the ones Rebecca held, as though to be sure no family treasure had inadvertently been included, which seemed funny until she said, "I want 'em back, though. They was his."

The phone rang and Leon's sister went off to answer it. Rebecca spent a few more minutes in Leon's room, looking around at the pictures and clippings on the walls. The sick man had turned this cramped space into a temple to a bizarre faith, one that must have many more adherents than she would have thought possible; hundreds, if not thousands were writing these articles and maintaining the websites that had lured Leon. She thought about what Mom had told her just last week. Forty years ago Escambia had been another country.

Maybe part of it still was.

There Is A Natural Order

hree folding tables had been pushed together for a makeshift
conference table at the We Care Center. Professor Fred and
Rebecca sat around it and worked their way through the stack of
brochures and newsletters Rebecca had piled in the middle. Carnetta
was stationed at a green metal desk before the glowing computer
monitor. When the professor would read out the name of a group
from one of the publications, she would run a Google search and
print out any interesting hits. Rebecca then went through the resulting
pages.

"You wouldn't think some of these people were smart enough to
even use a computer," she said as she read one printout.

Carnetta nodded. "Just the names of the groups are enough to give
you the creeps. 'White Citizens Defense,' 'Aryan Protection Corps,'
'White Might,' 'Confederate Future,' 'New Confederate Alliance.'" She
turned to Professor Fred. "You're the expert; have you heard of any of
these before?"

The old man closed the brochure he had been reading. "I'm not
sure. There were dozens of these groups in the old days and all the
names were rather similar. There are only so many ways to combine
confederate and white and protection."

"Speaking of names." Rebecca had just recalled the list she made in
Leon's room. She bent over to find the page in her steno pad, then
flipped to the right page and handed the pad across the table to
the professor. "Leon had these on a 'Roll of Honor.' There are one or
two I don't recognize."

The professor's lips moved slightly as he read. "Hmm" he said,
looking up at her. "Not a good group. Byron De La Beckwith
murdered Medgar Evers, who had integrated the University of

Mississippi." He thought for a moment, then said "Bryant, hmm" and turned in his chair toward the door to Ida's office.

"Ida," he croaked, "wasn't Roy Bryant the one who was convicted in the deaths of the three boys they buried in that dam?"

Ida Mae came to the door shaking her head. "I could have lived a lot longer and been just as happy not to hear that name again. That was him all right."

Fred turned back to the table, nodding, "OK, you've read about Bobby Frank Cherry, one of the Klansmen who bombed the church in Birmingham that killed those four little girls. That was in the fire hose days. The feds have been saying they're finally going to bring him to trial." He reached to hand the steno pad back to Rebecca. James Earl Ray did not require comment.

Rebecca looked back at the table and picked up another copy of "White Man's Burden," a newsletter published by something called the Alliance for White Progress. Several issues had been in the material Leon's sister gave her. This one was only eighteen months old. The cover story was an angry tirade against the city council of Chattanooga, Tennessee. Apparently the city had refused a request by the Alliance for White Progress for a parade permit through a predominately black neighborhood of Chattanooga.

"This high-handed denial of our rights to assemble comes from a city government that kow-tows to a noisy colored population while ignoring the interests of the majority race. This is not the first time the AWP has been victimized - we who stand for racial purity must expect this treatment because we speak the truth others do not want to hear. There is a natural order created by God and we must risk humiliation and victimization to stand up for that natural separation God created between the races.

"The city speaks of a fear of violence if we are allowed to march, but a great leader of our cause has said "there is a righteous violence: we become the hand of GOD to smite those who would overturn the laws of Nature. The race-mixers, the communists, the atheists, all of them will feel the wrath of the God whose laws they would ignore. *"

"We do not advocate violence until we have no other means of defense. But can anyone doubt that the opposition to our rights has been violent? Were not the hostile shouts against us in that council chamber a form of violence?"

Rebecca almost smiled at the asterisk. One didn't expect this kind of material to be footnoted. The note at the bottom of the page read "*Thanks to our brother Colton Jenner for finding this quote from the great days of resistance." It seemed odd to Rebecca that the writer would print the quote in bold and then not attribute it. And what did "great days of resistance" even mean? Maybe the quote was so old no one remembered who had said it. One thing for sure, these southerners loved to quote things. Leon's walls had been covered with…

A sudden memory jolted her upright in her chair and she read the quote twice more, and then excitedly reached for the professor's arm. "Look at this - the part in bold."

He read it quickly. "Pretty bad," he agreed, "but at least it's old."

"No, no," she said impatiently, "the newsletter it's quoted in was printed last year. But that's not the point anyway. Look at 'righteous violence.' Don't you see? It's in the note."

"What…?"

"It's in Leon's note."

She was already flipping through her pad to see where she had copied the note. She found it and passed the pad over.

"It can't be a coincidence. He got it from them."

He gave her a quizzical look. "How could you even remember that?"

Rebecca shrugged. "I'm a detail person."

She took the pad and newsletter back from him and continued reading the article. "Listen to this."

These noble words remind us that we have a sacred duty to protect our race, and a tradition from those great days of the 1960's when valiant defenders of the South were not afraid to match words with actions. The time for such bold action - has it come again?

Rebecca stopped reading and looked at the two men opposite.

"That's incitement, isn't it? Aren't they asking their readers to do what Leon did?"

Her heart was pounding as she thought about the story this would make. She was composing the lead in her mind when she remembered.

"Oh, damn."

"What?"

"We've got to go see Sergeant Murphy. I can't sit on the note any longer, not after seeing all this." She indicated the papers strewn on the table.

While the professor called Murphy's office Rebecca packed up her notes and the printed pages. She asked Carnetta to check the web for any mention of Colton Jenner. She and Professor Fred were almost out the door when she stopped suddenly and came back to where Carnetta sat.

"While you're at it," she said, "see if you can find out who Alexander Stephens is."

"Sounds like a pretty common name," Carnetta said. "Anything I can add to the search to narrow it down."

Rebecca clucked her tongue, thinking. "Yeah. Put in the word 'slavery.' That should narrow it pretty well."

* * *

Rebecca wasn't sure she could get used to calling the sergeant "Corky." He was a nice guy though, just a little surprised.

"What the hell are you talking about?" He had asked after Rebecca described the brochures and articles she had taken from Leon's house.

"You didn't know about this?" Rebecca asked. "His sister Diana said the police had checked out Leon's room."

"I'm sure we did," Corky said. "I hope my guys just figured it was a lot of garbage like you see sometimes and left it at that."

"Whatever," Rebecca said, uncertain how she was supposed to take that statement. "The point is that this material proves the note wasn't just an irrational outburst of some madman. This was intended to be a racial attack. If your department wants to make some statement I'll be glad to include it in my story."

The sergeant leaned into the table, propping his upper body on his elbows, and sighed heavily. "I just hate this, you know? This is not what the South's about, but it's all people outside ever see." He cupped his chin in one hand. "I'll bet you there's not five thousand people all told in all these groups put together. And half of them aren't even based in the South. Then if you take out the people like me who love to study the Civil War and admire the bravery of the men who fought, on both sides, that number comes down even more. It's just not fair."

Rebecca listened, interested but impatient. She wanted to get her story filed quickly—she wouldn't be the only one to find this connection. But she understood the sargeant's concerns. She thought about telling him that she had become a sort-of booster of the South in the last few days. But it wouldn't change anything. This was an important story and she had a part of it no one else had.

These Things Exist Out Of Sight

Greenville Gunman
Pushed by 'Net Racists
by Rebecca Tanner
Greenville, ES

The *Constitution* has learned that Leon Threadman, the mentally unbalanced shooter in the rampage that left six dead earlier this week in this small town in southeast Escambia, left behind a note stating his intention to kill African-Americans. Threadman was apparently motivated, in part, by self-styled "Neo-Confederate" web sites and other internet sites that foster white supremacy philosophies. The Constitution has also learned that one of these sites was the source of inflammatory language Threadman included in the note he left behind (the spelling and punctuation are in the original):

"The time has come for me to join the battle to save the South Way of Life. White people is being driven off this land we made, because the strong leaders we had in the '60s have gone on ahead and now we are timid and scarred to do whats rite. This got to change and I must help. God wants the white people to lead and for the race to be pure as he made them. God wants us for the soldiers. Violence is not the first thing we should do. But there is a righteous violence — we become the strong hand of God to smite those who break and laugh at the laws of nature. I saw our soldiers fighting the dark people in Iraq and I know I have to do the same here at home. I'm called to fight for the bless South."

Rebecca was pleased with the story, which went on to quote the Alliance for White Progress web site that originally contained the "righteous violence" speech, and to detail other racist content on the Confederate Defense Coalition web site. Jeff's e-mail, after this story

270

appeared on page 1, included another of his quotes, calling it, "good advice for an amateur historian, Becko." She gritted her teeth at the nickname but, reading the quote, decided he was probably right. Again. She printed the email at the Courier offices and taped the quote to the mirror over the motel sink.

* * *

Rebecca was rummaging in the trunk of her rental car, deciding what files she needed to move into the motel room and which she could leave in the car until she (finally) got home to Atlanta, when she came across the flier about the Confederate flag controversy she had been given that first day on the capitol grounds. The logo of the Sons of the Confederate South was centered at the bottom. Along the left margin she now noticed a list of names of the executive committee. She studied the names for a moment before going inside to use the phone. Carnetta answered on the second ring.

"Hi. While you're doing those searches I asked you for, how about adding these names to the list?"

* * *

The sergeant's office was a madhouse. Rebecca had thought (but kept it out of her stories) that, compared to Atlanta, on the normal day a lot of these little town offices seem like playhouses, they were so small and insignificant. If there were only 3,000 people in the "City" was it really that hard to be the Mayor? Or chief of police? It was like all these people were school kids playing at being grown-up.

But this was not the normal day and now, in the glare of lights from CNN, Fox and MSNBC, Corky Murphy — Sergeant Murphy — looked like a very grown-up figure indeed. Murphy opened the press conference by noting that Leon Threadman had been buried two days before, that the Cooper and Anders family fatalities would be buried tomorrow and that the immediate determination of guilt was over. He paused before continuing.

"Yesterday I said that I didn't think there was much hate in Greenville. I said that from my heart and with sincerity but now I have to change that statement at least a little and admit that there are strains of ugly racial hatred that do exist here. I have learned these ideas fester in our city out of sight of the decent people who make Greenville the community that it is. The presence of racism on the Internet is like an unseen virus working harm until it bursts out like a sickness when it reaches a certain level. But this evil is made even more repellant to us all when the hate-mongers tie it to a false and deceptive appeal to Confederate loyalty and memory."

Sergeant Murphy took questions for a half-hour, perspiring lightly under the TV lights. He ended the press conference with the words "I'm sure many of you plan to attend the funerals tomorrow. We are asking that there be no photos or filming on the grounds of the church itself and, I hope it goes without saying, inside the church building."

Far From The Peaceful Shore

A s a gray-haired lady in a summery print dress played an ancient organ that wheezed slightly out of tune, Rebecca thought that very few people her age ever had to go to two funerals in a week. Some people might say she should find a better job.

The concrete block structure was plain; even a stranger could tell this was not a prosperous congregation. It was, however, a large one. Looking at the crowd, she estimated more than four hundred, predominantly a segregated group. There were perhaps fifty white people — she saw Sergeant Murphy, of course, and she would bet that every white politician within a day's ride had shown up — but the majority of the crowd was black. A sizable part of the group was family. The child's obituary notice from the local paper ran almost six column inches. The list of "survived bys" included nine aunts and uncles, four great aunts and 22 cousins.

At the front of the church two caskets, one full-size the other much smaller, rested end to end, separated by a small table. Both caskets were open and the uncle and his young niece lay as though sleeping, hands folded on their chests. Rebecca had been part of the crowd that filed past before taking a seat. The man was dressed in a dark suit and crisp white shirt, the little girl in a frilly dress. An elderly woman standing a few places in front of Rebecca had leaned over the little girl's body and said "the Lord's gone be glad to see you, baby," as she patted her hand. Turning her head, Rebecca had seen on the small table a framed picture of the uncle holding the little girl high in the air, both of them laughing with every part of their faces.

Rebecca opened the program she had been given in the foyer, thinking she had not seen a program for a funeral before. A young woman came up on the podium when the first hymn had ended. She talked about learning English from Mr. Cooper, the uncle, when he taught at the high school. She told the crowd that she had been to visit him just six months ago. He had his niece with him that day, too, showing her off while he listened to this young woman who had come to tell him that she had recently won a job as an English teacher, something she wanted to be because of the example he had set for her.

The minister told his memories of baptizing little Rashanna. The great uncle had stood beside the girl's mother that Sunday morning, proud as a grandpa. Over the next few years, the girl had begun church school and, this past summer, her first vacation Bible school. She loved to finger paint.

The program indicated there would be six speakers, each a witness to some part of the life of James Cooper or his niece. Each providing some testimony of how much, in this community, they would be missed.

And between each speaker, a song. So that when the preacher finished the congregation began…

I was sinking deep in sin
Far from the peaceful shore

And as those voices rose round her singing in parts, with flourishes Rebecca could not recall in her own church, she was brought back to a memory of the thin singing of only two hymns she had heard at Leon's funeral. Was it only three days ago?

Thinking of that now, as Ida Mae Brown came to the front to speak, Rebecca knew she had a story for Jeff in the contrast of these two funerals. The same ritual for the same purpose, but entirely different in spirit, and message. At the end, the congregation had risen and formed a line all around the church to march in progression past the grieving family, giving hands and hugs and the eternal, ordinary, irreducible, words of consolation and concern, all the while singing yet another hymn, the walls reverberating with the refrain,

No more crying now,
We are going to see the King.

She Met One Of Those Guys
The First Day

A fter the funeral, Carnetta had come up to Rebecca in an agitated
state. "Are you coming back to the Center?"

"Well, I had…"

"No, you need to come now. I found some things."

When they got back to the conference room Carnetta had stacks of
paper to show. "Watch how this works, now. I did a search for Colton
Jenner like you said - that's these pages." She put down a stack of a few
sheets.

"We already knew he was a member of the Alliance for White
Progress," Carnetta continued. "But I found out that the web pages
that mention him also mentioned two other groups: the League for
Southern Unity and the Confederate Defense Coalition. She turned to
pick up more pages from the desk. "It gets a little complicated here.
The Internet is great but it's flat, there's no perspective."

Rebecca made a face. What was Carnetta talking about? The
teacher laughed at Rebecca's confusion.

"What that means is, unless you are careful with your search and
pay attention, you get items one after the other that could be fifty years
apart. That's what happened here. We've got references to the
Confederate Defense Coalition going back thirty years or more.
The L.S.U. is not quite that old but both groups broke off from
another group, the Sons of the Confederate South, which is still
around. Apparently the members of the old Sons of the Confederate
South had a falling out years ago over how they should react to the
Civil Rights Movement."

Carnetta was grinning wildly, so proud of what she'd been able to
find. She loved proving that women could be technically talented.

"Look at this one," she said, handing more pages to Rebecca. The printing was poor quality, at least on the original. The pages appeared to be old newsletters that had been scanned so they could be e-mailed. Carnetta had highlighted parts of one page that was dated at the top, May 6, 1992:

- Those were days of glory, when Southern heroes like Lester Maddox and Orville Faubus fought the oppression of a northern government dominated by the coloreds and Jews. Standing in the shoes of Jefferson Davis and Alexander Stephens, these statesmen fought to protect the legacy white people had created on this land over generations. No hero of the Southern way of life was ever greater than T. J. Davis. So it was a very great honor when he sent his most important personal aide to address our 1966 convention and inspire us with an impassioned speech. It is a privilege to reprint this section from that speech, delivered in a time of struggle, when the defenders of the South were not afraid to speak openly about the actions that must follow our words.

- (Excerpt from January convocation speech, January 26, 1966):

- The liberal papers up North are constantly whining about violence in the South. Nobody is wantin' violence in everyday life. We'd all be plumb happy if violence was never necessary, in war or to protect our families. But we all know that sometimes it is the right thing and, sometimes, violence can be down-right required. We all know, deep down, there is a righteous violence — we become sorta like the hand of God to smite those who defame the laws of nature. The race mixer, the communist, the atheist, all of them will feel the wrath of the God whose plan they would overturn so callously. The glory days of the South ain't behind us, as they try to say. Not if men like us can make ourselves be brave enough to fight the battles that are gonna be necessary, to earn the days of glory that are ahead.

"That makes another reference to Alexander Stephens," Rebecca said. "Did you…?"

Carnetta was already reaching for yet another piece of paper. She glowed with accomplishment as she read: "Alexander Stephens, 1814 — 1898. Vice President, Confederate States of America 1864 — 1866." She looked at Rebecca, bright-eyed. "The slavery quote you saw in Leon's bedroom is from Stephens's inauguration speech in Montgomery, Alabama, on March 14, 1864."

Rebecca sucked her bottom lip over her teeth. "This is great staff, but what's the connection again?"

Carnetta came over to Rebecca's side of the table and pointed at different pages. "Colton Jenner is mentioned in several places, see?" She pointed out a small box of announcements in the 1992 paper that named Jenner as a member of something called the 'senior brigade'. "You remember the first newsletters you found in Leon's room identified Jenner as the source of the quote he used in the note? When I looked up the name I found other mentions, like here," she pointed, "there's a one-line mention in a newsletter from the League for Southern Unity."

"That's great work." Rebecca said excitedly.

Carnetta held up a hand. "Hold on, though, there's a problem." She held out a black and white picture of a group of men in casual clothes. Under the picture was a list of names and Rebecca could see Colton Jenner was one of those. Rebecca could instantly see the problem. No one in this photo from the 1970s appeared to be any younger than 60.

"So the Colton Jenner in the current newsletter can't be the same man."

"Right," Carnetta said, "but there's another possibility. See, each of the issues has other names somewhere on the newsletter, so I made a list to cross-reference and I've found five names that all are on two or more of these pages and are the same as, or very close to, the names of current members of Sons of the Confederate South; we know that group because they've been leading a movement to put the Confederate flag back on the capitol building."

"I met one of their guys the first day I was here."

"They've always been a sort of mainstream Confederate group, if there is such a thing," Carnetta said. "For years, in the eighties, the Sons of the Confederate South leadership tried to distance themselves from racism and the Klan. They seem to feel sincerely that the history itself is not racist." She paused and wrinkled her nose. "That's hard for me to get, as a black woman, but I think the old guys were pretty sincere."

Rebecca grimaced. Carnetta was a terrific researcher but she didn't always explain things well. After hours of searches she knew the material so well it was apparently hard for her to remember that not everybody had been at it as long as she had.

"I'm lost," Rebecca said. "What do you mean by the "old guys?" The ones I met last week couldn't have been much more than 40."

Carnetta shook her head. "That's what I'm trying to say. Those guys were probably the new guys. That's what these are," she shook the list of names in Rebecca's face.

Rebecca's look of puzzlement just made Carnetta talk louder.

"See, these guys that are in League for Southern Unity, Confederate Defense Coalition and Alliance for White Progress, the ones you asked me to look up, these are the ones who are pushing the racist views and in the last few years they have taken over the Sons of the Confederate South. It's like a revolution; they're creating a racist front movement inside the Sons of the Confederate South, using that group's moderate image as cover. The Colton Jenner who's in the AWP now must be the son or a grandson of the first Colton Jenner who was fifty-six in 1982. If we knew enough I'll bet we'd find that all these new guys are the latest family members in these groups." Carnetta blew a deep sigh. This was the most she had talked since Rebecca met her.

"I don't know how we'd ever prove it, Rebecca, but I'll bet that's true."

"Rebecca?" she said again.

Rebecca heard her name called but she was no longer listening. She did not mean to be rude, but as Carnetta was talking and handing her publications a recent issue of the Watchman, the newsletter for the League for Southern Unity, the most extreme of the racist groups, fell open on the table to a picture of a group of middle-aged men. What Rebecca saw tied together everything Carnetta been trying to say. She frantically clawed through the pages on the table to find the black and white pictures Carnetta had shown her before.

A row of five men and there, second from the right, the sturdy build, the heavily muscled forearms and, she knew though his hands were out of sight, the ragged scar across the top of the left hand. She looked at the names in the caption finding one she recognized and knew, beyond a doubt, she had the story that would finally make Jeff really proud of her.

By the time she finally clicked the "send" button it was nearly one a.m. She had never been so tired, but almost never so pleased with a story. Brushing her teeth before falling into bed, she read the quote from his email she had taped on the mirror and wondered if Jeff would agree that she had taken his advice.

In analyzing history, do not be too profound, for often the causes are quite superficial —Emerson

You're One Of Us, Gordon

T he headline was below the fold and was only two columns, but it was front page. On Sunday:

Former Governor's Aid
Linked to Racist Shooting

"Great story," Jeff had said in a voice mail. "It's exactly what I'm always saying. The story is not just the shooting; everybody reports that. The story is the context in which the shooting takes place. You're good at this. I thought you would be. Congratulations."

She called her dad to brag and walk him through the steps to see the story on the Internet. Then she returned the call to Jeff. As she expected, the tone of congratulations had faded, pushed to one side by more questions.

"Some of the newsletters make it seem that the violence was not just encouraged, but actually planned by these groups," he said, all business. "You know the U.S. attorney in Birmingham, Alabama, is prosecuting old Klansmen in the church bombing that happened there. Could some of the violence over the years in Escambia be tied to these groups, too, rather than just random bad guys like Leon they influenced?"

Rebecca grimaced at the phone. This story was taking over her life.

* * *

On Sunday morning Gordon had already read most of the paper and had his coffee when he heard Margaret call to him from the kitchen.

"Honey, do you have the TV on? Turn on Channel 12. You should see this."

He reached for the remote and watched as the CNN announcer came into focus.

"Welcome back to Headline News. As we told you before the break, the *Atlanta Constitution* is reporting that a key aide to civil rights era governor and former presidential candidate, Thomas Jefferson Davis, has for decades been supporting an extreme pro-white, pro-Confederate political organization. The paper claims that this organization, the League for Southern Unity, was the source of hate literature that may have driven Leon Threadman to kill six black people in Greenville, Escambia, earlier this month. The paper was in the middle of running a multi-part series on the legacy of the former governor, who is critically ill, when the Greenville shooting occurred."

"Oh good Lord." Gordon looked up to see that Margaret had come into the room. "Did you know anything about this?" she asked. For an awful moment Gordon was afraid she might be thinking the story referred to him. He shook his head and turned back to the screen.

"The *Constitution* has printed excerpts from dozens of newsletters published by various groups over forty years to build its case against Billy Trask, the chief of staff and closest advisor to Governor Davis during the sixties. The paper claims Trask was a frequent speaker before such groups and was instrumental in shaping a white supremacist, anti-government message. That has become more extreme as these groups have become more isolated."

As the reporter talked the screen showed images of cheaply printed newsletters.

"The *Constitution*'s story is sure to generate controversy since many of the quoted speeches do not identify the speaker."

The on-screen picture changed to a shot of the front page of the Atlanta paper.

"The *Constitution*'s article claims, however, that Trask was always present at meetings where the most extreme speeches were made. It also claims that membership in these organizations is passed down through generations, so that sons and grandsons carry on the tradition. One picture published with the article from a "white rights" rally includes a man the paper identifies as the son of Billy Trask.

The screen now showed a reporter standing on a tree-lined street of small houses.

"A friend of the Trask family has told CNN that the *Constitution* story is based on conjecture and a young reporter's overactive imagination. This source said, quote, the deaths in Greenville are tragic. But to try to link this tragedy to Southerners who celebrate their heritage is not only wrong but also grossly unfair. Mr. Trask is 81 years old and has done nothing wrong. He deserves to be left in peace. End quote"

Gordon pushed the power button on the remote and the screen went black. He thought how nice it would be to be left in peace.

"What do you think?" Margaret asked.

"I think our young friend from Atlanta has gotten a little overheated from being in the Deep South. It'll all blow over in a day or two."

She gave him a smile, then turned in her chair and hummed away toward the kitchen. Gordon picked up the paper and had just found the Sports section when the phone rang. It was Edward, asking if he'd heard about the *Constitution* story and moaning that the *Courier* had been scooped again. Then the phone rang with another call.

"Who does that little bitch think she is?" an ancient voice croaked in his ear.

"Why are you asking me?" Gordon said.

"You're the one's been talking to her, damn you."

"Only about T.J. That's all she's asking about."

"Well, looks like that's changed, don't it?"

"Because of the killing," Gordon said. "You expect her to ignore something like that?"

"I expect her to say what happened. Crazy man killed somebody." Billy snorted in the phone. "I don't expect her to drag me into it. I ain't her business." Gordon could hear signs of the old Billy, the mean one who had things his way, sooner or later.

"You tell her that," Billy said. "You're one of us Gordon. You tell her."

Gordon hung up the phone thinking the reporter from Atlanta had ruined another morning for him. He had done quite well all these years without listening to Billy Trask throw his weight around. It angered Gordon to think he was being treated as a messenger, as though he was still on staff and, worse, would have been subordinate to Billy in any case. On the other hand, he didn't want Billy contacting the girl directly. The old fool would probably threaten her, or worse. He picked up the *Mayor of Casterbridge*, but five minutes later he was still staring at page 206. Something Billy had said kept coming back to him. *Was* Gordon one of them?

* * *

On Tuesday morning, Miss Amy greeted Rebecca back at the *Courier* morgue.

"I read your piece on Sunday. You've got things stirred up around here I can tell you. Edward has reporters running around like chickens with their heads cut off, trying to catch up.

Rebecca introduced Carnetta, who had taken time off to help, and they got to work in the old files. Hours later, her head was throbbing both from trying to keep all the violent acts straight and from the disturbing details in the old clips. She had seen the story of the man who had been castrated by Klansmen who then poured kerosene over the wound. The pain was excruciating but the cauterizing effect probably saved the maimed man's life. She read of the fourteen year old white Boy Scout, returning from a troop meeting in his uniform, who shot and killed a black boy of the same age riding on a bicycle with his brother. And she read again the accounts of the bombing of Phillips High School and the murder of the three civil rights workers who had been tortured, then buried in an earthen dam.

Certainly the last two acts were tied to extremist groups, at least by rumor. But there were so many acts of violence over the years - how could anyone show which ones might have been part of a conspiracy and not just the act of one evil person?

"That would be an important story," Carnetta said. "But most of these crimes seem pretty haphazard. Look at Leon. He pretty clearly got a half-baked, evil idea, probably thirty minutes or less before he started shooting. Bless his heart, I doubt he could plan a picnic.

Rebecca was silent for a moment.

"You're right. Really, the only time I've ever heard people even gossip about a planned killing was when the older black people at the Center would talk about Michael DeWitt. The car wreck always seemed suspicious to them because it was right before the election. But DeWitt was known for liking to drive fast."

"Well, there you are."

"Yeah," she said. "Probably."

You Just Want To Play
Woodward And Bernstein

When she looked back at it, Rebecca thought fate must have intervened. She had intended to drop the subject of DeWitt's death altogether. There seemed no reason not to, but after her talk with Carnetta the very next stories she looked at in the morgue contained references to Michael DeWitt. The first recounted the murder of a woman from Michigan who had come to Montville as a volunteer in the voter registration drive. Rebecca had found this story because one of the Klansmen who committed the crime was a member of the group that later became the League. The story quoted DeWitt saying violence was repulsive to the people of the South, and contrary to what they all knew from being in church every Sunday. At the time he spoke he was about to challenge T. J. Davis in the 1970 primary and, though he could not have guessed it, he would not live out the year.

In the very next story she read another Klansman referred to DeWitt as "traitor" to Southern heritage who deserves "a traitor's fate." She decided to call Jeff for some advice.

* * *

Wednesday morning, Rebecca stopped by Miss Amy's desk before getting to work. She came with two cups of coffee from the pot near the door.

"Didn't you tell me," Rebecca began, "that you remembered the Michael DeWitt race against T. J. Davis?"

"Oh my goodness, yes I do. It was the only race the governor ever had that was even close. You understand, though, it wasn't for governor, per se. It was for the Democratic nomination. It amounted to the same thing, of course, back then. The Democrat always won," Miss Amy giggled. "That must seem strange to all you young ones who've come along since Mr. Reagan's years."

When they had finished their coffees, Miss Amy helped Rebecca find clippings on the DeWitt wreck. She remembered it, and wasn't surprised when Rebecca mentioned that black people thought it was no accident.

"There was a good bit of that kind of talk back then, just because of the timing. It was so sudden, and close to the election, so lot of folks just couldn't think of it being at random. But there was no real evidence of a crime that I ever heard of."

"How close to the election was it?" Rebecca asked.

"Real close, right at the end of the campaign."

The *Courier* had done a long front-page story on the accident, in two double-width columns. Rebecca thought the tone odd, almost as though the state had been deprived of a savior. It must have seemed strange to readers who knew that the publisher's son worked for the opposition.

There were follow-up stories on the details of the wreck, and tributes from state leaders including T.J. Davis. What Rebecca did not see, after reading issues covering the next month, was any speculation that the crash was anything other than an accident. Rebecca was puzzled.

"I thought there was lots of talk that this might not have been an accident? I don't see any of that."

"There was." Miss Amy was unflappable. "But lots of things were talked about that didn't get in the paper." She could see Rebecca found that unlikely. "This was thirty years ago, Hon," she continued. "When the papers still had standards."

Rebecca recognized the clips she had seen in the notebook kept by Professor Fred. Of course, there were many more. But the volume didn't make up for the difference in styles of reporting, then versus now. The lack of speculation in the stories was odd, but she could understand that modern stories would have lots more of that than the *Courier* would have then. What puzzled her more was the lack of detail. The stories were almost squeamish in the avoidance of specifics about the cause of death. Having seen so many fictional gunshot victims bleed out in realistic dramas, Rebecca found the reticence of these old news stories weird. And what about witnesses? Hadn't she read something about witnesses? Weren't there old women who heard something?

Miss Amy looked blank. "Whatever we have, I think, would be in the clips."

"What about reporter's notes?" a pointless question, since Rebecca knew the answer.

"The reporter would have them, in a box in his attic. They wouldn't be in our files."

Rebecca was re-folding clippings to return to a file box when her eye was caught by a photo of DeWitt's car at the bottom of a small ravine. Of course.

"What about pictures? There must have been lots of pictures that weren't used."

Most of the afternoon was spent in the basement of the building, Rebecca's nose and head clogging with dust. Miss Amy was resourceful as ever and found a taped up envelope of pictures. The black and whites were like something from a noir film festival. Rebecca had to make a mental adjustment to realize the splotchy areas of black would be blood.

There was a lot of it. The face of the body sprawled across the seat was mostly covered in it. And the steering wheel, an enormous thing like a bus would have, with a center hub as wide as a dinner plate, it, too was covered in black. There were pictures from outside showing the dented car, somehow less damaged than she expected. The front and hood were largely crumpled in, but nothing was completely collapsed, as she had seen in modern high-speed crashes. Light from the old-fashioned flash set bright white smudges on the fender, door and windshield.

Rebecca couldn't get out of her mind that there were supposed to be witness statements. Where had she seen that? She looked at the interior picture again, at the blood-soaked hub of the steering wheel. The hub you'd press to blow the horn.

"Wasn't there supposed to be something about the horn blowing?" She didn't realize she had spoken out loud until she saw the puzzled look on Ms. Amy's face.

"I could have sworn I saw that somewhere."

Miss Amy stroked her chin. "I have no idea what you're talking about."

Rebecca tapped her teeth with the pencil, wondering where to go next, when she thought of what Jeff would tell her. Context. Put the fact in its context. The fact was the accident. The context was the campaign. Of course. She could fill in the details later.

"Miss Amy," she asked, "can we pull the stories that would show what was happening in the campaign right around this time?"

Most of the stories were dry-as-ash coverage of speeches. But one was different. It was the editorial in which the Editor of the *Courier* endorsed Michael DeWitt for Governor. It had run three days before the candidate's car ran off the road.

On her way to Gordon's for another talk, Rebecca stopped by the motel to check the notebook on DeWitt that Professor Fred had given her. After flipping pages for a few minutes she found what she was looking for. The page was a slick and crinkly copy from an old-fashioned photocopy machine. A handwritten note on the page read *Escambia Bugle* with the date "10/26/70." Yep, she was right about that horn.

* * *

"You've been busy," Gordon said when Rebecca had settled into what she now thought of as "her" chair in his den. "Your story about the League for Southern Unity has gotten some people stirred up."

"I guess." she said. "That's our job isn't it?"

"Hmm."

She had used the word "our" intentionally, but he didn't comment on it.

"Anyway," she went on, "I was looking at some of the stories near the end of the campaign against DeWitt. That was…"

"1970," Gordon said without looking up. Rebecca wondered if the interruption was intended to break her chain of thought, a mind game like lawyers play.

"Yes," she said slowly. "1970 it was. Anyway, one of the stories I found was that editorial in which your father endorsed DeWitt."

Gordon looked at her with great weariness and she thought that, for the first time, he looked like a sickly old man.

"You 'found' it?" he said sarcastically. "Aren't you giving yourself rather too much credit? It has not been lost, to my knowledge."

"I know you've told me you don't want to talk about it," she said guardedly, "but you know this business. I have to keep asking how that came about."

"He decided to write the endorsement." Gordon was curt. "That's how those things normally come about." He rested his head in his hand, elbow on the desk, stroking his temple with the middle fingers.

Long seconds went by.

"The election was only a few weeks away," Gordon said at last, "and perhaps my father thought the race was close enough that an editorial would matter. He was wrong, of course. And he may have known it would not matter. He only wanted to…" He let the sentence trail away.

Rebecca debated following up, then decided against it.

"How did Governor Davis react?"

Gordon smiled grimly. "He was not greatly pleased."

"I'll bet. But he was a powerful man. Didn't he do something?"

She saw immediately that she had somehow gone too far — asked one question too many. He seemed to tense around the eyes and she imagined something similar inside his mind. The pathways to that memory were hard to keep open on the best days; now she could sense that the gates, which had been slowly raised in the last week, were fully down.

"The governor was far ahead. I told my father the endorsement was a waste of time. It would embarrass me but serve no other purpose. You're naïve to think the governor needed to do anything."

"My question is, *did* he do anything?" Having already gone too far, Rebecca decided she had nothing to lose by pushing.

Now his look was different. For the first time Gordon seemed to resent a question, as though he were a witness for the other side.

"He won." He turned to reach for his coffee cup, as though the point had been made, but she wasn't ready to let it drop.

"He won against a dead man."

He froze for a split-second, and then replaced the cup. She thought she might actually have surprised him, which she had not often been able to do.

"That again? You want to know if Davis was involved in DeWitt's death?" Gordon's voice was sharp. "I should have known that would excite the young reporter. The sensational trumps the true every time, doesn't it? Isn't that how you run journalism these days?"

"I simply stated a fact. T.J. Davis did not actually defeat Michael DeWitt in 1970. Michael DeWitt died before the election. That is simple fact."

"That crash was investigated 'til the cows came home. There is no story there, and you know it. You just want to play Woodward and Bernstein don't you? Stir up something and make a little Watergate?"

Rebecca didn't answer immediately, partly because she knew Gordon had a fair point. Every reporter had to be sensitive to the fact that most readers thought they would sensationalize any story. Finally she said, "We're a paper, Gordon. I don't work for Fox News."

She asked a few more questions but it was obvious she had all she would get in this session. When she had packed up her notebook and recorder, Gordon walked her out, through the garden to the back gate. In a few minutes her skin was damp from the heat.

"I hate to see it get like this," Gordon said.

Rebecca thought for a second he meant their relationship, but when she turned he was staring at the plants wilting in the brutal sun.

"I should get an irrigation system," he said with a deep sigh. "I can't take care of things as I once did." He took her arm with a look to continue walking toward the gate, then said, "You need to wrap this up."

Seeing her expression, he added: "This story. You know as much about T. J. Davis as anyone can. You need to wrap it up."

"You mean I should forget about DeWitt's death?"

"DeWitt's accident," he snapped, then caught himself. "Forget about it," he said more quietly, "because there's nothing there."

"I'm a reporter, Mr. Halt. You remember what that's like. I can't just drop it."

"You can drop it when the story's finished — there's nothing wrong with that."

"But there are questions…"

He bent slowly and broke a dry branch off a hydrangea bush.

"This is life, Rebecca. There will always be questions. But not all of them have answers. Some questions are just tricks played with words, like 'this sentence is not true.' It sounds like a real statement but it has no meaning."

She watched his wrinkled hands fumble with another small limb. "That's kinda zen for me, Mr. Halt. What's the real reason I should drop it?"

He dropped the dead branches into the flowerbed and she saw his jaw tighten. "I've told you the 'real' reason," he said. "Another reason, however, is that there are people who've been gossiped about for years, when there has never been the slightest evidence against them. They don't want that to start up all over again for no good reason, when there is nothing new. Frankly, I agree with them."

Rebecca squinted slightly, as though in a glare. "Maybe." She turned and continued to walk toward her car, leaving Gordon where he stood. Opening the driver's door, she turned back to him and yelled.

"Do you know more than you're telling, Mr. Halt?"

He knew he should yell back at her, even knowing she was the impertinent type who wouldn't stop, whatever he said. But she didn't wait for an answer. By the time he looked up, he heard the car door slam. Besides, standing there in his dying garden, he wasn't at all certain of what he *did* know.

Night Music

A s Miss Amy had predicted, the Sunday story in the Atlanta paper had created a competitive furor at the *Courier*. On Tuesday the paper published three stories on the League of Southern Unity and Association for White Progress. One dealt with the effect of internet-based literature on violent crime, one revealed that links to the AWP had been found when several incidents of violence and arson, which had been closed by arrest, were re-examined. The last was an analysis of white supremacy groups like the LOSU and AWP in other parts of the country.

On Wednesday, Councilwoman Amanda Salter, who had marched in voter right's demonstrations as a high-schooler, rose in the council chambers to display racists pamphlets she said had been downloaded on a computer in the county library and demanded that internet access to racist web sites should be barred on those machines. The white-haired Ms. Salter was dismayed to learn that it would be very difficult to block the more than four hundred sites known to be operated by Klan, neo-Nazi, skin-head and similar groups. On a moment's reflection, she opined that the best solution might be to simply remove the computers from the library.

The *Courier* duly covered the Tautman speech and, in its other stories, duly credited Rebecca as the reporter who discovered the link between the AWP and the crimes of Leon Threadman, but not everyone in Montville read the stories. Even so basic a civic duty as regular newspaper reading assumes a certain minimum quantity of leisure time. People in Weeda's situation, however, found their days consumed with such immediate concerns that civic duties had to take a back seat.

Weeda's daughter had left the baby with her for a week and the constant needs of a toddler were taking a toll on the old woman. Partly as a result, she was not sleeping well. She could not decide if there actually was more gunfire in the neighborhood or if she just noticed it more because she was exhausted.

* * *

Across the city, in what was, in fact, a different world, Gordon awoke, as usual, and made his middle-of-the night trek to the bathroom.

When he returned to bed, Margaret shifted to make room for him, but her breathing remained regular. He closed his eyes hoping to rest, but his mind raced away from sleep.

Behind his closed lids was only darkness, but in his ears the sounds were many and as vivid as waking. It took only an instant to realize they were the sounds of the past: the radio in his father's study, crickets outside the open windows, an occasional car driving past.

Then, suddenly, vision joined the sounds and Gordon was there, once more, to ask Father not to endorse Michael DeWitt.

"Michael DeWitt is what the state needs if we are to avoid barbarity," Father had said. "Or at least avoid more than has already been committed." He was obsessed, had been for days, with the story of the three civil rights workers who had vanished. Everyone assumed they were dead; that was taken for granted. No one yet knew their bodies had been bull-dozed into an earthen damn. But something terrible had happened and the weight of it was on his father's shoulders.

"Those poor boys," Father had said over and over. Of course, Gordon agreed it was a tragedy, *if* they were dead. But why always assume the worst, as Father did? Just because it happened in the South did not mean the worst had happened. And there was more to it than that. It was as though Father blamed Governor Davis, or not even that, blamed *him*, Gordon, just because the administration opposed forced integration. How could he be so unfair?

Gordon had tried to reason with the old man. "You'll humiliate me if you write this."

"Everything is about you? Aren't you going to try to reason with me? Give me reasons why I shouldn't endorse DeWitt?"

"You know what I mean."
Father had looked at him as though some awful scar crossed his forehead.

"No, God help me," he had said slowly. "You're my son and I don't know what you mean. Or what you want or believe. Sometimes I think I don't know anything at all about you."

"Don't talk in riddles." Gordon's exasperation caused his voice to rise before he realized it. "This endorsement doesn't mean anything. It won't do a thing for Michael; it will only hurt me. Is that what you want? DeWitt can't win, you know that."

Father had capped his fountain pen with great concentration, before answering. "Is that the only reason to do a thing, so that you'll win? And therefore if the majority does not favor the right thing you just don't do the right thing? He sagged back into his leather desk chair. "Good God, Son, is that the way your mind works?"

Even now the memory made Gordon's face sting. He rolled over slowly onto his side. Moonlight through the drapes was enough to outline the old mahogany chest against the lighter wall. He was almost surprised not to find his father standing in front of it, the voice in his head had been so real.

He clinched his eyes shut again and, as though a switch had been thrown, heard his mother speaking on his behalf.

"So many people ask you for help, yet you begrudge your own son. How can that be?" She had been shaking with emotion.

"This is not about him. Everything is not about *us,* Amelia. " Father had picked up his pen and removed the cap, preparing to return to his work. "Gordon has made a life without seeking my approval. He can't pretend now to be disappointed that he doesn't have it."

Mother had taken his hand — he could still feel hers, so small yet hard, refusing to be frail — and led him across the hall to the parlor, settling on the velvet settee and patting the cushion for him to join her. She reached up to pick a piece of lint off the lapel of his jacket, brushed her fingers over the spot, then laid her hand on his shoulder.

"He's jealous of you, you know." She smiled, but so tightly it seemed painful. "Don't look so shocked. Why shouldn't he be? I don't mind saying it. Your are a senior advisor to our greatest modern governor while he is editor of a once-great newspaper that he has made irrelevant."

She fiddled with his tie. Gordon said nothing, knowing that was expected. She might say things about a husband that, even as an adult, he could not say about a Father.

"You are doing such important work for the South. Don't let what he does make you doubt yourself." Her voice changed, and she made an elaborate sweeping gesture with her right hand. "I release you from that," she said grandly, "from that tyranny a Father has over his son. I release you now and forever."

She stood and glided him to the door, stopping only long enough to offer her cheek to his kiss. Even now, Gordon could feel that warm skin under his lips and that comfort and support that had once made it seem nothing really bad could ever happen to him.

He seemed to hear his shoes on the wooden steps as he left the big white house, each remembered step bringing him closer to certainty that he would not be going back to sleep this night. He was suddenly panicky at the thought and willed himself to take deeper breaths, more slowly, in the hope that rest would come.

* * *

Weeda had finally succeeded in falling asleep about 1:30 a.m., two hours before Gordon's memory of kissing his mother's cheek and three before the first 9mm round exploded into the aluminum siding on the Douglass Street side of her house. Before the shots there had been the sounds of pounding bass notes from a car sound system mixed with shouted profanities, but these were the natural background noises of Weeda's night, equivalent to the cricket song and drone of multi-ton air conditioners Gordon was used to. Night music. Even when the shouting became angrier and louder it was not different enough to bring Weeda out of the sleep she was so desperate for.

But when that bullet hit the metal siding it reverberated like a bomb blast. Ripping through wallboard, it then slammed into the framed picture of Weeda with her girls that hung on the opposite wall. The shattered glass crashed to the floor, yanking Weeda from sleep as though by a rough rope.

Before she had time to be fully terrified, bullets two, three and four exploded into the walls, splattering window glass, splitting a door frame, pocking wallboard. Weeda's heart pounded. Then an engine roared, tires squealed and the bullets stopped. When the engine faded in the distance, she got out of bed and found the phone.

"This is police emergency," a sleepy woman's voice.

"Help me! My house has been shot up, I…"

Not sleepy anymore, the voice said, "Yes m'am, try to be calm. I'm showing 14569 Ninth Place North. Is that the right address?

Weeda said that it was.

"Who did the shooting?"

"I don't know," Weeda cried into the phone. "Somebody outside. Those hoodlums."

"I am sending the police now. Are you hurt, do you need an ambulance?

"I'm okay I think, but my house is all…" Weeda stopped, suddenly more dizzy and confused.

"M'am?" The phone buzzed at her. "Are you there m'am?"

She let the phone slip from her hand. She remembered the neighbor girl feeding the baby and putting her to bed, but was that this night or was that last week? Was the baby here tonight? That *little* angel always sleeps so solid, maybe she didn't wake up. There was more buzzing from the phone receiver as Weeda felt her way up the hall.

Light from the street lamp filtered through bullet holes torn into the window shade. So faint it gave no color, the light was enough to find the baby quiet in its bed, but with what looked like a heavy black shadow on the sheet by its head. A heavy black shadow that, when she touched the baby's head, spread to Weeda's fingers.

In a cinder block building in downtown Montville, the concerned 911 operator was re-checking the phone connection when she heard what sounded like static from the other end. Listening closer she realized the raspy, broken keening was human, and terrible. She dispatched an ambulance.

Can't Somebody DO Something?

I n his bedroom Gordon was visited by his ghosts, in sleep that brought no rest. Pieces of dreams followed one another without order or sense, like random scenes at a time traveler's multiplex. So now he is with T. J. Davis in the executive office. The governor waives a newspaper in Billy's face. He has been doing so for forty years.

And now he is with Mike DeWitt, in black tie at the same fancy ball Michael has attended in this dream, with Gordon, T. J. and Billy, year after year after his death. And now he is with Billy, in the back seat of a car that still runs after forty years, with those seats as large as a sofa and itchy as burlap and the windows down and blasts of air hitting his face. None of the scenes has sound and all are blurry. But he's been here before; he knows that will change.

The light is shifting and wavering, as though he is falling through water and he is again in T.J.'s office. The newspaper is still in the governor's hand, still being wielded like an ax, but now the dream has sound.

"I ask you for one fucking thing and you can't do it?" T. J. bellows. His voice booms to every corner of the large office, his anger replacing the oxygen Gordon desperately needs, and compressing Gordon's chest as though T. J. was physically pushing him against the wall. The newspaper he holds contains the editorial Gordon's Father has published, endorsing DeWitt.

Suddenly T. J. snaps the paper open. "Escambia will make an historic choice," he reads, contorting the words with sarcastic emphasis. "Michael DeWitt gives us a chance to move toward a politics of unity and progress. Governor Davis has built his career on divisiveness and demagoguery, suspicion and fear. The people of Escambia deserve better."

Davis flings the paper at Gordon, who jerks sideways as though avoiding a brickbat.

"God*damn*, doesn't your old man know I pay your fuckin' salary? I told you to talk to him."

"I tried."

"Well, that's a piss-poor job of trying, if I ever seen one." The effort to think of something strong enough to say causes T. J.'s face to glow red. "God*damn*, Gordon, whatever made me think you were such a great communicator. Your own damn daddy won't listen to you; what the hell use are you to me?"

He spins and strides across the room, as though to get as far away from the repulsive Gordon as he could, then paces rapidly back and forth, his anger driving him like a tightly wound spring. Only Billy has the nerve to break the silence.

"You know, T. J., Mike DeWitt is crap. He's fifteen points behind and the election is three weeks away." Billy stops to spit into his cup. "Gordon's daddy is a fuckin' Commie anyway. Nobody's gonna give a damn about his endorsement."

"Maybe," T. J. says without conviction, as he continues to pace. "But DeWitt has tried to beat me everyway he could for my whole damn life. Everywhere I turn, he's there. He never gives up; he's like me that way."

T. J. turns on Gordon again, as though mention of the newspaper reminds him who the real enemy is. "Your Daddy is throwing this bastard DeWitt in my face all over again. It's like some curse was put on me at birth." His voice spiraled up in volume, until he was shouting. "It ain't right. Can't I ever get away from this bastard DeWitt? Can't anybody *do* something?"

Again the light changes, dimming then glowing in shifting patches of intensity before dropping to near darkness. Gordon, in his dream, is aware of movement but whether his own or his surroundings he can not guess. A roar fills his head as he again feels wind blowing in his face, and rough fabric against his arm and through his shirt. Within the roar he hears voices, but cannot detect words. He is tossed about from side to side, as though on a raft in rough water. The impressions wash over him but he can make no sense of them.

The wind dies and the voices become louder. A light flares up to blind him for a moment, then just as suddenly dies. The voices, too, fade away and he becomes aware of his nausea. He feels himself sinking into a darker place and fights desperately to wake up.

Suddenly a horn blares through the dark. Gordon's body jerks violently at the sound, then it comes again like a lighthouse klaxon warning of danger. Suddenly he was awake in his bed, the spasm of his body having been real. His heart was pounding, his blood roared in his ears, and he wondered if the last horn blast had been real, outside on the street, or part of the imaginary world of that awful dream. Lying there with sweat beading in the hair at his temples, he realized there was a third, terrifying possibility.

* * *

Rebecca had been sleeping peacefully until the phone rang. Carnetta's voice was ragged.

"Hey. I'm sorry. But I knew you would want to know."

* * *

T. J. Davis, lying in his hospital bed, was undisturbed by external forces that night, though it would have taken a medical expert to say if he merely slept. Or, if so, whether the dreams of eighty years played in the random nerve firings of his brain. And the greatest expert could not have said if those dreams would have brought him peace or misery.

For even the most famous, the really important events normally happen away from public scrutiny; never more so than at life's end. The reporters maintained their vigil in the lobby, his family waited to be offered hope, and his political allies and enemies calculated the loss of his name and memory as tools in the continuing political struggle.

But none of that reached the former governor. At the end, the only influences on T. J. Davis were chemical and electrical; the former in the regimen of drug cocktails that flowed into his veins with his I.V. nutrients, the latter in the firing of impulses across neural synapses in his brain. These few electrical signals, detected by the monitor beside the bed, were the only signs of life other than the warmth of the old man's skin. The doctor had said even these feeble impulses would soon end and the family should be close by. T.J's wife (to Margaret's renewed annoyance) had called Gordon mid-morning.

Walking through the lobby once more, Gordon saw the handful of reporters who could not have looked more bored if they were covering a shopping center opening. None of them looked as old as forty. They lived in the world T. J. Davis had made, Gordon thought, but they were oblivious.

Gordon grimaced, thinking the governor would not be happy with this coverage. Better that he didn't know the shooting down in Greenville had been on CNN hour after hour. Other than this desultory crew in the lobby, there was almost no coverage of the passage of a state leader. Only the girl from Atlanta and the *Courier* were doing pieces in depth, and the stories the girl was writing after the Greenville shooting made Gordon wish for less coverage, not more.

Looking around the depressing room for the fiftieth time, he thought T. J. would be glad there was no television coverage up here. The visuals were really terrible. Gordon had been there for an hour or so when the doctor came in, checked some equipment, and told Barbara, "he's gone."

Just like that. Death. The lack of fanfare seemed almost obscene. No change was visible from across the room. T. J. seemed to be resting, as he had seemed to be for the last eight days. The difference between life and death, at this stage, was so little that we needed an expert to interpret it for us. Gordon did not like the thought.

We Shall Not See His Like Again

The funeral took place on Thursday, three days later. Gordon's paper - he still thought of it that way, though it really was Edward's now - ran a special section entitled "The End of an Era," without implying anyone should regret the end. There was fair coverage of the years opposing integration but the emphasis was on Davis as a sort of elder statesman, who had reached out to black Escambians in his later years.

A memorial service the day before had drawn 5,000 people. Confederate flags were visible among the crowds but there was no formal gathering by the Sons of the Confederate South. Speculation in the press was that Rebecca's stories had generated so much publicity that the best thing was for such groups to lie low.

Gordon sat a few pews behind the family at the service, feeling distanced from the proceedings. Seeing Billy Trask sitting beside Barbara he thought again how few people in this crowd - in the whole country - were as old as they. Few of the mourners were even alive when T.J. was a powerful governor.

The current governor, a Republican (who thought he'd live to see that?), spoke the eulogy in a perfunctory performance. Gordon thought his manner suggested he might have been opening a new section of highway; but then he would have been five years old when T. J. Davis left office.

"Few men have affected any state the way Governor Davis planted his mark upon Escambia," he intoned, fearlessly embracing the obvious while avoiding a value judgment. Gordon snorted.

The language was affirmative, but dispassionate, as though T. J. had been a house-guest, an eccentric uncle who had dropped in unexpectedly but could not be turned away. Certainly the visit had been enjoyable, but how unfortunate he had been so ill-mannered as to seriously overstay his welcome. Gordon thought he sensed this tension in all the politicians at the church; that pull between "I have to be here," on the one hand, and "Is it really smart to be here?" on the other.

The burial was to be at Memorial Gardens. Billy had let everyone know he disagreed with this decision. He thought T.J. should be going back down south to Clayman County where it all began. But a number of former governors were at Memorial, as were, much more importantly, the earthly remains of that secular saint, Coach Butler from the University, so Gordon thought Memorial seemed about right.

The line of cars proceeded from the church through busy streets then past the new housing development where saplings were guy-wired like telephone poles to stand in the graded earth. At the cemetery the cars pulled to the winding curb and, almost in unison, the doors spread like wings from the long bodies. The mourners emerged and slowly filed toward the green tent some distance away.

Perhaps a hundred people clumped around the tent, many of whom Gordon felt sure he was supposed to know. He wandered up to the edge of one cluster.

"They made him look real good, didn't they," a portly matron was saying. Gordon thought she might have been legislative staff ages ago but could not be sure. He saw several faces with familiar contours, faces that tilted toward his or creased slightly in recognition, faces attached to names buried more deeply in his memory than T. J. would soon be in this ground. And no more easily recovered.

One person he did know was Ethel Toomey, a friend of Margaret's from church. Ethel noted how good God had been in not making T. J. suffer. "From all I hear," she said, "he was asleep the last few days, and isn't that a blessing?"

Ethel the philosopher, Gordon thought. Leave it to her to prove one of his favorite theories, which was that the more important an occasion was the more likely people would be banal in talking about it. Had anything the least bit meaningful been said at any wedding, birth or funeral since time began? It seemed to Gordon that the human mind was completely overwhelmed at any reminder of life's transience.

Apparently to prove the point, a stooped and frail gentleman beside him said, "We shall not see his like again." This seemed highly unlikely to Gordon; T. J. Davis's 'like' seemed pretty common in politics, but he did not express himself.

Beside the incongruously glossy casket, the preacher was well into the familiar words about returning to the earth that which was hers. It occurred to Gordon that he had not seen Rebecca since leaving the church. He wondered if this represented some attempt on her part to be discreet, but rejected that idea out of hand. The younger reporters seemed not merely to avoid tact as a mode of behavior but to actively repudiate it, as though the least expression of civility would signal a fatal weakness. No, she was here somewhere.

It was at that moment, as the preacher was consoling the few family members seated in the front row, that Gordon caught sight of Billy across the crowd. Three uniformed State Troopers accompanied the old pol (Gordon wondered if it was odd that he never thought of himself in those terms) as though he was a football coach after the big game. Gordon assumed the security was intended to shield Billy from the press, but it was absurdly out of proportion. Though it was true that Billy had figured prominently in the stories about the shootings in Greenville, especially after Rebecca's stories first linked the killer to the League and Alliance, and then showed how involved Billy had been (still was? Gordon wondered) in those groups.

When their eyes met, Billy jerked his head up slightly as though he had been searching the crowd for Gordon. He raised a brow and cocked his head toward the roadway, away from the crowd. *I want to see you*, was the message, as clear as if it had been telegraphed. Gordon nodded to Billy, *message received*, but searched for an escape route. After the phone call two days ago Gordon did not imagine that Billy merely wanted to be sociable. Whatever problems Billy had with the girl reporter, Gordon saw no advantage whatsoever to being in the middle.

I Guess You Just Decided Not To

G ordon said goodbye to Ethel and backed away from the group, trying to lose himself in the now-dispersing crowd. Across the road, Billy and his escort moved toward the driveway and, Gordon feared, his own car.

He moved away from the drive, toward a stand of stout trees, which broke up the huge swath of carefully mown grass. The trees had obviously been saved when the grounds were originally developed and now provided some cover for Gordon, who stood behind a large oak trunk, feeling foolish. Billy would soon realize that unless Gordon had jumped into the grave himself, these trees were the only place he could not be seen. And if he were behind these trees it could only be because he was hiding, like a schoolboy. He rested against the tree to gather his thoughts, feeling the rough trunk against his back, imagining the bark tearing into the wool of his suit.

The unnaturally green field spread away from him, studded with monuments in mathematically neat rows. He saw a small garden tractor pulling a flat trailer of some sort and as it came closer Gordon could see the trailer was loaded with plants, shovels and hoes, and bags of soil. Two black men sat on the tractor, the one driving blowing clouds of smoke.

Gravediggers, Gordon thought. That's what they had to be. Apparitions, like something out of Dickens. He realized they must have been there all along, at a discreet distance from where the cars would have lined up, waiting patiently for the family to leave so the last mundane activity could be completed. Gordon had the crazy thought that these men did not have to be concerned that new technologies would put them out of business. Their jobs could not be outsourced to India.

He looked back toward the tent over what would soon be T. J.'s grave. The crowd was gone now, only a few idlers talking by the cars. And Billy, Gordon could just see, waiting there for him to finally come. It was obvious now that Billy saw him and knew Gordon was not talking with old friends nor had any other excuse. Oh well, get it over with. He was turning toward the cars, bracing himself with a hand against the rough trunk when he heard the familiar voice.

"Mr. Halt!"

He looked back to his right, past where the groundskeepers waited in the tractor, and saw Rebecca moving toward him with terrible slowness. She was beside the oldest human being Gordon thought he had ever seen, since he was becoming something of an expert on the subject. They were making turtle progress because the black woman was trying to use a walker on the uneven ground. He could not see the ancient face but suddenly he knew, of course, who she had to be.

He walked over to where the old and young women tottered in the direction of the green tent. He motioned and pointed for the grounds men to meet him.

"Weeda," he said, placing one hand on the walker rail the other on her frail bony arm.

She leaned heavily on the walker and squinted up at him. Then she spoke, in a tone he could not interpret. "Master Gordon." She looked down and shook her head. "You remember that. Your mama wanted you called Master Gordon." She cackled, a form of laugh rattling in her throat, but joyless.

She let Gordon help her into the passenger seat on the tractor after one of the men climbed out. The tractor advanced at a walk toward the tent, quiet now and alone except for rows of folding chairs, the gaping grave with the casket now at rest, and the mound of clay-orange soil.

Gordon saw Weeda turn to the driver. "What's your name, son?"

"I'm Carl, ma'am."

She seemed satisfied with that. "You work here regular?"

"Yes'm, been here four years."

She thought about that for a moment. "So tell me something. Why do white folks bury they people so *fast?*"

Carl laughed and said that was a good question.

Weeda let Gordon help her off the seat and took back the walker. "This time I'm glad of that," she said, though it was not clear to whom. "This here's a man needed to be in the ground a long time ago."

She tottered up onto the fake grass carpet, close to the open grave, and then lowered herself into the center chair in the first row, where the widow had sat earlier. She breathed heavily for a time, before turning to Carl, the driver.

"You boys gonna cover him up now?"

"No hurry, ma'am." Carl said. "You just take all the time you need to pay your respects."

The old woman snorted.

"I got no respects," she said. "I came to see you put him in good and deep." She held Carl's eye for a long second and Gordon could imagine some telepathic communication between them, some digitally compressed packet of data that, in one second, could let Carl know of the years of living that made this woman want to be in this place at this very moment. The connection must have been a good one for Carl smiled at Weeda, gave a small nod and turned to his companion, picking a shovel off the cart as he spoke.

"Let's don't be keeping this lady waiting."

Gordon was aware that Rebecca had taken a seat a few rows behind Weeda and, as always, was writing in a steno notebook. But he couldn't take his eyes off Weeda.

Carl and his companion pushed the shovel blades deep into the mound, then turned and tossed the dirt into the hole. The first clods landed with a hollow thud, as though hitting a drum.

During the process, Gordon heard Weeda hum at intervals, *um-hum, um-hum,* as though indicating approval. As though she were directing the entire activity. *Um-hum, Um-hum,* in unison as each shovel load was pitched.

Soon the dirt rose above the surrounding lawn, formed into the oblong mound that says 'grave' in any culture. Carl dropped his shovel and walked over to Weeda, wiping his face with a large cotton handkerchief.

Um-HUM. Weeda hummed emphatically, as though Carl had done especially well.

"We about done now," he said. "Got to take down the tent and fold up these chairs. Not much to see. You want me to ride you over to your car?" Rebecca spoke up and pointed out her blue rental, on the far side of the lawn.

Gordon stepped to Weeda's side to help steady her at the walker.

"I'm sorry about everything," he said. "I haven't been out to see you; I don't get around all that much. And then Rebecca told me about the baby. Terrible thing."

Weeda looked up at him and her face seemed as deeply creased as a Greek tragedy mask, each line more eloquent of loss than a volume of words would be.

"No tellin' what she coulda been," Weeda said. "We won't know now anyway." She looked around the tended field. "Wish she was gonna be buried in some place pretty like this."

"I wish there was something I could do," Gordon said, "but..."

It sounded like what should be said, though he was not sure himself what the words meant. That he wished he could have the baby buried here? That he wished he could have prevented her death? That he was sorry he couldn't tell Weeda what the child would have grown up to do?

Weeda was turned back to face Gordon and he saw something in her sunken eyes, a glare, a burning, he had not noticed before.

"But...it's too late? Isn't that what you was gonna say, Master Gordon? That whatever you was gonna do shoulda been done a long time ago? Maybe if you had a done something then, things would be different now. Maybe they wouldn't be selling drugs in my yard, shooting up my neighborhood. Maybe that baby would be alive."

The old woman shuddered against the walker, making the flimsy aluminum frame wobble. Gordon stepped closer, afraid she might fall, but not certain he could hold her up. Weeda didn't appear to notice.

"But you wanted to be like him." She motioned to the grave, stared at it for a second, then lifted the walker and moved closer to it. When she was beside the mound, she turned to face Carl.

"I always planned to dance on this grave, if God let me live long enough." She cackled dryly. "Cain't do that no more, but..." She worked her mouth around as though a denture had come lose, then leaned forward over the walker and spat on the dirt.

"Guess that'll have to do," she said with a snorting sound. "Don't seem like enough for the pain he caused, but I guess it'll have to do." She looked back at Carl. "I think I'm ready now, if you'll help me, please." He went to her and slowly they moved toward the tractor. They passed close to Gordon, who still stood as though planted, and Weeda motioned that she wanted to stop.

She leaned so that her face was close to Gordon's before speaking. "Your Daddy wanted to do something about how we was treated. He was a fine man. You know that don't you?"

Gordon was struck mute, as though a small boy again.

"I used to think you would be like him," Weeda continued. "You was kind to me and smart as a whip. With him as a guide, I always thought you coulda made a difference." She looked at Gordon for a moment as though waiting for him to defend himself, then said, "Humph. I guess you just decided not to."

Gordon could feel Rebecca's eyes on him as he stood in the blazing heat of Weeda's scorn. He prayed she would not say anything and she did not. Instead she helped Carl get Weeda and the walker onto the tractor. They moved slowly away. Gordon watched them until the blue rental car disappeared in the distance.

Gordon turned to begin the slow walk toward his own car, head down, his mind full of Weeda's words. A horn sounded, abrupt and loud, ahead of him. Looking up, he saw Billy leaning in the half-opened driver's window. Another horn, he thought.

"I'm coming. Hold your horses." He didn't need this. He had enough on his mind without having to deal with Billy's bluster. But Billy couldn't stop being the tough guy and Gordon had never found a way to defuse him. The horn sounded again, Billy being a spoiled child; Gordon could imagine him behaving exactly this way when he was six years old. Well the hell with him. I'm coming as fast as I can.

"That was her, wadn't it?" Billy asked when Gordon approached the car. For a moment he was puzzled; did Billy even know what Weeda looked like?

Billy was exasperated. "The girl, goddammit. The reporter. That was her?"

"It was."

"We gotta talk to her."

"We?" Gordon had done a good job of staying away from Billy's business for the last thirty years. He didn't plan to change things now.

Billy's eyes narrowed and his noisy breathing made him sound like a dangerous animal.

"Don't get senile on me, Gordon. You're part of this and you gotta help control her." Billy took several steps toward him, so that Gordon had to look up into his eyes. "Otherwise, it's gonna get bad for all of us."

Gordon hated that fuzzy, disoriented feeling he felt more and more lately. He had been a leader in the Davis administration; he was not a flunky Billy could push around. How had he come to this, his mind crowded with flashes of memory, with Weeda's words of disgust, with dreams and visions, and now this wild belligerent face in front of him. And suddenly he felt something had clicked, between Billy's face tormenting him in present time and the dreams that tormented him from the past. Billy should be in those dreams, he suddenly felt, but could not think why. A fit of coughing from Billy interrupted Gordon's thought.

"Don't ignore me, Gordon." Billy said when he had composed himself. "I'm giving you a chance to be there, but I'm talking to her by God either way."

And then it occurred to Gordon why Billy might have a place in his strange dreams. The idea made him cold inside.

"We can talk to her," Gordon said, a vague sense of dread building inside him; he wanted to get home to Margaret and his book.

The other man leaned forward, blustering with impatience. "Speak up, dammit. What are you saying?"

Gordon looked up, but said nothing else.

Whatever Got Done, WE Did It

S he really didn't want to be here.

Her footsteps echoed creepily in the vacant marble halls, an effect increased by the lightning storm outside and the reduced, late night lighting within. She had been surprised that it was even possible to get into the Escambia state capitol at almost midnight, but she had used Gordon's name with security, as he had told her, and the bored, minimum wage guy let her right in. Standing in the lobby, shaking the rain off her cheap umbrella she listened to thunder that seemed to shake the massive columns and thought again, I don't want to be here.

Rebecca could not imagine anything Gordon wanted to tell her that couldn't have waited and she didn't know whether to be angrier with him for making such a stupid request or with herself for agreeing to it. Probably the latter; she had let herself lose all proportion about this story and so when he asked her to meet she threw good sense out the window.

He had told her to go to the second floor and walk to the center of the building. Under the dome, a vast rotunda was open for three floors, accessed by a spiral stair. She saw Gordon ahead, standing at the rail where the rotunda opened.

"I enjoy being in the building at night." Gordon said as she walked up. "In my mind I can populate all these offices with the faces and voices that used to be here, back when important things were being done." He looked at her and laughed awkwardly, as though he realized how he sounded. "Edward thinks I'm senile. I suppose this would give him some evidence."

Rebecca leaned over the rail, looking across the vast opening to the statutes on the main floor, below. "The word 'rotunda,' does that mean the inside of the dome or the space under the inside of the dome? I wonder." She turned back to face him. "So, why all the drama, Mr. Halt? We couldn't have had this talk tomorrow?"

"Tonight is better."

They walked the circular path around the railing. High above, the mural-painted ceiling reflected warm light on the hallway. When they reached the opposite side of the opening Gordon stopped and drew Rebecca back to the railing, pointing down to the main floor.

"The first time I ever laid eyes on T. J. Davis, he was standing right down there. Mike DeWitt and I were high school boys and I don't think Davis ever knew we heard him. T. J. was standing there, just a boy, making a speech all by himself..." He looked up suddenly, giving Rebecca the impression he had just remembered she was there, as though he had been talking to himself.

"Have I told you about that?"

Rebecca yawned deeply, nodding her head at the same time. She was too tired to listen to another repetition of what she now thought of as the 'T. J.'s first speech story' and interrupted.

"You said we needed to talk, Mr. Halt."

He rubbed the side of his face. Rebecca thought he might be thinking over a difficult problem. Finally he said,

"I wish I could have told you more..." He pushed himself away from the railing and continued down the hallway. He opened a door off the main hall, into a large conference room and stepped aside for her to enter. Rebecca guessed they were near one of the large legislative chambers and that this room with its table and twenty over-sized leather chairs was used for committee meetings. Her train of thought was broken when she realized two of the large chairs were not empty.

"Mr. Halt?" she said, not pleased.

"Don't talk to him, talk to me!" A deep voice with a rasp like a rusted tool boomed from one of the chairs. "If you're going to ruin me in that goddamn newspaper, you can at least talk to me."

So, Rebecca thought, this is how I meet Billy Trask. He was surprisingly big, seated in the large chair. She guessed he might be older than Gordon, but he was robust. The other, younger, man seated beside him she did know. She still had the handbill he had given her on her first day in this awful city. For the first time since she had come to this place her mother had warned her about, Rebecca felt fear. The surroundings didn't help. This dingy hulking building in the middle of a thunderstorm and midnight. It was almost too much, like parody of a Faulkner story, which she now saw, must have been the intent. But why would Gordon have agreed to it? She couldn't understand it, but she couldn't worry about that now. She decided there was no advantage in being timid.

"If writing the truth is what ruins you, I can't control that." She hoped she sounded braver than she felt.

The younger man jumped from his chair.

"You smart-mouth bitch!" The table was wide, but still Rebecca jerked backwards.

"Sonny," the older man said. Just that one word, not even loud, but it stopped whatever the son was about to do or say. The old man turned his attention back to her.

"So you're the city girl that's gonna tell what the truth is, eh?" His noisy breathing seemed as sinister as the surroundings. "The rest of us are just village idiots, is that it?" He made a sound between a snort and cough. "Well, missy, why don't you tell us what you think you know."

The question caught her off guard, yet calmed her at the same time. This was probably a bad thing; surely fear was the appropriate emotion right now. But in different circumstances this was a question Jeff might ask about a story. He might even say it in something like that challenging way. And she couldn't help responding. She could always defend her work.

"I know you were one of the founders of the Alliance for White Progress and you've never been far from the leadership. I know you helped your son to take over the Sons of the Confederate South, to make it more extremist, and I know that not a word of racist provocation gets on the 'net or into the newsletter until you approve it." She paused to take a breath and decide whether to go further. "And I know that you pushed pitiful Leon Threadman over the edge as surely as if your hand had been on his back."

She saw the rheumy eyes narrow and felt what a mouse would feel if it knew the hawk was staring, but still she talked.

"And I know the car wreck by itself did not kill Mike DeWitt. His faced was crushed in the wreck, but the windshield was broken from the outside. The steering wheel should have hit his chest, but it was covered in blood from his face. That's strange isn't it? But what's even stranger is, Governor Davis wanted DeWitt to go away and suddenly he was gone. Is that enough or shall I continue?"

The old man leaned over the table, resting heavily on his elbows. He face was flushed and his breathing had become nearly as loud as the thunder that sounded every few minutes.

"I'm gonna cut you some slack because you're still a young'un and you don't know what the hell you're talking about," he said, the words coming out in an angry rush. A flash of lightening lit up the tall windows. "You think it's racist to care about your history, about where you came from? But what is Black History month, if not racial pride? Why is there a Little Italy in New York, and a Chinatown in every large city. Is that racist? But if the Sons of the Confederate South does something for white culture then you think that's racist?" His smirk underlined his words. "You are a traitor to your own people."

"And that poor fella in Greenville," he continued after catching his breath, "shame on you for picking on him when he's dead. I know he did a terrible thing. But look at the pressure he was under. He lost a promotion when his boss gave it to a colored fella. Did your friends tell you that? That man lived in a world where the government says a white fella who ain't old has no rights at all. Did you write that in your damn stories? Hell no! But you wanna pretend like you're shocked when he broke like a twig under that kind a pressure. And then you got the damn gall to take all that and try to blame it on us? Just to have a story? I don't think I'm gonna let that happen."

He twisted his face into a snarling smile and took several deep, noisy breaths. He punched his son on the arm.

"You know, boy, ain't but a handful of people reading her paper will remember who Mike DeWitt was, and even they won't give a fuck." He laughed noisily at this, then turned back to face Rebecca. "But hey, Sweetie, it's a free country. Knock yourself out playing in that ancient pile of horse turds. But before you get too much of it sticking to your fingers, you might want to have a nice long talk with your buddy here," he motioned toward Gordon, "'cause there's lots of us got reasons not to want to resurrect all those old fairytales."

Rebecca turned to Gordon with a quizzical look. "I don't understand."

Gordon did not look at her, she wasn't even sure he had heard her. His gaze was fixed on Billy Trask. Then he spoke.

"She doesn't understand, Billy."

The big man seemed confused by this, as though he had forgotten Gordon could speak.

"Explain it to her!" Gordon shouted, just as a crack of thunder shook the windows. Then all was silence. Billy's eyes were wide, his mouth slack.

"Tell her what you did," Gordon said, this time speaking just above a whisper. There was no sound except the rain hitting the windows and the rasping of Billy's ragged breath. This gradually became more regular as Billy seemed to regain control of his facial muscles, recomposing an ugly snarl.

"Don't get cute with me you son of a bitch," he said, staring at Gordon. "Whatever got done, *we* did it, not just me." He grunted for air. "And don't you forget it."

Billy leaned back in his chair and focused on Rebecca once more.

"Don't let him confuse you with his damn riddles, little miss. Mike DeWitt was a weakling who never stood up for nothing. He would never have beat T. J. and everybody knows it. It wasn't necessary for nobody to reach in and jam his head into that steering wheel a couple of times, cause it didn't matter anyway. He didn't lose no worse by being dead than he would have lost if he'd been alive. So what's the difference?" He turned to Sonny, and grunted. "Besides, DeWitt was kinda like you boy, he was a piss-poor driver."

The old man chuckled at this, exposing his teeth. Rebecca was frozen in place, as though strapped to her chair.

"One more thing," Billy Trask leaned forward, his eyes narrowed. "You keep on writing this bullshit about me and my boy and I'm gonna sue your pretty little ass and the fancy-pants *Atlanta Constitution* for a couple of million dollars. And then you gonna have to find yourself a line of work you're a little bit better at doing."

"I don't think the paper's lawyers are afraid of you." Even to Rebecca this was unconvincing. Billy's face showed he was not impressed. He leaned back, enjoying himself.

"Maybe you better ask them before you stick your neck out. And make no mistake, missy, your neck is sticking way, way out. 'Cause you see I don't have to go over to Atlanta to sue you all. You'd love that. But I can sue you right here in Montville. Right at home." His face brightened "Hell, we'd probably get a judge I helped appoint! Go ask your lawyers how they feel about coming over here. You might get educated pretty quick."

He sighed deeply and waited. Rebecca couldn't decide if the silence was her ally, but she couldn't stop herself from breaking it.

"You've said a lot, Mr. Trask, but you haven't said my stories weren't true."

Billy stretched a threatening grin across his wrinkled face.

"She *is* a young 'un, ain't she Gordy? We're talking about lawsuits, honey. I'm not sure I got to worry too much about what's true. I just got to worry about what you can prove. Since I know who your witnesses would have to be, I reckon I'm in a pretty good spot here."

He stood up, his arms straight, palms braced on the table so he could lean his face close to hers.

"Now you on the other hand," he said low and slurred, "you got to worry about Sonny."

Gordon rose from his chair while speaking.

"That's enough, Billy. You wanted to talk to her, but I won't have threats made. These are not the old days."

Billy straightened and glared at him.

"And ain't that a goddamned shame? But you know, Gordy, maybe the old days can come back."

Billy rose from the chair, motioning to Sonny with a twist of his head, and started walking around the table. Gordon moved Rebecca toward the other end, a movement Billy caught in the corner of his eye. He laughed, a dry cackle, and continued toward the door.

"Y'all take care now, ya hear?" he said.

It Was Only Thirty Years

A fter the two men had gone, Rebecca sat at the conference table, holding her head between her hands, and tried to make herself stop shaking. She had been intimidated by local politicians and crooked businessmen, but before tonight she had never considered that it was actually possible someone would harm her to stop a story. She felt Gordon's hand on her shoulder.

"I'm sorry," he said. "I didn't think it would be like this. He's actually somewhat stupider than I remembered. I am sorry."

Gordon sounded terrible, but he should. Rebecca twisted her shoulders to get his hand off her.

"How could you do that to me?" She asked the question but was too angry to accept any answer.

"I thought I had no choice," he said miserably. "I was afraid he might come to your hotel or accost you on the street if I didn't agree to meet. I wanted to be with you."

Rebecca sighed. That, at least, she could agree with. Besides, Jeff would want her to use what had happened for the story if there was a way, and knowing that helped to calm her. Her mind raced over the last half hour and she turned to Gordon as she fumbled in her bag.

"He said that you would not want the death of DeWitt brought up any more than he would?"

She pulled out the recorder and saw with relief that it had not run out of tape. Putting it back in the bag, she heard Gordon groan.

"Are you all right?" she asked.

Gordon was looking down at his hands, folded on the table, and breathing in shallow breaths. He seemed to be trying to sort out words, as though English were not his best language. He spoke without looking up at her.

"I had a selfish reason for wanting this meeting; the truth is I don't know what Billy meant when he said that because," he hesitated, "I don't know just what I *do* know. I can tell you this much. my father decided to endorse DeWitt. You know that. When the *Courier* came out that day, the Governor was enraged. His anger was like a storm in the room. He raged about my father and my own pathetic lack of influence. But more than that, he raged about Michael. He said that he had always been tormented by Michael, silly things like that, but said with incredible anger."

Gordon turned to her. He was biting his upper lip before he spoke.

"But then Davis said, 'do I have to deal with DeWitt all my life?' Not to anybody in particular, but to the whole room. Like he was questioning his fate. And the next day we heard that DeWitt had died in the wreck."

Rebecca had grown used to hearing the same stories repeatedly so, tired as she was, she almost missed this entirely new one. It occurred to her that Gordon probably couldn't keep straight what he had told her before, which might be useful. He might say more than he meant to, if she prodded a little.

"None of that is new, though," she lied. "Billy had to mean something more than that."

"But there is nothing more that I *know.*"

"Then tell me what you suspect. This isn't a perfect world, Mr. Halt, we have to go on hunches sometime."

"This is not even that." He looked up at the ceiling and took a deep breath. "This is a dream."

Rebecca was suddenly glad she had gotten new batteries for the recorder. Gordon proceeded to tell her about the watery light and the scratchy fabric and the wind so strong across his face. He felt sure that sensation was riding in a car; he couldn't be wrong about that. He had done it too many times. But he could not be sure about anything else; lights coming on and going off, Billy being there or was he, nothing was certain — except the sound of horns.

"I have had the dream more often since you mentioned the newspaper reports about horns, so that may be the source. I had not thought of that for many years. But in my dream a horn blows, two times at least, maybe three." A flash of lightning from the window washed the color from his face for an instant and he startled as thunder boomed. "I had always thought it might be a foghorn but I don't know anymore."

Rebecca tapped the table with a fingernail. "My God, Mr. Halt, you must have been there! When Michael crashed his car. How else could you know about the horns? This isn't a dream you have, it's a memory."

Gordon shook his head with some energy. "That's not possible," he said emotionally.

Rebecca watched his face, deciding how hard to push.

"Look," she said, "let's go back to what you remember about that night before the accident."

Gordon took another deep breath. "Everybody was shaken by T. J.'s anger and I more than the others. After all I was the one whose failure had precipitated it. We were all as traumatized by the outburst as though T.J. had our life in his hands. Anyway, we went to Billy's office where he kept a quart of Old Forrester and I can remember I drank right from the bottle. The other guys did that a lot but I never had, until that night. Billy talked about that for days. He thought I was finally loosening up after all my years of being what he considered formal. That, of course, only made me more determined to have no such lapses in the future. Gordon fidgeted, pulling on his shirt cuffs, and seemed surprised to find he was wearing a watch.

"We should go," he said suddenly. "I had no idea..."

"Wait." Rebecca could hardly believe that Gordon would even think of stopping here. He was a newspaperman himself. He must know he had only now gotten to the essential part of the story. "What happened next?"

Gordon looked genuinely puzzled. "After the drinking?"

Rebecca made a gesture her friends would have understood to mean "duh." Gordon got the drift.

"I woke up on my living room sofa, in my clothes."

"Mrs. Halt must have loved that."

"This was before dear Margaret."

Rebecca knitted her brows and chewed her bottom lip.

"So you are inside the capitol drinking one minute and on your own sofa the next. And you must have gotten home by car, right? I'm guessing someone else drove?"

"I don't think I would have been foolish enough to drive."

"But Billy might have?" Rebecca tilted her head in his direction. This was like guiding a toddler.

"He certainly had more experience drinking than I did," Gordon said. "He could have decided to drive."

"So let's think of what we know. We know this all happened the night before you learned DeWitt had been killed. We know that you were in a car at some point. We suspect that Billy was with you, and possibly driving. We know that in your dream/memory you heard horns. And we know at least some witnesses heard a car horn that same night."

She could see on Gordon's face that he recognized the implication and, just as clearly, that he had never thought of it before.

"I was there when he died." It was little more than a whisper.

For a moment he seemed so crushed that Rebecca was sorry they had started down this path. She was afraid he might cry. She reached out and touched his hand.

"Or, you were very close by. That's what it looks like." She had to think a moment about whether to go on. It seemed clear now what Billy had been implying, but did she want to be the one to point out to Gordon that some people might think he could be a conspirator in what Rebecca now thought of as another murder.

"It doesn't seem possible." He did not seem to know he had spoken aloud. He seemed more addled than she'd ever seen him, so his next words surprised her.

"Who told him," Gordon asked angrily, "anyone bashed Michael's head on the steering wheel?"

"I didn't know if you caught that," Rebecca said. "I think that came out from his subconscious somewhere, like God wanted us to know it. I'm sure he didn't mean to say it."

"But you think that's what happened."

"Yes I do. I think your dream of being in a car is a memory, that probably Billy and the others thought they'd find DeWitt and it looks like they did. Then who knows? Did they run him off the road, or did he speed up to escape them and lose control? I don't know. But I believe at some point he was off the road, and may have been seriously hurt anyway. Then Billy would have pulled over and got out..."

"The dome light would have come on when the door opened. I remember that light in the dream I could never understand..."

"And I think he may have walked down to the wrecked car and found Michael still breathing and ...

"just like he said..." Gordon interjected.

"reached in and smashed his head against the steering wheel

"and the horn blew...

"Once, twice,

"and again...

"three times. That's what the news clipping said. The sisters who heard it had thought it was a plea for help."

Gordon was breathing heavily and every muscle in his body seemed to have gone slack. Rebecca patted his hand again. He bit his lip and then shrugged. "It's been a tough few days." He rubbed his face with his hands. "Billy's right though, isn't he? No one could ever prove what we're talking about."

Rebecca was already running through the possibilities in her mind. How far would they let her stretch a hunch, how much do you ask readers to take on faith, how hard do you attack someone over the ancient past. Even, how much do libel suits cost? It didn't take long to realize what Gordon had already guessed.

"No, probably not. But you know what, at least I know. I found a story and I believe I've gotten to the bottom of it. I can't print it, but I know what the truth is. I can live with it."

As she spoke she saw Gordon's face change, the muscles tightening so that he seemed to flinch, betraying such sadness that her breath caught in her throat. She had been at the graveside and, without meaning to, she had heard what Weeda said to him. Now he was dealing with this. She regretted her choice of words. The bigger question was could *he* live with it?

Finally it was time to leave. Gordon stopped, as she knew he would, at the railing under the beautiful dome, and looked down at that spot on the first floor and she waited for him to tell her once more that he and Mike had heard T. J. Davis addressing an imaginary crowd all those years ago. She found herself disappointed when he did not speak.

She turned and leaned backward slightly to look up at the dome murals.

"Do you know Carnetta, my friend who works with the center in Greenville? She brought me here. I think she really only wanted me to come so she could tell me a story." She turned to Gordon gesturing to the arched ceiling. "Have you noticed the paintings up there?"

Gordon slowly looked up, like an obedient but not engaged child. "Rebecca, I've been coming here for nearly 60 years. I'm sure I've seen them hundreds of times. They haven't changed."

"Well, actually they have." She kicked herself mentally for her tone. "The whole thing got a major facelift 10 years ago." The dome, which arched up to a circular skylight, was divided into six segments, like an orange. Each segment featured a painting recalling some part of Escambia history, with a title for each framed at the bottom, and the dates covered by that particular historical period.

"Look at that one." Rebecca turned Gordon with one hand while pointing up to a panel on which a mediocre artist had rendered a large white house with giant columns that she thought must have been based on Tara, in the movie. On a magnolia-lined drive in front, an elaborately attired squire sat astride his dark horse, his lady riding beside him on her white one.

Gordon sagged under her hand. "It is very late, please"

"You dragged me out here, Gordon. This is important. Look at it."

Gordon reluctantly looked again at the panel.

"O.K." She stood up straight and abruptly took Gordon's shoulders in her hands and turned him toward her. "Now, look at me. This is a test. That picture is called "The Golden Period of Antebellum Life in Escambia." What are the dates under that picture?" His eyes moved upward reflexively, but she caught him.

"No," she said sternly. "Look at me. What are the dates for that period of your history?"

Gordon closed his eyes in thought.

321

"The War started in 1861," he said softly, "so I imagine that has to be the end date. And, let's see, Escambia became a state in 1820, but it was mostly forest then. Plantations would have taken awhile. So, say, 1830 to 1861." A cloud came over his face.

Rebecca smiled. "But...?" drawing the word out.

"But that is only thirty-one years." He spoke softly, his brows close to-gether. "It should be longer than that, shouldn't it?"

"Look for yourself."

Gordon turned his face to the light and read aloud.

"1840-1860. Can that be right?"

"That's what Carnetta wanted me to see. The whole "golden" era was only about Scarlet O'Hara's age in that movie. The people who settled Escambia in the first place did not know the antebellum style of life, and would probably have been appalled by it. Yet that style became this myth that supposedly "defined" what the South is all about. It was only twenty years, but one hundred thirty years later you were supposed to live your whole life by those rules."

Gordon didn't say anything. The corners of his mouth were pulled down, whether in sorrow or simple concentration she could not tell. She wondered what he must be thinking, but then decided she might be happier not knowing.

Gordon's friend on security was still at the door and let them out. The rain had stopped, but silent streaks of lightning still ripped the sky to the northwest as she said goodbye in the parking lot. Gordon said that yes, he was fine to drive home. She made him say it twice.

Things To Do Differently

R ebecca was still upset the next day about the confrontation with Billy and his son. She went to see the Professor, only to talk her way through the lingering tension she felt. But he insisted on calling Sergeant Murphy.

"I can tell you how to swear out a warrant if that's what you want," Corky had said. "It sounds like it's justified."

"It would kinda kill my credibility as a reporter though, wouldn't it? I've already written about these guys."

"Yeah, I guess." The phone was quiet for a moment. Rebecca could hear a baseball game on a radio in Corky's office. "Let me speak to Professor Middlebrooks again."

Rebecca passed the phone back. He spoke a few sentences, then hung up with an odd grin.

"That was funny," he said. "The Sergeant said if you left that tape you made lying around somewhere, I should get it and send it to him. He wouldn't tell me why, but he said the Trask family would be too busy for the next few months to give you a hard time."

* * *

Margaret had been waiting up for him when Gordon returned from the capitol. His distress was evident to her as soon as he entered the house. For his part it was made worse seeing how tired and worried she looked. He agreed to tell her everything that was troubling him, but only after they had both had a good night's sleep.

The dream returned that night, but now he clearly heard road sounds as he sat against the rough fabric. He heard men's voices he had never heard in the dream before and, in the hazy light he now thought he saw Billy's features, as they were so long ago. But what part of that came from the events of the last weeks? He could not begin to tell.

He and Margaret did talk for hours in the days that followed and, as the best wives do, she assured him he had lived a good and honorable life and was not to blame for the outcome of decisions he had made in good faith.

Gordon was pouring a cup of coffee when the doorbell rang. He heard Margaret's chair as she went to answer it. Then he heard her call for him.

The young deputy held his hat in one hand, a folded piece of blue paper in the other.

"Mr. Gordon Halt?" he asked. "I am directed to serve this subpoena for your testimony before the grand jury of Montville County on the 15th of next month, sir." He reached out to Gordon with the folded paper.

Gordon took the paper without opening it. He could probably trust the young man to be right about what it was. "Can you tell me what this is about?" he asked.

The deputy shrugged. "I don't know, sir. Pretty much whatever the D. A. wants to ask you, I guess."

* * *

Rebecca had been back at her desk in the *Constitution*'s newsroom for more than a month, covering meetings and interviewing county officials. She had not forgotten her time in Escambia by any means, but she had begun to feel that she had her life back.

Her reverie was interrupted when she heard someone clear his throat rather theatrically and turned around to see Jeff, standing across the desk, just as he had done when the Escambia adventure had begun.

"Just wanted you to know," he said with fake casualness, "the editors have nominated your T. J. Davis series for the Associated Press In-Depth Coverage Award." He grinned liked she'd already won it.

* * *

Sonny Trask was over for a visit at his daddy's house on Thursday afternoon when the doorbell rang. He opened the door to see an officer in uniform and another in a suit. The suit held his badge out, but Sonny didn't to examine it.

"Sorry to ruin your day, Sonny, but I have warrants for you and your father. He's here isn't he?"

"Yeah," Sonny snarled, "He's here. What's this about?"

The suit spoke calmly. "You two are charged with conspiracy and incitement to commit manslaughter. You'll need to come down to the station with us."

Sonny led the men to the back room where Billy sat. "Daddy," he said. "These men say we been arrested. We have to go downtown."

Billy rose unsteadily from his chair and walked to the dresser where he picked up a brush and ran it through his hair. "I don't want to look raggedy."

Sonny's eyes watered and he turned to the officers. "You sons of bitches have turned on your own kind."

The suit put a hand on Sonny's thick arm, not unkindly, just in charge. "This doesn't have to be a big deal. You just go down there and make bail and come on home. That's all there'll be to it, unless you let your mouth overload your ass."

Sonny did not say anything else and the four men left in the police car. When they arrived at the Montville Police Department the suit placed a call to Greenville to advise Sergeant Corky Murphy that his arrest warrant had been served.

* * *

The elegantly engraved envelope stood out in her in-box like a jewel in a pencil tray. Rebecca turned the envelope over to see the logo of the We Care Center, and removed a bordered card announcing a banquet in honor of the Reverend Fred Middlebrooks. She noted the date on her calendar, then finished the sandwich she had been eating at her desk. When the wrapper had been scrunched up and tossed in the trash, she scrolled through the article she was writing on her monitor. *A chapter in the long and troubled civil rights history of the state of Escambia,* she read, *came to a close today when..."*

Not bad, she thought. Just needs a few more quotes. She picked up the phone and dialed the Greenville Sheriff's Department.

* * *

The next morning, the phone rang in Gordon's study. He found a bookmark and wedged it into *Common Sense*.

"Gordon, this is Whitey Burgess. You know we're counting on you for this committee to build a suitable monument for T. J. There's a planning committee meeting we're trying to set up for Thursday. Can I put you down?"

"I don't think so, Whitey."

"Gordon, it's gonna look funny if you're not a part of this thing. People gonna think we left you out." The voice in the phone cackled nervously.

"People are going to think something no matter what we do, and whatever they think will probably be wrong."

"But damn now, Gordon."

"I'm sorry to let you down, Whitey, but there are some things I've got to do differently in the little bit of time I've got left. And this is one of those things."

His manners prevented him from ever hanging up on anyone, so Gordon let Whitey say "damn, Gordon," a few more times and he said "Sorry, Whitey," a few more. Finally he heard a loud sigh and a click.

PAIR PLEAD GUILTY
IN HATE CRIME DEATHS

By Rebecca Tanner

MONTVILLE, ES

A chapter in the long and troubled civil rights history of the state of Escambia came to a close today when Billy Trask, 78, and his son, Sonny, 56, both pleaded guilty to six counts of misdemeanor criminal incitement in connection with the sniper murders in Greenville, Escambia, last June. The two men had been charged with incitement to commit manslaughter and faced possible imprisonment for sixteen years if found guilty. Under the terms of the plea agreement each man will serve four years of house arrest, monitored by electronic devices. The younger Mr. Trask will serve an additional 2,500 hours of community service in an interracial environment.

The guilty pleas came at the end of an extensive investigation by Escambia law enforcement officials and the Federal Bureau of Investigation. As originally reported in the *Constitution*, the sniper in the Greenville incident had been a frequent visitor to numerous white supremacist web sites and may have been influenced by their fiery rhetoric. The Trasks were found to be frequent contributors to, and financial supporters of, these groups that include the League for Southern Unity, the Alliance for White Progress and the Sons of the Confederate South.

In conjunction with today's guilty pleas, the District Attorney of Greenville announced that the web sites of the three groups had been shut down permanently and all three of them had entered into consent decrees by which they agree to eliminate any encouragement or support of violence from any future communications. "This is an important day of healing for all of us in Greenville,' said District Attorney Charles Garrick. 'The attempt by these groups to tie love of the South to racism is something every decent person will reject and abhor. I am grateful to our law enforcement agents for their tireless efforts in closing this case. Special thanks are due Sgt Collins Murphy, who initiated the investigation and pushed it to this successful conclusion."

When contacted by the *Constitution* for comment, Sergeant. Murphy asked to respond with a written statement, saying "I've never been that good off the cuff." His statement is reprinted here:

"It is not only false, it is foolish to pretend that the Confederacy was not committed to insurrection, and dedicated to the destruction of the Union and the preservation of slavery. But the Confederacy was a political movement. Being Southern is something different.

"Southerners believe that courtesy is more important than politics, that it is far better to be neighborly than to win an argument, that patriotism is not old-fashioned, that children say "M'am" and "Sir" to their elders because the elderly know more than we do and are entitled to respect. None of these things that matter so much to us as Southerners has much to do with the Confederacy and none has anything whatsoever to do with racism.

"Leon Threadman, that tortured soul, may have been tricked into believing he represented a resurgent Confederacy. But I tell you, he did not represent the South."

Gordon Is Invited

"Gordon! Atlanta is calling!" Margaret's voice echoed into the den. He reached for the cordless phone and heard the familiar voice in his ear.

"How are you?" Rebecca asked.

"Well, I'm still old," he said, "but not bad altogether. At least things have quieted some since you left."

Her laughter tinkled through the phone.

"I talked to Corky Murphy in Greenville. He said you were a great witness before the grand jury."

Gordon snorted. "I hope that merely telling the truth does not qualify one as a great witness. I simply responded to their questions."

"If you say so," she said. "It's good to hear your voice again. I've been thinking about you because I got an invitation to a dinner honoring Fred Middlebrooks; you remember him. I wondered if you'd like to be my date."

Not for the first time, he thought, the girl from Atlanta had surprised him. "I am quite speechless. You are most kind, but I cannot imagine that I'd be welcome. I'm afraid the professor and his people probably think of me as the enemy. It would be awkward for them."

A few seconds went by. Gordon could imagine the young girl was trying to think of a tactful response.

"Don't say no," she said. "Think about it a few days. You were a big part of the past and Sergeant Murphy tells me you've been a big part of what's happened now."

Gordon let out a long breath. "Whatever I've done now is very late and probably..."

"No," she interrupted. Her manners, he thought, could still use some work.

"My dad says it is never too late to do the right thing. You should give yourself some credit."

So, Gordon thought, her father makes another appearance. He thought of their discussion in his library.

"You're too generous. That's very appealing in a young person. Let's leave it that I'll think about it. Would that be satisfactory?"

He heard her giggle. "That's great," she said, "but I'm not going to forget. I'll call you in a week or so."

Gordon sighed, and then remembered what he had meant to say. "Speaking of your father, please tell him I congratulate him on his parenting skills. He did a fine job." He heard her say "awwww" and imagined she might be blushing. "You may also tell him that I quite agree with his thoughts about Dickens."

* * *

Gordon put the phone back on the table. Margaret called to him from the kitchen: would he like a cup of decaf? Indeed he would. He looked down at his copy of *Common Sense*, thinking as he always did of the ironies of the title. He did not pick it up.

Hearing from Rebecca had brought back to mind all that he had been going over in his thoughts these last weeks. He had imagined she must consider him a form of ogre after everything she had learned and made him relive; he almost felt that way himself. But apparently not. Perhaps he would go to this banquet. He'd ask Margaret when they had their coffee.

He turned toward the far wall and walked unsteadily to the bookshelf. He scanned the highest row until he found the book Rebecca had pulled down that day when she talked about her father. He walked carefully back to his chair with it and sat, squirming until he was as comfortable as his creaky body permitted. He stared at the cover of *David Copperfield* for some moments, until he felt ready, then he opened the cover and began to read:

Whether I am to be the hero of my own life, or whether that station will be held by anybody else, these pages must show.

ACKNOWLEDGMENTS

Any author of historical fiction owes a very large debt to the real historians. Whatever the merits of *Heart in Dixie,* it would be a much poorer effort without the valuable details and context provided by these important works, among many others:

Carry Me Home, by Diane McWhorter, is a magisterial account of the manner in which systemic racism was fostered in her home town by the white power structure, to the detriment of both white and black working people.

The Politics of Rage, by Dan Carter, is widely considered the definitive political biography of George Wallace. The book provides a thorough and cogent consideration of his philosophy and tactics, as well as his effect on national politics over generations.

George Wallace: American Populist, by Stephen Lescher, is the authorized biography of Wallace and is sometimes said to have the weaknesses to be expected when the cooperation of the subject is a factor. That said, Lescher's title has turned out to be amazingly prescient to our most recent election and it is hard to argue with his implication that Wallace has had the greatest impact on our presidential elections of anyone in the last century.

Bull Connor, by William A. Nunnelley, is the only in-depth biography of the notorious Commissioner of Public Safety who unleashed police dogs and fire hoses on school children and galvanized national public opinion in favor of the civil rights demonstrators. His vivid and gripping account makes Connor a fully realized character and demonstrates why he, like so many of us, could only have been produced in the South.

I doubt any reader needs to be told that "southern-born and southern-bred," though in common usage down here, is best known nationally as a lyric by Terry Gentry and Randy Owen. When I was very young "born and bred" was the expected answer to the question, "Are you from the South (or Alabama/Georgia/etc.)?"

Wendy Tunstill, Marilyn Cash, and Lare Willson read early drafts and made valuable suggestions. Jake Reiss, owner of The Alabama Booksmith, read an excerpt and provided guidance from his career of dealing with publishers.

Not just myself, but the entire nation owes a debt of gratitude to the Southern Poverty Law Center and its founder and former head, Morris Dees. Despite years of intimidation and threats of violence, Dees and the Center have developed the most complete database in the nation on terrorist groups working under the white-power banner. Without the incredible bravery and persistence of Dees and the Center, this dangerous and deranged subculture would be unknown to most of us, and seriously underestimated by law enforcement.

I don't know how many marriages have been ruined by men trying to write a novel, but I am blessed to have a wife who was willing to put up with a very long effort. In addition to her many other gifts, she is a more prolific writer than I am, having three books herself, so she understands. Jean has been a constant source of encouragement, affection and good advice. Her years as a newspaper reporter made her suggestions and hours of proofreading especially valuable and she is solely responsible for making me put the book into print, after letting it lie fallow for more than five years. "A trucker's dream if I ever did see one."

CPSIA information can be obtained
at www.ICGtesting.com
Printed in the USA
LVHW111552190719
624656LV00003B/474/P